New York Times and U
Barbara Dunlop has wr
Mills & Boon, including
series for Mills & Boon
stories regularly hit bestseller lists. Barba̲ ̲ ̲ ̲ ̲
time finalist for the Romance Writers of Amer̲ ̲ ̲
RITA® Award.

Brenda Jackson is a *New York Times* bestselling author
of more than one hundred romance titles. Brenda lives
in Jacksonville, Florida, and divides her time between
family, writing and traveling.

Email Brenda at authorbrendajackson@gmail.com or
visit her on her website at www.brendajackson.net.

Also by **Barbara Dunlop**

Sex, Lies and the CEO
Seduced by the CEO
A Bargain with the Boss
His Stolen Bride
From Temptation to Twins
Twelve Nights of Temptation
His Temptation, Her Secret
The Illigitimate Billionaire

Also by **Brenda Jackson**

Zane
Canyon
Stern
The Real Thing
The Secret Affair
Breaking Bailey's Rules
Bane
The Rancher Returns
His Secret Son
An Honourable Seduction

Discover more at millsandboon.co.uk

THE ILLEGITIMATE BILLIONAIRE

BARBARA DUNLOP

AN HONOURABLE SEDUCTION

BRENDA JACKSON

MILLS & BOON

First published in Great Britain 2018
by Mills & Boon, an imprint of HarperCollins Publishers
1 London Bridge Street, London, SE1 9GF

The Illegitimate Billionaire © 2018 Barbara Dunlop

An Honorable Seduction © 2018 Brenda Streater Jackson

ISBN: 978-0-263-93601-8

51-0518

MIX
Paper from
responsible sources
FSC™ C007454

This book is produced from independently certified FSC™ paper to ensure responsible forest management.

For more information visit: www.harpercollins.co.uk/green

Printed and bound in Spain
by CPI, Barcelona

THE ILLEGITIMATE BILLIONAIRE

BARBARA DUNLOP

For Shaina, Jacob, Karl and Heidi

One

In an absurdly masculine room, deep in the halls of Clarkson Castle, Deacon Holt carefully neutralized his expression. He wouldn't give Tyrell Clarkson the satisfaction of seeing anger, envy or any other emotion.

"Drink?" Tyrell asked, making a half turn toward Deacon from the inlayed walnut bar. He held up a cut-crystal decanter that Deacon could only guess held decades-old single malt.

Tyrell was well-known in Hale Harbor, Virginia, for indulging in the finer things.

"No," Deacon answered. He had no idea why he'd been summoned today, after being shunned his entire life, but he was positive this wasn't a social occasion.

Tyrell shrugged and poured two glasses anyway. He cut partway across the library and bent at the waist to set the glasses on opposite sides of a dark wood coffee table.

"In case you change your mind," he said and gestured to one of two brown leather armchairs flanking the table.

Deacon preferred to stand. He wanted to be on alert for whatever was coming.

"Sit," Tyrell said and folded himself into the opposite chair.

Though he was in his late fifties, Tyrell was obviously in good shape. He had a full head of hair, and his wrinkles were few, giving his face character. By any objective measure, he was a good-looking man.

Tyrell was rich. He was clever. He was powerful.

He was also detestable.

"What do you want?" Deacon asked.

The rest of Hale Harbor might jump to Tyrell's commands, but not Deacon.

"A conversation."

"Why?"

Tyrell lifted his glass and turned it in the light that beamed down from the ceiling fixtures. He gazed at the amber liquid. "Glen Klavitt, 1965."

"Am I supposed to be impressed?"

"You're supposed to be curious. When was the last time you tasted fifty-year-old single malt?"

"I forget." Deacon wasn't rising to the bait, even though they both knew he wasn't in a tax bracket that would allow him to casually spend whatever 1965 Glen Klavitt cost. Not that he'd be foolish enough to blow his money on it anyway.

"Sit down, boy."

"I'm not your dog."

One of Tyrell's brows went up.

Deacon expected Tyrell to react with anger. He mentally braced himself for the onslaught, realizing he'd been looking forward to a fight from the moment he walked through the oversize castle doors.

"But you are my son." Tyrell's words, though softly spoken, fell like cannonballs into the cavernous room.

Deacon held still, half expecting eight generations of Clarksons to rise from their graves and rattle the crested shields hanging on the stone walls.

He tried to gauge Tyrell's expression, but it was inscrutable.

"Do you need a kidney?" he asked, voicing the first theory that came into his mind.

Tyrell's mask cracked, and he almost smiled. "I'm in perfect health."

Deacon didn't want to be curious about anything to do with the Clarkson family. He wanted to turn on his heel and walk out the door. Whatever was going on here, he wanted no part of it.

Tyrell had two healthy, living legitimate sons, Aaron and Beau. He didn't need to reach out to Deacon for anything—at least, not for anything that was honorable.

"Will you relax?" Tyrell asked, gesturing to the empty chair with his glass.

"No."

"Stubborn—"

"Like father, like son?" Deacon asked mildly.

Tyrell laughed.

It was the last thing Deacon had expected.

"I don't know why I thought this would be easy," Tyrell said. "Aren't you even a little bit curious?"

"I stopped caring about you a long time ago."

"Yet, here you are."

Deacon knew Tyrell had him there. Despite his anger, despite his hatred, despite the twenty-nine years of resentment, Deacon had come the first time Tyrell called. Deacon told himself he was here for a confrontation with the man who had impregnated and then abandoned his mother. But the truth was he'd also been curious. He was still curious.

He sat down.

"That's better," Tyrell said.

"What do you want?"

"Do I have to want something?"

"No. But you do."

"You're not stupid. I'll grant you that."

Deacon wasn't sure if Tyrell expected a *thank you* for the backhanded compliment. If he did, he was going to be disappointed.

"Why am I here?" Deacon pressed.

"I assume you know about Frederick."

"I do."

Tyrell's youngest son—and Deacon's half brother, though they'd never been introduced—Frederick had died of pneumonia six months ago. Rumor had it that Frederick's lungs had been seriously damaged as a child, when he'd been thrown from a horse. The fall had also broken his spine and confined him to a wheelchair.

"Did you know he lived in Charleston?" Tyrell asked.

Deacon hadn't known where Frederick lived. He'd only known Frederick had left home after college and never returned. Everyone in Hale Harbor knew Frederick had a falling out with his father and walked out of the Clarkson family's life. Deacon had silently admired Fredrick for doing it.

"Frederick has two sons," Tyrell said. His gaze didn't waver.

Deacon was surprised at that news. He wasn't an expert on spinal cord injuries, but he wouldn't have expected Frederick to father children. He supposed they could have been adopted.

He didn't know what Tyrell anticipated as a response to that particular revelation. But Deacon didn't have anything to say about Frederick's sons.

"The oldest is four, the other eighteen months," Tyrell said.

"Congratulations?" Deacon ventured.

"My only grandchildren, and I've never met them."

"I don't get where this is going." Deacon had sure never met Tyrell's grandsons.

The entire Clarkson family did their best to pretend Deacon didn't exist. Aaron and Beau knew perfectly well who he was, though he'd never been sure about Tyrell's wife, Margo. It was possible Tyrell had been successful in keeping Deacon a secret from her all these years—which begged the question of what Deacon was doing in the castle today. Surely Margo would be curious.

Tyrell took a healthy swallow of the scotch.

Deacon decided to try it. What the heck? It might be the one and only thing his father ever gave him.

He lifted the expensive tumbler to his lips and took an experimental sip. The whiskey was smooth, rich and peaty, not bad, but he'd sampled better. Then again, the company might be tainting the taste.

"I want to see my grandsons," Tyrell said.

"So see them."

"I can't."

"What's stopping you?"

"Frederick's widow."

It took Deacon a beat to comprehend what Tyrell meant. Then he grinned. Poetic justice had visited Tyrell. Deacon took another sip of the whiskey, silently toasting the widow. The scotch tasted better this time, really quite good.

"You find that amusing?" Tyrell's words were terse.

"Someone keeping the powerful Tyrell Clarkson from something he wants? Yes, I find that amusing." Deacon saw no point in shading his feelings. Tyrell couldn't possibly think Deacon gave a damn about Tyrell's happiness.

Tyrell seemed to gather himself, leaning forward, his chin jutting. "Down to brass tacks, then. Let's see if you think *this* is funny. I'll trade you what I want for what you want."

The words unnerved Deacon. At the same time, they put him on alert. "You haven't the first idea of what I want."

"Don't be too sure about that."

"I'm completely sure about that." Deacon had never even had a conversation with his father, never mind confided his hopes and dreams to him.

"I'll acknowledge you as my son," Tyrell said.

It was all Deacon could do not to laugh at the offer. "I could have proved our relationship through DNA years ago."

"I mean, I'll make you an heir."

"Put me in your will?" Deacon wasn't falling for a promise like that—a promise changeable with the stroke of a pen.

"No. Not when I die. Now. I'm offering you twenty-five percent of Hale Harbor Port. You'll be equal partners with me, Aaron and Beau."

Hale Harbor Port was a billion-dollar corporation that had been owned by succeeding generations of the Clarkson family since the 1700s. Deacon tried to wrap his head around the offer. He couldn't.

His entire childhood he'd dreamed of being a part of the Clarkson family. He'd spun fantasies that Tyrell truly loved Deacon's mother, that he secretly wanted Deacon in his life, that he would one day leave Margo and welcome Deacon and his mother into the castle.

But then Deacon's mother had died when he was barely nineteen, and Tyrell didn't so much as send condolences. Deacon accepted the reality that he meant nothing to Tyrell, and he stopped dreaming.

And now this offer came completely out of the blue. What could possibly be worth twenty-five percent of a billion dollars? Nothing legal, that was for sure.

"You want me to kidnap them?" Deacon asked.

Tyrell shook his head. "That would be too easy. Also temporary, because we'd be sure to get caught."

"But you're not morally opposed to it?" Maybe it should have surprised Deacon that Tyrell would consider committing a capital crime. It didn't.

Tyrell drew in an impatient breath. "Give me credit for a little finesse."

Deacon knew he should walk away from this conversation. "I don't give you credit for anything."

"But you're still listening."

"I'm curious, not tempted."

Tyrell gave a smug smile, polishing off his drink. "Oh, you're tempted all right."

"Spit it out, or I'm leaving." Deacon rose to his feet. He wasn't going to play this game any longer.

"I want you to romance and marry Frederick's widow and bring my grandsons home." Tyrell watched intently for Deacon's reaction.

Deacon didn't have a reaction. He would have bet he hadn't heard right, but Tyrell's words were crystal clear.

"Why?" Deacon tried to fathom the complexity that had to lie behind the request.

Tyrell was reputed to be a master conspirator.

"Why would she marry me?" Deacon voiced his own thought process as he searched for more information. "And what does it gain you? Just offer her money to come home."

"I can't offer her money to come home. I can't even risk contacting her. I'm positive Frederick poisoned her against the family. If I make that play and fail, it's game over."

"You have a whole lot of money to offer."

However Frederick might have disparaged his family, surely most mortal women would be attracted to the family's immense wealth.

"Frederick may have walked away from the company," Tyrell said. "But he didn't walk away from his trust fund. She doesn't need money."

Again, Deacon smiled. "Something you can't buy. Must be frustrating."

"She doesn't know you," Tyrell said.

"Does she know Aaron and Beau?" Deacon still wasn't getting the play here. It had to be galling for Tyrell to approach Deacon for anything.

"Aaron's already married," Tyrell pointed out. "And Beau... I'm not naïve where it comes to my children, Deacon. Beau's nobody's idea of a good husband and father."

Deacon didn't disagree with that statement. Beau had always been the wild one, parties every weekend and a different girlfriend every month. His exploits had been splashed across local gossip columns dozens of times.

"You, on the other hand," Tyrell continued. He gestured Deacon up and down with his empty glass. "I recognize you have a certain sophistication. Women seem to like you. Nice women seem to like you."

Deacon couldn't help but be amazed that Tyrell had paid any attention to him at all.

"You're not publicly connected to the family," Tyrell continued. "You can move in under the radar, romance her, marry her."

"Then blindside her with the news about you?" Deacon had always questioned Tyrell's morality, but this was beyond belief.

Tyrell rolled his eyes. "Ease her into it, boy."

"No." An ownership position in Hale Harbor Port might

be Deacon's lifelong dream, but he wasn't going to use Frederick's widow as a pawn.

Tyrell came to his feet. "You have a moral objection?"

"Yes. And you should, too." Deacon peered into Tyrell's eyes, searching for some semblance of a soul. "You do know that, right?"

"Go meet her," Tyrell said.

Deacon started to refuse again, but Tyrell talked right over him. "Just meet her before you decide. If you don't want to do it, don't do it. But don't give up hundreds of millions of dollars without looking at all the angles."

"You're the angles guy, not me."

"You're my son," Tyrell repeated.

Deacon wanted to protest. He might be saddled with Tyrell's DNA, but he wasn't anything like him. He had a moral compass. He got it from his mother.

But he found himself hesitating.

In that second, it was clear he'd inherited some traits from his father. And they couldn't be good traits. Because he was weighing the harm in meeting Frederick's widow. Was there any harm in meeting her before refusing Tyrell's offer?

It was on days like these that Callie Clarkson missed her husband the most. Frederick loved springtime, the scent of roses wafting in the bakery windows, mingling with the cinnamon and strawberries from the kitchen. Today the sun was shining in a soft blue sky, and tourists were streaming into Downright Sweet for a midmorning muffin or warm berry scone.

Their bakery, Downright Sweet, occupied both floors of a red brick house in the historic district of downtown Charleston. The first floor held the kitchen that they'd refurbished when they bought the place five years ago. It also held the front service counter and several tables, both inside and out on the porch. The second floor was a dining room with screened windows all the way around, plus a covered sundeck that over-looked the tree-lined, shade-dappled street.

The lunch crowd was diminishing, and Callie's manager, Hannah Radcliff, breathed an audible sigh of relief.

"My feet are killing me," Hannah said.

She was in her early forties, with rounded curves from a self-described weakness for buttercream. Her voice was soft. Her eyes were mocha brown, and she had a perpetual smile on her very pretty face. Both of Callie's sons, James and Ethan, loved her to death.

"Go take a break," Callie said. "Nancy and I will be fine."

"Rest your feet," Nancy echoed from where she was wip-ing down the espresso machine. "I'll do the tables."

"I'll take you up on that," Hannah said. "Wait. Hello."

Callie followed the direction of Hannah's gaze to see Mayor Watkins striding past the front window, toward the Down-right Sweet entrance.

Nancy gave an amused laugh. She was a college student who had come back to her family in Charleston for the sum-mer. She didn't see the attraction of the Mayor.

Hank Watkins was single, slightly younger than Hannah and equally quick to smile. His dark hair was short at the sides, with a swoop across the top that didn't particularly appeal to Callie. But he was attractive enough, in a distinguished way that was beneficial for a politician.

She'd describe him as burley, with a deep, booming voice. He was the son of one of Charleston's most prominent families. They traced their ancestry all the way back to the Mayflower.

The classic little gold bell jingled as the door opened.

Callie stepped away from the cash register, busying her-self with tidying the displays of cupcakes and giving Han-nah a clear field.

"Hello, Mr. Mayor," Hannah said.

"You know to call me Hank," the Mayor answered.

"Hank," Hannah said. "What can I get you?" She gestured

to the glass case on her left. "A lemon puff pastry? Or coconut buttercream? The cupcakes are popular today."

"What do you recommend?"

"You can't go wrong with the pecan tart."

"Done."

"Whipped cream?" Hannah asked.

"Of course." The Mayor pulled his wallet from his suit jacket pocket. "Callie?" He turned his attention to her.

"Whipped cream is always a nice addition," Callie answered lightly. She kept her attention on the cupcakes, not wanting to intrude.

"I was hoping I could talk with you," Hank said, his tone going more serious.

She went immediately on edge. "Is everything okay?"

Following the unexpected death of her husband six months ago, Callie's optimism had taken a hit. She realized her years with Frederick had made her complacent. She'd forgotten life mostly dished out pain and disappointment. She intended to be braced for it from here on in.

"Nothing too worrisome," he said, handing Hannah a ten-dollar bill. He smiled again as he spoke to her. "Keep the change."

"Thank you, Hank," Hannah said.

He looked at Callie again. "Will you join me?"

"Sure." She untied her hunter green apron and slipped it over her head.

Beneath, she was wearing a white blouse and a pair of pressed khaki slacks. Her hair was up in a casual twist, and her earrings were small diamond studs that Frederick had given her for her birthday last year. She wore them every day. And as she walked around the end of the display case, she twisted her engagement ring and her wedding band round her finger.

She feared Hank was here with bad news about her deck permit.

He had offered to talk to the board personally to advocate for its quick approval. She'd turned down the offer, but now she wondered if that had been a mistake. Maybe she should have let him help.

Frederick had always advised her to keep the local politicians on their side. *You might not love them*, he'd said. *You might not even like them. But it costs nothing to be congenial, and you never know which way the wind will blow.*

If Downright Sweet didn't get the permit to renovate the deck, they couldn't replace the support beams, meaning they'd have to close the deck down while they came up with a new plan. It was May, the beginning of tourist season, and she was counting on running at full capacity by the end of June.

They took an empty table next to the window.

"Is this about the permit?" she asked.

"I'm afraid so."

Callie's heart sank. "It's been denied."

Hank organized his napkin and fork. "Not yet. But Lawrence Dennison is hesitating."

"Why?"

The bakery, along with all of the buildings in the historic district, was subject to stringent renovation conditions. There were bylaws to protect the character of the area. But Downright Sweet's plans had taken that into account. The deck would be larger, but it would be in keeping with the existing architecture.

"Lawrence is Lawrence," Hank said with a shrug. "He remembers the 1950s fondly."

"I can't believe he keeps getting re-elected."

While she spoke, Callie's mind pinged to potential solutions. She could shrink the size of the deck, maybe do only the structural renovations and keep the cosmetics exactly as they were. But it would be a shame to spend all that money and not improve the functionality. And to do a modified application, she'd have to start the process over again, losing time, and she'd definitely have to close the deck for the entire summer season.

"His pet project is the City Beautification Committee," Hank said, a meaningful look in his eyes.

Callie squinted, trying to read his expression. "And?"

"And, if somebody was to…say…join that committee and show a particular interest in city beautification, Lawrence might feel kindly toward that person." Hank took a forkful of the whipped cream and slid it into his mouth.

Callie found the suggestion unsavory. "You want me to bribe Lawrence to get my permit."

Hank gave an amused smile. "Joining a committee is not a bribe."

"It might not be money."

Hank reached out and covered her hand with his.

It was a startlingly familiar gesture. Her first instinct was to pull back. But Frederick's words echoed in her mind. *It costs you nothing to be congenial.*

"Do you have something against city beautification?" Hank asked.

"Of course I don't." Who could have anything against city beautification? "But I'm busy, the boys, the bakery, taking care of the house."

When they'd first moved to Charleston, she and Frederick had bought a roomy, restored antebellum house. It was beautiful, but the upkeep was daunting.

The bakery door opened again, and a tall figure caught Callie's attention. The man glanced around the room, seeming to methodically take in every aspect.

For some reason, he was fleetingly familiar, though she was sure she hadn't met him before. He looked to be a little over six feet, with thick dark hair, blue eyes and a strong chin. His bearing was confident as he took a step forward.

"It wouldn't be much work." Hank's words forced her attention back to their conversation. "I'm the chair of the committee, and I promise not to assign you anything onerous. We meet once a week. There are six members. Depending on the topic, there's usually some public interest, so citizens attend, as well. It's all very civilized and low-key."

Once a week didn't sound like much, but it meant skipping story time with the boys that night, getting a babysitter, doubling up on housework on another evening.

"It's not a bribe," Hank repeated, giving her hand a light squeeze. "It'll demonstrate your commitment to the city, your participation in the community and that you care about the culture and flavor of the historic district."

"I do care about the culture and flavor of the historic district. I live here, and I work here."

"I know." He gave her hand a firmer squeeze. "So join the committee. Join in a little. Make Lawrence happy, improve your city and unblock the permit for your deck."

When he put it that way, other than the babysitting challenge, there seemed little wrong with the plan. It felt opportunistic, but she wouldn't call it unethical.

Hank leaned in and lowered his tone. "With Frederick gone, I'm sure you want Downright Sweet to be as successful as possible."

"I do."

Callie had grown up severely impoverished, never knowing from week to week how her dysfunctional family would afford food, never mind clothes and electricity. Frederick had pulled her out of all that. He'd been a wonderfully sweet man, vital and full of life. The wheelchair had never held him back.

He'd had enough of a nest egg to buy both their house and Downright Sweet here in Charleston. The business had no capital debt, but it was still a struggle to keep operating costs manageable.

A shadow crossed the table, and a deep male voice interrupted. "Excuse me?"

Callie glanced up, startled to see the tall stranger. She looked into his blue eyes and felt a strange pressure build against her chest.

"Are you Callie Clarkson?" he asked. "The bakery owner?"

"Yes." She slipped her hand from beneath Hank's, wondering if the man was a lifestyle reporter or maybe a restaurant critic.

He held out his hand to shake hers.

She took it, and felt a surge of comfort and strength. He was gentle. He didn't squeeze her hand. But his palm was solid, slightly rough, not too warm, not cool, but an identical temperature to her own.

"Deacon Holt," he said.

Hank pulled back his chair and came to his feet, putting on his practiced political smile. "I'm Mayor Watkins. Are you new to Charleston?"

"A tourist," Deacon Holt said, without breaking his eye contact with Callie.

She knew she should look away, but there was something in the depths of his eyes that was oddly comforting.

"Well, welcome," Hank said in a hearty voice. "I hope you've checked out the Visitor Centre on Meeting Street."

"Not yet," Deacon said, slowly moving his attention to Hank.

"They'll have everything you need—hotels, dining, shopping and, of course, the sights."

"I've already found dining," Deacon said.

Callie felt a smile twitch her lips.

"Well, then I hope you have an enjoyable stay."

Deacon didn't seem fazed by Hank's dismissive tone. He looked back to Callie. "What do you recommend?"

"Everything's good."

He grinned at her answer, and the feeling of familiarity increased. "That was diplomatic."

Hank cleared his throat. It was obvious he wanted to get back to their conversation, to hear Callie's decision.

She'd made a decision, but it could wait two minutes for whatever Deacon Holt wanted. On the chance he could offer free publicity, she was going to make him feel more than welcome.

"The sourdough is terrific," she said. "Any sandwich made with that. If you have a sweet tooth, I'd try a cupcake. The buttercream frosting is to die for."

"Buttercream frosting it is," he said. "Thank you."

"Callie?" Hank prompted as Deacon walked away.

"My answer is yes," she said.

Hank beamed. He really did have an extraordinary smile. He took her hand in both of his. "I'm so pleased."

"When's the next meeting?"

"Thursday. Six thirty."

"I'll be there."

Deacon had been surprised to find Callie in an intimate discussion with Mayor Hank Watkins. Deacon had only been in town a couple of days, but he'd already learned all about the Watkins family. They were the Clarksons of Charleston—all the power, the prestige and the local money.

He'd also been surprised, even more surprised, that Callie was poised, polished and so stunningly beautiful in person. He hadn't expected that of Frederick's wife. Frederick hadn't exactly been suave with the opposite sex.

Deacon had gone to a different high school than Aaron, Beau and Frederick. Deacon had been at PS-752. His three half brothers had gone to Greenland Academy. But there had been enough cross-pollination through sporting events and in social circles, that he'd known the basics of each of them.

He and Beau were the same age. Aaron was a year older, and Frederick was two years younger. Aaron was blond, Beau dark like Deacon and Frederick had ended up with ginger hair and freckles. He was thinner than his brothers and shorter, and always seemed to live in Aaron's intellectual shadow, as well as Beau's athletic one.

Even in the best circumstances, Deacon couldn't see a woman like Callie falling for a man like Frederick. He supposed it could have been the money. It was often the money. Heck, it was usually the money.

For some reason, Deacon didn't want to think that of Callie. But he'd be a fool if he didn't consider the possibility.

After first meeting her yesterday, he'd waited overnight, waited through the morning, and now he was eating lunch at Downright Sweet for a second time. He was looking for more information, particularly for information on her relationship with Mayor Hank Watkins.

From what Deacon could see, Callie was way out of Hank's league. But Hank obviously thought he had a shot. She must have given him encouragement of some kind.

Fact was, Hank had money just like Frederick. There was a chance Callie's charming personality was an act, hiding a shrewd woman who knew exactly what she wanted.

She was behind the counter now, serving customers and looking as enchanting as yesterday. Her dark blond hair was in a jaunty ponytail. Thick lashes framed her blue-green eyes, and her cheeks were flushed with heat and exertion. Her apparent work ethic didn't dovetail with a gold digger. Then again, most people had contradictions in their personalities. And he hadn't even begun to get to know her.

She'd been right about the sourdough bread. It was beyond delicious. Yesterday he'd gone with black forest ham. Today he was trying sliced turkey and tomato. He hadn't decided on dessert yet. There were too many choices.

His gaze moved from the tarts to the cupcakes to the pastries and cookies. He was tempted by the peanut butter white chocolate. Then again, he could practically taste the strawberry cream tarts. Maybe he'd have two desserts. Maybe he'd have to run ten miles before he went to bed tonight.

He was just about to bite into the second half of his sandwich, when the café door opened. Two young boys rushed inside, followed by a perky teenage girl in a T-shirt, shorts and white runners.

Deacon set down his sandwich and watched the boys with amazement. There was no question that they were Callie's two sons. The four-year-old was a mini version of Aaron, while the eighteen-month-old looked exactly like Beau.

"Mommy, mommy," the younger one called out. He trotted through the maze of tables, while his brother followed at a more measured pace.

Callie smiled at her toddler. "Hello, my little darling."

"We were going to stop for ice cream on Parker Street," the teenage girl said.

She looked to be about sixteen. Her blond hair had a flashy blue streak in it that swooped across her forehead. "But the lineup was nearly an hour long, so they decided to bring all the kids back to the preschool early."

"Did you have fun at the waterpark?" Callie asked.

"Sprinkley," said the compact Beau.

"I went down the big slide." Little Aaron made a long swooping motion with his hand.

"Ethan squirted everything that moved." The teenager ruffled Little Beau's dark head. "He has good aim."

"Squirted James head," Ethan sang out with pride. He turned his thumb and index finger into a gun and pointed at his brother.

Deacon watched the interplay with amazement.

"I was already wet," James said philosophically.

"I'm glad you had fun," Callie said.

"Can we have cookies?" James asked.

"Since you skipped the ice cream, you can each have one."

"I want peanut butter," James said.

"Color candies," Ethan sang out.

"What about you, Pam?" Callie asked the teenager.

"I'm fine."

"We just took some oatmeal monster cookies out of the oven."

Pam laughed. "You talked me into it."

She ushered the boys to a table by the wall.

Deacon rose and crossed to the counter.

"Those are your sons?" he asked Callie.

The question obviously took her by surprise. "Yes, they are."

"They seem terrific."

Her expression stayed guarded. "Thank you."

"Did I hear you say you had warm monster cookies?" Deacon asked.

"Fresh from the oven," she said, putting on a professional smile.

"I'll take one."

"Coming up." She pressed some keys on her cash register.

He held up his credit card. "Your advice was good yesterday."

She looked puzzled.

"You suggested the sourdough bread. You were right."

"I'm glad to hear you enjoyed it." She pointed to the small terminal, and he swiped his credit card over the window.

"I'm back today for more."

"That's what we like to hear."

The machine beeped its acceptance of his payment, while another staff member set his cookie plate on the counter.

He knew his time was almost up.

"I was wondering," he said to Callie.

Her pretty brows went up in a question.

"Would you join me for coffee?"

The question clearly unnerved her. She touched her wedding ring, and her gaze darted to her sons.

"I don't mean right now," he clarified. "Maybe later?"

Her forehead creased.

"Or tomorrow," he hastily put in, sensing her imminent refusal.

"It's really nice of you to offer," she said.

"I hear a *but* in there."

Was she dating the Mayor? She'd certainly say no to coffee with Deacon if she were dating the Mayor.

"The *but* is that I'm really, really busy."

"I understand," he said, pocketing his card.

Being busy was probably just an excuse. It likely had more to do with Mayor Watkins. But pushing her wasn't going to get Deacon anywhere—better to regroup.

Not that he'd made a decision to romance her. He was still assessing the situation.

He wasn't about to take advantage of an innocent woman. But if she was gaming the rich Mayor now, she might have been gaming Frederick before him. And that changed the equation entirely.

"Maybe another time," he said to her.

"Are you staying long in Charleston?" she asked.

"I haven't decided." He gave her an intimate smile. "It depends on how well I like it."

Her cheeks flushed.

He lifted the plate with his cookie. "Thanks for this."

"Any time."

"I'll hold you to that."

She didn't seem to know how to respond.

He backed off. He'd ask around town. Maybe he'd get lucky and someone would know if Hank Watkins was in a relationship with Callie.

Two

In the small office in the back of the bakery, Callie's gaze rested on the framed photo of Frederick and the boys. She was struck by how much the boys had grown since Frederick passed away. She lifted the picture into better lighting.

It was the last one taken of her sons with their father. It was on their road trip last September. They'd traveled north along the coast, all the way to Virginia Beach.

Frederick had loved driving holidays. She suspected that sitting in a car made him forget about his disability and feel just like everyone else.

James was patient with the long rides, but Ethan was less than enthusiastic about spending so much time in his car seat. Frederick had done his best to entertain Ethan, who had just turned one that trip, while Callie had done the driving. It seemed like such a long time ago.

In November, Frederick had come down with a cold, just a routine cold that James had picked up in preschool. It settled in Frederick's chest, which was normal for him. He insisted it was nothing to worry about, since both James and then Ethan had run fevers with the bug, coughed a few nights and then recovered.

But in the morning, Frederick's fever had spiked alarmingly. Callie had rushed him to the hospital, where he lost consciousness and was diagnosed with pneumonia. They started antibiotics immediately. But his lungs had been severely bruised in his fall as a young teenager, and the scarring had left them weak.

He never woke up, and she'd said a final *goodbye* to him within hours.

Now she looked at the photo, Ethan grinning on Frederick's lap, James standing with his head on Frederick's shoulder. James still remembered Daddy, but Ethan only knew him from photos and video clips. Both boys had changed so much, grown so strong, learned so much. Frederick would be proud of them both.

"Callie?" Hannah poked her head through the open doorway.

"Is it getting busy out there?" Callie set the picture back down.

It was nearing the lunch hour. Pam had the boys until two today. With Frederick gone, Callie had modified her schedule. Pam was a godsend of a babysitter, and Hannah kept the bakery running like a well-oiled machine when Callie had to be at home.

"The lineup's growing," Hannah said. "The Spring Berry Cheesecake is still really moving."

Callie was happy with the news. They'd created the recipe and introduced the new item just this month. It was gratifying to hear it was a success.

"I'm on my way." Callie rose and followed Hannah through the kitchen to the café.

The lineup was halfway across the seating area. A few tables had just been vacated. Callie moved quickly to clear them and make room for more customers to sit down.

As she freshened the last of three tables, she was surprised to spot Deacon Holt sitting in one of the window booths. It had been a week since he was last in the café, and she'd assumed his vacation had ended and he'd left town.

Since she never expected to see him again, she'd allowed herself to fantasize the past few nights. Her fantasies ranged from hand-holding in the park to kissing under the stars to more, much more. She felt her face warm thinking about it. She knew he couldn't read her mind, but looking at him now felt oddly intimate.

He spotted her. "Hello, Callie."

She shook off her discomfort and went to his table. "Hello, Deacon."

His smile went broad at her use of his name.

"I thought you would have left town by now," she said.

"Still here in Charleston."

She glanced at his sandwich plate. "And back for more sourdough?"

"I couldn't stay away." His tone sounded flirtatious, and she raised her gaze. "I was hoping you'd reconsider my invitation."

She wished she didn't feel the same way. She knew she had to fight it. It would be unseemly to rush out and date this soon after her husband's death.

It wasn't that Frederick had been the love of her life. They were dear friends, companions, parents together. Frederick had rescued her from hopeless poverty, and she'd given him the family he desired.

"I wish I could," she said honestly.

"Something is stopping you?" His tone was gentle, even concerned.

"A full and busy life." She wasn't about to get into details.

"Someone else?" he asked.

She drew back in surprise. "What?"

"Are you dating someone else?"

"I don't date." She glanced over her shoulder to check the lineup, feeling suddenly guilty for standing and talking while Hannah and the others were so busy.

"Everyone dates," Deacon said.

"No, they don't. Case in point, me." Why was she still here? Why was she indulging herself in something that couldn't happen?

"Maybe not in the formal sense, but the opposite sex is always checking each other out."

"I'm not checking you out," she lied.

There was a gentle amusement in his blue eyes. "Well, I am most definitely checking you out."

"Don't."

"It's not something I can control. But to be clear, I'm only suggesting coffee and conversation."

She gestured to the lineup. "I have to get back to work."

"Okay."

"I can't go out with you. I don't have time." The excuse was perfectly true. Between the bakery and her sons, she had no time for a social life.

"Okay." He gave up easily.

She didn't regret saying no. She wouldn't allow herself to regret it.

She gave him a nod and firmly turned herself around, heading behind the counter.

"What was that?" Hannah asked in an undertone.

"Just a customer." Callie wished she didn't feel overheated. Then again, she was in a bakery, and it was May. It would be odd if she didn't feel overheated.

"He was in last week."

"He was," Callie acknowledged.

Hannah finished ringing up a cheesecake order and handed a customer some change.

Callie took a clean plate from the stack and loaded it up with a slice of Spring Berry Cheesecake, a drizzle of chocolate sauce and a generous dollop of whipped cream. She set it on top of the case, then assembled another identical one.

"What did he say?" Hannah asked.

"Nothing," Callie answered.

"That was an awfully long nothing."

"He asked me to coffee," Callie admitted.

"That's fantastic."

"I said no."

A new customer stepped up. "Two pecan tarts and a dozen peanut butter cookies. Can you make the cookies to go?"

"Cookies to go," Hannah called over her shoulder.

Callie plated the tarts. "Whipped cream?" she asked the man.

"Only on one."

She decorated the tart, while another staff member bagged the cookies.

The staff worked efficiently until the lineup disappeared. Hannah followed Callie into the back, where cinnamon twists were cooling on racks, and the bakers were rolling out pastry.

"Why would you say no?" Hannah asked her.

Callie knew exactly what Hannah was talking about. "I'm not going to date a tourist. I'm not going to date anyone. I don't have time, and it's only been six months."

"It's been a lot more than six months."

"Nobody knows that." Callie and Frederick had never let on that their marriage was anything other than normal.

Hannah's voice went singsong. "I'm just saying, what's wrong with a little flirting, a little kissing, a little…whatever with a handsome stranger?"

"I'm not answering that."

"Because the answer you wish you could give is opposite to the answer you want to give," Hannah said with authority.

"That didn't even make any sense."

"Your hormones want one thing, but your brain is fighting it."

"I have two sons, a bakery and city beautification to think about."

"Callie, you're a healthy and vibrant young woman who's never—"

"*That* has nothing to do with anything."

Hannah knew Frederick hadn't been able to engage in intercourse. James and Ethan were conceived through in vitro fertilization.

"You're going to have to take the plunge someday."

"Sex is not the only kind of intimacy."

"I get that," Hannah said, backing off.

"It doesn't sound like you get that."

"I'm not trying to push you."

Callie let out a laugh at the absurdity of Hannah's last statement.

"I'm only saying…you know…don't write off a guy like that too quickly. Think about it."

Callie had thought about it. She was still thinking about it. That was her biggest problem. She couldn't seem to stop thinking about it.

Deacon recognized a losing strategy when he was engaged in one. Callie wasn't going to date him. It was probably because of the Mayor, but it could be something else. In any event, if he wanted to get closer to her and find out, he had to change tactics.

He spent another week in town, researching Callie and Hank Watkins. People considered them both pillars of the community. They hung with the same crowd, attended the same functions. People mostly thought the Mayor was a good catch, and a few seemed to have speculated on the two of them as a couple.

When Deacon learned Callie was on the City Beautification Committee, he jumped on the opportunity and showed up at a meeting. He sat in the back, obscured by the shape of the room. But he was close enough to watch her interactions with Hank.

Hank whispered in her ear at one point, and she smiled in return. He touched her arm, and she didn't pull away. He filled her water glass and offered her a pen. She took the pen and drank the water.

Watching her cozy up to the wealthy, powerful, but much older, Hank Watkins renewed Deacon's suspicion she'd married Frederick for his money. It also confirmed that Deacon had competition.

He realized he didn't have the Watkins name and power, and he sure couldn't tell her he was a Clarkson. But he'd achieved a reasonable level of success in life, and he could make himself sound better than he was—richer and more powerful.

But he was going to take a more subtle approach this time, let her come to him. At the end of the meeting, when coffee and cookies were served over friendly chitchat, he struck up a conversation with a few Charleston citizens. He stood where he was sure he'd be in Callie's line of sight.

"Deacon?" Her tentative voice behind him said the approach had worked.

He turned, feigning surprise. "Callie. It's great to see you again." He cheerfully excused himself from the others.

"Exactly how long is your vacation?" she asked, brow furrowed as they moved a few steps away.

He feigned a guilty expression. "I'm afraid I have a confession to make."

She waited.

He'd rehearsed his lines. "I'm more than just an ordinary tourist."

She looked apprehensive. "Who are you?"

"I'm thinking of relocating to Charleston."

The words seemed to put her off guard. "Why didn't you say so?"

"It's complicated. There were things to check out, arrangements to make. I didn't want people to know I was considering the city."

"Considering it for what?" Now she seemed annoyed and distinctly suspicious.

He realized he was messing this up. "I'm a partner in a national transportation company."

The claim was an exaggeration, but not a huge one. He was a minor partner, and they were more regional than national. But it was true enough to get by.

"We're based out of Virginia," he continued. "But we're looking to expand. We'd need a lot of land, commercial industrial land. If the real estate community knew we were in the market, well, funny things happen to prices when a large corporation expresses an interest."

He stuck as close as he could to the truth. Mobi Transport was always looking to expand. It could as easily expand into Charleston as anywhere else. And local land prices did get jacked up when the real estate community knew a big corporation was in the market.

"You're saying dishonesty was in your best interest."

He wasn't sure how to answer that. "I wouldn't call it dishonesty."

"You're keeping Charleston citizens in the dark about the value of their property."

"I'm keeping the value realistic."

"By lying about your intentions."

"I'm not—"

"That's how market forces work, Deacon. When something is in demand, it becomes more valuable."

He was surprised the conversation had taken this turn.

At the same time, he was curious about her immediate leap to skepticism. Honest people were trusting. Devious people looked for deceit in others.

"I don't want to have to pick another city," he told her. "I like Charleston. If land costs too much here, we'll choose another city where it costs less."

She gave a little shrug, as if the easiest solution in the world was at hand. "Just tell the people that's the case."

"That's one way to approach it."

"It's the honest way to approach it."

"Are you an honesty-is-the-best-policy type?" He watched her reaction.

She hesitated, her expression flinching ever so slightly. "It *is* the best policy."

She hadn't exactly answered, but he didn't press.

"Check out the Mobi Transportation website. See if you think it would be good for Charleston."

The Mobi website was slick and professional. It was designed to encourage sales by making the company look bigger than it was.

"We do long-haul trucking. We have six terminals across the northeast."

Her expression relaxed a little. "That sounds...interesting."

"In the internet age, goods transportation is primed for expansion. There's a whole lot of opportunity in the sector."

Out of the corner of his eye, he could see Hank Watkins making his was toward them.

Deacon gestured to the refreshment table on the other side of the room. "Would you like a coffee? A cookie? They're okay, but not as good as yours."

"Flattery, Deacon?"

"The truth, Callie." He didn't have to exaggerate there. "Your cookies are the best I've ever tasted. How long have you been a baker?"

She made a move toward the refreshment table. "I worked in a café from the time I was fourteen."

He fell into step beside her. "That young?"

"We didn't have much money when I was growing up. I did whatever it took. I lied about my age. I bused tables at first, but then I was promoted to waitress."

He was starting to form a picture of her. She was a survivor. He could relate to that.

"Did you grow up here in Charleston? Decaf?" He reached for the labeled pot.

"Decaf would be best."

He poured them each a cup.

"It was a small town in Tennessee, Grainwall." She flinched almost imperceptibly as she said the town's name.

He kept watch on Hank's progress. "You didn't like it there?"

"Nobody likes it there. My husband, Frederick, and I chose Charleston because it was so beautiful." A look of sadness passed over her face.

"I was sorry to hear about your husband."

Deacon was genuinely sorry about Frederick's death. Frederick had seemed like the nicest of the entire Clarkson clan. He was certainly the most honorable. Neither of his brothers seemed to ever stand up to their father, who—if employees of the company were to be believed—was an ill-tempered, self-centered control freak.

"Thank you," Callie said, her expression pinched. "We miss him. He was a wonderful man."

Deacon silently acknowledged that she played the delicate widow very well.

"I met him at the Fork 'n' Spoon," she said.

"You worked somewhere called the Fork 'n' Spoon?"

"It was aptly named, since we provided both forks and spoons." She gave an engaging smile. "It was mostly burgers and chili—not the best clientele. I don't know how Frederick found it, but he kept coming back."

Deacon wasn't surprised that Frederick kept coming back, and it sure wouldn't have been for the burgers. Callie was enough to draw any man back again and again. Like Hank, who was slowly getting closer.

"He said he liked the chili." Callie held her coffee mug in both hands, but didn't take a drink.

"Was it good?"

She laughed lightly. "I've seen it bring down a man twice Frederick's size. He may have been in a wheelchair, but he had the stomach of an ox."

Deacon decided to let the wheelchair comment slide. "So you moved to Charleston together?"

"That's when we opened the bakery. We had no idea what we were doing. But Frederick had a little bit of money."

A little bit? Deacon couldn't help but be curious about her definition of a lot of money.

"I knew something about the café business," she continued. "And I wanted to work somewhere nice, somewhere pleasant, somewhere that customers were happy. Desserts seemed like a good idea. When Hannah came on board, we managed to make it come together."

Hank was closing in, only one persistent senior citizen holding him back. Deacon glanced at his watch, wondering how he might get Callie outside.

She followed suit and glanced at her watch. "I've got a babysitter waiting."

Perfect.

She set down her cup and started for the door, and he went along.

"You're interested in city beautification?" he asked as they walked.

"I am now."

He held open the door, taking note of Hank's frustrated expression. "Well, that answer has me intrigued."

"I..." She looked flustered.

He couldn't imagine what would fluster her about city beautification. Had she joined the committee to get close to Hank?

"I thought... I should...get engaged and support my community."

Well, that was the worst lie Deacon had ever heard. She was all but begging him to call her on it.

"Will you tell me the real story?" he asked, assuming that's what she expected him to do.

Her face flushed under the community center's porch lights. "It's embarrassing."

"We all do embarrassing things. I promise, I'll understand."

Deacon was ready for her to walk to the parking lot. Instead, she turned the opposite way down the sidewalk. That worked for him.

She took an exaggerated breath, as if she was about to own up to grand larceny. "I joined the committee to butter up Lawrence Dennison."

The unexpected answer threw Deacon. "Isn't Lawrence pushing eighty?"

"Downright Sweet is in the historic district. My deck needs repairs, or I'll have to close it down. I can't do the repairs without the permit. Lawrence is holding up the permit. And the beautification committee is Lawrence's pet project. I'm buttering him up by joining the committee."

Deacon was impressed. By guiltily confessing to such a trivial lie, she looked like the most honest woman in the world.

If Deacon didn't believe she was using the story to manipulate him, it would have been enchanting.

For the next three days, Callie glanced up every time a customer walked through the bakery door. She thought Deacon might stop by Friday. He'd walked her all the way to her door Thursday evening.

He hadn't judged her for joining the committee. He'd understood. He'd even told her his own story about planning a lavish party when a particular state politician was in town, with the aim of getting an introduction to him in order to help Mobi Transportation expand. He couldn't say for sure if it had worked, but he'd definitely put out the effort.

They'd laughed and talked for ten blocks. She would have invited him in, but she had to tuck the boys into bed. She'd found herself hoping he'd kiss her. But he didn't.

Then she'd fully expected him to show up at Downright Sweet and ask her out again. He didn't do that either.

By Monday, she feared he'd left town. Maybe the right land wasn't available. Or maybe taxes were too high. There were a hundred reasons why he could have decided against Charleston.

"Callie?" Hannah came out of the kitchen with a phone in her hand. "It's for you. Lawrence Dennison."

Callie didn't know whether to be optimistic or worried. Was Lawrence calling to thank her for joining the committee, or had he seen right through her ruse?

"Does he sound annoyed?" she asked Hannah.

"Not that I could tell."

"Happy?"

"No. What's going on?"

"Nothing." Callie took the phone. She steeled herself. "Hello?"

"Hello, Callie." Lawrence sounded happy—maybe too happy.

"Hello, Councilman Dennison."

"Please, please, call me Lawrence."

She couldn't help but think the invitation was a good sign, but she didn't want to hope. "All right. Lawrence."

"I'm calling to thank you personally."

She felt a wave of relief. "For joining the committee."

"For the donation."

"The donation?"

Hannah, who was watching, cocked her head in curiosity.

"Two-thousand dollars was very generous of you."

Two-thousand dollars? Had Callie accidentally signed something, or agreed to something? She couldn't afford to donate two-thousand dollars. "I—"

Lawrence didn't seem to hear her. "The beautification committee will definitely put the money to good use."

"Lawrence, I think there's been—"

"And on your building permit, I've reviewed the architectural drawings, and I'm optimistic it can be approved this week."

"Approved?"

She knew she should protest. She hadn't made any donation. And if she had, would it have been a bribe?

Hannah's brown eyes went wide as she whispered. "The permit?"

Callie wanted to nod, but she was afraid to jinx it. Could this really be happening?

"You should hear something by Wednesday. If the office doesn't call, feel free to contact me directly."

Hannah touched her arm, pointing to the bakery door.

Callie turned to see Deacon walk in. He looked tall, handsome and crisply cool in a pair of designer jeans and a dress shirt with the sleeves rolled up and the collar open.

"I...uh..." Her gaze met Deacon's secretive, self-satisfied smirk, and she immediately knew what had happened. "Thank you, Lawrence."

"My pleasure. Goodbye, Callie."

"Goodbye." Without taking her gaze off Deacon, she handed the phone to Hannah. "I have to talk to Deacon."

"Are we getting our building permit?"

"Looks like we are." Callie wasn't sure how to feel about that: happy, guilty, annoyed, grateful?

What kind of man would do that for her?

While she wondered, he came to a stop on the other side of the display case. "Hello, Callie."

"Can we talk?" she asked.

"Sure." He glanced around at the customers. "Can you get away for a few minutes?"

"Yes." She untied her apron and lifted it over her head.

He gave an admiring glance at her white, short-sleeved blouse and fitted black skirt. The interest in his eyes sent a pleasant sizzle down her spine. He had a casual, earthy sexuality that reached out to her.

She had to remind herself she was...at least possibly...annoyed with him.

A good person would be annoyed with him.

Wouldn't they?

Winding her way through the dining tables, she followed him to the door. Her gaze moved involuntarily from his broad shoulders, down the taper of his back, to his attractive rear. He had to be in incredible shape. A good person wouldn't be watching his rear end either.

She wanted to be a good person.

"It's a hot one," he said as they exited to the sidewalk.

"It was you, wasn't it?" she blurted out.

"I don't know," he said easily. "What are we talking about?"

"The *donation*."

It was clear from his expression that he immediately understood. "Ahhh."

"I'm taking that as a yes."

"Yes. It was me. Can I hold your hand?"

"What?" Her brain stumbled on the question.

"Your hand. I'd like to hold your hand while we walk."

"Why are you saying that?"

"Because it's true."

"We're talking about *you* letting *Lawrence* think I made a big donation to the beautification committee."

"We can't do that while I'm holding you hand?"

"Deacon."

"What?" Instead of waiting for an answer, he took her hand as they walked beneath the arching oak trees.

She knew she should pull away, but she didn't seem to have it in her. "Lawrence just called me," she persisted.

"Good." They took a few more steps. "Right?"

It was definitely good holding hands. In fact, it was great holding hands. His was strong. It felt manly. It was a manly hand, and she liked that.

"Callie?"

"Huh?"

"What did Lawrence say?"

"Oh." She put her focus back on track. "He said my permit will be approved on Wednesday."

Deacon squeezed her hand, lifting it to his lips to give it a kiss. "That's fantastic!"

She let his action sink in for a moment.

He'd kissed her.

It was on the hand, sure. But he'd kissed her, and she'd liked it. Her lips tingled as she thought about the kiss. They were jealous of her hand.

She ordered herself to get a grip. She got a grip, tamping down her wayward reaction.

"You bribed him," she said, making sure she sounded disapproving.

"That wasn't a bribe. It was inspiration."

"It was *money*."

"A bribe would be if you called him up and said 'I'll give you two-thousand dollars if you approve my permit.'"

"I didn't *do that*." Her brained clicked through the implications. "Did I break the law?"

He chuckled. "You're too much." Then he lifted her hand to kiss it again.

He held it still against his lips. He stopped walking, and she stopped too.

He turned to gaze into her eyes. She felt a wash of helpless desire warm her body and flush her skin.

He wrapped his free hand around her upper arm, urging her gently backward into a narrow, cobblestone alley.

"Can I kiss you?" he whispered. "I want to kiss you."

She didn't even think to refuse. "Yes."

Three

Deacon's anticipation of the kiss went way beyond the role he was playing. He truly wanted to kiss Callie senseless. But he forced himself to take it slow.

He brushed the back of his hand over her cheek, marveling at the softness of her creamy skin. "You're beautiful."

Her red lips parted, softening, while her blue-green eyes went opaque. She looked slightly tremulous, compellingly innocent. Even as he questioned her authenticity, he reacted to the sensual image with a rush of passion and an overwhelming surge of possessiveness.

He leaned down and brought his lips to hers.

She tasted like honey. Her lips were tender and malleable. She returned his kiss, and a tidal wave of desire hijacked his senses.

He spread his fingers into her hair, releasing its lavender scent into the summer breeze. He placed his palm on the small of her back, drawing her close, reveling in the touch of her soft, toned body. She molded against him.

Her head tipped to the side, and he deepened the kiss. She welcomed his tongue, answering it with her own. He could feel his arousal build. He was dimly aware they were on the street, barely masked by the stone buildings on either side. He could feel himself stop caring.

But then her palms went to his chest, and she gave the lightest of pushes.

He immediately broke the kiss and backed off. His breathing was deep and ragged, and his head was swirling with a cocktail of hormones and emotions. What on earth had just happened?

"I'm sorry," she said, with a tremble to her tone.

He took another half step back and blew out a breath, struggling to get his bearings. "I'm the one who's sorry. That was my fault."

"It's just…" She glanced to the sidewalk behind him.

"Anybody could have seen us." He finished her thought.

"It's complicated," she said.

He couldn't help but wonder if she meant it was complicated because of her feelings for Mayor Watkins or because of Frederick's recent passing. She still wore her wedding ring.

"I understand," Deacon said. Whether it was Hank or Frederick, Deacon's job right now was the same, behave like a perfect gentleman. "I wasn't trying to rush you or push you. I'd be happy just to take you out for coffee."

A man's voice sounded behind Deacon. "Callie?"

Concern crossed her face.

Deacon turned to see Hank Watkins on the sidewalk behind them.

"Hello, Hank," she said, shifting from behind Deacon, putting some more space between the two of them. "You remember Deacon Holt?"

Hank's attention shifted to Deacon for a brief second, just long enough to be dismissive.

"I was looking for you at the bakery," Hank said to her.

"Oh?" Guilt was pretty clear in her voice.

Deacon would bet she was either dating Hank, or at least stringing him along.

He decided to test his theory by shifting closer to her. "I don't know if Callie mentioned it, but my company, Mobi Transportation, is looking to open a new terminal in North Carolina."

As Mayor, the prospect should have pleased Hank. But as Callie's boyfriend, it would annoy him.

It annoyed him.

"I see," Hank said, jaw tightening and eyes going hard. "Am I to understand you're considering Charleston?"

"He wanted to keep it quiet," Callie said in a rush, putting

the space back between her and Deacon. It sounded suspi-
ciously like she was making an excuse for keeping the information from Hank. "For business purposes," she finished.

"Callie has been very kind in helping me understand the
city," Deacon said.

Hank's nostrils flared.

"Did you need to talk about something?" she asked Hank.

Hank refocused his attention on her, and his expression
smoothed out. "I spoke with Lawrence this morning. I understand it's good news all around."

"You mean the permit?"

"I mean the donation. Well played, Callie."

"It wasn't—"

"She was just telling me about the positive outcome," Deacon put in.

Hank's gaze hardened on Deacon. "She was, was she?"

"I agree with you," Deacon told Hank, pretending to be
oblivious to the undercurrents. "The donation was a good
move. The permit should be in place this week, and she can
get moving on the renovations."

"*She* doesn't need your support," Hank said.

"I'm standing right here," Callie said.

"Forgive me." His tone dripping with remorse, Hank
stepped forward and took her hands.

Deacon wanted to rip her from Hank's hold. He waited for
her to break it, but she didn't.

Part of Deacon wanted to repeat his invitation for coffee,
nail it down here and now. But the smarter part of him wanted
to keep Hank in the dark about his intentions. If Hank knew
Deacon was interested in Callie, he'd block him from every
angle. Better to make a strategic temporary retreat and let
Hank feel overconfident.

"I have to be on a call in a few minutes," Deacon told Callie.

"Sorry to have kept you." She finally withdrew from
Hank's hand-hold.

"See you later," Deacon told her in a breezy tone that masked his frustration.

He left them, taking swift, long strides along the sidewalk.

Half a block away, he pulled out his phone. He dialed Tyrell's private number.

"Yes?" came Tyrell's gruff answer.

"I'm in," Deacon said.

There was a silent pause on the line. "You'll romance Callie?"

"Draft the paperwork." Deacon ended the call.

Callie wasn't going to think of this as a date. It was true that coffee with Deacon had turned into dinner. But that was only a matter of convenience. It was easier for her to get away in the evening. Downright Sweet catered to the breakfast and lunch crowd, closing at six, after patrons picked up takeout on their way home.

She didn't know where she and Deacon were going for dinner, so she'd gone neutral with a sleeveless midnight blue cocktail dress. Its scoop neckline sparkled with a spray of subtle crystals. The waist was fitted, and it flared slightly to mid-thigh.

She'd popped her little diamond studs into her ears, pairing them with a delicate gold diamond chip pendant. Her black, high-heeled sandals were classic and comfortable. Her makeup had turned out a little heavier than usual, and when she caught a glimpse of herself in the mirror, she realized there was a shine of anticipation in her eyes.

She spotted her wedding set in the mirror.

She lifted her hand, spreading her fingers and touching the solitaire diamond.

She was too jazzed tonight for something that wasn't a date.

She closed her eyes. Then she pulled off the rings. Before she could change her mind, she opened her jewelry box and set them on the red velvet. She'd already kissed Deacon once.

If she was going to do it again, she had to admit to herself that Frederick was in her past.

She smoothed her dress, taking a last look at herself in the mirror.

Then her phone rang, and she felt a sudden rush of anxiety. Was it Deacon? Had he changed his mind?

She was afraid to look at the number, afraid to see it was him.

"Hello?"

"Callie?" It was Pam.

Callie breathed a sigh of relief. "Are you running late?"

"Yes. I mean, no." Pam's tone was high, her words rushed. "I mean, I'm not running at all."

"Whoa. Slow down. Is everything okay?"

"I fell down the front stairs."

There were voices in the background.

"Are you hurt?" Callie asked. "Who's there with you?"

"I twisted my ankle. My mom's taking me to the hospital for X-rays. It's swelling up fast."

"I'm so sorry." Callie's heart went out to Pam.

Pam was an avid cyclist and tennis player. A broken ankle would be devastating for her.

"I can't babysit tonight," Pam said.

"Don't worry about it. Take care of yourself."

"I'm so sorry."

"It's fine. Get to the doctor. Call me when you know something, okay? And if there's anything I can do."

"Ouch! Mom, I can't bend that way."

Callie cringed in sympathy.

"I better go," Pam said.

"Good luck," Callie called as Pam signed off.

"Mommy, Mommy," James shouted up from the kitchen.

"I'm coming, honey."

The front doorbell rang.

"Ethan squirted his juice box," James cried out.

"Ethan," Callie admonished her youngest son as she trotted down the stairs. "You know better than to squirt."

"Purple," Ethan said with an unrepentant grin.

"Do you want to use a sippy cup instead?"

Ethan's smile disappeared, and he shook his head.

The doorbell rang again.

"Then don't squeeze," she told him firmly.

"Can we have macaroni?" James asked, opening the refrigerator door. "With orange cheese?"

"We'll see," Callie said, swooping the juice box out of Ethan's hand to set it on the counter.

"Juice box!" Ethan cried, reaching up for it.

So much for her date. Or her non-date. Whatever it was, she was sorely disappointed to miss it.

"I have to get the door," she told James.

"Juice box!" Ethan screeched.

"You'll have to wait a minute," she said to Ethan, walking quickly down the hallway to the entry foyer.

She drew open the door to find Deacon on the porch.

"Hi," he said. Then his attention was immediately drawn to Ethan's cries from the kitchen. "Is everything okay?"

"Juice box disaster," she said, pulling the door wide and standing out of the way. "Come on in."

He wore a white dress shirt, a steel blue blazer and dark jeans.

"You look fantastic," he said, closing the door behind him.

She smiled, her heart warming at the compliment. She hated to tell him the night was over before it even got started.

"I'll be right back." She headed for the kitchen to quiet Ethan.

He'd come up with another plan of attack and was pushing a chair toward the counter.

She retrieved the juice box. "No more squirting?" she asked him in a grave voice.

"No squirt," he agreed, abandoning the chair to trot over to her.

"I'm hungry," James said.

"I know." She rubbed her hand over his tousled hair. "Pam can't come tonight."

Ethan took a pause in his drinking. "Pam, Pam."

"Pam hurt her ankle," Callie told them both. "She has to go see a doctor."

"Does she need a bandage?" James asked. "We have horsey bandages."

"Yes, we do," Callie agreed.

The boys were currently big into cartoon bandages. Since they got a lot of cuts and scrapes, it was helpful that they thought of the bandages as a treat.

"The doctor will probably give her a white bandage. It might be a big one."

"Big owie?" Ethan asked.

"I hope not," Callie said.

She was already thinking about tomorrow morning and what she could do about work. With Pam out of commission, she was going to have a problem.

Deacon's voice joined the conversation. "Somebody has a *big owie*?"

Callie turned to see him in the kitchen doorway.

Both boys fell silent and stared at Deacon.

"I didn't mean to abandon you," she told Deacon.

"No problem."

"James, Ethan, this is my friend Deacon Holt."

"Hello," James said.

Ethan stayed silent.

Deacon stepped into the kitchen and crouched on his haunches. "Hello, James. Hi, Ethan. You probably don't re-member, but I saw you at Downright Sweet last week. You were having cookies."

"Color candies," Ethan said.

"That's exactly what you had."

"I had peanut butter," James said.

"I had a warm monster cookie," Deacon said.

"Purple juice," Ethan said, holding up his juice box as proof.

"I see that." Deacon's gaze took in the purple streak that ran across the white patterned linoleum.

"Oh, dang," Callie said, remembering the spill. If she didn't get it wiped up, it would stain.

She crossed to the sink and soaked a cloth with hot water.

"I'll get that." Deacon's voice directly behind her made her jump.

"Oh, no you don't." She wasn't about to let him scrub her floor.

"You look way too good to be cleaning floors." He gently but firmly took the cloth from her hand.

"Deacon, don't," she protested.

But he was down on one knee, wiping up the spill.

"Ethan squirted," James said.

"I see that," Deacon answered.

"He got in trouble."

"Trouble," Ethan called out with glee, jumping in place.

"Careful," Callie said, afraid of another stream of purple, afraid it might hit Deacon's white shirt.

"Gone, gone," Ethan said and shook the box.

Callie took it from him, while Deacon rinsed out the cloth.

"It's my babysitter that got hurt," Callie told Deacon. "She's getting an ankle X-ray. I'm sorry, but I'm afraid we'll have to postpone dinner."

Deacon shut off the taps and squeezed the excess water from the cloth. "You're going to have to eat something."

"The boys want me to make them macaroni." It wasn't Callie's favorite, especially when she'd been anticipating music, wine and adult company.

"With orange cheese," James said.

"How do they feel about pizza?" Deacon asked.

Ethan's attention immediately perked up. "Pizza?"

"It has white cheese," Deacon said to James.

"Pineapple," Ethan called out.

"With pepperoni?" James asked.

Callie couldn't believe Deacon was making the offer. Was he actually willing to stay here amongst the grape juice stains with two rambunctious boys and eat take-out pizza?

"What's your favorite topping?" he asked her.

"I don't think you know what you're doing," she said.

"I have ordered pizza a time or two."

"You're volunteering to stay?"

"You're staying."

"Of course I am."

He gave a shrug. "Then that's settled. What's the best pizza place in the neighborhood? And do you want me to run out for some wine?"

On the sofa, Ethan's sleeping head cradled in her lap, Callie sipped a glass of cabernet sauvignon.

"It's the biggest castle in all of England," James said, putting a final colored building brick on the tower he was assembling with Deacon.

"Who lives inside?" Deacon asked, making Callie smile.

"The King," James said. "And the Queen, and five little princes."

"Five? That's a lot of princes."

"They play together in the tower. It has winding stairs, and they have practice swords."

"Are there any princesses in the castle?" Deacon asked.

"Nah. Girls are no fun."

Deacon looked up to catch Callie's eye and give her a light-hearted grin. "I think girls are pretty fun."

"They play with dolls," James said, scooting backward on the living room carpet to survey their creation.

"I suppose that's true. But boys can play with dolls," Deacon said.

"I know they *can* play with dolls. But why would they?"

"They could pretend they were the daddy."

"My daddy had a wheelchair," James said matter-of-factly.

Callie's breath caught for a second. James rarely mentioned Frederick.

"I heard he did," Deacon said with a nod.

"I sat in it once. I like my bike better." James took the remaining few blocks and built a square near the front gate. "That's the statue."

"Guarding the front gate?"

"It's a statue. It can't guard."

"Some statues are built to look fierce and scare off the bad guys," Deacon said. "Like lions."

"Or dragons."

"Or dragons."

"James," Callie said softly, so as not to disturb Ethan. "It's bedtime, honey."

"It's always bedtime," James said on a whine.

"Same time every day," Callie said, although it was half an hour later than usual. She hadn't wanted to interrupt the castle building.

"It's not fair," James said, screwing his mouth into a mulish frown.

"Why don't we take a picture of the castle," Deacon suggested, producing his phone. "That way, you can always remember it. Do you want to be in the picture?"

Callie couldn't help but admire Deacon's distraction technique.

"I want to be in the picture," James said, coming up on his knees beside the castle.

"Smile," Deacon said as he snapped a few pictures. "I'll send these to your mom, and you can see them in the morning."

"Okay," James said, and then he magically came to his feet.

Grateful, Callie gathered Ethan in her arms.

"Do you need help?" Deacon asked in an undertone.

"He's not too heavy." She stood, wrapping her arms beneath Ethan's bottom, supporting his head with her shoulder. "I'll be right back."

"I'll be here."

She followed James up the stairs, where he tiredly climbed into his pajamas, alternating between jabs with an imaginary sword and wide yawns.

She tucked Ethan in, and then supervised while James brushed his teeth. James was asleep as soon as his head hit the pillow.

Barefoot now, but still wearing her dress, she padded back downstairs to the family room.

Deacon was on the floor, disassembling the castle and packing the blocks into their bins.

"You don't have to do that," she said. "I can clean it up in the morning."

He kept at it. "You're not going to Downright Sweet in the morning?"

"I will if I can find a substitute babysitter."

"Then you don't need to be picking up toys before breakfast."

"Fine. We'll do it now." She lowered herself to the floor to help.

"Am I doing this right?" he asked, indicating the various sizes of bins.

"You're doing it very right. I never thought to ask, but do you have children?" She didn't know why she'd assumed he didn't.

"No."

"Nieces or nephews?"

He hesitated over his answer. "No children in my life."

"Funny."

"Why?"

"Because you're very good at this." She was definitely impressed.

"Good at building toy castles?"

"Good at dealing with children. James was about to make a huge fuss about going to bed, but you distracted him. And you didn't ask if he wanted to demolish the castle. You asked whether or not he wanted to be in the picture. Either answer was a de facto agreement to end the game."

She finished talking and realized he'd stopped putting the building blocks away and was watching her.

"I really hadn't thought it through," he said.

"So it's instinct."

"I don't know what it is, logic and reason, maybe."

She leaned forward, stretching to put a handful of blocks in a bin. "Then I admire your logic and reason."

He didn't respond, and when she looked up at him, she realized the neckline of her dress had gaped open, giving him an expansive view of her lacy bra.

She knew she should move or cover herself. She didn't.

"Wife?" she asked him.

"Huh?" He didn't wear a ring, but that didn't make it a certainty.

"Are you married?"

He raised his gaze to meet hers. "I wouldn't be looking at you like this if I was married."

"Girlfriend?" she asked, not ready to take anything for granted.

"I *kissed* you."

"That's not a guarantee."

"It is in my case. I wouldn't have kissed you if I had a girl-friend." He eased closer. "Boyfriend?"

"No."

"Potential boyfriend?"

She drew back in confusion. Did he mean himself?

She wasn't sure how to answer.

"I don't really know. I haven't given it much thought."

As she said the words, she recognized they were a lie. She'd given plenty of thought to Deacon. Maybe not as formally as a boyfriend, but definitely in the romantic sense, absolutely in the sexual sense.

"Okay," he said. His gaze returned to her neckline. "You're killing me, Callie."

"You want to kiss me again?" She saw no reason to be coy. "And how."

She straightened to her knees, and he scooted forward, rising to wrap his arm around her waist, meeting her lips in a deep kiss that sent instant arousal zinging through her. She wobbled for a second, but he held her tight.

On their knees, their thighs were pressed together. Her breasts were flush against his chest, their bodies pressing intimately.

His kiss deepened. She tipped her head back, giving herself up to the taste and scent and sensation of Deacon.

She wrapped her arms around his neck, and he eased them both to the carpet. The strap of her dress slipped from her shoulder. He kissed the tip. The intimacy of his hot lips on her skin made her soften with escalating desire.

Her body liquefied, melted against him. He slid his hand up her bare thigh, firm, certain and direct. He kissed her neck, then her mouth. He traced her lips with his fingertip. She touched his finger with her tongue, and he groaned, his other hand flexing on her inner thigh.

She knew what was coming.

She wanted it badly.

But she had to be honest. She had to be fair.

"Deacon," she tried, but no sound came out.

"Deacon," she tried again, managing a whisper.

"Hmm?" he asked before kissing her neck.

"You know," she said on a groan as his tongue laved her tender skin.

"I know," he said.

She ordered herself to focus. "You know Frederick."

Deacon interrupted the kiss.

She wouldn't allow herself to stop. "Frederick had a spinal injury."

Deacon drew back, looking somewhat dazed. "Are we really going to talk about your husband right now?"

"No. I mean…" She was afraid of getting this all wrong. "Yes."

"Why?"

She could feel the atmosphere cooling. She had to get on with it. "Because…well…there's something you should know. The boys were conceived through in-vitro fertilization."

Deacon didn't move. He didn't say a word.

"I'm not telling you I'm a virgin," she rushed on. "I mean, not technically. I've had two children. But…the truth is… I've never…" She felt her face heat in embarrassment.

He took his hand from her thigh.

"I'm afraid of doing this all wrong." She took in his stunned expression. "I'm doing this all wrong, aren't I?"

His mouth worked for a moment. "You've never had sex before?"

"I was young when I met Frederick."

"That's a yes? I mean, a no? I mean…"

"I've never had sex before."

He rocked into a sitting position, raking a hand through his hair. "I like you, Callie."

She hated where this was going. She was embarrassed and hurt "But not enough to have sex with someone so inexperienced."

"*What?* No. *No.*" He emphatically shook his head. "I'm angry with myself. I keep trying to take you on a date. I want to take you on a proper date. I don't want to just—" He gestured around the family room.

She felt instantly better. "Have a quick roll in the toys?" She reached beneath her shoulder blade and extracted a stray building brick, holding it up as her sense of humor returned.

He gave a self-deprecating half smile as he took it from her. "Not my most charming moment."

"It felt pretty good to me."

He reached out to smooth her hair from her face. "Let me take you to dinner."

"I tried to let you. Events conspired against us."

He chuckled low. "They did. Let's try again." He put her strap back onto her shoulder and smoothed her hem into place.

"Is our date over?" she asked, telling herself not to be disappointed.

He was being noble. She should appreciate that.

"Tonight might be over, but our date hasn't even started."

Four

Deacon wanted to get it right this time. He couldn't remember ever having so much trouble getting a woman on a date.

He wasn't big on labels and designers, but he spent an afternoon in Columbia decking himself out with the subtle symbols of wealth and privilege. He bought a ridiculously expensive watch, a beautifully cut suit, a pair of diamond cufflinks and shoes that cost as much as a new refrigerator.

He hated to admit they were comfortable.

Callie hadn't denied having boyfriend prospects, and Deacon could only assume she'd meant Hank. It seemed she was carrying on with an upwardly mobile life. Frederick had lifted her from poverty, and now she was moving to the next rung, power and societal position.

Deacon could understand that. He might not admire her methods, but he had no quarrel with her objectives. And if wealth was what she wanted, wealth is what Deacon would project.

It was dead easy to guess at Hank's interest. Callie was absolutely a prize. She would be good for his political career—a beautiful young widow, a business owner in the community, the mother of two little boys. The four of them would look spectacular on the Mayor's Christmas card.

She'd suggested they meet at the restaurant, so he'd arrived at the Skyblue Bistro a few minutes early. When he saw her coming across the walkway, her motivations flew from his mind.

Her hair was loose, billowing around her face in the fresh breeze. She wore a burgundy cocktail dress, slim fitting, with a halter neckline. It molded over her breasts and hugged her trim waist, highlighting a shape that made men turn their heads. The skirt showed off several inches of toned thigh, while her shapely calves ended in strappy sandals that decorated her ankles and polished toes.

He walked forward to meet her. As she drew closer, her turquoise eyes sparkled under the hundreds of little lights in the trees around them.

"Hi." He held out his crooked arm, anticipating her touch. She took it. "Hi, yourself."

"You look stunning." He covered her hand with his, impatient for skin-on-skin contact.

She cocked her head and took in his outfit. "As do you."

"The most attractive thing about me is walking beside me."

She grinned, and he felt her essence rush through him.

"How was your day?" He told himself to get a grip.

"Hectic. One of the ovens broke down, and we had repairmen there for three hours."

"I'm sorry to hear that."

Before she could respond, they came to the hostess podium.

The woman gave them a professional smile. "Good evening."

"A reservation for Holt," Deacon said.

"Would you like to sit inside or on the patio?" she asked. He looked to Callie.

"It would be nice to overlook the river," she said.

"The wind's coming up," the hostess said, as she stacked two leather-bound menus. "But I can put you behind a plexiglass divider."

"Does that work for you?" he asked Callie.

"It sounds perfect."

"We'll take it," he said.

The hostess led them to a small table at the edge of the patio. The wind was gusty, but it was calmer behind the divider, and they had a great view of the lights across the river. Clouds were gathering to block out the stars, but the roof above them would keep away any rain.

"Did they fix the oven?" Deacon asked, picking up the conversation thread, as Callie got settled into the padded chair.

"Not yet. They had to order a component from Philadelphia."

"How long will that take?"

"About three days. We bought that oven used when we remodeled the kitchen. I'm not sure it was good value."

"You bought a used oven?" Deacon was confused by that decision.

She gave an absent nod as she opened her menu. "I'm sorry we did. It's been a money pit ever since."

"Why would you buy a used oven?"

"It was reconditioned. We also bought two that were new, smaller ones. To get *that* size, in a decent brand, would have cost the earth. You probably haven't eaten here yet. The steaks are amazing, but the fish is their feature. It's always market fresh."

"Frederick bought a *used* bakery oven?"

She looked up, her brow wrinkling. "Why is that so surprising? Back then, we had to economize where we could."

"Why?"

It took her a moment to answer. "The usual reasons."

Deacon gave himself a shake, realizing he was grilling her. "I'm sorry. I don't know where I got the impression Frederick had a lot of money."

"He had some. Way more than I ever imagined having, that's for sure."

Deacon wanted to probe for more information, but he didn't dare.

"Shall I order a bottle of wine?" he asked instead.

"I'd drink a glass or two."

"Red or white?"

"What are you ordering for dinner?" she asked.

"You say they're good with fish?"

"It's hard to go wrong with the catch of the day."

He flipped to the white wine page and turned the list to-ward her. "What looks good to you?"

"I don't know anything about wines."

"Frederick did the wine ordering?" Deacon guessed.

"We weren't that big into them. We pretty much went with what was on sale."

That didn't sound even remotely right to Deacon. She was obviously downplaying her lifestyle. The question was why?

The waiter appeared, along with an assistant who filled their water glasses.

"My name is Henri, and I'll be serving you tonight, along with Alex and Patricia," he said, gesturing to the woman be-side him. "Can I start you off with a cocktail or an appetizer?"

Deacon looked to Callie. "A cocktail?"

"Wine is fine for me."

Deacon looked down at the wine list and pointed to the most expensive white on the page.

"The Minz Valley Grand Cru," Henri confirmed. "We re-ceive excellent feedback on that one."

He placed their napkins in their laps before withdrawing.

The wind picked up, flickering the flame in the glass hur-ricane lamp and billowing the tablecloth.

Callie brushed her hair from her face, but it blew right back again. "Will it totally ruin my look if I pull my hair back?"

"Nothing could ruin your look."

"Good answer."

She fumbled with her purse, producing a clip that she set on the table. Then she worked against the wind to pull her hair to the back of her head.

"Do you need some help?" he asked.

"Can you hand it to me?" She nodded to the tortoise shell clip.

He handed it over, and she snapped it into her hair.

"That's better," she said.

"We can go inside," he offered.

"No, I like the breeze. I just don't like my hair blowing into my mouth while I'm trying to eat."

"Understandable."

Henri arrived with the wine, along with Patricia, who set up an ice bucket in a stand next to the table.

Henri showed Deacon the label. It was pretty dark, and Deacon couldn't really read it. But he decided to trust the waiter wasn't substituting an inferior bottle.

At Deacon's nod, Henri opened it with a flourish, pouring a small amount into Deacon's glass. Deacon offered the taste to Callie, but she waved him off. So he did the honors. It tasted fine to him.

"Good," he said to Henri, who seemed inordinately pleased that the wine hadn't gone off.

Henri poured some for Callie, then filled Deacon's glass.

As Henri and Patricia left the table, Deacon raised his glass.

"To a beautiful woman, on a beautiful night." As he finished the toast, the wind suddenly gusted, and a splatter of rain hit the deck's roof.

Callie glanced above them at the worsening weather. "I'm not quite sure how to take the comparison."

"To a beautiful woman, on a not-so-beautiful night?" he tried.

"That works." She touched her glass to his, and they both drank.

"Oh, that's good." She kept her glass aloft, gazing at the wine inside.

His second taste was more impressive too. He had to admit, it was a very fine-tasting wine.

"Nice choice," she said.

"Thank you." He pretended there'd been some level of knowledge behind it.

Henri appeared again. "Excuse me, ma'am."

Callie tipped her head to look at him. "Yes?"

"The gentleman over there." Henri pointed. "Would like to buy your wine tonight."

Annoyance flared in Deacon. He looked past the waiter to the table Henri had indicated.

It was the Mayor. Hank Watkins was going to buy Callie a drink? Deacon didn't think so.

He set his napkin on the table, rising from his chair.

"The wine stays on my bill," he told the waiter as he passed.

Then he crossed the patio to Hank and his party of four businessmen.

"Deacon Holt, isn't it?" Hank asked heartily as he arrived.

"I know you consider yourself a bigshot around here," Deacon said to Hank, keeping his voice low, ignoring everyone else at the table. "But where I come from, you don't buy a woman a drink when she's with another man."

Hank squared his shoulders, setting his beefy hands on the tablecloth. "I'm only being neighborly, sir."

Deacon leaned slightly forward, keeping his gaze locked on Hank's. "And I'm being neighborly by telling you plain. Back off."

"Touchy?"

"You don't know the half of it."

Henri arrived, looking concerned. "Mayor? Mr. Holt?"

"It's fine, Henri," Hank said. "Mr. Holt was just leaving."

"So long as we're clear," Deacon said, hardening his gaze.

"I believe you've been perfectly clear." Hank gave a practiced smile to the rest of his party. "Mr. Holt prefers to take care of his own bill."

"Indeed, he does," Deacon said. He straightened and turned away.

Back at the table, Callie looked puzzled. "Is everything okay?"

"It is now." He sat down and repositioned his napkin.

"Why did Hank want to pay for the wine?"

"It was a power play. It had nothing to do with the wine." She looked confused.

"He wanted to impress you by proving he's rich."

Now she looked amused. "By paying for a bottle of *wine*?" She lifted her glass. "Exactly how much did this cost?"

"Seven-hundred dollars."

Her expression fell. The glass slipped from her fingers, bouncing on the table.

She gasped, while Deacon reached for the glass, saving it before it could roll into her lap.

She stared at the widening, wet circle in horror. "I just spilled a hundred dollars' worth of wine."

"Good thing it was white."

"*Deacon.* What were you thinking?"

"About what?" He used his napkin to blot the spill.

"Spending so much money?"

"I thought it would be good. And it was good. It *is* good. Don't worry about the price."

"How can I not worry about the price?"

"I can afford it," he said. "I can easily afford it."

It was true. Just because he didn't choose to spend his money on luxury items, didn't mean he couldn't afford to buy them.

Alex and Patricia bustled over to the table.

"We can move you to a new table," Alex said.

"It's fine," Callie said.

"If you're sure," Alex said.

Patricia blotted the spill, replaced Callie's wineglass and produced a new napkin for Deacon.

In the blink of an eye, the table was almost back to normal.

Henri joined the trope. "Is there anything I can do to help?"

Callie started to giggle.

Henri raised his brow, looking concerned.

"We're really not batting a thousand on this, are we?" she said to Deacon.

He felt himself relax. He could see the humor in the situation, and he chuckled along with her. "But we do keep getting up to bat."

"You have to admire that about us."

Henri looked from one to the other. He didn't seem to know what to say.

"I think Mrs. Clarkson might like some more wine," Deacon said.

"Indeed, she would." Callie held up her glass.

"Of course," Henri quickly answered, gesturing to the bottle.

Patricia retrieved it from the ice bucket, dried it and poured.

"I can take your order whenever you're ready," Henri said, seeming to recover his poise.

"Give us a few minutes," Deacon said.

As Henri withdrew, Deacon raised his glass again. "To…?"

There was a spark of mischief in her eyes as she put her glass to his. "To a slightly crazy man, on a slightly crazy night."

"I'll drink to that."

"You have to tell me about last night." Hannah sidled up to Callie at the front counter.

It was the late-morning lull, and Callie was refilling the coffee-bean dispensers.

"I had a good time," Callie said, feeling a warm surge of emotion at the memories: laughing over dinner, then walking along the river path, Deacon's jacket draped around her shoulders against the cold.

"You gotta give me more than that." There was a thread of laughter in Hannah's voice. "I like the way your eyes are shining. So, did you…"

Callie glanced up from her work and immediately understood Hannah's meaning. "No, we didn't."

"Too bad. Why not?"

"It didn't seem… I don't know. It wasn't what I expected. He wasn't what I expected."

Deacon had called her a cab. His good-night kiss was passionate and wonderful, and it lasted a very long time. But he hadn't suggested anything more.

Hannah's enthusiasm dimmed. "Oh. Not so good, then?"

"Not *not* good. More…" Callie searched for the words. "Intriguing, maybe. It's like he's got this polished thing going on at the surface, but you break through and he's super down to earth. He's got a good sense of humor. He seems smart."

Hannah cocked her head. "I'm not hearing any good reason to hold back."

"I'm not holding back. I wasn't holding back." Callie hadn't made any overt sexual moves, but she hadn't been standoffish either.

"He's holding back? That seems odd. I mean, for a guy."

The bell on the door tinkled, and Hannah looked in that direction.

"Oh, heads up," she said.

Callie looked, her chest contracting with the expectation of seeing Deacon. It had only been twelve hours, but she was more than ready to see him again.

But it was Hank who walked in.

"I got this," Hannah said, stepping up to the counter.

Disappointed, Callie went back to scooping varieties of coffee beans into the glass cylinder dispensers.

"Hello, Hank," Hannah said behind her.

"Good morning, Hannah."

"What can I get for you today?"

"A cappuccino and one of those chocolate-dipped shortbreads."

"You got it." Hannah rang up the order.

"And, Hannah?"

"Yes?" There was an expectant lilt in her voice.

"Can you ask Callie if she has a moment to talk?"

Hannah paused for a second. "Sure."

You had to be looking for it, but Callie caught the disappointment in Hannah's response. Hannah was such a fun, compassionate and beautiful woman, and Hank had never been married. Callie didn't understand why he couldn't seem to see the potential for the two of them.

Hannah turned. "Callie?"

Callie pretended she hadn't been paying any attention to the conversation. She glanced over her shoulder. "Yes?"

"The Mayor wants to talk to you."

"Sure." She washed her hands and dried them on a towel.

Hank had moved partway down the counter while Hannah worked on the cappuccino, so Callie followed him there.

"I won't ask you to sit down," Hank said.

She was relieved. "We are pretty busy today."

She would rather keep Hank at arm's length.

She might agree with Frederick on the wisdom of having a cordial relationship with the city's politicians. But getting too close was inviting trouble. And Hank had been unusually friendly the past few weeks.

She'd already joined a committee and been a party to a donation. She didn't want to be drawn any further into any political web.

"I can see that," Hank said. "I just wanted to make sure there was no misunderstanding."

She could only assume he was talking about the building permit for the deck. As far as she knew, everything was in order.

"My gesture at dinner last night, it was meant to be friendly and welcoming, nothing more. I fear Deacon Holt misconstrued my motives. I don't want you to think badly of me."

The unexpected turn of the conversation surprised her. "I don't think badly of you."

Even if Deacon was right, and Hank had been showing off that he was rich, she wasn't going to worry about it. It seemed unlikely Hank had known the price of the wine. In fact, it would be odd if he had. In which case, Hank's version was the more plausible. He was trying to be welcoming to a potential city investor.

"I'm very glad to hear that," Hank said. "Will you be at the meeting Thursday?"

Callie wished she could skip it. But she'd promised herself she was joining the City Beautification Committee for more than just her permit. It was how she'd soothed her conscience. She wasn't about to stop attending now that she had her permit in hand.

"I'll be there," she said.

"Good. That's good. You should know there's talk of putting a rose garden and a water feature at Fifth and Bay Street."

It took Callie a moment to picture it in her mind. "Do you mean blocking off the through traffic?"

"Traffic would reroute on Balsam Crescent."

"But…" A feeling of dread slid through her. "Whose idea was that?"

Blocking off Bay Street would significantly impact traffic flow to Downright Sweet. They'd stand to lose a huge percentage of their tourist business.

"I'm looking into it," Hank said, concern clear in his expression. "Can I get back to you?"

"Yes, please do."

Hannah broke into the conversation. "Your order is ready, Hank."

Hank put his public smile back on as he turned to Hannah. "Thank you so much, Hannah. You're a treasure."

Hannah looked pleased by the compliment.

Callie was still absorbing the news. She counted on impulse purchases from the passing tourist traffic. Her local customers were a stalwart base to her business, but Downright Sweet couldn't survive without the money they made from tourists in the summer months to offset losses over the winter.

Frederick hadn't had life insurance. His health condition had made premiums far too expensive. And they'd spent all they had buying the house and the bakery.

He'd once told her he'd donated significantly to charities before they'd met. He'd said he regretted that decision. At the time, he'd never expected to have a family to support. She never imagined she'd someday be sorry he'd donated.

But what was done, was done. Now she needed the bakery

to be profitable. She had the boys' education to worry about, upkeep on the house and day-to-day living expenses.

"Something's wrong," Hannah muttered to her as Hank chose a table.

"Nothing huge." She sure didn't want to worry Hannah.

"What is it? What did Hank want?"

"It's the beautification committee. Some of their ideas are pretty out there."

"That's because they're all geriatrics with short-term memory loss. Well, except for you and Hank, of course," Hannah hastily added.

"I am definitely going to have to keep attending those meetings."

Beautification was one thing. But the city's economy was important, too. If the committee's decisions started impacting businesses, everyone was going to suffer.

"Maybe Deacon will come with you."

"Maybe."

The meetings would definitely be more fun if Deacon came along. And perhaps he'd be willing to lend a voice of sanity. His transportation business wouldn't need property in the downtown core. But if he was planning to live here, he'd probably care about the overall success of the city. Maybe he'd be willing to side with her.

"And then, after the meeting…" Hannah let her voice trail off meaningfully.

Callie rolled her eyes. "You have a one-track mind."

"You should have a one-track mind, too. You're dating a hunky guy, and your level of sexual deprivation has got to be off the charts."

"Hannah!"

"I'm just calling it like it is."

"That's not *like it is*." Callie didn't have a one-track mind. She wasn't obsessed with sex. Okay, she was a little obsessed with Deacon. And she'd like to have sex with Deacon. And she did think about that an awful lot.

But she wouldn't say she had a one-track mind.
She thought about other things.
A little bit.
Sometimes.

Deacon accepted the video conference call from Tyrell, bringing the man's face up on the tablet screen in the hotel suite. Tyrell was obviously in his office.

"I need an update," Tyrell said without preamble.

"I'm here. I've met her. I'm making progress."

"What kind of progress?"

"The getting-to-know-her kind of progress." Deacon wasn't about to share anything personal with Tyrell.

"I heard you went on a date."

"What do you mean, you heard?"

Who would Tyrell have heard from? Did Tyrell have contacts in Charleston?

"Are you spying on me?" Deacon demanded, rocking back in his desk chair.

"Of course I'm spying on you. I don't trust you. And I need to know what's going on down there."

"Then ask your spies."

"My spies weren't on the date. And they're not inside her house. What's going on with the Mayor?"

Deacon told himself not to be surprised by Tyrell's behavior.

"I don't exactly know," Deacon answered honestly. He'd been giving a lot of thought to the Mayor. "Hank is definitely interested in Callie. I can't tell for sure if she has any interest in him."

Deacon couldn't definitively say she wasn't. Hank was quite a bit older than her. But it was possible she was drawn to political power. It was an explanation that had been rolling around in Deacon's head.

"Get her interested in *you*," Tyrell said.

"I'm *trying*." Deacon found it easy to get annoyed with Tyrell. "I'm succeeding. I think."

Callie had seemed to enjoy their date.

Deacon had been the one to stop at a good-night kiss. It wasn't like she'd pushed him away. In the moment, he'd thought taking it slow was the best decision. But he was only guessing at that, as well.

"You've met my grandsons." Tyrell's words weren't a question.

"A couple of times. I don't know if you've seen pictures—"

"I've seen pictures."

"Then you know they're Aaron and Beau 2.0."

Tyrell gave a genuine smile.

Deacon wasn't sure he'd seen that before. "What can you tell me about Frederick's trust fund?"

"What do you want to know?"

"How much was in it? Ballpark?"

"Enough. Millions. Why?"

The answer hit on the heart of Deacon's confusion. "Because Callie doesn't act like a woman with money."

"Oh, she's got money all right."

Deacon tapped his index finger on the desktop. "Why doesn't she want me to know she has money?"

"Did you mess up? Does she think you're a gold digger?"

"I didn't mess anything up. I've done everything in my power to prove to her that *I* have money. I pointed her at Mobi Transportation. I've upgraded my wardrobe, my accessories. I've got the most expensive hotel suite in town, a high-end car. There's no way she thinks I need money."

"Well, you better figure it out."

"I am going to figure it out. Millions, you say?" Deacon's brain went back over the bakery oven conversation. It didn't make any sense.

"She was a waif when Frederick found her," Tyrell said.

"That's what she told me."

"It worked for her once."

"So you think she's playing the part of the damsel in distress."

"Yes. Go rescue her, Deacon. Time's a wasting."

Tyrell's theory didn't feel right to Deacon. But he didn't have a better one, and something was definitely up with Callie and money.

"And get that mayor out of the picture," Tyrell demanded.

"I'm working on it."

"Work harder. My people tell me she's with him right now."

"She's *what*?" Deacon glanced at his watch. It was only five fifteen.

On Mondays, Callie didn't leave the bakery until six thirty.

"They just left the bakery together."

"I'm on it." Deacon signed off the call, grabbed his wallet and phone and left the hotel.

It was a short walk to the bakery, and he was there in minutes, looking up and down the street for signs of Callie.

It didn't take him long to find her. She and Hank were at a table on the patio of a nearby café. They sat side by side, heads close together, intense emotion in their expressions.

Callie was upset about something.

Hank seemed to be comforting her.

He took her hand.

She shook her head.

He spoke at length, clearly trying to talk her into something.

Deacon took two steps forward before stopping himself.

What could he say? What could he do? What was she up to?

She raised her head, and Deacon quickly stepped back, shielding himself from her view with an oak tree.

Then she nodded, and Hank squeezed her hands with his. Hank smiled, and Deacon wanted to punch him in the teeth.

Deacon acknowledged the danger in his reaction. He should be frustrated that he had competition from the Mayor. But he shouldn't be jealous. It shouldn't hit him on an emotional level.

Callie was a means to an end. She was a complicated woman, who obviously had an agenda of her own. He needed to harness that. He needed to use it by pursuing their relationship. But he also needed to stay detached.

The smart play was to coolly and dispassionately focus her attention on him, instead of Hank. Whatever Hank could do, Deacon would do better. That meant eliminating the differences between them.

He pulled his phone from his pocket and dialed Tyrell.

"Yes?" Tyrell answered in a gruff tone.

"It's Deacon."

"I know."

Deacon could hear male voices in the background. "Can you talk?"

"Give me a minute."

It went silent.

"What is it?" Tyrell asked.

"I need a political future."

"Explain."

"It needs to be something convincing, maybe a shot at the state legislature. I want Callie to believe there's a powerful political career in my future. Who do you know who can help?"

"Everyone."

"Okay, who do you trust?"

Tyrell was silent for a minute. "Senator Cathers."

"Seriously?" Deacon couldn't help but be impressed. Senator Cathers was the Senior Senator from Virginia.

"He's speaking at a Chamber of Commerce event in Richmond tomorrow. I'll have him mention your name."

It took Deacon a second to respond. Just like that, Tyrell could put words in a Senator's mouth?

"Make sure you record it," Tyrell continued. "Figure out a way to put it in front of her. Yada, yada."

"Yeah, I get it. I get it."

"Good."

Deacon glanced back at Callie and Hank. Every instinct he had told him to march up to the table and drag the two of them apart. But he had to be smart about this. He had to be methodical. He had to make her come willingly to him.

Five

Callie left the City Beautification Committee meeting, anger propelling her forward. She made it through the door and halfway across the porch before she heard Hank's voice.

"Callie, wait."

She ignored him and kept walking.

"Stop." His hand clasped around her upper arm.

"Let go of me." She tried to shake him off.

"Just listen for a minute."

"Listen?" she demanded, rounding on him. "I *have* listened. I listened really good back there while you threw me and Downright Sweet under the bus. I didn't ask you for anything, but you promised to support me."

If she'd known what he was going to do, she could have been better prepared.

"There was nothing I could say to them that would have made a difference," he said.

"You didn't even try. Never mind try, you jumped on the bandwagon with the other side."

They hadn't formally voted on the rose garden tonight, but it was only a matter of time until they did. It would pass, and her business was going to suffer. She was going to lose money. She couldn't afford to operate at a loss, and Hank knew that.

"This is only the first round," he said.

"No, Hank. This was a knockout punch. There's nobody on my side. Everyone loves the rose garden proposal. Nice PowerPoint by the way."

"You have to look at the long game, Callie."

"There's no long game. There's no game. There's only the demise of Downright Sweet."

"You're getting hysterical."

"No. I'm getting angry."

"Please calm down." His patronizing tone was offensive.

"I'm leaving." She looked pointedly at where he held her arm.

He let go of her arm but took her hand. "I know what it is you need."

Why did he insist on touching her so much? It was really annoying. But his grip was firm enough that she couldn't easily slip out of it.

"It's hardly a secret," she said.

"What I mean is I know how to help you."

"You didn't help me." When she'd needed his help, he'd sat mute in the committee.

He seemed to gather his thoughts. "This is going to sound bold, but I think there's a way we can help each other."

She wanted to jerk her hands from his. Every instinct she had told her to ignore Frederick's advice and walk away. Being friendly to the Mayor wasn't helping her one little bit.

"You're an incredibly beautiful woman, Callie."

His words took her by surprise. "What's that got to do with—"

"Let me rephrase," he rushed on. "You're a wonderful woman. And your boys, well, I think they're terrific."

Unnerved, she searched his expression. Was he threatening her boys?

He eased a little closer, lowering his voice. "You and I, Callie. We should think seriously about teaming up."

"What do you mean?" But she was afraid that she knew exactly what he meant.

"I'm saying that I'm attracted to you."

Something shriveled inside her.

"I'm more than just attracted to you," he continued.

She'd always considered him a fairly distinguished man. But she'd never had a single romantic thought about him.

"You, me, a perfect little family…think of the possibilities."

Forget Frederick's advice. She jerked her hand free of Hank's.

"Nobody knows this yet." He talked faster. "But I'm running for Governor next election."

She couldn't think of a single response.

Should she have seen this coming?

He'd been friendly, sure. But he was friendly to everyone. She'd never given him the slightest cause to think she was romantically interested in him.

His enthusiasm was obvious. "I have dozens of well-placed supporters. Contributions are pouring in. Our future would be—"

"I can't," she blurted out.

What had she ever done to make him think she'd be swayed by his political aspirations?

He took a moment. "Is it the age difference?"

"Yes." It seemed like the simplest answer. It was the age difference and so much more.

"There are a few years between us, I know. But it happens all the time."

"Hank, please stop. I'm sorry." She didn't know why she was apologizing. She only knew she wanted out of this conversation.

"You're a practical woman, Callie. It made sense for you to marry Frederick when you needed him, and it makes sense for you to marry me now."

There was no comparison between Hank and Frederick—none at all.

"You and your sons will have everything you could ever want."

"This isn't going to happen, Hank."

His gaze narrowed. It seemed like his patience was wearing thin. "You've considered it for all of two minutes."

"It's not something I'm—"

"Is that all I get? A whole two minutes of your time?"

She didn't know what to say that wouldn't make the situation worse.

His voice took on a harder edge. "The rose garden would get out of your way." He snapped his fingers in the air. "Just like that. Gone. I can do that. I can fix things."

"You think I'd marry you to move a rose garden?" The idea was both preposterous and revolting.

"It's not just the rose garden. That's small time. I'm talking about the Governor's mansion, Callie."

She took a small step back. Like there was a house in the world that would entice her to marry him.

His voice turned gravelly, his expression darkening. "I make a much better ally than an adversary."

A chill ran through her, and she realized she might be better off with another tactic. She forced herself to lighten her tone. "Hank, I'm flattered. But you have to know this is very sudden."

The words seemed to mollify him, and he gave a thoughtful nod. "Fair enough. You need to think about it. I can understand that."

"I'll think about it." She would. But not in the way he meant.

She wanted to appease him for the moment, to put an end to the drama. She wanted out of this conversation and to go home to her boys.

Luckily, three people chose that moment to exit the main door and join them on the porch.

Callie took advantage of the distraction. "Good night, Hank."

She trotted down the stairs and walked quickly to the sidewalk, resisting the urge to break into a sprint. She wanted to leave Hank far, far behind.

She made it fifty yards.

"Whoa," came a voice from the street side.

It took her a second to realize it was Deacon. Her heart was beating fast, and she was breathing deeply.

"Where's the fire?" he asked.

She ordered herself to pull it together as she looked over at him. "You missed the meeting."

He fell into step beside her. "I was hoping to catch the tail end. How did it go?"

"Not great."

"No? What happened?"

She opened her mouth. Then she hesitated, unsure of how much to share.

Deacon had felt an immediate lift in his mood when he spotted Callie.

She had energy. She sparkled. The air seemed lighter around her, the world a more interesting place.

If something had gone wrong for her, he wanted to help.

"Tell me?" he prompted.

"Everyone *loves* that rose garden," she said, her sarcasm crystal clear.

Deacon had heard about the garden, and he knew it was going to be a big problem for Callie.

"What about Lawrence?" he asked. As far as Deacon was concerned, Lawrence owed Callie his loyalty.

"Lawrence and Hank put on a PowerPoint together. It swayed everyone who might have been on the fence."

"I'm really sorry to hear that." Deacon impulsively took her hand as they walked along the edge of the park.

It felt good. It felt ridiculously natural to be connected to her.

At the same time, it was disturbing to learn that Lawrence had abandoned her. Could Lawrence be naïve about politics? Or maybe two-thousand dollars didn't buy much goodwill these days.

"They didn't vote yet," she said. "But it would have been seven to one if they had."

Deacon looked for a way to help. "What's your next move?"

A pained expression came over her face.

"Is there more?" he asked.

It took her a second to answer. "No. Not exactly." Then she rushed on. "I don't know *what* to do next. All I want to do is run a business, a simple little bakery that gives people tasty treats. I don't want political intrigue. I don't want favors and tactics and counter-schemes." She abruptly stopped and turned to face him. "Is that so much to ask?"

"No." His answer was simple.

And she was beautiful in the moonlight.

He smoothed her windblown hair. "How can I help?"

"You're listening to me complain. That's a help."

"I'm happy to do it. But it's not very practical."

"Hank's offered to help." There was an odd inflection in her voice.

Deacon's hackles rose. He didn't want Hank anywhere near Callie's problems.

"How?" Deacon asked, his question clipped and short. Too late, he wished he'd been more careful with his tone.

But Callie didn't seem to notice. She gave a dismissive wave with her free hand and started walking again. "He wasn't any help tonight, that's for sure."

Deacon wanted to press, but he also wanted to move past the topic of Hank.

"What about you making a donation?" he asked, watching for her reaction to the suggestion. With this much at stake, would she finally admit to having money?

"Even if I could afford it, I'm not going down that road."

"There's no way for you to come up with the money?" He covertly watched her expression.

"No. I'm not taking out a loan against my business to bribe a city politician. Wow. That sounds really unsavory, doesn't it?" Her expression was inscrutable.

He knew she was lying about the money. She could be faking the moral outrage, as well. She seemed completely genuine, but he had to be smart about this.

"Can I ask you a question?" he asked.

She hesitated. "You can."

"It's about Frederick."

"I don't mind talking about Frederick."

Deacon weighed the pros and cons in his mind. "Were you in love with him?"

Callie slipped her hand from Deacon's hold, and he could have kicked himself.

They walked in silence for a several minutes, passing the end of the park and turning onto a residential street.

He was about to apologize, when she spoke.

"It was complicated," she said. "I was young. I'd been through a lot. My family was severely dysfunctional. My mother died, and I was all alone in the world with nothing. I'd already dropped out of high school. I could barely keep a roof over my head. And Frederick was kind. He wanted children. And I, well, I wanted security. We each wanted something the other could provide. Frederick was a decent man. I respected him. And I liked him."

She made it sound almost noble, marrying a handicapped man for his money to give him children.

"I don't regret it," she said.

The cynical part of Deacon wondered why she would. She had two boys she clearly loved, all of Frederick's money, and she was free to embark on a new relationship and better her circumstance even more.

He shouldn't care. He didn't care. It wasn't like she was robbing banks. And her pragmatic attitude suited his purposes. All he had to do was make sure he was the next rich husband on her list.

"I understand," he said.

She paused once again, turning toward him. "Do you?"

He took both her hands in his, happy to pretend he was buying the image she projected. "You're kind. You're generous. You're devoted, a paragon really." It wasn't hard for him to say those words. He believed them.

She smiled with self-deprecating humor. "That's ridiculous. You should see what goes on inside my head."

"I'd like to," he said, moving in. "I'd love to hear your innermost thoughts."

That wasn't the only thing he'd love. His gaze focused on her lips, dark and soft under the faraway streetlight.

"Deacon," she sighed, her eyes fluttering closed.

He cradled her cheek with one hand, leaned forward and kissed her soft mouth.

He instantly stopped caring who was pretending and who was playacting. It didn't matter. Nothing mattered except the taste of Callie.

"Come in," she whispered against his lips.

It took a moment for her words to penetrate, and he realized they were in front of her house.

"You're sure?" he asked, not wanting to seem too eager.

"I'm sure."

He held her hand as they took the walkway and entered the house.

There, Pam said a breezy good-night before she limped to her car.

"She's off the crutches," Deacon noted, moving closer to Callie in the living room.

"The sprain is healing fast."

"That's good." He couldn't stop himself from touching Callie, so he brushed her shoulder.

The fabric of her simple T-shirt was thin, and he could feel her warmth on his fingertips.

"A drink?" she asked, the slightest quaver to her voice.

"Whatever you're having." He kissed her temple.

She stood still for the length of the kiss.

Then she turned toward him and tipped her chin. "I think I'm having you."

As her words hit his brain, the world disappeared. Passion obliterated everything.

"You are incredible," he whispered as he drew her into his

arms, kissing her mouth, slanting his head to deepen the kiss. Her taste filled his senses.

He pressed her fast against him, sliding his palms down her back, reveling in the tone of her body, the indentation of her waist, then the flare of her hips and her rear.

He held her close, his arousal building.

She moaned in response, the sound vibrating against his lips.

His hands convulsed against her.

"Upstairs," she whispered.

He didn't need another invitation. He scooped her into his arms and headed for the staircase.

"Right," she said. "End of the hall."

He walked as fast as he dared, and in seconds they were through the double doors, into an ornate, cream-toned bedroom with a fireplace and a massive canopy bed. It was lit by a small Tiffany lamp on the dresser. Impatience screeched inside his head.

Instead, he set her on her feet. His hands all but trembling, he cradled her face. He kissed her tenderly, ordering himself to take it slow and gentle. She'd never done this before.

Her hands went to the buttons on his shirt. They were trembling.

"Are you okay?" he asked, worried he'd frightened her.

"Huh?" She looked up at him, her blue-green eyes glazed in the dim light.

"You're hands are shaking."

"Help me," she said.

It took him a second to realize she meant with his buttons.

"I can't get them." She looked at one of her hands. "Is this normal?"

"Are you afraid?"

"What? No. *No.* I'm… I don't know what I am. But could you please take off your clothes?"

"Yes, ma'am." He practically ripped his buttons open.

While he did that, she peeled her T-shirt over her head,

revealing a lacy white bra. It was irresistible. She was irresistible.

She pulled off her slacks and stood in front of him in equally tempting panties, wispy and lacy, minuscule and sheer.

"Deacon?" she asked.

He gave himself a shake. "Yeah?"

"You're overdressed."

"I'm in awe." He drew her toward him, wrapping his arms around her, feeling her melt into him. "You are stunningly beautiful."

"You might be, too," she said, pushing his shirt off his shoulders. "But I can't tell yet."

He chuckled, half at himself and half at her. She wasn't anywhere near what he'd expected.

He quickly stripped to his black boxers.

"That's nice," she said, gazing at him, reaching out to stroke his chest.

Her fingertips sent flares of passion across his skin. He closed his eyes, arousal hammering along every nerve. Her hand moved lower and lower, until he grabbed it to stop her.

"Pace yourself," he rasped. "Pace me," he corrected.

He wrapped one arm around her waist, and with the other hand, he covered her breast.

She gasped, and when he kissed her mouth, she met his tongue, tangling with it.

He unhooked her bra, sliding it away to touch her skin, skimming his knuckles over her nipple, drawing it between his thumb and forefinger, watching in satisfaction as her head tipped back, her eyes closed, and her mouth dropped open.

He settled her gently on the bed, lay down beside her.

"Let me," he whispered, using his hands and his lips to kiss and caress her, finding her sensitive spots, doing his utmost to bring her to a perfect arousal.

She touched him back, exploring his body, testing his concentration and his resolve.

When her hand wrapped around him, he spun her onto her back, knowing he was beyond his limit.

He looked deep into her eyes. "Now?"

She nodded.

He was quick with a condom, and then he was above her. Her legs went around him, and he slid them to a slow and perfect meld.

Her eyes were wide, her cheeks flushed, and her lips formed a perfect *oh*.

"Good?" he asked her, loving the expression on her face.

"Oh, Deacon."

"I know." He cupped her breast again, touching her nipple, bringing it to a peak.

He withdrew and surged, withdrew and surged.

Her fingertips grasped his shoulders, clinging tightly.

"What?" she gasped. "What do I...?"

"Nothing," he told her. "You're perfect. You're amazing. You're wonderful. Just let go." He kissed her deeply, canted her hips toward him, pressed deep, pulled back, feeling her body, listening to her sounds, guessing what made her feel best.

Her chopped moans guided him. He increased his pace, driving harder and harder. Insistent waves of pleasure drove deep in his abdomen. He lost his focus, lost control, lost his very mind.

Then she cried out his name, and he tumbled with her, wave after wave after wave of infinite pleasure washing through him and over him and all around him.

When he came back to earth, she was panting in his ear.

He eased his weight from her, giving her lungs some space.

"You okay?" he asked between his own gasps.

"Wow."

"Is that a good *wow*?"

She seemed to blink him into focus. "Wow. So that's what people were talking about."

He struggled not to laugh. But her expression was amazing, endearing and funny all at the same time.

He turned them together, putting her on top, wrapping himself around her and wishing he never had to let go.

He didn't know what to say. He couldn't find any words. So he stroked her hair and whispered her name, while her body went lax on top of him.

Callie woke up alone. The ceiling fan was whirring above her head. Two windows were open, and she was buried in a comforter, in the middle of the big bed.

She threw off the blanket, squelching her disappointment that Deacon had left while she was sleeping. Last night had been nothing short of magical. He was passionate, attentive and so incredibly sexy. Whatever happened between them after this, she would never regret making love with him.

It was bright in the room, brighter than normal. She glanced at her clock, shocked to see that it was nearly nine. The boys never slept this late.

She sat upright, worried something was wrong.

But then she heard their voices.

Ethan laughed, while James whooped.

Then she heard another voice. Deacon. He hadn't gone home last night.

She dropped her head back down on the pillow. Instead of going home, he'd gotten up with her boys, letting her have a rare sleep-in. Could he have made himself any more perfect?

She brushed her teeth, pulled on a pair of exercise pants and a T-shirt and wandered downstairs.

The voices were coming from the kitchen, and she walked to the doorway to find Deacon and the boys clustered around the stove. James was on the step stool, Ethan on a chair, while Deacon wielded a spatula in one hand. The kitchen counter was a mess of bowls and utensils and baking ingredients.

James spotted her first. "Deacon's making pancakes. They're shaped like race cars."

"Zoom cars, Mommy," Ethan called out.

Deacon turned with a smile. "Morning."

"Morning," she said, walking barefoot into the room. "Looks like you've been busy."

He glanced around the room, and his smile dimmed a little. "Won't take long to clean it up."

"Smells good," she said, realizing she should be appreciating his efforts, not criticizing them.

"They're banana," James said.

"And tasty syrup," Ethan sang out.

"I'm guessing that's a quote," she asked Deacon.

"Tasty syrup is the very best kind of syrup." He carefully flipped a pancake. "We're going to need plates."

James started to hop down.

"I'll get them," Callie said. "Can you get forks and knives?" she asked James.

"Wheels," Ethan announced, pointing to the pan.

Callie noticed Deacon was using a back burner, and the position of Ethan's chair made it impossible for him to reach the hot surface. More points for Deacon.

She set four plates out on the table, while James carefully arranged the cutlery. She added butter, syrup and juice to the mix. Then she started the coffee maker.

"I hope we're not keeping you from something," she said to Deacon.

He reached along the counter and wrapped his hand around her forearm, urging her closer, while leaning in, speaking in an undertone. "There's nowhere else I want to be."

After a quick glance to make sure the boys weren't watching, he gave her a tender kiss.

She smiled, her heart feeling light.

"Pancakes one and two are ready for eating," he announced to the boys.

James put his arms out like wings and made an engine noise as he trotted to the table. Deacon wrapped an arm around Ethan's waist, making a matching noise as he swooped Ethan to the table, settling him in his booster seat.

He took their plates to the stove and placed an impressively shaped car pancake on each of them.

"Where did you learn to do that?" Callie asked.

"My mom was creative."

"I can see that." She spread some butter on Ethan's pancake and added a drizzle of syrup.

"Any requests?" Deacon asked her.

She didn't understand the question.

"What shape do you want your pancake?"

She smiled as she cut Ethan's car into careful squares. "Round is fine for me."

"I'm going to need more information," Deacon said.

"You need me to explain round?"

"Do you want an orange, a beach ball, the moon? You're going to have to be specific."

"Get the moon, Mommy. Get the moon," James called.

She couldn't help laughing. "I'll take the moon."

"One moon, coming up."

"What are you having?" she asked, moving to stand beside him at the stove.

"I'm going with a base drum."

"You must be hungry."

"I am." He paused. "I worked up an appetite last night."

Her cheeks grew warm. "Yeah." She didn't know what else to say.

"Don't tell me you're feeling shy."

"A little," she admitted. She'd never had breakfast with a lover before. She had to wonder if children were often part of the equation.

"You should feel great. I feel great." Deacon put a hand on her shoulder. "You're amazing."

"You're pretty amazing yourself."

She could see him smile out of the corner of her eye.

"Any chance you can take the day off?" he asked.

She hesitated. She wasn't sure she wanted to hop immediately back into bed. Well, part of her did. But part of her wanted to take a breath.

Deacon must have guessed the direction of her thoughts, because he nudged her playfully with his hip. "I thought we could take the boys to the beach."

"Oh, uh, let me check with Hannah."

"I didn't mean *that*." His tone was teasing.

"I know."

"Don't get me wrong. I'd do it again in a heartbeat. But that wasn't where I was going."

Her self-consciousness rose again. Then she told herself to quit being foolish. She wasn't some blushing teenager.

"Juice, Mommy, juice," Ethan called from the table, his little heels banging against the chair legs.

She stretched up to whisper in Deacon's ear. "I would too."

Then she sashayed across the room to pour the orange juice.

Deacon was right behind her with the pancakes.

He set them down and pulled out her chair. Then he leaned in behind her as she sat. "Teasing me?"

She gave him an unrepentant grin. "Just being honest."

His blue eyes twinkled in response.

"Anybody want to go to the beach today?" she asked the boys. She was confident Hannah wouldn't mind holding down the fort at the bakery.

"Beach," Ethan shouted.

"Can we build a sand castle?" James asked.

"We sure can," she said, cutting into her pancake.

"Castle," Ethan sang out.

"He doesn't seem as noisy when you're outside," Callie told Deacon.

"I don't mind. I get it. I was a boy once myself."

She took a bite of her pancake. It was delicious. "Secret recipe?"

"It's all yours if you want it."

"I do."

"Mommy, can I take my orange wagon?" James asked.

"I don't think the wheels will roll on the beach."

"They might."

"They might get stuck in the sand."

"Why do you want your wagon?" Deacon asked.

"It's big. It'll fit a whole mountain of sand." James made an expansive gesture with both hands.

"Watch your fork, honey." Callie could live without syrup drops flying through the kitchen.

"Do you have buckets?" Deacon asked James. "Your mom's right. The wagon wheels will probably get stuck. But I'm pretty strong, I can carry big buckets."

"Can we take the bubble tub?" James asked, his eyes wide with excitement.

"The bubble tub?" Deacon asked.

"It's a laundry tub. We play bubbles in it in the backyard."

Deacon lifted his brow to her in a question.

"I have to warn you, it's pretty big," she said on a laugh. She didn't imagine the beach would do it any harm.

"Done," Deacon said. "Let's see how much I can lift."

Six

Callie's sons were slightly sun-kissed, thoroughly exhausted and now sound asleep. Deacon gave one last look at Ethan in his crib and James in a sports car bed, still marveling at how much they looked like their uncles, Aaron and Beau. Then he followed Callie out of their bedroom.

"You wore them into the ground," she whispered to Deacon.

"They were the ones who did that to me." He'd been impressed at their energy levels all day long.

They'd slowed down around one o'clock, but half an hour of shade, a couple of hotdogs and some hydration, and they were ready to go all over again. They'd built a sandcastle, rented bikes, tossed a beach ball around and played endlessly in the waves, finding tiny shells and sea creatures.

"Should we eat something?" she asked.

"I don't know. Are we hungry?" He smoothed back her hair and kissed her neck, like he'd been dying to do for hours.

Her creamy, copper limbs and bare midriff had been teasing him all day long.

"You want to stay?" she asked, stopping at the top of the stairs and turning to face him.

"Do you mean overnight?" He didn't want to misunderstand.

"Yes, I mean overnight."

"Absolutely." He couldn't think of anything he'd rather do.

"Then, we can probably take time out to eat."

"I suppose I can wait."

"Yes, you can wait." Her tone was mock-stern. "It's barely eight o'clock."

"I can wait." In fact, he wanted to wait. He wanted to hang

out with her in this big, comfy house, enjoy her company, have a little dinner, all the while anticipating that he would be holding her in his arms, making love with her, sleeping curled around her lithe body.

"I can order something in," he offered as they started down the stairs.

"There are leftover pancakes."

"You've been living in mom-world way too long."

She grinned over her shoulder.

"I was thinking of braised duckling and wild mushrooms," he said.

"You can get that delivered?"

"You can get anything delivered. They'll throw in salad, wine and dessert."

"I leave it in your capable hands."

He gave her a mock salute. "On it, ma'am."

"I'll pick up the toys."

He gazed around the jumble of the living room. He didn't mind the lived-in look, but he knew Callie was more comfortable when things were tidy.

"I'll help in a minute," he told her, borrowing her tablet and bringing up a food delivery app.

It was quick and painless to place the order. And then, though he preferred to stay with her in the fantasy and forget about the outside world, he did his duty and set the tablet to a Virginia political news page.

"We've got thirty minutes," he told her, placing the tablet on the coffee table.

"No," she said, seeming to randomly throw the word into the conversation, as she finished lining up stuffed bears across an armchair.

"No what?"

"No, we're not tearing our clothes off for thirty minutes, while we wait for dinner."

"Did I say that?" Not that he'd turn her down. He definitely wouldn't turn her down.

"It's in your eyes."

He moved toward her. "You haven't even looked in my eyes."

"Then it's in your tone."

He looped an arm around her waist. "The only thing in my tone is a desire to get you to sit down and stop working. You have to be just as tired as I am."

She let herself be led to the sofa. "I didn't carry anywhere near as much sand. And you had Ethan on your bike."

"He's not heavy." Truth was Deacon had been entertained by the little guy's chatter throughout the ride.

She sat at one end of the sofa, while he moved to the other to keep himself away from temptation. Because, despite his protests, he was having a very hard time keeping his hands off her. And it was time for him to focus on impressing her.

He pretended to bump the tablet as he sat down, lighting the page he'd queued up. He'd enlarged his name in the title of the article, hoping she'd notice.

She didn't, and the page soon went dark.

"Are you thirsty?" he asked, looking for another excuse to touch the tablet. "I ordered wine, but I can get you something while we wait."

"I'm fine."

"Well, I'd like some water." He rose, touched the tablet screen again, surreptitiously turning it her way. Then he headed into the kitchen.

"You sure I can't grab you one?" he called back.

"No, that's…okay, maybe, sure. Bring me one."

He took two bottles of water from the fridge door, breaking their seals as he returned.

Bingo. She was reading the article.

She looked up. "What's this?"

"Hmm?" He set a water bottle down close to her and took a drink from his own.

"It's about you."

"Me? Really?" He feigned surprise. "I must have typed my name in the wrong box. Is it the Mobi Transportation family picnic? I killed in the ring toss."

"No. It's Senator Cathers. He was talking about you."

Still pretending to be confused, Deacon reached for the tablet. "When?"

"At some event last week."

He scanned the article. "Oh, man. This is embarrassing. I told him not to do that."

"Is it true? Are you going into politics?" She didn't look particularly happy at the prospect.

"No. Well, maybe someday. There are a few people out there who think it's a good idea."

"For the power and influence?" she asked.

"To help my fellow Virginians." It was such a pat answer, it was almost laughable. But it was still the best answer. "There's a lot of work to be done in streamlining regulations, cutting red tape and creating jobs."

"Are you sure it's not for the power and influence?"

He lounged back, trying his best to look nonchalant. "That's not my focus at all. Why so skeptical?"

"I don't know."

He didn't buy it, and he wanted to get to the bottom of her thought processes. "Why?"

It took her a minute to answer. "I don't... It sure seems to be working for Hank Watkins."

Deacon tried to read her expression, but it was carefully neutral. For some reason, she was hiding her feelings about Hank's political power. Deacon couldn't tell which way to play this. So he waited.

She leaned forward and lifted her bottle of water, twisting off the cap and setting it down. "Hank says he can make the rose garden go away."

Deacon hid his reflexive annoyance. "He offered to fix your rose garden problem?"

"He did."

"Did you take him up on it?" Deacon hated the thought of Hank having leverage over her.

She frowned, her eyes hardening. "No."

"Good. I'll donate to the committee again." And this time, he'd make the donation big enough to make sure Lawrence stayed loyal.

"No," Callie said.

"What do you mean no? That's how we do an end run around Hank."

"It feels too much like bribery."

"It's not bribery. It's maybe, at most, gaining a little influence."

"You just said you didn't care about power and influence."

"I don't." What he cared about was helping Callie and disempowering Hank.

"Then why are you using it?"

"I'm not a politician, Callie." Deacon could see that he'd gone down the wrong path on that one, but it didn't mean he'd leave the field open for Hank to fix her problem.

"Not yet," she said.

"Maybe never. I'm a long, long way from a decision like that."

The doorbell rang.

She rose.

He stood with her. "I'll get that."

She nodded, looking sad and dejected. Their mood was completely ruined.

He moved to face her and took her hand. "I'm sorry."

"I am, too." Her eyes were wide and glassy.

"I won't make another donation."

"Thank you."

"Do you want me to leave?"

She hesitated. Then she slowly shook her head. "Stay."

He felt a huge weight come off his chest.

* * *

Callie had postponed long enough. It had been nearly a week since Hank had showed his true colors, and she owed it to Hannah to tell her the truth. The last staff member had just gone home for the evening, so it was only Callie and Hannah finishing the paperwork and calculating the day's bank deposit.

"You should get home to the boys," Hannah suggested as she sorted through the cash, putting it in neat stacks into the deposit bag.

Callie pulled a second chair up to the small round table in the compact office. There wasn't much room next to the bookshelf, so she leaned forward. "There's something I've been wanting to tell you," she opened.

Hannah smiled without looking up. "About a certain hunky tourist who's been hanging around every day, gazing at you like a lovesick calf?"

Callie didn't think that was a particularly accurate description of Deacon. But she was determined to stay on topic. "It's about Hank."

Hannah did look up. "Is something wrong? He hasn't been in for a few days. Did he catch that flu that's been going around?"

"It's not the flu."

"What is it? What's happened?"

"I saw him last Thursday, at the beautification committee meeting."

"Uh-huh."

"I didn't say anything to you then, but he went against me on the rose garden."

Hannah straightened a stack of twenties and put a band around them. "I'm sorry he did that. But maybe he had his reasons."

Callie slid a round mesh pencil holder over in front of her, absently separating the pens by color as she talked. "You really like him, don't you?"

"Everybody likes him. He's a great guy."

"Thing is." Callie put the four reds pens in a row. "He might not be such a great guy."

"Just because he's in favor of the rose garden?"

"I was mad about that. I admit it. But then…" Callie drew out a black sharpie that didn't match anything else and tapped it on the table. "He said something, Hannah. I'm so sorry, but he… I guess…propositioned me."

Hannah's chin dropped.

Now that she'd broken the ice, Callie wanted to get it all out in the open. "He told me he was attracted to me. He said we could be a perfect little family, and if I agreed to be with him, the rose garden and all my other problems would go away."

Hannah swallowed. She seemed to be having trouble finding her voice. "What did you say?"

"I said *no*."

"Okay."

"I'm not interested in Hank." The only man Callie was interested in was Deacon.

She didn't want to insult Hannah by sharing her true feelings about Hank. She only wanted to stop Hannah from fantasizing about him. Hank was no good for Hannah. But Callie hated to hurt her friend's feelings.

Hannah began flipping through a stack of fives. "I sure called that one wrong, didn't I? Oh, well, what could I expect? The good ones always go for younger women."

Callie covered Hannah's hand with hers. "That's not always true. And Hank isn't one of the good ones."

"Just because he's attracted to you instead of me? That's perfectly normal. Look at you. You're extraordinary."

"I'm not extraordinary. I'm completely ordinary. And Hank was more interested in how the four of us would look as a family for his political career than he was in me personally. He doesn't even know me."

"Well, I know you," Hannah said with conviction. "And you are amazing."

"So are you. And you're beautiful. And any man would be beyond lucky to date you. But it's not Hank. You're way too good for Hank."

"That doesn't seem to be the way Hank sees it."

"Hank's a fool."

A sheen came up in Hannah's eyes. "I'm the fool for thinking I had a shot."

Callie squeezed her hand, not sure what else to say.

"You should go home," Hannah told her. "James and Ethan will be waiting."

"I wish this hadn't happened," Callie said.

"Well, I'm glad it did. No point in an old woman like me pining for someone who's never even noticed her."

Callie smiled, hoping to lighten the mood. "You're not old. And you're not pining. You just had a misguided crush."

"Crushes are for high school."

"Crushes are for everybody. And you'll have another one. And it'll be soon. It's almost June, and the town's filling up with tourists, and new customers walk through that door every day. Heck, if Mobi Transport opens up a new terminal, the town may be crawling with single men."

Hannah cracked a smile. "You are an optimist."

"Not really." Callie was mostly a pessimist.

Before Frederick, her life had been a series of disasters and disappointments. She'd simply learned how to move forward in life, no matter what happened. A person could take a lot of hits and still get up.

Hannah went back to counting the cash. "I'll be fine. I'm glad I know. Thank you for telling me."

"Do you want to stop for a drink somewhere? We could grab something to eat." Callie had planned to meet Deacon after work for the sixth night in a row. But she was sure he'd understand if she cancelled.

"No thanks," Hannah said. "Do you mind if I take home a couple of the red velvet cupcakes?"

"Take as many as you need."

Hannah gave a brave smile. "Nothing a little buttercream won't fix. I'll see you tomorrow."

"If you're sure."

"I'm sure."

Callie's phone pinged with a text message.

"That'll be your hot guy," Hannah said.

Callie checked. Sure enough, it was Deacon. The message said he was out front waiting.

"Go do something wild," Hannah said. "I'm going to live vicariously through you for a few weeks."

"Something wild, huh?"

"Tell me all about it in the morning."

"If it's what you want, I will gladly share." Callie texted back to Deacon that she was on her way.

Then she logged out of her computer and headed through the dimmed dining room.

It felt good to see Deacon's face.

"What's wrong?" he asked, as she locked the door behind herself.

"Long day." She forced a smile. "I'm glad you're here."

He swung an arm over her shoulders. "I'm glad to be here."

They took a few steps along the sidewalk, but Deacon slowed, stopping.

"Tell me," he said.

"Tell you what?"

"Your shoulders are tense. Tell me what's wrong." He turned to face her head on.

She didn't want to tell him, but she didn't want to hold back either. "I had to talk to Hannah about Hank."

Deacon's eyes narrowed. "Hank?"

"At the meeting Thursday. I didn't want to make a big deal about it. But she's had a thing for him for a while now, and after what he said to me on Thursday…"

"About the rose garden?"

"Partly. He also…" Callie hesitated. She wasn't sure telling Deacon was the right thing to do. "He kind of, sort of, propositioned me."

Deacon drew back, his expression turning to thunder. "He *what*?"

"It wasn't exactly that blatant. He suggested a relationship between the two of us. He seemed to think I would be a political asset, and he could use his power as Mayor to solve problems for me."

Deacon was still. "What did you tell him?"

The question surprised her. "That I wouldn't even consider it."

"In those exact words?"

"Yes." Then she rethought the vehemence of her answer. "I mean at first, yes. That's what I said. But I may have hinted later, a little bit, that I'd think about it. But—"

"Are you thinking about it?"

"It was a ruse. I wanted to get out of the conversation."

Deacon leaned in a bit. "Does he believe you're still thinking about it?"

"It doesn't matter. I'm not."

"Don't."

"I won't."

"Good."

"Deacon?"

"Yeah?"

"Are you angry?"

He looked angry. "No."

"That wasn't very convincing."

He wrapped her hand in his and started walking again. "Hank ticks me off."

"I used to think he was a decent guy."

"He's not."

"I know that now."

"You shouldn't—" Deacon raked his free hand through his

hair and gave his head a quick shake. "You know what? We're not going to talk about him anymore. Home to the boys?"

She liked the way that sounded. It was a relief. "Yes. Home to the boys."

Deacon knew he had to speed up his plan. Hank wasn't going to go away quietly. He was going to use every bit of leverage to win Callie over. She might not particularly like Hank, but Deacon couldn't be sure what factors she'd take into account. He couldn't afford to wait for Hank's next move.

Though it was too early in their relationship, making it more of a risk than Deacon would like, three days later he headed into a jewelry store.

It was quiet and cool inside. Thick grey carpet cushioned his feet, and he was surrounded by bright turquoise tones and curved glass display cases that sparkled under suspended lights.

"Can I help you, sir?" A crisply dressed and very professional-looking thirtysomething woman approached him.

"I need something fantastic," he said. He didn't have a particular style in mind. He only knew he wanted to knock Callie's socks off when she opened the box.

"In a ring?" the woman asked.

"An engagement ring," he clarified.

She gave him a warm smile. "You've definitely come to the right place. Were you leaning toward traditional or modern?"

"I was leaning toward fantastic."

Her grin widened. "Did you have a price range in mind?"

"No. If it's the right ring, price doesn't matter."

"Okay." She gestured to a round display case in the middle of the store and moved gracefully to it. "Let me show you what we have here in the 'fantastic' case."

Her joke got him to smile, and he felt himself relax. It was a strange situation to be sure. But there was no reason he couldn't be friendly with the clerk.

"Please do," he said.

She slipped through an opening into the middle of the round display. Then she unlocked a glass door and selected one…and then two…and then three diamond rings.

"These are the most common solitaire shapes," she said. "Round, emerald and marquis. If you're interested in overall brilliance, the round cut is most popular."

"What about quality?" he asked.

She pulled out a fourth ring. "This is a D flawless, excellent cut."

She handed him a magnifier.

He dutifully took it, and he had to admit the diamond looked great. But he didn't think Callie would look that closely.

He handed back the magnifier and set down the ring. "How about this? If I was asking you to marry me, which ring would you want me to buy?"

The sales clerk looked surprised by the question.

"You must have a favorite," he said.

"I have a few favorites. What are you trying to say? Beyond the proposal itself, what are you trying to say to her with the ring?"

"That I'm the best choice, and I'll take care of her and her children forever." The answer popped out before Deacon could think it through.

"Ahh." The woman's eyes danced with delight. "I know just the ring."

She crossed to the opposite side of the display, slid open another case, before returning with a snow-white leather box. It held a ring with a large, round center stone, set within a whimsically swirled and twisted band of platinum and yellow gold, further decorated with tiny diamonds.

"It's our finest stone," she said, her voice almost reverent, as she leaned forward to look with Deacon. "In a timeless but modern setting." She drew back. "I'd marry you if you gave me that."

Deacon chuckled. "Sold."

"Really? Do you want to know the price?"

He drew out his wallet to extract his credit card. "Not particularly."

She laughed as she took the card. "I'd so marry you." As she backed away, she waggled the card in his direction. "If she turns you down, keep me in mind."

Deacon grinned in acknowledgement of her joke, but inside, he was anxious all over again. Callie could turn him down. She could easily turn him down.

The sales clerk rang through the purchase and packaged the ring. She seemed to see something of the uncertainty in his expression.

"It is returnable within sixty days," she told him gently.

"I'll know the answer a whole lot before then."

"Good luck."

"Thanks." He returned his credit card to his wallet and his wallet to his pocket.

On the way out of the store, his phone rang.

A glance at the screen told him it was Tyrell. He didn't want to talk to the man right now.

He had good news. Tyrell would be thrilled to know Deacon was about to propose. But Deacon didn't want to share that information.

He wanted Callie to be the first person to hear.

The ring box tucked in his shirt pocket, he pulled his rental car from the parking space and entered the downtown traffic. Downright Sweet was only ten minutes away, and he'd arranged to meet her for a late lunch.

A fancy candlelight dinner might be a better choice. But he didn't want the audience they'd have in a restaurant. He could ask her at home, after the boys went to sleep. But as much as he found the toy-cluttered living room relaxing and comfortable, it didn't exactly shout romance.

He'd take her to the patio of the View Stop Café. They could take the winding river path from the parking lot. They could step off into the flower garden. Amongst the bright azaleas and the swaying willow trees, he'd pop the question.

He drove to Downright Sweet and saw Callie standing on the sidewalk. She was gorgeous in the sunshine, her hair freshly brushed and taken down from her usual ponytail, a soft white lace-trimmed blouse topping a pair of fitted dark slacks.

She'd changed her shoes. He knew she wore flats in the bakery, but she was wearing a pair of strappy black heeled sandals. They accentuated the length of her toned legs and showed off her pretty feet.

He came to a halt.

Before he could hop out and open the door, she was inside, buckling up.

"Having a good day?" he asked.

"Hank came by."

"What? Why? What did he do?" The last thing Deacon wanted to think about today was Hank.

"I didn't come out of the back. Hannah gave him the cold shoulder. He didn't stick around long."

"He'll be back." Of that, Deacon was sure.

Deacon touched his hand to the bulge in his shirt pocket. He wanted Hank out of the picture for good.

"View Stop Café?" he asked.

"Perfect."

Deacon drove the mile to get them there. Traffic was light that summer afternoon, and the lights seemed to be in his favor. He was breezing through the second green in a row, counting his good fortune, when a white pickup barreled through the intersection, against the red, heading straight for Callie's door.

Deacon spun the wheel to turn her out of the way a split second before the pickup smashed into the back quarter panel, sending them into an uncontrolled spin. His car slammed into a light pole on the passenger side, all but folding in half.

Deacon shook his head to clear his vision as he turned to Callie. "Are you all right?"

She moaned.

"Callie?" He was afraid to touch her.

He released his seatbelt and leaned around to look at her. People were rushing to the windows, shouting at him from outside. He barely heard them.

Callie's eyes were closed, she was slumped sideways and her forehead was bleeding.

Callie had only been stunned for a couple of minutes. She tried to tell the ambulance attendant that she was fine, but he only responded with soothing words, telling her to lie back on the stretcher and relax. Eventually she gave up, closing her eyes while the vehicle swayed beneath her.

She didn't hear sirens. She had to think that was a good sign.

Her head did hurt, but it wasn't unbearable. She reached up to touch the spot, but the attendant gently grasped her hand, stopping her.

"You'll need stitches," he said.

She opened her eyes again. "Really?"

"Only a few. Your hair will hide the scar. Does anything else hurt? Can you wiggle your fingers and toes?"

Callie tested. Everything seemed to work fine. "I think I hit my shoulder."

"You did," he said. "You have a bruise. But it doesn't seem to be broken. They'll x-ray you at the hospital."

"I don't need a hospital." Now that the shock was wearing off, embarrassment was setting in. She was about to arrive at the hospital on a stretcher. It really was overkill.

"Deacon is okay?" She looked for confirmation. "The driver?"

She remembered him talking to her in the car, and then she'd seen him speaking to the police while she was wheeled away. He'd looked okay, but she didn't know for sure.

"I can tell you there was only one ambulance called to the scene."

She assumed that was good.

"Here we are," the paramedic said.

The ambulance slowed and came to a stop.

The back doors opened, and sunlight flooded in.

Callie closed her eyes against the glare. The movement of the stretcher made her dizzy, so she kept them closed.

She could feel the temperature change when they entered the hospital. She heard voices, a nurse directing them and then the swoosh of a privacy curtain closing. The movement stopped, and she opened her eyes.

There was a woman standing over her.

"Hello, Mrs. Clarkson," she said. "I'm Dr. Westhall. You've been in a car accident."

"I remember," Callie said.

"Can you tell me what day this is?"

"Wednesday. It's May 30th."

"That's good," the doctor said, flashing a little light in Callie's eyes.

"I didn't lose my memory."

"I'd be surprised if you had. But you've had a good bump, and you'll need three or four stitches."

Deacon suddenly appeared beside the doctor, his face pale, his expression grave. "Callie. Are you all right?" He took her hand.

"Are you Mr. Clarkson?" the doctor asked.

A pained expression crossed Deacon's face. "No. I'm her boyfriend."

The words surprised Callie. Her boyfriend? Deacon considered himself her boyfriend?

Her chest warmed, and she couldn't hold back a smile.

He sat down on the opposite side of the bed to the doctor and held Callie's hand in both of his.

"I'm fine," she said.

"I'm so sorry."

"It wasn't your fault. The guy ran that light."

The doctor wrapped a blood pressure cuff around Callie's arm, and it whined as it tightened.

"I should have seen him coming."

"You turned," she said. She had a sudden memory flash of the truck's heavy duty grill coming straight at her. "If you hadn't turned..." She would have been crushed.

He pressed her hand against his lips.

"I'm going to put in some freezing," the doctor told her as she inspected Callie's forehead.

"Sure."

"I'm thinking I'll go with five stitches. The smaller the scar, the better."

"I'm not worried about a little scar," Callie said.

Deacon's attention went to the cut. "Your hair will probably cover it."

"I'm really not worried." She wasn't sure why everybody seemed so concerned about a little scar on her forehead.

Life happened. People got banged up. Nobody stayed pristine.

"When I'm done, we'll take an X-ray of that shoulder."

The concern came instantly back to Deacon's face. "You hurt your shoulder, too? Anything else?"

"It's just a bruise," Callie told him. She could feel the freezing start to work, and the stinging went away from her forehead.

"I'll feel better when we get an actual medical diagnosis. What else did you hit?"

"Everything else feels normal. Did you call Hannah? Can Pam stay with the boys?" Callie glanced at her watch. She didn't know how long an X-ray would take, but Pam was due to drop the boys off at the bakery at four.

"I've talked to Hannah. And I've talked to Pam. She has plans, but I'll pick up the boys. I can take them home. Unless you want me to bring them here?"

"No." She started to shake her head.

"Hold still," the doctor said.

"Sorry. Don't bring them here. I don't want to scare them." Callie couldn't help but think that the last time her sons were at a hospital, their father had died.

Not that Ethan remembered. But James might.

"I'll arrange for a car to take you home," Deacon said.

"I can call a cab."

"I'll set something up."

His offer warmed her. She felt cared for. It was an odd experience.

From her earliest memory, she'd struggled to take care of her sickly mother. Her older brothers had been lazy louts. At eight years old she'd already been cooking and cleaning for them.

Frederick had been wonderful. But his physical limitations meant she was the caregiver. She was the one who managed the physical necessities of life for herself, the boys and Frederick.

But now Deacon was her boyfriend. That's what boyfriends did. They took care of their girlfriends, and their girlfriend's sons. She couldn't help but smile again.

Deacon was her boyfriend.

Seven

Deacon finished reading a story to James and Ethan. He'd told them their mommy had a headache and was going to bed early. Luckily, they didn't ask any questions. They both seemed content to let Deacon give them a bath—an exciting experience for Deacon—and get them into their pajamas and tucked into bed.

Ethan had fallen asleep during the last pages of *Wilbur the Little Lost Pony*, and James was giving slow blinks, looking cozy under his rocket ship comforter. Deacon quietly closed the book and left their bedroom.

He made his way to the opposite end of the hall, through the open double doors to Callie's room. She was sitting up in bed, with a tablet on her lap and a small white bandage on her forehead. She was wearing a pretty pastel nightie with lace around the shoulders and across the neckline. Her hair was lustrous in the yellow lamplight.

"You're awake," he said softly.

"It's only eight o'clock."

He came forward to sit on the edge of the bed. "Sleep would be good for you."

"I have a boo-boo," she said. "I'm not sick."

"You almost got a concussion." He couldn't help himself, he smoothed her hair back on the uninjured side of her forehead.

"I came nowhere near to getting a concussion." She paused, and her eyes shadowed. "Thanks to you."

"I'm just glad you were okay." He moved closer and drew her gently to him.

She set aside the tablet and hugged him back. She felt perfect in his arms.

"Did the boys fall asleep?" she asked against his shoulder.

"Ethan did. James is almost there. I read them the pony story."

There was a smile in her voice. "They love that one."

"They're amazing kids."

"I'm so lucky to have them." She wiggled against him, then suddenly drew back. "What *is* that?" She pointed to his shirt pocket.

It was the ring box bulging out against her.

The circumstances were hardly ideal. He knew he should wait a couple of days. He knew he should give her a chance to feel better. He knew he should do it somewhere more romantic.

He wanted a yes.

Above everything else, he wanted a yes.

But he suddenly didn't want to wait another second.

He let his emotions rule his judgement and reached into his pocket. He extracted the box and handed it to her.

Looking half perplexed, half intrigued, she flipped it open.

Her expression froze as she stared at the diamond ring.

He knew immediately that he'd made a mistake, and he had to fix it somehow. "I know this might seem sudden. But, Callie, if one thing has become clear to me these past weeks, it's my feelings for you. I'm crazy about you. I'm crazy about your sons. We're good together. We belong together. We can have such an amazing and wonderful life together."

She lifted her gaze to his. "Are you…"

"Marry me, Callie. Make me the happiest man in the world."

"I…" She seemed to stumble over her words. "When… Why… How…"

"Why? Because you're amazing. When? I think the second I saw you. And how, well, a very nice woman at the jewelry store helped me buy this."

"Deacon, this is…" She hadn't said yes, but she hadn't said no either. She was hesitating.

He couldn't tell if she was simply acting the part of a tentative, newly widowed woman, or if she thought another man, someone like Hank, would be better for her.

"I can give you a fantastic life," Deacon said. "Both you and the boys. You'll have everything and anything you need."

Her voice was soft, cautious, nervous. "Do you love me, Deacon?"

He couldn't bring himself to utter the ultimate lie. "I am head over heels," he said instead.

"I love you, too." Clearly, she was a woman who could go all in.

He admired that, even as it put him slightly off balance.

"Is that a yes?" he asked.

"Yes. It's a yes." She wrapped her arms around his neck, and he gathered her close against him.

"Don't let me hurt you," he said, restraining himself, trying to be gentle.

"You're not hurting me."

There was a sheen in her eyes as she drew back, holding out her hand. It trembled ever so slightly.

As he took the ring and slipped it on, a cramp formed in the pit of his stomach.

It was happening. She was going to marry him, and his impossible childhood fantasy was going to come true.

He should have been thrilled.

He should have been over the moon.

But something didn't feel right. No, something felt too right.

Callie was too good at playing her part. She was taking his emotions along on the ride, and there seemed to be nothing he could do to stop it.

"Make love to me, Deacon."

He hesitated, his conflicting emotions trampling all over each other. "I don't want to hurt you," was his excuse.

But she stripped her nightie over her head. "You're not going to hurt me."

She was beautiful. She was beyond beautiful. She was perfect.

There was nothing he wanted more than Callie in his arms.

He wanted this to be real. Once again, he asked himself, *where was the harm?* She was getting what she wanted. And he was definitely getting what he wanted.

Why not delve completely into the fantasy?

He kissed her mouth, wider, longer, deeper. He closed a hand over her breast, feeling her nipple bead into his palm. He firmed his forearm across her lower back, easing her down on the mattress, resting her head on the white pillow.

The words *I love you* formed inside his brain. But he didn't dare let himself go that far.

His phone rang in his pocket. He knew deep down it would be Tyrell.

He shut if off without looking, then he stripped off his clothes, pulled back the covers and lay down beside Callie.

She cradled his face with her hands. "The boys adore you."

"I'll do right by them." He promised himself as much as he promised her.

He'd bonded with her sons in a way he hadn't expected. They'd be his responsibility from here on in. As his half nephews, they were his blood relatives on top of everything else. No matter what happened, he'd make sure they were cared for and protected forever.

She kissed him. "I can't believe this is happening."

"Neither can I." That part was the absolute truth.

Callie's life galloped forward at breakneck speed.

The Mobi Transportation project was still just an idea on paper, so Deacon wanted Callie and the boys to move to Hale Harbor. Deacon said it made sense to keep her house in Charleston, because they'd be back and forth quite often.

At first she didn't see how she could up and move out of Charleston. But Hannah eagerly offered to take over management of the bakery. Deacon confessed to having made another donation to the City Beautification Committee to get them to move the rose garden.

At first Callie was stunned and annoyed that he'd gone

against her wishes. But then she saw Hannah's reaction, and she knew he'd solved a big problem for them. He'd also circumvented Hank. And, on Hannah's behalf, Callie appreciated that. So she decided to forgive him.

Before long, Callie realized that living in Hale Harbor was a realistic option.

She'd expected they'd have a small wedding, but Deacon was in a hurry for that, too. He wanted to rush down to the courthouse and sign the paperwork. She found the idea sorely lacking in romance.

But Deacon argued that couples were wrong to fixate on the wedding. Personally, he was focused on the marriage, and he wanted to get to the heart of their relationship as quickly as possible.

She had to admit, he actually made the courthouse idea sound romantic. She also had to admit she admired his practicality. She also admired his efficiency. And she found herself anxious to get started on their new life.

So newly married, they'd landed at the small airport in Hale Harbor. Deacon had chartered a plane, explaining that the number of connections they'd need to get in and out of small airports would be hard on the boys.

She hadn't stopped to think about Deacon's wealth before now. She knew he had money, but somehow, she hadn't expected it to be at this level—maybe first-class tickets and maybe five star hotels, but chartering an entire jet? She experienced a new wave of uncertainty at the pace of everything.

But when they arrived at his house, she was relieved. It was nice. It was beautiful. It was even generous in size. But it wasn't a mansion. She'd been worried that he might have a household staff and a dozen luxury cars lined up in air-conditioned garages.

Then when he showed her into the boys' bedroom, her heart nearly burst.

It was larger than their old bedroom, and the windows were

in different places, and there was a connected bathroom, but otherwise, it was identical to their room in Charleston.

"I wanted them to feel at home," he told her as the boys hopped onto James's bed.

"How did you do this?" She took a step inside, even James's rocket ship comforter and the train pictures hanging on the wall were the same.

"I took some pictures and sent them to my housekeeper. She's a miracle worker."

"You have a housekeeper?" Callie asked, getting nervous again.

"She comes in a couple of times a week."

James scooted across the blue carpet to his dresser. "Our clothes go here."

"Don't tell me you changed the carpets," Callie said, realizing it was a near match to her house.

Deacon shrugged. "They were getting worn anyway. I wanted to go all in." He raised his voice a little. "If your mom wants to give you a bath, I'll bring up your suitcases and unpack."

"You're too much," she said.

She wanted to ask him exactly how much money he had to throw around on frivolous things, but the question was going to have to wait. It had been a very long day, and the boys were going to get cranky soon. She wanted to have them tucked into bed before exhaustion set in.

By the time she had them bathed and toweled off, Deacon had their clothes unpacked and their pajamas laid out on the bed. Callie couldn't help but appreciate the extra help. It took only minutes for the boys to be happily tucked into bed.

Outside the boys' room was a loft overlooking a curved staircase, with a spare room next door, facing out the front of the house. Past the staircase, a short hallway led to the master bedroom. It was magnificent, a very large room with a high ceiling, an adjacent sitting room, a huge master bathroom and a giant walk-in closet that was only about a third filled with Deacon's suits and clothing.

"This is gorgeous," Callie said, turning to look from all angles.

"It was one of the things that sold me on this house plan. I like space around me. I don't like feeling cramped."

"When did you buy it?" she asked.

"Three years ago. The company had a good year, and the dividend payment was unusually high. Besides, I'd never intended for my apartment to be permanent."

"Was it new when you bought it?" Callie hadn't seen anything in the house that looked remotely worn.

"I'd bought the building lot a while ago, so it was just a matter of finding the right plan. Do you want to unpack, or look around a bit first?"

"Can I look around?"

"You can do whatever you want."

She made her way back to the staircase, passing another loft that overlooked the two-story living room. At the bottom of the stairs, the foyer opened to a library on one side and a formal dining room on the other. Moving to the back of the house, she came to the two-story living room with an arched bank of windows facing the yard and connected to an open-concept kitchen, breakfast nook and family room.

"There's a covered porch off the family room." Deacon flicked a switch and lit up a generously sized deck with padded all-weather furniture and a hot tub.

"Is the hot tub secure?" The thought of Ethan accidentally falling in made her nervous.

"I put a lock on the cover."

She turned to glance behind her, taking in the sparkling kitchen, the pristine family room furniture, the art work and fixtures.

"I don't know how to ask this," she said, walking back, trailing her fingertips along the burgundy leather sofa.

He followed. "Ask away."

She abruptly faced him. "I didn't think… I mean, we never discussed… How, um, rich are you?"

"On a scale of one to ten?"

"You know what I mean."

His expression became a little guarded. "I have enough to support us."

It was a nonanswer.

From what she'd seen, he had far more than enough to support them.

She tried to put her concerns into words. "It's a little… This wasn't exactly what I was expecting."

He crossed his arms over his chest, his lips pursing as if she'd annoyed him. "You don't waste any time, do you?"

She didn't understand. She struggled with how to phrase it. "I can't help wondering how much my life is going to change."

"I didn't really want to do this tonight," he said.

"This?"

He kept talking. "I hoped we could have a little dignity about it."

"Dignity?"

Was he secretive about his money? If he wanted to keep it private, she supposed she could live with that. But it was an odd way to start a marriage.

"Why don't you go first?" he said.

The question baffled her. "Go first at what?"

"Why did you hide Frederick's money?"

"Hide it where?"

Did he mean by buying the bakery? That wasn't hidden. And hidden from whom?

"I think we're past playing coy, Callie."

"Deacon, if you don't want to talk about your money…"

"I don't want it to be one sided."

She peered at his expression, trying to figure out what was going on. "Okay…"

"Good," he said. "What's your net worth?"

The question confused her even more. He'd seen her house, her business. He knew her lifestyle.

"You mean the house and the bakery?"

Deacon looked impatient. "I mean Frederick's money."

She cast around for an answer. The few thousand dollars in her savings account didn't seem worth talking about.

"Frederick didn't have a life insurance policy," she said. "Not with the injuries to his lungs."

"I meant his family money."

"What family money?"

He threw up his hands. "This is getting us nowhere."

She was feeling as frustrated as he sounded. "Then tell me what you want? What are you talking about?"

"I'm talking about the Clarkson family fortune?"

He was joking. He had to be joking.

She waited for him to laugh, but he didn't.

She braced her hand on the back of the sofa. Something was terribly wrong with this conversation.

Deacon couldn't figure out what Callie had to gain by continuing to pretend. They were married now. The deal was done.

They'd played each other. But they'd both done it. They were both bringing something to the table, and they were both getting what they wanted.

"I know all about Frederick's family," he said. "So let's just figure out how this is going to work."

She still didn't drop the act. "What about Frederick's family?"

"I grew up in Hale Harbor."

She didn't respond. If anything, she looked even more confused.

"Everyone in Hale Harbor knows the Clarksons. The castle, the Port, their history, their *money*."

"Frederick's family lives in Miami."

The statement stopped Deacon cold.

Either she was the greatest actress on the planet, or she believed what she'd just said.

Plus, there was no reason for her to have made that up. There was no benefit to that particular lie. Was there?

"They don't have a fortune," she continued. "They sure don't have a castle."

A feeling of unease crept into Deacon. If Frederick had lied to her, where had his money gone?

Deacon frantically reframed a world where Callie hadn't known about Frederick's money.

Her hold on the sofa tightened. Her expression hardened, and she gestured around the room. "Is this all a sham, Deacon? Are you a con artist? Are you under the impression that, by marrying me, you'll get your hands on a fortune? Are you in debt, is that it?"

"No!"

"You didn't want a prenup. I thought that was odd. I should have listened to myself." She turned to leave the room.

His brain was struggling to make sense of everything. "Callie, something's wrong."

"You bet it is," she called over her shoulder.

"Frederick lied to you."

She gave a slightly hysterical laugh. "It's *you* who lied, Deacon." She kept walking.

He rushed across the living room and caught up to her in the foyer.

"You can divorce me," she said. "And go find yourself some other rich woman to marry."

"I don't want your money."

The front doorbell rang.

"I'll be out of here in the morning," she told him.

"Deacon?" a man's voice called through the door.

Deacon recognized Tyrell's voice and swore under his breath.

Callie started up the stairs.

"I can explain," he called after her.

She didn't answer.

"Deacon," Tyrell called out again.

Deacon was torn between going after her and getting rid of Tyrell. The last thing he needed was Frederick's father in the mix of all this.

He dragged open the door. *"What* are you doing here?"

Before the words were even out, he saw that Margo was with him.

"Where are my grandsons?" she asked, a desperate hunger in her eyes.

"They're asleep," Deacon said.

"But they're here."

"You were supposed to call," Tyrell said.

"And I *will*," Deacon countered.

Margo started forward.

"You have to *leave*," Deacon said, blocking her from entering and glancing behind him.

He was fairly sure Callie wouldn't come back downstairs, but he didn't dare chance it.

"I want to see them," Margo said.

"I told you, they're asleep."

"I won't wake them."

Deacon looked at Tyrell. "Take her home or you'll blow everything."

He could see the hesitation on Tyrell's face.

"Now," Deacon said.

"I've waited so long," Margo wailed.

"Darling." Tyrell put a hand on his wife's arm. "We have to—"

"You can't make me wait," she cried, shaking Tyrell off. "And *him*." She pointed to Deacon. "He's the last person who should stop me from seeing my grandsons." She surged forward.

Deacon planted himself directly in front of her. "You may not like me. You may even hate me. But this is my house, and Callie is my wife, and you are not getting past me to see those boys."

"How *dare* you."

He heard a noise behind him.

"Deacon?" Callie asked.

His stomach turned to lead.

"What's going on?" she asked.

"Is that her?" Margo asked.

"Go," Deacon hissed.

"Grandsons?" Callie asked.

He turned to face her, blocking the opening of the door. "I told you I could explain."

"Who are those people?"

Deacon fought it for several seconds, but then gave in to the inevitable. "They are Frederick's parents."

The color drained from Callie's face.

"They've been estranged from Frederick for years," Deacon quickly explained. "He didn't tell you about them, because he didn't speak to them."

She looked like she might keel over, and he rushed forward to support her. He grasped her shoulder and put an arm around her waist.

"Are you Callie?" Margo asked.

Deacon saw that the door was wide open, and Margo had stepped inside.

"I'm sorry," he whispered in Callie's ear. "I'm so sorry."

"I'm Frederick's mother," Margo said.

Tyrell entered, as well. "I'm Tyrell Clarkson. This is my wife, Margo."

Callie tipped her head to look at Deacon.

"Can we do this tomorrow?" he asked Tyrell.

"I've waited so long," Margo said. "Can I please see my grandsons?"

"They're asleep." Callie's whisper was paper dry.

"I promise I'll be quiet," Margo said. Her longing was so painfully obvious, that even Deacon felt sorry for her.

"You don't have to do this," Deacon said to Callie. "She has no right to ask."

Margo glared at Deacon.

"You're their grandmother?" Callie asked Margo. The bewilderment was clear in her tone.

Margo nodded.

"You knew this?" Callie said to Deacon.

"I was trying to figure out how to tell you. I thought—" Deacon stopped himself. There was no way he was having this conversation in front of Tyrell and Margo. "I'll explain. But not right now."

"I don't have Frederick's money," Callie told Deacon.

"I don't want Frederick's money."

"What happened to Frederick's money?" Tyrell asked.

"Back off," Deacon ordered.

"He gave it to charity," Callie said. "Spinal cord research."

"His entire trust fund?" There was skepticism in Tyrell's tone. "Millions of dollars?"

"He never told me how much. He once said he regretted it. He didn't know he'd have the boys."

"I have no interest in Frederick's money," Deacon said to Callie. To Tyrell, he said, "Can you not see that you should leave."

"But—" There was a tremor in Margo's voice.

"Not tonight," Deacon said.

"You can come up and see them," Callie said.

Deacon looked at her, dumbfounded.

Hope rose in Margo's expression.

"For a quick minute," Callie said. "If we're really quiet."

Margo gave a rapid nod.

Callie disentangled herself from Deacon. "This way."

She started up the stairs, and Margo was quick to follow.

"You better start talking," Callie said to Deacon as she marched into the family room.

She'd sat in the boys' room for an hour after Margo left. Instinct had told her to curl up next to James for the night and try to block out everything she'd just learned. But she knew she'd never sleep. There was no point in putting off the confrontation with Deacon.

"Will you sit?" he asked.

He was in a leather armchair, next to the stone fireplace, a tumbler of amber liquor on the table beside him.

There was nothing to be gained by standing. So she took the opposite chair. The thick cushions cradled her weight.

"Something to drink?" he asked.

"No."

"Okay." He sat forward. "From the beginning. When I first came to Charleston, I already knew who you were."

"What did you want from me?"

"I wanted to meet you. Tyrell was curious about his grandsons. He was also afraid of approaching you. He thought Frederick had turned you against them, so he didn't want to introduce himself."

"Why you?"

Deacon hesitated.

She peered at him. "Are you making up a lie?"

"I'm thinking about how to phrase the truth."

She scoffed at the semantics, wishing now that she'd said yes to a drink.

"It was because I'm only tangentially connected to the family," Deacon said. "Tyrell thought you'd know the rest of them, but not me."

"What does *tangentially* mean?" She hated the way he was talking in riddles.

Deacon was hiding something. He was probably hiding a lot. When she let herself think about what she'd lost here tonight, her stomach curled into a ball, and tears burned behind her eyes.

"I'm Tyrell's illegitimate son."

Callie sat up straight, nearly coming out of her chair. "You're Frederick's *brother*?"

"Half brother. And we never knew each other. I'm not sure he knew I existed."

"But his father did."

"Oh, yes. Tyrell has known about me all along."

Callie sat back, trying frantically to digest the information. Deacon rose and crossed the room.

When he came back, he handed her a glass.

"Brandy," he said.

She thought about refusing, but it seemed like a better idea to drink it down.

She accepted the glass and took a healthy swallow.

"You don't love me," she noted as he sat down. Of everything that had been revealed, that was the fact that burned most sharply in her mind.

Deacon sat back down and again took his time responding. "I was amazed at how much I liked you."

"Am I supposed to be grateful for that?" She could add mortification to her list of unwelcome emotions. She'd honestly thought she loved him, that she was *in love* with him, that he was the love of her life.

He, on the other hand, had been faking it the whole time.

"I thought you were after my money," he said.

"I wasn't."

"I don't mean that in a bad way."

"There's a good way to accuse me of being a gold digger?" She took another drink.

"You as much as admitted to marrying Frederick for his money. I thought I was the next step on the ladder."

"But you stayed after that. It doesn't make sense that you stayed."

She knew she was tired. She was emotionally drained. This was probably the very worst day of her life, and her brain was foggy. But it was nonsensical that he'd stuck around if he thought she was using him.

"There are a lot of different relationships in the world. I guess I didn't mind that you were pragmatic about bettering your circumstances."

"You thought I was pretending to fall for you?"

What kind of a man was he? She thought back to the time they'd spent together, the fun they'd had, the nights in her house, the beach with the boys. All that time, he'd thought she was playing him?

"I liked you a lot," he said, toying with his glass, turning it in a circle on the wooden coaster. "I didn't know where it was going, and I wanted to find out."

"So you *proposed*? You *married* me to find out where it was going?" She took another healthy swallow of the brandy.

"I knew Watkins was pursuing you, and, well… I couldn't afford to wait."

"I had no interest in Hank." She was revolted by the thought of even kissing Hank. There was no way she would have embarked on a relationship with him.

"I know that now," Deacon said.

She polished off her drink. "I don't know what you thought was going to happen here. But I'm leaving in the morning. I'm filing for divorce. You've messed up my life—"

"I wish you wouldn't do that."

"Too bad."

"I think we can make this work."

She laughed. It sounded a bit hysterical. It probably was.

"Make it work?" she repeated. "In what universe is there anything here to make work?"

"I was wrong. I thought I was giving you what you wanted, another wealthy husband."

"It had nothing to do with wealth." She didn't know why she made the point. She didn't care anything about Deacon's opinion of her. "Frederick begged me to marry him. He knew I wasn't in love with him. But he was kind, and he said I made him happy, and I wanted to be a mother. I didn't want to stay in Gainwall and—"

"You don't have to explain it to me."

"I hate what you thought of me."

"I was wrong. I knew the Clarksons wanted their grandsons. I thought you wanted money. We got along fine. We got along better than fine."

Memories of their lovemaking—the ones she'd been desperately trying to keep at bay—suddenly surfaced. She felt her body heat up from her toes to her cheeks.

"Is that how you see it?" she asked. "You had everybody's best interests at heart?"

"I'm saying I knew what they wanted. I thought I knew what you wanted. And it was easy to talk myself into doing it."

"You got it completely wrong."

"I just admitted that."

It was true. He had. She didn't know what else to say.

"Don't leave right away," he said. "It's always an option. It'll stay an option. But there are a lot of people…"

She waited, wondering how he'd intended to end the sentence.

"More brandy?" he asked instead.

She looked down at the empty glass in her hand. She wasn't leaving in the next five minutes. She still had to make it through tonight. "Why not?"

He rose to pour. "You saw how Margo feels."

Callie couldn't help but think back to Margo's expression when she saw her sleeping grandsons. There had been tears in her eyes. She'd slowly crouched down beside James's bed and just stared at him.

"There's no love lost between me and Tyrell, but he is their grandfather. And they have two uncles, Aaron and Beau." Deacon finished pouring her brandy and turned back. "James and Ethan are the spitting images of their uncles."

"I don't care," she said.

This wasn't about uncles. It was about her and her sons. Her chest tightened again thinking about what this would do to her boys. They adored Deacon.

They were barely recovering from the loss of their father. She'd just ripped them away from their lives in Charleston, and now she was going to ruin their foundation all over again. How had this gone so wrong?

"Family matters," Deacon said as he handed back her glass.

A question rose up in Callie's mind. "What happened with Frederick and his family?"

"Something between Frederick and Tyrell. Beyond that, I don't know."

"I don't believe you."

"All I know is that Frederick went off to college and didn't come back afterward. There were rumors that he'd had a falling out with his father."

"You never asked?"

"Asked Tyrell?"

She nodded.

"Tyrell and I don't talk much."

Callie was struggling to put the pieces together. "But he sent you to Charleston."

"That was an anomaly. I was probably his last choice."

She gazed into her glass, the rich amber glowing in the lamplight. "I am leaving." She had no other choice.

"I know," he said softly. "I'm only asking for a few days."

Her heart actually hurt. "I'm not sure if I—"

"You can have your own room. I'll stay out of your way. Let the boys meet their grandparents. Just take it slow, methodical, make the best choices for the three of you. It'll be the right thing in the long run."

She studied his expression, wondering if he was playing her all over again. "What do you get out of this?"

"I like you, Callie. I adore the boys. We're...compatible." The sensual glow in his eyes told her what compatible meant. "We could make it work."

He wasn't wrong. They were compatible in every way possible.

But staying with him, knowing all this, accepting what he'd done and how he felt about her? She couldn't do it. It was more than her heart could take.

"That's not going to happen," she said, her voice breaking over the words.

Eight

It was 4 a.m. Deacon was in bed, but he wasn't anywhere near to sleeping.

How had he judged her so wrong? Callie wasn't acting. She's wasn't playing him or Hank or anyone else to work her way up the societal ladder.

Down the hall, Ethan cried out in his sleep.

Deacon was on his feet and halfway across the room before he realized he couldn't go to the boy. Callie would go to him. Deacon no longer had the right.

He sat on the edge of the bed, his gaze going to the glowing red numbers on his bedside clock. It was four eleven.

Her heard Callie's voice, indistinct as she tried to soothe Ethan.

Deacon rose again, moving to his open door, listening while Ethan continued to cry.

He heard James's voice, and realized Ethan had woken him up.

He started down the hall. He didn't care how Callie might be feeling about him. It was clear she needed help.

He walked into the room and went straight to James, who was sitting up in bed. Deacon sat down, and James climbed into his lap. He hugged the boy close and looked to Callie.

"He's burning up," she said in a hoarse voice.

"Does he need a doctor?"

"There was a bottle of acetaminophen drops in one of the suitcases."

"I put them in the medicine cabinet." Deacon rose, carrying James with him into the bathroom.

In the glow of the nightlight, he located the medicine. Behind him, Ethan coughed weakly and cried harder.

"Owie," Ethan whimpered.

"I know, sweetheart," Callie said. "We're getting you some medicine."

Ethan sobbed, coughed and sobbed some more. He sounded wretched, and Deacon's heart went out to the poor little guy. Deacon measured out a dose and brought it to Callie.

"We can call a doctor," he said.

"Let's see if this helps first."

Deacon would rather call a doctor right away, but he knew he had to leave the decision to Callie.

She put the medicine dispenser to Ethan's lips. "You need to swallow this, honey," she crooned.

"Yucky," Ethan cried.

"You can have some juice after."

"No."

"It'll make you feel better."

"No, Mommy, no," Ethan wailed, turning his head.

"Ethan." Callie's voice was firm.

"Daddy," Ethan cried, launching himself to Deacon, catching Callie completely off guard.

Deacon quickly grabbed for him, holding James fast in his other arm, gathering the sobbing Ethan against his chest before he could fall to the floor.

Deacon locked onto the staggered expression in Callie's eyes.

"Let me try," he told her softly. "James, can I put you down on the bed?"

Ethan's sobs turned into an uncontrollable cough.

"Mommy?" James asked, his voice trembling. "Is Ethan going to die?"

Callie's eyes filled with tears. She reached for James, taking him from Deacon to hold him in her arms. "No. No. Sweetheart, Ethan is going to be fine. I promise. We just have to give him some medicine."

Deacon took the medication from Callie and sat down on

James's bed, holding Ethan close, the little boy's damp face against Deacon's bare chest.

"Does your throat hurt bad?" Deacon asked in a calm voice.

Ethan gave a miserable nod.

Deacon kissed the top of Ethan's head. "I'm sorry, buddy. Do you want it to go away?"

Ethan nodded again.

Deacon was vaguely aware of Callie and James watching him.

"I think I can help." Deacon smoothed Ethan's soft hair. "Do you like honey?"

"On toast," Ethan rasped.

"Not on toast right now. On a spoon. It'll help. Do you think you could swallow some honey on a spoon?"

Ethan nodded.

Deacon rose, carrying Ethan. "Let's go to the kitchen and find some."

"Owie," Ethan whimpered again, as Deacon walked out of the bedroom.

"You know what will work even better than honey on your owie?" Deacon took the stairs. "The yucky medicine."

"Nooo."

"The trick is, you swallow just a little bit of medicine, and before you can even taste it, you pop the honey in your mouth."

James spoke from Callie's arms behind them. "Can I have honey?"

"Sure," Callie said, sounding dazed.

Deacon turned on a small light in the kitchen. He located a bottle of honey and a spoon.

"What do you say, buddy?" He looked down at Ethan. "A quick squirt of yucky medicine and then a big spoon of honey?"

Ethan looked skeptical, and Deacon was afraid his ploy wouldn't work. If it didn't, he was calling a doctor whether Callie liked it or not. Ethan was burning up. They had to get his fever down.

"'Kay," Ethan said in the quietest of voices.

"That's my boy." Relief rushed through Deacon. He held up the medicine dispenser. "I know you can do it, buddy."

Ethan gave a brave nod.

Deacon squirted the medicine into Ethan's mouth.

Ethan screwed up his face in a scowl, but he managed to swallow it.

Deacon quickly put the honey to his lips, and Ethan sucked the spoon into his mouth. His expression slowly cleared.

"That was fantastic," Deacon praised him, wrapping his arms fully around Ethan's sweaty little body.

Callie slumped against the counter, James still in her arms, a single tear escaping to run down her cheek. He held her gaze, and she gave him a shaky nod of thanks.

"Do you want to go back to Mommy?" Deacon asked Ethan.

"'Kay," Ethan squeaked out.

Callie set James down, and Deacon handed her the limp Ethan.

Then Deacon crouched to talk to James. "Honey for you too?"

"Is Ethan okay?" James asked.

"He's going to feel better really soon," Deacon said. "After your honey, you'll need to brush your teeth again."

"Okay," James agreed.

Deacon got a fresh spoon and gave James a small dollop of honey.

He grinned as he licked it.

Callie was sitting at the breakfast table, rocking Ethan in her arms.

Deacon took James's hand. "Back to bed for you."

"Okay," James said, with a last look at his brother.

Deacon helped James with his teeth, got him tucked back in and then returned to the kitchen. Callie was still at the table, rocking Ethan.

Ethan had stopped crying. But his eyes were open, and he cringed in pain as he swallowed.

Deacon crouched beside them.

"Thank you," Callie said, her voice breaking.

"No problem." Deacon was incredibly glad to have been here to support her. "We can still call a doctor."

Callie glanced at her watch. "Let's give the acetaminophen time to work."

"Do you want to move to the family room?" He rose and held out a hand to help her up. "It'll be more comfortable."

She hesitated, but then accepted his offer.

Deacon resisted the urge to put his arm around her. Intellectually, he knew their relationship had irrevocably changed. But emotionally, he still felt protective of her. He still felt close to her. He still felt like her husband.

She sat down in the same armchair as earlier, leaning back with Ethan stretched across her chest.

"Do you want a blanket?" Deacon asked her.

"He called you daddy."

"Yeah." Deacon's chest tightened with the memory. It had taken him completely off guard.

Callie looked wretchedly unhappy, her voice half whisper, half wail. "What am I going to do?"

After Ethan recovered, circumstances seemed to conspire against Callie.

The boys were very obviously bonding with Deacon, and Hannah called full of excitement and ideas as she ran the bakery solo. Margo had had a playroom specially built, and couldn't wait to show it off to her grandsons.

So on Saturday, with Ethan back at full strength, Deacon pulled the car up to the front of the castle.

Callie couldn't do anything but stare in awe at the imposing stone structure. "It looks like a hotel."

"This is where Frederick grew up."

"Daddy used to live here?" James asked in wonder from the back seat.

"He did," Deacon confirmed.

"Was Daddy a prince?"

"He was just a very lucky little boy." There was something in Deacon's voice, but Callie couldn't pinpoint the emotion.

"I wish I was a prince," James said.

Callie had to fight a smile. It was the first time she'd seen humor in the world since she'd discovered the truth.

"When I was a boy, I wanted to be a prince, too," Deacon said.

"There's a tower," James said, excitement growing in his voice. "A real tower. Can I have a sword?"

A part of Callie couldn't help being interested in Frederick's childhood home. But mostly she was plotting their exit from Hale Harbor. The sooner she moved the boys back to their old life, the better it would be for them.

While she helped Ethan out of his car seat, Deacon opened the opposite door for James.

The castle's grounds were vast. Summer flowers were blooming in dozens of garden beds. The lawn was a smooth emerald carpet. Oak trees lined the wide, exposed aggregate driveway. And two lion statues flanked a wide staircase that led to arched oversize wood-plank doors.

The castle was three stories high, with a tower on each of the front corners. She could see at least three gardeners on the grounds. While off to the left side, there was a six-car garage.

"This is ridiculous," she muttered under her breath.

"Down," Ethan said, kicking his legs.

Callie set him down.

He immediately ran for the lawn.

"Don't touch the flowers," she called after him.

James trotted after his brother, while Ethan dropped and rolled in the lush grass.

The door to the castle yawned open. Callie half expected a butler to emerge. But it was Margo and Tyrell who appeared.

With them was a young woman who looked to be in her early twenties.

"Who's that?" Callie asked Deacon, dividing her attention between the porch and the boys.

Ethan had spotted a row of rhododendron bushes, and she could almost see his little mind working.

"I don't know. It's not Aaron's wife."

"Another long-lost relative?"

"Not that I know about."

The trio started toward them.

Although it was a warm Saturday, Tyrell was dressed in a business suit. Margo wore tan slacks and a sleeveless patterned silk top. Her grey hair was wispy around her face, while a pair of designer sunglasses were perched on her nose. The other woman was dressed in jeans, a white capped-sleeve T-shirt and flat sandals. She had long blond hair in a sporty ponytail.

"James," Callie called out. "Can you bring Ethan back?"

James trotted over to his brother and took his hand. Ethan pointed at the pink rhododendrons, but James tugged him along.

"I just can't get over it," Margo said as she watched the boys come toward them.

"The genes are strong," Tyrell said.

Callie had learned from Deacon that James and Ethan bore an uncanny resemblance to their uncles, Aaron and Beau.

"I'll have to show you some pictures," Margo said to Callie.

Although she greeted Callie with a squeeze on the arm, Margo didn't acknowledge Deacon.

It was growing clear to Callie that Margo didn't like Deacon. It didn't take a genius to figure out why. It wasn't Deacon's fault that Tyrell had an affair with his mother. But it seemed as though Margo was determined to hold Deacon responsible.

"Callie, this is Dee Anderson," Margo said. "Dee has a degree in early childhood education, and she's joined our household staff."

Callie let the phrase "joined our household staff" roll around in her brain for a moment.

"Hello, Mrs. Holt." Dee offered her hand.

The name jolted Callie, and she stumbled in her response. "Please, call me Callie." She studiously avoided looking Deacon's way.

Deacon had spent a lot of time at work the past few days. In the evenings, he'd been a big help with the boys. But they'd tiptoed around each other when they were alone. She hadn't talked to him about her immediate plans to stay or go, and he hadn't brought it up.

"Grandma has something special to show you," Margo said to James and Ethan.

James hung back, but she captured Ethan's attention.

"Candy?" asked Ethan.

"It's not candy," Margo said with an indulgent smile.

Ethan frowned

Callie moved to take each of her sons' hands, putting a cheerful note into her voice. "Why don't we see what Grandma wants to show us?"

James hung on, while Ethan tried to pull out of her hold.

"Do you want some help?" Deacon asked Callie.

"We'll be fine." Margo waved him away and started walking.

"My name is Dee." Dee introduced herself to the boys as she fell into step. "You must be James, and you must be Ethan."

"Ethan," Ethan said.

"It's nice to meet you, Ethan."

"Have candy?"

"Ethan," Callie warned. "You've only just finished breakfast."

"Dessert," Ethan said with authority.

"You know we don't have dessert with breakfast."

"Do you like slides?" Dee asked.

James spoke up. "I like towers." He craned his neck as they walked toward the castle.

Instead of heading for the front door, they took a walkway along the south side of the castle, coming to a chain-link gate that led to a fenced area with a giant, colorful playset of swings, slides, bridges and ladders with safety rails.

James's eyes went wide.

"Slides!" Ethan squealed.

Dee opened the gate, and both boys dashed inside.

"It's…" Callie didn't even know what to say.

"It's consumer tested and very highly rated," Margo said.

"The best safety rating," Dee said.

"I was going to say enormous." Callie stared at straight slides, covered slides, curving slides.

Ethan started up a ladder.

Callie checked his path, looking for the danger zones, deciding where best to stand to spot him. But she didn't see any flaws in the design. There were no spaces where it looked like he could fall. And Dee was right behind him, laughing and asking him what he wanted to try first.

"They seem to like it," Margo said.

"I don't know any kids who wouldn't." Callie looked a little further around. The area was completely fenced. The boys couldn't wander away.

"Would you like to sit down?" Margo gestured to an umbrella-covered table. "I'll have some iced tea brought out for us."

Callie got the feeling she'd been separated from Deacon for a reason. But the boys were happy. Margo was being very hospitable, and Callie preferred to keep her distance from Deacon anyway.

It didn't matter where he was, or what he was doing. She wasn't even going to think about him.

As Deacon signed the paperwork at the boardroom table in the castle's business wing, Beau burst through the door.

"You can't *do* this," Beau shouted at his father.

Tyrell glared at his son for a beat before answering. "Hello, Beau."

"Aaron just told me what's going on."

Tyrell's tone was clipped and even. "Had you not missed the last three board meetings, you might have known sooner."

Beau stalked across the room, making a beeline for the paperwork in front of Deacon.

When Beau reached out to grab it, Deacon jumped from his chair, grabbing Beau's lapel and pushing him back into the wall.

Beau doubled up his fist, and Deacon braced himself for a hit.

"Stop!" Tyrell bellowed.

Beau glared into Deacon's eyes.

"You need a two-thirds majority," Beau spat.

Deacon narrowed his eyes, trying to gauge if Beau was bluffing.

"No," Tyrell said, staying in his seat at the head of the long table. "You need a two-thirds majority to overturn the decision."

Beau broke eye contact with Deacon to look at his father. Deacon took a chance and relaxed his hold.

Beau pushed to break free. "Are we going to let the lawyers duke it out?"

Aaron appeared in the doorway, and Deacon felt distinctly outnumbered.

"Do you have the authority to make this deal?" Deacon asked Tyrell.

"Yes," Tyrell said, his voice definitive.

"I will fight you," Beau said. "You are not having this…" He rounded on Deacon. "This *person* replace Frederick."

"He's not replacing Frederick," Tyrell said.

"No?" Aaron walked in and took the chair to the right of his father. Aaron's tone was far more reasonable. "You're giving him Frederick's company shares. He married Frederick's wife. He's here. What more is there to replacing Frederick?"

"We should throw him out," Beau said.

"Beau," Tyrell snapped.

"You're not helping," Aaron said to his brother.

"You're welcome to try," Deacon said easily.

"I'll tie you up in court so long, you'll be bankrupt or retired before we're done."

Deacon sat back down and signed the final paper with a flourish. "Do that, and you'll never see my sons again."

Deacon knew full well Callie could walk away at any moment, and he'd be the one who'd never see James and Ethan again. But for the moment, they were his best leverage point with the Clarksons.

"The price is too high," Beau said to his father. "Even *you* have to know it's way too high."

"They're my grandsons," Tyrell said. "They're the future of this family."

Beau walked around the table and dropped into a chair. "I'll get married," he said. "You win. I'll get married and give you legitimate grandchildren."

"You had your chance," Tyrell said.

Deacon couldn't help but glance at Aaron. Aaron was married. Was there some reason he wasn't having children? From the tight expression on Aaron's face, Deacon guessed that must be the case.

The reason for Tyrell's offer to Deacon was becoming clearer. James and Ethan weren't just his first grandsons. They might well be his only grandsons.

"What's your beef with me?" Deacon asked Beau.

Beau shot a sneer across the table. "Are you kidding me? The mere sight of you is a knife in my mother's heart."

"Not my fault," Deacon said.

"Shouldn't we be talking about his credentials," Aaron asked. "What does he know about running the port? We don't need a useless drain on the system with twenty-five percent voting power."

Deacon was getting tired of this argument. He looked to Tyrell. "Do we have a deal, or don't we? Because I'm the legal guardian of those two boys, and their mother is madly in love with me." The last part was a gross exaggeration at this point, but Deacon liked the way it added to his threat.

Tyrell stood. "There's something you need to see."

At first, Deacon thought Tyrell was talking to him. But it was clear he meant Aaron and Beau.

"What?" Beau asked.

"You can't run this place by decree," Aaron said.

"Will you follow me?" Tyrell's exasperation was clear.

Both men reluctantly followed their father out of the room.

Curious, Deacon went along. Whatever it was Tyrell had up his sleeve, Deacon could only hope it settled the deal.

They made their way along a hallway, through a formal dining room, to a set of glass doors. The doors led to a patio. And when they walked outside, Deacon could hear James's and Ethan's shouts. He also heard a woman's laughter. He guessed it was Dee.

The play area was off the edge of the patio, and both Aaron and Beau moved closer to look. They stopped at the concrete rail, and Deacon watched their expressions as they stared: Aaron at James and Beau at Ethan. It was clear they saw what everyone else did. It was as if they'd been cloned.

Aaron spoke first. "How could that..."

Beau brought the heels of his palms down on the rail, a note of awe in his voice. "Do you think Frederick could see it?"

Tyrell's bet seemed to have paid off. It looked like Aaron and Beau would close ranks around their nephews.

Deacon caught a glimpse of Callie. She was laughing, looking relaxed while she chatted with Margo. She looked unexpectedly happy, and he was jealous. He saw her every day, but he missed her desperately.

His fingertips itched from wanting to touch her. He was

longing to hold her. Every time she smiled at her sons, he wanted to kiss her. And at night, he lay awake in a near-constant state of frustration.

She was only steps down the hall in the guest room. He pictured her silk nightgown, her creamy shoulders. In his mind he saw her sleeping, eyes closed, cheeks flushed, lips slightly parted. He'd kissed her awake more than once. And then...

He gritted his teeth and gave himself a shake, focusing his attention on reality.

As he did, and as he surveyed the scene, a cold realization came over him. It was the boys they wanted. It was Callie they needed. If Callie walked away from him, the Clarksons would welcome her with open arms.

Deacon was entirely expendable.

Callie had let ten days go by.

First Ethan had been sick. Then Margo wanted some time with her grandchildren. She'd asked to take them shopping and to the funfair at the pier. Dee always came along and lent a hand, making Callie feel quite spoiled.

Deacon had stayed busy, working all day, coming home late, making it easy for her to push their problems to the background. He never asked if she was staying, never asked if she was going.

She wanted to leave. But leaving meant telling the world she'd made a mistake, telling Hannah and everyone back in Charleston she'd been a fool. Telling Margo she was taking the boys away. It meant giving a final decision to Deacon and maybe fighting with him about it.

She didn't want to fight with Deacon. She wanted to laugh with him again, talk to him about anything and nothing. She wanted to hold him, kiss him, make love with him and sleep in his arms again. Her soul ached with missing him.

She walked back out onto the deck, in the cool dark of the evening. She'd played with the boys in the hot tub before bundling them off to bed. Now, she picked up the discarded towels and reached in for the floating toys.

Her hand skimmed the warm water. She'd pulled on her cover-up, but her bathing suit was still damp underneath. She was chilled now, and the hot water felt wonderful.

She knew that just inside the door was the wet bar, with wine and brandy, and anything else that might strike her fancy. The moon was full, the lights in the garden glowing, with a view overlooking the town and the dark ocean beyond.

She hadn't spent much time, really no time at all appreciating her surroundings. Deacon had a wonderful house, in a beautiful spot, with every amenity a person could wish for.

Making up her mind, she padded inside, the carpet soft against her bare feet. She found a small snifter, chose a pretty brandy label and poured herself a drink.

She dimmed the lights, discarded her cover-up and lowered herself into the hot water, turning the jets to high and facing the view. She sipped the brandy as the water pulsated against her lower back and surged between her shoulder blades.

"You look comfortable," Deacon said from behind her, his voice deep and melodious.

For a moment, she let the sound wash over her, leaving her skin tingling.

"I didn't know you were here," she said, craning her neck to look at him.

He moved into her view. "I just got home."

"Working late?" A part of her wanted to laugh at the banal conversation, as if they were a normal couple, on a normal night, in a normal circumstance.

He crouched on his haunches and trailed his hand through the water.

She watched with rapt attention, imagining it on her skin.

"Growing pains," he said.

"Hmm?" She forced herself to look up.

"The port is growing, and there are some tough decisions to make."

She was surprised he was sharing. He didn't seem to ever talk about work. She knew he'd lied about Mobi Transportation looking at relocating to Charleston. It was a minor lie in the scheme of things.

It was true that he was a shareholder at Mobi, but his real job was in the family firm of Hale Harbor Port. That was where he worked, with his half brothers, Beau, who seemed hostile, and Aaron, who seemed cold to everyone, not to mention his father, who had, despite Margo's resentment of Deacon, apparently brought him into the family business anyway.

"Mind if I join you?" Deacon asked.

Her heart skipped a beat.

He took in her expression. "I won't if it makes you uncomfortable."

"No. It's fine. It's your hot tub."

He looked like he wanted to say something, but he clamped his lips together.

"Please," she said, gesturing to the water. "It's nice."

He rose. "I'll grab a suit."

She watched him walk away, wishing she could tell him to forget the bathing suit. She'd seen him naked dozens of times. And he'd seen her. And it was silly for them to feign modesty now.

She lowered herself deeper into the water and sipped the brandy, while her mind went on a flight of fancy about making love with Deacon.

He was back before she expected, startling her.

She sat back up, while he climbed into the hot tub with his own glass of brandy. He also set the bottle at the edge.

"Margo mentioned a ball today," Callie said, latching onto a neutral topic.

"The Summer Solstice?" he asked.

"That sounds right."

"It's famous around here, the social event of the year. Everyone wants to be invited to the castle to dance in the grand ballroom."

"The Clarksons apparently have a tailor. She wants to make matching suits for the boys."

Deacon blinked at her. He didn't have to ask the question. They both knew what it was.

The ball was a week away. Would James and Ethan be here to wear their custom-made suits?

"I don't know," Callie told him honestly. "I don't know what to do."

Deacon might be the source of her problem, but he was also the only person who knew the truth. Everyone else thought their marriage was real.

"You know what I want." His tone was deep, sincere, like the words had been pulled from his very core.

She couldn't take her gaze from him. She couldn't speak. She couldn't move.

When he shifted to the seat next to her, her pulse jumped. The water temperature seemed to inch up several degrees.

"Stay," he said. "For as long as you want. I'll give you space." Even as he made the promise, he seemed to grow closer. His gaze moved to her lips. "I'll give you—"

And then he was kissing her. And it was magic. It took her breath away. And she kissed him back, the water sloshing between them. His arms went around her. Her body slid against his. Her breasts plastered again his chest.

A crash shattered the night around them.

They jumped apart, and she realized she'd dropped her brandy snifter on the concrete deck.

"I'm sorry." She couldn't believe she'd been so careless.

She rose to her knees to look over the edge.

"Don't move," he told her, setting his own glass down.

"I'm so stupid," she said.

"I'll clean it up."

"You have bare feet."

"I'll get some shoes."

He turned back to her, wrapping his hands around her

shoulders, gazing into her eyes. "I will give you space," he promised.

"That was my fault, too." She had to make the admission.

"What do you want?" he asked. "Just tell me what it is, and I'll do it."

What she wanted was impossible. She wanted the fantasy that had never been true. She wanted their marriage to be what he'd pretended.

"I don't think you can," she whispered.

"Okay," he gave a nod of acceptance. "Okay. But that doesn't mean I won't stop trying."

She watched him rise from the water, the droplets sliding off his broad shoulders, the arms that held her so tightly, his abs, his thighs, everything she'd kissed and touched as they'd made love so many times.

How could he try? What could he possibly do?

There was no way to go back and turn his lies into the truth.

Nine

Deacon dug in and worked hard to learn about Hale Harbor Port. Callie didn't know that his interest in the company was tied to her. She assumed he'd been working there for years, and he hadn't corrected her. So he was on eggshells, thinking she might ask a question he couldn't answer.

Aaron and Beau sure hadn't made the learning curve easy. They wouldn't answer a single question, and Deacon was convinced they were actively turning staff members against him.

But he'd persisted. He'd poured over their billing, accounts payable and receivable, their terminal schedules, traffic volume, even cargo manifests. After hours and hours of work, he'd come to a simple but startling conclusion. Hale Harbor Port was losing money.

He presented his findings to Tyrell, Aaron and Beau at the boardroom table in the castle's business wing.

Tyrell showed little reaction. "We're aware of it," he said.

"It can't continue." Deacon didn't have to fully understand the port business to know that much.

"It's won't continue," Beau said. "It's a temporary slump."

"You have to revise your pricing structure." Deacon didn't buy that it was a temporary slump. He knew from his work at Mobi that the transportation sector had fundamentally changed over the past decade. Everyone had to look at new approaches.

"And price ourselves out of the market?" Beau asked. "It's competitive out there."

"That's obviously not what I meant," Deacon countered.

"What do you mean?" Aaron asked.

Beau turned on his brother. "You're going to take him seriously? He's been here all of five minutes, and you're ready to take his advice."

"Nobody's taking his advice," Tyrell said.

Deacon rocked back in his chair. "Sure. Ignore me. Stick your head in the sand and—" As he spoke, he caught a glimpse of movement through the boardroom window.

He could see all the way across the courtyard, through a window into another part of the castle. It looked like… It was. Callie was in the next wing. He leaned forward for a better view.

"We should at least monitor it," Aaron said.

"We are monitoring it," Tyrell said.

Then Deacon spotted James. He looked disproportionately tall, and Deacon realized he was standing on something. He raised his arms, holding them out to his sides.

"We do have accountants," Beau drawled.

A man approached James, reaching across his outstretched arms. Deacon all but cheered. The man was the tailor. The boys were being measured for suits. They were staying for the ball. Callie was staying for the ball.

A wave of relief passed through Deacon.

"Is that funny?" Tyrell asked.

Deacon refocused his attention. "What?"

"Is it funny that we have accountants?"

"Of course not." Deacon stole one more glance across the courtyard.

James and Ethan were going to look terrific in little tuxedos. Deacon was buying one for himself. He didn't think a tuxedo would come anywhere near to changing Callie's mind about him. But it couldn't hurt either.

"We're not making a major decision today," Tyrell said.

"I'm only suggesting we gather more data," Deacon said, refocusing. "We should look at options."

"What kind of options?" Aaron asked.

"Will you stop humoring him," Beau demanded.

"Vertical integration," Deacon said.

Beau threw up his hands in frustration, but Aaron looked interested.

"Again," Beau said. "He's been here five minutes."

"I've been alive longer than that," Deacon said evenly. "I've been in the transportation industry for years. There's money there. Global supply chains are growing, trade agreements are popping up all over the world. At the retail level, bricks and motor are out, delivery is in. Hale Harbor could be at the nexus of a game-changer."

"Vertical integration." Aaron's head tilted thoughtfully.

"We've operated steady as she goes for hundreds of years," Tyrell said.

"Exclusive agreements," Deacon said to Aaron. "With a firm like Mobi Transport."

"There it is," said Beau. "He wants to use Hale Harbor Port to beef up Mobi."

"It was only an example," Deacon said. "And I meant the other way around, use a company like Mobi Transportation to beef up Hale Harbor Port."

"How?" Aaron asked.

"I've had enough of this." Beau came to his feet.

"We have other business on the agenda," Tyrell said. "But let's break for lunch." He also came to his feet.

Deacon allowed himself another glance across the courtyard, seeing Callie in profile. She was talking to Margo, and the two were watching the tailor try to wrangle Ethan.

Beau and Tyrell left the room, but Aaron stayed seated. He tapped a pen on his leather folder. "How?" he repeated to Deacon.

"Does it matter?" Deacon asked. He knew Aaron was as hostile toward him as Beau. Aaron simply hid it better.

"Do you have a good idea or not?"

Deacon figured he had nothing to lose. "Buy or take an equity position in Mobi, or in another company along the chain, like a maritime shipping company. Mobi is nice because it's local, it's small. So a good place to start and test the methodology. Give them preferential pricing, so they use Hale Harbor exclusively."

"*Lower* prices? Lose more money?"

"Increase volume, streamline processes, make the port itself revenue neutral, then get profitable through the subsidiary businesses."

"Do you have *any* idea what you're talking about?"

"I'm only saying it's worth exploring."

"The magnitude of that change is ridiculous."

"You got a better idea?"

Aaron came to his feet. "Not yet. But there has to be a dozen better ideas than that. Beau's right. You've been here five minutes."

Squelching his disappointment, Deacon let his gaze rest on Callie. He might have lost this round with Tyrell and the boys, but Callie was staying, at least for another week. It was a win for him on that front.

"The slump could be temporary," Aaron said.

"Maybe." Deacon didn't think so.

Aaron started for the door. "It always has been in the past."

"This isn't the past," Deacon tossed over his shoulder.

Given the choice between lunch and seeing Callie, he was taking Callie.

He left the boardroom and made his way along the second-floor hallway. The castle was big and rambling, with circuitous hallways, dead ends, multistory grand halls and winding stairways. He had to go up to the third floor and make his way along an open loft hallway, then come down to traverse a kitchen, drawing curious looks from a couple of staff members.

But he finally made it to the other side of the courtyard. He found the second floor and heard the boys' voices.

They were in a dressing room of some kind, though it was the size of a dance hall. He wondered if Margo had all her clothes custom made and if Tyrell and their sons did, as well.

"Daddy," Ethan cried, jumping down from the stool to the obvious chagrin of the tailor.

"What's going on here?" Deacon asked cheerfully as Ethan trotted toward him.

"We're getting new clothes," James answered, heading for Deacon.

"Special, special clothes," Ethan spun around.

Deacon caught Callie's gaze. "You're going to the ball."

Ethan made a throwing motion with his hand.

"There will be dessert," James said.

"You know I like dessert," Deacon said, ruffling Ethan's hair.

Margo kept her attention on the tailor, doing her best to pretend Deacon wasn't there. He wondered how long she planned to keep giving him the cold shoulder. He wasn't going away.

He crossed the room to Callie. "You made a decision?" he asked her on an undertone.

"Time for lunch," Margo said brightly to the boys. "Who wants grilled cheese?"

"Me, me," Ethan said.

"Yes, please," James said.

"Let's go find Dee." Margo hustled the boys out, while the tailor retreated to a table at the far end of the room.

"I should go," Callie said, watching the doorway where her sons had left.

"I'm glad you're staying," Deacon said.

"Don't make any assumptions."

"I'm not."

"It's not for you."

"I know." He wished it was, but he acknowledged full well it wasn't.

"Margo is… She's really grown attached to the boys."

Deacon hadn't seen himself ever being grateful to Margo. But he was now. In this moment, he silently thanked her for her doting ways. It bought him some time.

He didn't know what he was going to do with that time. He had absolutely no plan. But it was better than the alternative.

* * *

As she tucked the boys into bed, Callie hoped she was doing the right thing by staying for the ball. It was a form of torture being around Deacon, wanting him, missing him, trying desperately to stay angry with him.

"Mommy," James said as she smoothed the covers around him.

"Yes, sweetheart?"

"Is Grandma very smart?"

"I think so. She seems pretty smart."

"Okay."

"Why do you ask?"

"She says a red tie will make me shine."

"I bet you'll look terrific in a red tie."

"Ethan's snoring again."

Callie listened for a moment. "Just a little bit. It's a quiet snore."

"It sounds like an angry dog."

She gave James a hug. "Your brother's not an angry dog."

"Okay. You're smarter than Grandma."

"I'm glad you think I'm smart." Callie came to her feet. She couldn't help but be warmed by the compliment. She also couldn't help but be curious about the scale James was using to make his assessment.

"Grandma gets mixed up," James said.

"About what?"

"She calls Ethan Beau."

Callie stilled, unnerved, but not completely sure why. "Ethan looks like Uncle Beau did when he was little."

"Uncle Beau looks like an angry dog. He frowns all the time."

"Does Uncle Beau frighten you?"

"No." James sounded completely unconcerned. "I bet he snores."

Callie breathed a sigh of relief. "Good night, James."

"Good night, Mommy."

She left the door partway open as she walked into the hall.

She'd heard Deacon come in while she was reading the boys a story. He was home earlier than usual. She toyed with the idea of going straight to bed. It would be better if she didn't see him tonight. It was emotionally safer to keep her distance.

But she'd left some dishes in the sink, her book was on the table in the family room and she'd been looking forward to a cup of tea. She might struggle with her feelings around him, but she didn't want to hide in her room either.

She started down the stairs.

Deacon was talking, she assumed on the phone. But then she heard another voice. It was oddly familiar, but she couldn't place it.

She followed the sounds into the living room to find the two men standing, facing each other.

Deacon saw her.

The man turned. He was shorter than Deacon, stockier, his hair was long, straggly, and he wore a pair of wrinkled jeans, scuffed black boots and a navy blue T-shirt. The skin of his face looked soft. He had a stubble beard and familiar blue eyes.

"Hello, Callie." His voice sent a shiver down her spine, and she flinched as she recognized him.

"Trevor?" It was her oldest brother, but he sounded frighteningly like her father.

"Long time, no see, baby sister."

"*What* are you doing here?" She hadn't seen or heard from him since the day he stormed out of their tacky little house in Grainwall.

He'd been eighteen. She'd been only nine.

"Is that any way to greet your brother?" He moved toward her.

She was too stunned to move, and he gave her a hug.

She was suddenly transported back to her childhood, to the screaming matches between her brothers and father, to the barked orders for her to bring them beer, make them sandwiches and *to clean that kitchen the hell up*. Everything inside her cringed.

After what seemed like an eternity, he stepped back. "I hear you got married."

She struggled to find her voice. "How did you find me?"

Why had he looked?

After her father had died, one by one, her three brothers had left home, until she was alone with her mother. None of them had ever come back. None of them had helped, not when her mother got sick, not when her mother had died. None of them ever cared that Callie had been orphaned at sixteen.

"Social media. It's a wonderful thing."

"Can I offer you a drink?" Deacon asked. "Please, sit down."

Callie wanted to shout *no*. If Trevor started drinking, he'd never stop.

"Don't mind if I do." Trevor popped himself down on a sofa and patted the seat next to him.

She took an armchair.

"What would you like?" Deacon asked.

"A brew if you've got one." Trevor glanced around the room.

"Merlot, Callie?" Deacon asked, knowing it was one of her favorites.

"I was going to make tea."

"Sure." Deacon left for the kitchen.

"Done real well for yourself, Callie," Trevor drawled.

Now that Deacon was out of the room, Trevor's eyes hardened in appraisal.

Callie's stomach started to hurt. The sights and sounds and smells of her childhood swelled up inside her head. She hadn't thought about her father in years, or her brothers, or even her mother for that matter. But now she pictured her father yelling, her mother sobbing in the corner and Trevor laughing drunkenly.

She couldn't remember who hit whom. There were frequent

fistfights amongst the boys, and her dad was quick to slap her mother. Callie herself hadn't been a target. They yelled at her and shoved her, but she didn't remember getting hit.

She did remember being terrified.

"Cat got your tongue?" Trevor asked.

She swallowed. She wanted to tell him to leave, to go away, to never come back. But she couldn't bring herself to do it. The frightened little girl inside her didn't have the courage to stand up.

"Never mind." Trevor looked her up and down. "You don't have to say anything for me to get how it is. You've landed on your feet. I've got my trouble, but you landed on your feet."

Deacon came back, and Callie was incredibly grateful to see him. He carried a mug of tea in one hand and two bottles of beer in the other. He set her tea down beside her, then handed Trevor a beer.

"Are you visiting Hale Harbor?" Deacon asked Trevor. Deacon chose the armchair opposite Callie and twisted the cap off his beer.

"Came to look in on Callie," Trevor said. "Been kicking around Alabama for a while now." He guzzled half his beer.

"Oh. What is it you do?"

"Little of this, little of that."

Deacon glanced at Callie.

She was frozen. She couldn't speak, and she couldn't move. A part of her knew it was ridiculous to be afraid of Trevor. He couldn't do anything, especially not with Deacon here. But she couldn't shake the visceral fear.

Deacon guzzled a good measure of his beer, and Trevor grinned at him in a way that said he'd met a kindred spirit.

"You married my sister," Trevor said.

"I did."

"Didn't get a wedding invitation."

"It was a small wedding."

"Really." Trevor seemed surprised. "I thought you well-to-do people put on posh parties."

"Sometimes," Deacon said politely.

Callie ordered herself to speak up, to say something. It wasn't fair to force Deacon to carry on this conversation with her brother.

Trevor took another long guzzle of his beer.

Callie asked, "Are you married?"

Trevor swung his gaze to her. "Never met the right gal."

Callie was silently grateful on behalf of womenkind. If Trevor had turned out anything like her father—which it seemed he had—then no woman deserved to end up with him.

"No kids either," Trevor said.

Callie did *not* want to talk about her sons. "Have you heard from Joe or Manny?"

She lifted her mug of tea, willing her hand not to shake.

"Can't say that I have. But maybe we should look them up. Maybe we should have ourselves a family reunion."

Callie immediately regretted asking the question.

Deacon polished off his beer and pointedly set down the bottle. "It was nice of you to drop by," he said to Trevor and came to his feet. He glanced at his watch. "Why don't you leave your number, and we'll be in touch."

Trevor looked flummoxed and then annoyed. "Well..." He looked to Callie, but she focused on her tea. "I was..." He didn't seem to know how to counter Deacon's dismissal.

Callie was immensely grateful.

"Sure," Trevor said, polishing off his beer.

He set the bottle on the end table with a thud and rose to his feet.

Deacon walked to a side table and produced a pen and paper. "Just write it down," he said to Trevor.

Trevor scrutinized Callie as he passed, but thankfully he didn't say anything to her.

She was vaguely aware of Deacon seeing Trevor out, and then Deacon was back.

He dropped to one knee in front of her, concern in his expression. "What on earth?"

"They're *awful*." The words burst out of her, and she started to shake.

Deacon quickly took the mug from her hands and set it aside.

"All of them," she said. "They're mean and violent."

"Did he hurt you?"

"Not me. Not physically. Not much."

Deacon pulled her into his arms, holding her close.

She couldn't help herself. She tucked her head against his shoulder and closed her eyes, absorbing his strength as fear and dismay shuddered through her.

"I thought I was over it," she said.

"Tell me what happened."

Everything inside Deacon told him to go after Trevor. Whatever it was that Trevor had done to Callie in the past had hurt her badly. He should be held responsible. Deacon wanted justice for the way Callie was shaking in his arms.

But Callie needed him.

He eased her to one side of the big chair and sat down himself, drawing her into his lap, cradling her close and rubbing her arms.

"Tell me," he gently urged.

Whatever it was, he was going to make it better. Somehow, some way, he was going to make it better.

"How could they do that?" she asked, her voice a rasp. "How could they be so cruel? I was just a little girl."

He listened while she told him about the family's abject poverty. There was never enough money for food and clothes. She'd gone to school in castoffs from the church rummage sale. Their electricity was often turned off. They barely had heat, never mind air conditioning in the summer. And she'd slept for years on a damp mattress on the floor.

Meanwhile, she and her mother had waited on her father and brothers hand and foot, enduring shouts, curses and shoves. She told Deacon about the terror she felt when her parents fought, how her father slapped her mother, and how she'd been relieved when her father had died of a heart attack.

But her brothers hadn't let up. It wasn't until they finally left home, one by one, that she had any peace. Money was still tight, and then her mother got sick. At fourteen, she'd found a part-time job and tried desperately to hold it together financially. But then her mom died, and the hospital bills came due, and Callie had quit school.

While she spoke, her shaking slowly subsided. "Frederick was the first person to care for me. He was so kind. He was so gentle. I was never afraid of him."

She was a limp bundle of heat in Deacon's arms. Twin tear tracks glistened on her cheeks. Her hair was tousled, her legs were curled up.

"Have you ever told anyone about this?" he asked gently.

"There was no one to tell. Frederick had more problems than I could imagine."

"He had different problems."

"I couldn't tell him. I didn't want to tell him. It was in the past by then." She gave a shaky laugh. "I wanted to pretend it had happened to someone else. I wasn't her anymore, that defenseless little girl, exploited like a servant." She fell silent.

"I'm glad you told me." Deacon kissed her temple.

She sighed and rested her head against his shoulder.

He kissed away the tear track on her cheek. Her lips were dark and soft and sweet, and he gave in to temptation, kissing her tenderly, trying to will away her pain and heartache.

She kissed him back.

But then she gasped and turned her head away. "Deacon."

"I know," he said, wrapping his arms fully around her, holding her desperately close. "I won't let it get away from us. I promise."

"We can't."

"We won't." He rocked her. "Just let me hold you."

Minutes ticked past before he felt her relax.

He wanted to kiss her again, but he knew he'd be lost. And

he couldn't let himself do that. She needed his comfort, not his lust.

He sat for an hour.

He didn't know exactly when she fell asleep, but she did.

He didn't want to put her down. He didn't want to let her go. But he had something to do, and he wasn't going to let it wait.

He carried her upstairs, laid her gently on her bed and pulled a comforter overtop of her.

Then he set his jaw, trotted down the stairs and took the paper with Trevor's phone number. He dialed as he walked to his car and opened the driver's door.

"Yo," Trevor answered, music twanging in the background.

"It's Deacon Holt." Deacon climbed in and shut the door, pressing the ignition button.

There was a brief pause on the line. "Well, Mr. Holt. That didn't take long."

"I want to meet," Deacon said, an adrenalin buzz energizing his system. He pictured Trevor in a seedy bar.

"Sure. Can do. When would you like this meeting?"

"Now. Where are you?"

There was another pause and a muttered voice. "It's called The Waterstreet Grill."

Deacon knew the place. It wasn't a dive. Too bad.

"I'll be there in ten minutes."

"You got it," Trevor said.

Deacon hung up the phone and pulled out of the driveway. It was after ten o'clock, so the roads were mostly clear. He lowered the windows and let the breeze flow in, trying to cool his temper. He kept picturing Trevor, who was six feet tall, shouting at a miniature Callie, her lugging cans of beer, and him chugging them down.

He smacked his hands on the steering wheel, swore out loud and pressed his foot on the accelerator. He made it to The Waterstreet Grill and swung into the curb out front. It was a no parking zone, but he really didn't care if they towed him.

He left the car, crossed the sidewalk and shoved open the heavy door.

It was dim inside the grill. The restaurant section was almost empty, but the bar was full. Country-pop came out of ceiling speakers, and cigarette smoke wafted in through an open door to the side alley.

He spotted Trevor talking with two other men at the bar. He made his way over.

"Yo, Deacon," Trevor said with a wide smile. He held up his hand to shake.

Deacon ignored it. He cocked his head toward the open door.

"You can talk in front of my friends," Trevor said. He clapped one of the men on the back. "This here's—"

"I don't want to talk in front of your friends," Deacon said. Trevor's expression fell. "Chill, bro."

Deacon grimaced. "Shall we step outside?"

"Is this a fight?" Trevor asked with an uncomfortable laugh.

"No. But it can be." Deacon turned for the side door, confident that Trevor would follow.

Deacon passed two groups of smokers in the alley and went a few feet further.

"You're the one who called me," Trevor said as he caught up.

Deacon pivoted. "Callie is not your gravy train."

Trevor's eyes narrowed and crackled, his passive demeanor vanishing. "She's my sister. We're family."

"What you were to her isn't family."

"Got a birth certificate that says different."

"She owes you nothing."

"Let her tell me that."

Deacon stepped forward into Trevor's space. "You're never speaking to her again."

"Are you threatening me?"

Deacon reached into his jacket pocket and withdrew a check. He knew exactly why Trevor had come back into Callie's life, and he was taking the most direct route to sending him away.

"Consider this the carrot," he said, planting the check against Trevor's chest. "If it doesn't work, I've got a stick."

Trevor stepped back, grabbing at the check. He looked down, his widening eyes giving away his surprise at the amount.

"You're gone," Deacon said. "And you're never coming back."

"Is this good?" Trevor asked.

"Gone," Deacon repeated and turned to walk away.

He hoped he'd made his point.

Ten

James and Ethan looked adorable in their matching tuxes. James wore a red bowtie, while Ethan's was royal blue. Callie was a ridiculously proud mom.

Deacon looked magnificent, while Callie couldn't help but feel beautiful in her designer gown, with its glittering bodice, peekaboo back and flowing chiffon skirt. Deacon had insisted she buy it. And she'd been inclined to make him happy, since he'd been so supportive about Trevor.

Deacon said he had spoken to Trevor and promised her that her brother wouldn't be back. She hadn't asked Deacon what he'd said. She didn't care. It was enough that she didn't have the weight of her family hanging over her head.

"Mommy, Grandma gave us pudding," James said with excitement as he arrived holding Dee's hand.

"Mousse," Dee told Callie.

"Chocolate?" Callie asked.

"We were careful of their white shirts."

"It's nearly eight o'clock," Callie said. She didn't give the boys sugar, never mind chocolate, after five.

"Oh, don't worry so much," Margo said, arriving with a fluttery wave of her hand.

"We should probably take them home soon." Callie looked around for Deacon. She didn't mind driving the boys home on her own if he wanted to stay.

"What's the rush?" Margo asked.

"They'll be getting tired," Callie said.

"I'm not tired," James said.

"They're doing fine. Their grandpa and I still want to show them off."

Callie hesitated. The boys did seem to still have energy. It was probably the chocolate, but she understood Margo's perspective. She had gone to a lot of trouble for tonight.

"A little while," Callie agreed.

"I'll stay with them," Dee said.

"I can come along." Callie knew she should keep an eye on their moods.

"Don't be silly," Margo said. "Go find Deacon and have a dance."

In the face of the onslaught, Callie gave in. A selfish part of her did want to dance in her new gown. A foolish part of her wanted to dance with Deacon.

To do that, she'd have to throw caution to the wind.

She paused to give her saner side an opportunity to talk her out of it. Instead, she admitted this was a caution-to-the-wind kind of night. Her toddler had just eaten chocolate pudding at eight o'clock.

She caught sight of Deacon across the room.

He met her gaze and smiled.

She felt the attraction arc between them. She returned his smile and started toward him.

He must have seen something in her eyes, because he looked puzzled. Then he looked pleased, then he looked flat-out sexy.

"Dance?" she asked without giving herself a second to hesitate.

"Absolutely." He took her hand and led her toward the dance floor.

There was a small orchestra in the corner of the grand ballroom. The polished floor was smooth under her feet. Deacon's lead was sure, his steps perfect, his arm wonderful around her waist.

"This is some party," she said as they twirled across the floor.

"It's been a tradition for two hundred years."

She drew back. "Seriously?"

"The Clarksons are big on tradition. Take a look at the

walls. Those are real swords and shields from the ancestors back home. The Clarksons came over on the Mayflower and fought in the civil war."

"Which side?"

"This is Virginia, ma'am. Both sides."

Callie grinned. "That's hedging your bets."

The music changed to a slower rhythm, and Deacon went quiet. His hand moved against the small of her back, gently stroking, his thumb touching the skin revealed by the open back of her dress.

She knew she shouldn't sink into the sensation, but she couldn't help herself. She shifted closer and closer, until she was flush against him. He put his cheek to her hair, and she burrowed into the crook of his neck.

Desire pulsed deep into her body. The music flowed louder. Voices around them disappeared. The other dancers faded to a swirl of color.

Then she heard it, faint but unmistakable. It was Ethan's cry.

She jumped back from Deacon.

He seemed stunned. "What?"

"Ethan," she called. "Something's wrong." She rushed toward the sound.

"No," Ethan was shouting.

Callie rushed as fast as she could on her high heels.

She could see Margo talking to Ethan.

Ethan screwed up his face and shook his head.

Tyrell said something, and Ethan looked up. At first he looked scared, but then he dropped to the floor and squealed.

Tyrell reached down and pulled him back to his feet as Callie came within earshot.

"—and behave yourself!" Tyrell's tone was sharp.

Callie quickly crouched to put her arms around her son. "Sweetheart? What is it?"

Ethan started to cry.

She stood, wrapping him in her arms.

"I don't think coddling him will help," Tyrell said.

Callie glared at him. She didn't care that this was his house, and that he was the party's host. Ethan was her son, and her parenting choices were none of Tyrell's business.

This was all her fault, not Ethan's. It was nearly nine o'clock.

James was watching the whole thing with wide eyes.

She took his hand. "It's time for us to go home, honey."

"Oh, there's no need for that." Margo's tone was soothing.

Deacon arrived. "Is everything all right?"

Margo spoke directly to Deacon. It was the first time Callie had seen her do that.

"I was just telling Callie there's no need for her to leave early. We've set up the nursery for the boys."

Callie didn't want the nursery. She didn't want to stay here any longer. She wanted to take her boys home to their own beds.

"Ethan?" Dee came up close to him. "Would you like me to read you a story? You can have a bubble bath, too."

Callie didn't like the idea. "I think it's better if we —"

Ethan's voice was watery. "Which story?"

"The Pig and the Duck."

"The whole thing?" Ethan asked.

"I like *The Pig and the Duck*," James said. "And I like bubbles."

Ethan stopped crying and raised his head, looking at Callie.

"Do you want Dee to read you a story?" she asked.

Ethan nodded.

Deacon touched her shoulder and whispered in her ear. "It's completely up to you."

"There's a room made up for you, too," Margo said. "It's right across the hall from the nursery. You wouldn't have to disturb them at the end of the party."

Against her better judgement, Callie took the path of least resistance. They were only moments from the nursery. It would take at least half an hour to get the boys loaded into the car and back home. By the time they got there, Ethan would be truly miserable.

"Okay," she said. "Dee can put you to bed." She handed Ethan to Dee, who took James's hand to walk away.

"You shouldn't encourage that kind of behavior," Tyrell said to Callie.

"Don't," Deacon warned him. "Callie is a fantastic mother."

"It was the chocolate." Callie felt the need to defend Ethan. It might not have been his finest hour, but he wasn't the one to blame.

"Shall we dance again?" Deacon asked her.

She took him up on the offer. It might not be the smart thing, but she missed Deacon's arms, and she wanted to get away from Margo and Tyrell.

She knew Tyrell had a big personality, that he preferred things his own way, but this was the first time it had touched her personally. And on the heels of her brother's unsettling visit, it was more than she could take.

Deacon heard Callie open then close the bedroom door. She'd been across the hall, checking on James and Ethan, and now she set the baby monitor on a small table.

It was after midnight, and the party was quickly winding to a close. Although there were still dozens of guests, not to mention the staff, in the halls below, the castle walls were thick, and here on the second floor, it was completely quiet.

The room was large, with warm wooden walls, recessed windows showing the original stone structure, heavy ceiling beams and a thick woven carpet. There was a massive carved wood canopy bed in the center, flanked by two armchairs around a fireplace and a small table and chair set. The walk-in closet and the connected bathroom were at opposite ends of the room.

Callie looked tired but beautiful in her flowing gown. Her upswept hair was wispy around her face, and when she reached down to strip off her high heels, Deacon felt a surge of desire. It was pathetic, really, finding her bare feet that sexy.

"Are the boys okay?" he asked as a conversation opener. He didn't want to address the sleeping arrangements head on.

"Did it seem weird to you?" she asked. "Earlier, I mean." She looked around the floor, settling on putting her shoes beneath the upholstered bench positioned at the foot of the bed.

"Did what seem weird?" All Deacon remembered was holding her in his arms on the dance floor, watching her talk and smile with the other guests, not being able to take his gaze off her all night long.

"Margo with the boys. I mean, Tyrell was a jerk. I don't want him alone with the boys, especially Ethan."

"I understand." Deacon had no intention of letting Tyrell babysit.

"But Margo." Callie perched on the bench. "Does she seem a bit possessive to you?"

"She adores her grandsons." That had been obvious to Deacon from minute one.

"That nursery." Callie pointed across the hall. "It's full of toys and clothes. They could live there forever if they wanted."

Deacon moved closer to Callie. "The Clarksons do have a lot of money."

She tipped her chin to look up. "I know. It's just a funny feeling I get around her lately. She called Ethan *Beau*. James told me that."

"They do look alike."

"Yeah. You're right. I guess it's not that strange."

"Are you okay staying here?" he asked.

"It doesn't make any sense to wake the boys up."

Deacon looked meaningfully to the big bed, the only place in the room for either of them to sleep. "I mean…"

It seemed to occur to her for the first time. "Oh." She drew a sigh. "I'm so exhausted, I don't even care. Will it bother you?"

"Not in the least." He was surprised by her pragmatic acceptance.

She sized up the bed again. "I doubt we could find each other if we tried."

He'd find her in about half a second. But he wouldn't.

He'd already hung up his jacket, and now he stripped off his tie. As he removed his white shirt, her gaze seemed to stall on his chest. He wanted it to mean something, but he doubted it did.

He held out the shirt. "Here."

"What?"

"You can sleep in this."

She blinked. She paused. "Oh. Okay. Thanks."

He gestured to the bathroom. "Go ahead."

She rose and took the shirt.

She shut the door behind her, and a vision of her changing bloomed in his mind. To distract himself, he removed his shoes and set them next to hers. Then he pulled the curtains on four separate windows. He flicked on a bedside lamp and turned off the overhead lights.

He turned down the bed and fluffed the pillows, folding the heavy spread and laying it across the bench at the foot of the bed.

The bathroom door opened, and Callie emerged. He told himself not to look. It was going to kill him. But he couldn't help himself.

She was backlit, his white shirt slightly translucent, falling to her mid-thigh, the sleeves rolled up along her slender arms, the top button open to make a V-neck.

The world seemed to stop.

"Is there a hanger...?" She removed the gown from a hook inside the door, the motion bringing his shirt against her breasts.

He nearly groaned out loud.

"The closet's over here," he managed.

She draped the gown over her arms.

"I can get that." He quickly took the gown from her arms.

"Thank you."

It took all his strength not to touch her, not to hold her like he had on the dance floor. Her green eyes met his in the shadowy light. She'd scrubbed off her makeup, and there was a fresh glow to her skin.

She was so incredibly, naturally beautiful. And she'd once told him she loved him.

But he'd ruined all that. Right now, he'd have done anything to rewind time, to fix his mistakes, to find a way back to where they'd been in Charleston.

Instead, he had to find a way to keeps his hands off her.

"Deacon," she said in a tentative voice.

"I can do this," he vowed on a whisper.

She looked at the dress, obviously misunderstanding his words.

He gave himself a mental shake. "Go to bed," he told her softly. "You should sleep."

She nodded.

While he hung the gown, she climbed under the covers.

Deacon shut off the bathroom light, stripped to his boxers and joined her, lastly turning the switch on the bedside lamp and plunging the room into darkness.

The blankets rustled, and he felt her move.

"I don't like it here," she said.

"Do you want me to leave?"

There was a short silence. "No. I mean I don't like this place, the castle. It feels, I don't know, dark."

"It is dark." He couldn't see his hand in front of his face.

He wondered if he'd made a mistake in drawing all the curtains. If the boys woke up, he and Callie would probably trip on the furniture getting to them.

"I mean somber. It feels like the walls want to suck the very joy out of life."

"It is cold and hard. Funny, from the outside it always looked grand."

"It's grand on the inside, too."

"It has no soul."

"That's it," she said.

He couldn't see her, but he heard her come up on her elbow. He did the same, facing her in the dark, barely able to discern her outline as his eyes adjusted.

"Do you think it could be haunted?" There was a joking note to her voice.

"By eight generations of Clarksons?" He gave a chuckle. "Now there's a daunting thought."

"Would you protect me?"

"From the ghost of Admiral Frederick Baines Clarkson?" Deacon deepened his voice, speaking with exaggerated drama. "Legend has it that Admiral Clarkson was murdered."

She matched his tone. "Here in the walls of Clarkson Castle?"

"I believe we may be in mortal danger." He gave a pause, glancing around at the tiny rays of light below the curtains. "Shh. Do you hear that?"

The wind was blowing through the battlements.

"Are you trying to scare me?"

"It's his ship's whistle. He's calling his men, still angry they didn't save him."

"You have a vivid imagination." She batted her hand against his shoulder.

The second she touched him, his world stopped.

She stopped.

Then she moved.

Her hand smoothed over his skin, to his neck, to his cheek.

"Callie," he breathed in desperation. "I can't... I won't..."

"I know," she said. "It's..." She shifted closer. Her breath brushed his face. Her lips touched his.

His reaction was immediate. His arm went around her waist, he pressed her into the soft mattress, his mouth opened wide, his kiss went deep. Every sense he had zeroed in on Callie.

Her hand burrowed into his hair, anchoring. Her arm

wound around his neck. Their bodies came tight together, and he absorbed her heat, her softness, her essence.

He kissed her mouth over and over again.

Then he moved to her neck, her shoulders, her breasts.

She gasped his name.

He stripped off her shirt, kicked off his boxers, and they clung naked to each other, limbs entwined. He breathed in her essence, tasted her skin, felt the softness of her lavender-scented hair between his fingertips.

"I've missed you so much," he rasped.

"Oh, Deacon." There was a catch in her voice.

He reached beneath her, tilting her body toward him. Her thighs softly parted. Her legs went around him.

He stopped, poised, holding himself back, wanting the magic to go on forever.

"Deacon, please," she moaned, and he plunged them together.

Her breaths pulsed against him. He kissed her deeply. He cradled her breasts, smoothed the backs of her thighs, captured her body, her core, over and over again.

Her arms convulsed around him, and her hips surged to meet him. Their passion heated the air of the cold castle. The thick walls absorbed their cries. The darkness cocooned them, and every shadow of his heritage disappeared.

The past didn't matter, only the future. And the future was Callie. It had to be Callie.

Her body contracted, pulling him over the edge, and he spiraled irrevocably into paradise.

Coming back home the next day, Callie realized how much she loved Deacon's house. It was welcoming, comfortable and functional. It was roomy, but really just the right size. The kitchen was brilliantly laid out, with every convenience. She could clean up from lunch while watching the boys play with building bricks in the family room.

It had been Deacon's idea to add a toy box to the family

room décor. So the boys could play and easily help clean up afterward. She was even getting used to a housekeeper twice a week. She was over the guilt of having someone else dust, vacuum and scrub her shower.

Now Deacon appeared by her side. She knew he'd been in his study making calls. He'd mentioned he was at odds with Beau over something, and he was trying to put together his own side of the argument. She'd learned he worked seven days a week. He might dial it back a bit on the weekends, but the port never closed, so there was always some problem to be solved.

He gave her a gentle touch on the shoulder. Still on a high from last night, she simply enjoyed the feeling. She'd have to come back down to earth soon. She couldn't simply pretend their marriage had turned normal. But not today—she wasn't going to let reality intrude just yet.

"I thought I'd take them outside for a while," Deacon said. "Maybe run around with the soccer ball and burn off some energy."

"I'm all for that," she said.

"Do you want to take a nap?"

She couldn't help but think the offer was a veiled reference to how little sleep she'd had last night. She'd slept in Deacon's arms, but mostly they'd made love and talked and made love some more. He'd said he missed her. She missed him more than she could have imagined.

"I'm fine," she said now. She really was. There was a spring in her step and energy in her veins.

"I think I'll call Hannah."

"Whatever you want." Deacon gave her a quick kiss on the temple and helped himself to the leftover cheese. "Who wants to play soccer?" he called to the boys.

Ethan jumped to his feet. "Soccer, soccer!"

"I need my red runners," James said.

"Let's gear up." Deacon swung Ethan up on his shoulders, giving Callie a parting wink as they headed for the foyer.

She returned the cold cuts to the refrigerator and wiped down the counter.

After stacking the dishes in the dishwasher, she took the kitchen phone and wandered onto the sundeck, where she could see Deacon and the boys playing on the far side of the yard. The sunshine was warm, and she stretched out on a padded lounger in her shorts and T-shirt. She put on a pair of sunglasses against the glare and dialed the bakery.

"Good afternoon, Downright Sweet Bakery." It was Hannah's voice.

"Are you busy?" Callie asked.

"Callie! Hi! How are you?"

Callie could hear the familiar sounds of the lunch crowd in the background. "I don't want to interrupt."

"It's steady but not bad."

The sounds faded as Hannah obviously moved into the back, probably into the office.

"I just wanted to check in," Callie said.

"It's turning into a good summer. Tourist business has been steady. The city rose garden is under construction. There wasn't another word about putting it at Fifth and Bay Street. I don't know what you said to the Mayor."

"It was Deacon."

"Well, he's magic."

Callie knew the magic was really Deacon's check book. She didn't like it, but she'd gotten over it. The important thing was that business was going well for Hannah.

"Speaking of the Mayor," Hannah said. "He has a serious challenger for re-election."

"I thought he was going for governor."

"Ha! That didn't pan out. Rumor has it his opponent has the support of two Congress Members and some financial backers."

Callie was afraid to hear the details. One thing she'd learned was that she wanted no part of the backroom power and deception, or the deals and betrayals, which often came along with politics.

"So long as he's staying away from you," she said to Hannah.

"Far away. We started a new product line this week."

"Do tell."

"I found a steady source of haskap berries in Colorado. They're supposed to be a superfood, all the rage and a wonderful color and flavor. We've done a muffin, a rainbow lemon loaf and syrup for the vanilla cheesecake."

"I can't wait to try them."

"How are the boys?"

"They're good." Callie focused on the soccer game. "They're kicking a ball around in the backyard with Deacon."

"He's super. You got yourself a great guy there, Callie."

"Yes," she managed. There were so many things about Deacon that were great.

If he hadn't lied about who he was, what he wanted, and his feelings for her, things would be downright perfect. Her heart hollowed out as she watched him laughing with James, passing the ball to Ethan. It was heartbreaking that it all had to end.

"Not yet," she whispered.

"What was that?" Hannah asked.

"Nothing. He's great." Callie could ignore his flaws, at least for a little while.

In the early morning, before Tyrell and Beau arrived in the business wing of the castle, Deacon sought Aaron out in his office. Tyrell occupied the large CEO's office in the corner, beside the boardroom. Tyrell's assistant and three other staff members worked in a common area outside. Aaron, Beau and now Deacon had offices along the north wall, overlooking the harbor and the port in the distance.

"I've fleshed out some more details," Deacon told Aaron, setting a file folder on his deck.

"The vertical integration?" Aaron asked.

"Yes."

"I thought you gave up on that."

"Why would I give up on it? It's a solid solution."

"Because without either Beau or my father's support, it's a nonstarter." But Aaron did open the folder.

"Tyrell might come around," Deacon said.

"You don't know him very well."

Deacon couldn't argue with that. Aaron knew both Beau and Tyrell far better than Deacon did. Aaron was probably right. But Deacon had to try.

Things were going so much better with Callie, that Deacon was beginning to see a future with her: a future with her, a future with the Clarksons and a future managing Hale Harbor Port—both for him and for James and Ethan.

That meant he had to take a long view, to push for what was best. Even if the odds were stacked against him, he had to try.

Aaron was his best bet. Aaron was smart. He was methodical. He wasn't anything like his hotheaded brother, Beau.

Aaron thumbed through the top sheets. "How optimistic are these numbers?"

"They're realistic. We've done a low, medium and high case scenario."

"It might be a range, but it's still only speculative."

Deacon was prepared for the question. "The base data was derived from—"

"Is this a private meeting?" Tyrell's tone from the open doorway was clearly a rebuke.

Deacon had learned Tyrell was an exacting man, a cantankerous man and also a paranoid man.

Aaron closed the file. "Volumetric data and route statistics."

It wasn't a lie, but it wasn't the full truth either. Deacon appreciated Aaron's discretion. It also told him Aaron wasn't completely opposed to pursing the idea of vertical integration. That was encouraging.

"I need to talk to you," Tyrell said to Deacon.

"Sure." Deacon left the file with Aaron in the hopes that he'd read further.

He followed Tyrell to his office, where Tyrell shut the door after them. Tyrell took his position behind the massive dark walnut desk. Beyond him were big recessed windows, the glass so old, it warped the city and mountains behind.

Sounds echoed in the big room, because unlike most of the rest of the castle, Tyrell had not covered the stone walls with paneling. Instead, he'd covered them with vintage oil paintings and coats of arms. The stone floor was worn, and the guest chairs were red velvet and ornate wood, anything but comfortable.

Tyrell sat down, and so did Deacon.

"You've had time to settle in," Tyrell said.

"I have."

"And Callie? And the boys?"

"Them, too." Deacon couldn't help but be curious about where this was going.

It wasn't like Tyrell to ask after anyone's welfare.

"It's been nearly a month," he said.

"Not quite," Deacon said. He was acutely aware of time passing, as he worried about Callie's ultimate decision to stay or go.

"Nevertheless," Tyrell said.

Deacon waited.

"It's time to make some changes."

Deacon's senses went on alert. "Changes to what?"

"To your circumstance. Margo and I have discussed it, and we want you to move into the castle."

The request gave Deacon a jolt. "That was never part of the deal."

And it wasn't something Deacon would ever consider. For one thing, Callie would hate it. For another, Deacon valued his independence far too much. And most importantly, it wouldn't be good for James and Ethan. Deacon planned to keep their exposure to Tyrell at an absolute minimum.

"It's not negotiable," Tyrell said.

"I wasn't planning to negotiate with you. The answer is no. We're not moving into the castle. I don't even know why you'd want us here. Margo can barely stand to look at me."

"That's not her fault."

"No, it's your fault."

"Nevertheless," Tyrell said.

"*Nevertheless* is not a rational argument for anything."

"You *will* move in."

"What part of *no* is getting past you?"

"What part of *will* is getting past *you*?"

"You can't force the issue," Deacon said. "You can't undo the contract. The shares are mine."

Deacon's lawyer had assured him that Tyrell could not renege on the contract.

"That may be true." Tyrell sat forward, bracing his hands on the desk. "But I have the power to change the class of your shares."

Deacon narrowed his eyes, focusing on Tyrell's unyielding expression, trying to imagine where this threat was going.

"With a two-thirds majority vote, I can change your shares from Class A to Class D. That means no voting rights, no position in the company, no dividends. Your interest in the company would be effectively worthless."

Deacon held his composure, refusing to let Tyrell see the news rattled him. Tyrell wouldn't be bluffing. Somehow, in the hundreds of pages of the contract agreement, Tyrell's lawyers had planted a loophole.

"I could sell," Deacon said.

There was nothing Tyrell could do to make the shares completely worthless. And Deacon could throw a wrench in the works by threatening to sell to someone hostile.

"You're forgetting the buyback clause. Hale Harbor Port would be happy to reacquire the shares at the price you paid for them."

"I would sue."

Tyrell laughed at that. "My dear boy, you can try. But you will lose. It will take years and the legal fees would break you."

Deacon clenched his jaw. He racked his brain, but he didn't immediately see another option. And deep down, he knew Tyrell's army of lawyers would have thought through every strategy.

Tyrell truly had no soul.

"I gave you everything you wanted," Deacon said. Though his effort was most certainly doomed, he had to try to reason with Tyrell.

"I wanted my grandsons."

"And they're here."

"No. They're not *here*. They're with you."

"They're with their mother."

"And she can live here."

"She won't agree to it." Deacon was completely sure of that. She'd probably walk out the minute he asked her.

"That's *your* problem," Tyrell said.

He took a pen from the ornate holder in front of him, slipped on his reading glasses and pointedly picked up a report.

"And if I can't convince her to do it?" Deacon asked.

Tyrell peered over the top of his glasses. "Then I convert your shares."

Deacon came to his feet. "You're the real bastard in this family."

"Is that a yes?"

"It looks as though I have no choice."

A smirk twitched Tyrell's mouth. "I'm glad you see things my way."

Eleven

Callie's heart sank as she stared at her brother Trevor in the doorway. Deacon had promised her Trevor wouldn't be back. And she'd believed him.

The boys were playing on the staircase behind her, building jumps for their little race cars.

"You shouldn't be here," Callie said to Trevor.

She felt instantly alone and vulnerable. Deacon wouldn't be home for hours.

"You're gonna want to hear what I have to say," Trevor drawled.

"No, I don't." She started to close the door.

He blocked it with a stiff arm, and her heart thudded hard against her chest.

"What do you want?" she asked, hating the fear in her voice.

"I want to know your game."

"What game? There is no game. Just go, Trevor."

"He paid me off. He paid me good."

Callie hadn't known Deacon had bribed Trevor. But it shouldn't have surprised her. At the moment, she was even grateful.

"So go away. You got what you came for."

Trevor gave a cold laugh. He unexpectedly shoved the door open and walked inside.

James and Ethan both looked up.

"Are these the little tykes?"

"James, take Ethan to the family room. You can watch cartoons."

Trevor moved toward them. "No need for them to skedaddle."

Callie's fear for her own safety evaporated, and she bolted between her brother and her sons. "James, honey, take Ethan. You can each have a cookie while you watch."

"Candy cookies," Ethan sang.

"Okay, Mommy."

"Thank you, sweetheart." She glared at Trevor and listened as the boys left the foyer behind her. "What do you want?" she demanded.

"More of the same."

"Deacon's not going to give you more money."

Trevor took a few steps across the foyer, his black boots glaring against the polished white tile. "I met a guy at the bar, a new drinking buddy of mine."

Callie kept herself between Trevor and the hallway that led to the family room.

"He's a gardener down there at that castle. Word is out on your scam, baby sister."

"I don't know what you're talking about." She wanted him out. She wasn't exactly afraid anymore, but she wanted Trevor out of the house.

"Oh, you know exactly what I'm talkin' about. The two of you are taking that family for millions."

She'd had enough. She marched back to the door and pulled it wide. "Get out."

"Not a chance."

"There is no scam," she said.

Trevor moved closer. "Then why's Deacon never been to the castle before? Why'd nobody even speak his name until he showed up with you? Now he's got the run of the place. Because of your kids." Trevor cast his gaze toward the family room.

"They're Tyrell's grandchildren," she said. "It's not a scam."

"Then it's a bribe," Trevor said with conviction. "And I want in on the action."

"It's not a—"

The word *bribe* echoed ominously inside Callie's head.

Bribes were Deacon's go-to tool. He did it all the time.

"You bribed the old man," Trevor said.

Callie hadn't bribed anyone. But had Deacon? Could Deacon have used the boys to worm his way into the Clarkson family?

If he had, everything suddenly made sense.

Deacon's voice boomed through the room. "What are you doing here?" He grasped Trevor by the collar and hustled him onto the porch.

Trevor only barely kept his footing. "Hey, man, I'm—"

"You're trespassing on private property." Deacon slammed the door in Trevor's face. He whirled to Callie. "Are you all right? Where are the kids?"

"Am I a bribe?" she asked, her voice quavering.

The enormity of what Trevor had just accused Deacon of, and the reality that he could be right, had shaken her to the core.

"What?" Deacon looked dumfounded.

"Trevor said—"

"You're listening to *Trevor*?"

"He said you bribed your way into the Clarkson family, using me and the boys."

The expression on Deacon's face told her it was true.

She gasped and took two steps backward.

He reached for her.

"No! That explains it all. It explains everything. You finding me, pretending to like me, lying to me, manipulating me."

"You have to listen, Callie."

"I don't. I really don't."

James came running through the foyer with his arms outstretched, as he made airplane noises.

Ethan followed in the same posture. "Hi, Daddy."

The two of them did a loop and left again.

"What have you done?" Callie whispered through a throat closing with emotion.

"Tyrell came to me with the offer. He promised me my

birthright, and I was tempted. I admit, I was tempted. It was everything I ever wanted in my life. Everything."

"You took it," she said. "You *took* it."

"No. I didn't. I only agreed to meet you."

"You lied to me and married me, and brought us home like some prize."

"By then I thought you wanted to marry me. I thought you had your own agenda."

"Your money," she said woodenly. "Yeah, I remember that lie, too."

"It all went horribly wrong," he said.

"Not for you. For you, it all went horribly right."

He turned from her and raked a hand through his hair. "Not anymore."

She didn't need to listen to this. She needed to get her boys, pack her things, get out of Hale Harbor and never come back.

Deacon was a liar, and she was never going to see him again. Ever.

Her heart shouldn't hurt this much.

"He wants us to live at the castle," Deacon said.

Callie mutely shook her head. No way, no how. That was *not* going to happen.

"He gave me an ultimatum today. I move you to the castle, or I lose it all."

"They want the boys," she found herself whispering. "They're trying to steal my sons."

"I told him yes."

"What?"

"Only to buy us some time. I came home to tell you everything. And to tell you, you need to leave."

James and Ethan buzzed through, playing airplane again.

"I *am* leaving," she said as her sons trotted out of earshot.

"Today. Right now," Deacon said. "I was going to tell you everything that happened, and then tell you to take the boys, take them to Charleston and never come back. I made a deal with the devil, and I was wrong."

"*Yes*, you were wrong!"

"Thing is…" he said, his tone turning reflective.

She refused to listen. "There's no *thing*. There is nothing."

"I kept trying to stay logical, to stay detached."

"Bully for you." She hadn't had the opportunity to stay logical and detached, because she'd been conned from minute one.

"But I couldn't."

"Stop talking."

"It took me way too long to recognize it, but I fell in love with you."

What was left of her heart shattered into pieces.

"You can't do that," she cried. "You can't say that. You can't wait until after everything else has failed and then throw that out on the table."

"I know."

"You can't."

"I can't. And I won't. Callie, I'm so sorry I let you down."

If the banging on the front door hadn't been so insistent, Deacon wouldn't have bothered answering. The house was eerily quiet with Callie and the boys gone. It had been less than twenty-four hours, and Deacon hadn't yet decided how to move forward.

This morning, he'd found one of Ethan's socks under a sofa cushion. He'd stared at it for a long time, trying to decide whether to wash it and mail it to Charleston or toss it out. Right now, it was sitting on a table in the family room, while he made up his mind.

Through the prismed window of his front door, he recognized Aaron. Deacon didn't particularly want to talk to him, but he didn't care enough to make an issue of it either. He'd rather face Aaron now and send him away than risk him coming back later and disturbing Deacon all over again.

Deacon opened the door.

He was shocked to see Beau standing next to his brother.

"What are you doing here?" he asked them bluntly.

"We want to talk," Aaron said.

Deacon coughed out a laugh of disbelief. "We've got nothing to talk about."

"I think we do," Beau said.

Deacon took in their determined stares. He didn't care enough to fight this either. He stepped back. "Come on in."

They glanced at each other, then stepped into the foyer.

The library was closest, but it was a small room, too intimate for Deacon's liking. He led them back to the living room, with its generous size, cavernous ceilings and huge bank of windows. Whatever they had to say could get lost in the space.

He gestured to a burgundy leather sofa and took the armchair across from it, putting a wide glass-topped table between them.

"We brought you something," Aaron said, placing a document on the table.

"You don't expect me to sign off on converting the shares." Deacon couldn't believe they had the nerve to show up and ask that. He was beginning to work up the energy to fight.

"It's not the shares," Aaron said. "After the last time you and I discussed vertical integration, I did some research."

"Why are you telling me this? I'm out. You both know I'm out."

"Will you listen?" Beau barked.

"Shut up," Aaron told his brother.

"He makes everything difficult," Beau said.

"You can leave anytime," Deacon told Beau.

"I remembered something Frederick worked on six years ago." Aaron pointed to the document. "It's dated, but it has a lot of the same ideas you had. It even mentions Mobi Transportation. Back then, Frederick suggested bringing you into the family fold."

Deacon tried to make sense of that statement.

"Now he's listening," Beau said.

"Frederick didn't even know me," Deacon said.

"He knew of you. He went off to college and came back with a sense of social justice and some big ideas for the port. He shared them with Father, who crushed him like a bug. Father called Frederick *pathetic*."

Beau sat forward. "But Frederick stood up to him. He said we had to modernize, and he said it was the family's responsibility to include you, because you were Father's son. Father went ballistic."

Deacon was speechless.

"I should have stood up for him back then," Aaron said.

"*We* should have stood up for him back then," Beau said.

"He was right about modernizing," Aaron said. "And he was right about you."

"That's why he walked out?" Deacon asked, trying to wrap his mind around it.

"He had more guts than either of us," Beau said.

"We didn't stand up for Frederick," Aaron said. "We're not going to make the same mistake again. Not with our long-lost brother."

Deacon couldn't believe he'd heard right.

But Beau came to his feet and stuck his hand out to shake. "We're with you in this, brother. We want to stand together."

Deacon rose, and so did Aaron.

"I'm out," Deacon said. "Didn't Tyrell tell you? I won't move to the castle, so he's converting my shares."

"Callie can't move to the castle," Aaron said.

"No kidding," Deacon said.

"Miranda's wanted to leave for a while now," Aaron said. "She's tired of dealing with Mother and Father all the time. I didn't have it in me before, but I do now. We're moving out."

"Well, I'm not staying there by myself," Beau said.

"What will the old man do?" Deacon asked Aaron.

"He can't do anything if we stick together."

"Are we going to shake on this?" Beau asked, sticking his hand out more firmly.

Deacon shook. "I'm flattered. I'm really overwhelmed." His emotions couldn't seem to sort themselves out. "But, like I said, it's too late."

Aaron smiled. He shook Deacon's hand then added his other hand overtop. "You haven't been paying attention." Aaron paused for what looked like effect. "Tyrell needs a two-thirds majority to convert your shares. We won't give it to him."

Beau pointed around the circle at the three of them. "And between us, we've got more than two-thirds."

Deacon could not believe what he was hearing.

"We're in favor of vertical integration," Aaron said. "Want to come with us and tell Dad?"

"We?" Deacon started speaking slowly. "The three of us? We're going up against Tyrell?"

"He's traveling, but will be back in two days," Aaron said. "I think we should do this in person. You in?"

"He's going to flip." Beau grinned as he said it.

"Where's Callie?" Aaron asked, glancing around.

"She moved back to Charleston."

Beau frowned. "Why?"

"She left." Deacon saw no point in hiding the truth. "She didn't like being used as a pawn. She particularly didn't like me exploiting her children for personal gain."

Aaron looked confused. "But I thought the two of you were…"

"Not so much," Deacon said, fighting to hide his despair.

"Man, I'm going to miss those little guys," Beau said.

Deacon missed them so much, he could barely breathe.

And Callie, Callie…

He might have his birthright and two new brothers, and he was grateful for both of those things. But none of it made up for losing Callie.

He'd made mistake after mistake. He'd hurt her badly, and he deserved his misery.

* * *

Being back at the bakery was surreal for Callie. In some ways, the past two months seemed like a dream—a breathtaking, bewildering, heartbreaking dream.

Her chest was hollow where her heart used to be, but everything else was normal. She looked the same. She talked the same. She acted the same. And the world around her hadn't changed at all.

Hannah nudged her elbow, and Callie realized she was standing at the counter, staring off into space, while a customer waited for service.

"Nancy?" Hannah prompted, gesturing to the customer.

Nancy stepped up to help.

In the meantime, Hannah reached into the display case and extracted two oversize vanilla cupcakes with mountains of buttercream and caramel sprinkles.

"We need to talk," she said to Callie.

"About what?" Callie asked.

"This way." Cupcakes on plates, Hannah headed around the end of the counter, into the dining area.

When Callie joined her at a corner table, Hannah handed her a fork and pushed one of the cupcakes in front of her.

"If ever there was a woman in need of buttercream..." Hannah said.

Callie had to admit, the cupcake looked unusually appealing. "I haven't had one of these in a very long time." She took a forkful of the rich, fluffy frosting and lifted it to her mouth.

"You haven't been this despondent in a very long time," Hannah said, digging into her own cupcake.

"I'm not despondent." Callie thought she was putting on a very brave front, especially considering how she felt inside.

Deacon was out of her life. It had only been three days, but it felt like a year. She'd lost count of the times James and Ethan had asked about Deacon.

Hannah's expression was full of sympathy. "What really happened?"

"It didn't work out." Callie had decided to keep her explanation simple.

"You were head over heels for that guy."

Callie felt her eyes mist up, and she covered her emotions with a bite of cupcake.

Hannah waited.

"It was a mistake," Callie said.

"It's never a mistake to fall in love."

"It is with the wrong guy."

Hannah tilted her head, her puzzlement clear. "Deacon was the right guy. He wasn't Hank, he wasn't—"

"He was worse than Hank." The words were out before Callie could think better of them.

"You're going to have to explain that." Hannah's tone was gentle but implacable.

Callie stopped eating. Her stomach couldn't take it.

"It was a con, Hannah. It was all a ruse." Once she started, she couldn't seem to stop herself. "Deacon's biological father, the rich and infamous Tyrell Clarkson—Frederick's father, too, by the way."

Hannah slowly set down her fork.

"Frederick was legitimate, but Deacon wasn't. Frederick hated his father, so he never told me anything about his family. I'm glad he didn't. It was the right decision to keep us apart. It would have been better if I'd never met any of them. But then Tyrell promised Deacon a share of the family fortune if he brought me back to Hale Harbor."

"How big of a share?"

"*That's* your question?"

Hannah gave a shrug. "Don't you wonder how much it took?"

"It was a lot."

"Millions?"

"Hundreds of millions."

Hannah's brow shot up.

"I suppose it's good to know I'm worth that much." Callie

gave a slightly hysterical laugh, quickly covering her mouth. "It wasn't so much me. It was the boys. Tyrell's grandsons. His only grandchildren."

Hannah's palm went to her chest. "Oh, Callie. Deacon only pretended to love you?"

Callie gave a miserable nod.

"I'm so sorry."

"He told me he didn't love me."

"That's brutal."

"It was…" Callie's brain flashed a kaleidoscope of Deacon. "And then…in the end…when it was all falling apart, he even used that as a tactic."

"I don't understand."

Callie felt her misery turn to bitterness. "When Deacon couldn't deliver, when he couldn't get me to move the boys to the castle, Tyrell pulled out the rug. He took back Deacon's share of the company. And at that point, Deacon said he loved me." She snapped her fingers in the air. "Suddenly, he'd fallen in love with me."

"The castle?"

Callie gave a small shudder at the memory. "The Clarksons have an actual castle. You should have seen it. It's positively medieval. I could never in a thousand years live there."

As she spoke, her mind was drawn back to the night she'd spent in Deacon's arms, making such sweet sexy love with him in that castle. Their whispered conversations, the laughter, his warmth, his scent, his taste—for those few short hours, she thought it was going to work out. She thought they could make a life together.

"Callie?" Hannah interrupted Callie's memories. "You zoned out on me there."

Callie dragged herself back to reality. "It was nothing but a ruse."

"He admitted he didn't love you."

"Yes." Callie picked up her fork and determinedly dug into

the cupcake again. She wasn't going to let Deacon, or anyone else, ruin buttercream.

"But then he said he did," Hannah confirmed.

"Only to get me to the castle."

"Walk me through it."

"What do you mean?" Callie asked.

"I'm trying to figure out why he'd change his story."

"It's simple. When Tyrell said 'move her to the castle or lose all the money,' Deacon suddenly decided he'd loved me all along."

"So he tried to convince you to move to the castle?"

"No." Callie cast her mind back to the conversation. "He told me to take the boys to Charleston and never come back."

She went over it a second time in case her memory was flawed. But that was how it had happened.

"Before or after he told you he loved you?" Hannah asked.

"Before. It was before."

"So, he'd already given up the money." Sounding like she'd made an important point, Hannah scooped a bite of her cupcake.

"No. He still had the option of getting me to change my mind."

"Which he didn't do. You said he didn't even try."

In the strictest sense, Callie knew that was true. But it was more complicated than that. "He didn't bother, because he knew it was hopeless."

"That's not what I'm hearing."

"What are you hearing?"

"I'm hearing he gave up hundreds of millions. He told you to go back to Charleston. *Then* he told you he loved you."

"Which, *believe me*, if I'd let it, would have led to a pitch to move me to the castle."

"Maybe," Hannah said, sounding unconvinced.

"I was there."

"You were upset."

That was true enough. Callie didn't think she'd ever felt

more upset in her life. Trevor's revelation had rocked her to her core. She hadn't told Hannah about Trevor. She tried to calculate how that would change the situation.

"You don't know what might have happened," Hannah said, polishing off her cupcake. "Eat."

"I know what *did* happen."

"Eat," Hannah said.

Callie took a bite.

"When you finish that cupcake," Hannah said. "I want you to consider that a man who gives up hundreds of millions of dollars for your well-being, then tells you he loves you, might…in fact…"

Callie couldn't let her mind go there. She couldn't survive another fantasy, another disappointment, another heartbreak.

"Love you," Hannah finished.

Callie took another bite of the cupcake, and another, and another, until it was gone.

"Well?" Hannah said.

"I can't go back. I can't let myself hope…" Callie wanted so desperately to hope, but she knew the stakes were far too high. She'd never survive another heartbreak.

"Then don't go back," Hannah said.

Callie was surprised. She was also a little disappointed. She realized she wanted Hannah to talk her into going to Deacon. That was beyond frightening.

"Call him. Text him."

"And say what?" It was the most preposterous idea Callie had ever heard.

"Anything. Text: *What's up? Where are you? What are you doing?* All you need is an icebreaker."

"I'm not doing that."

"Then text: *Can we talk?* If I'm right, he'll be on the next plane. If I'm wrong, he'll send some lame brush off answer, and you'll know for sure."

"He wouldn't have to wait for the next plane." Callie couldn't believe she was considering it. "He'd charter his own."

* * *

Tyrell swaggered into the boardroom, his expression dark. "What's this?" he demanded of Deacon, Aaron and Beau.

Deacon's phone pinged.

"We have some information to share with you," Aaron said.

Deacon watched Tyrell's suspicions rise. Deacon didn't feel the slightest sense of satisfaction or vindication. But he did feel a sense of justice.

His phone pinged again, and he glanced down.

His heart stopped when he saw Callie's name. Everything in the room disappeared.

He focused on her message.

Can we talk? her text said.

Yes, they could talk. Of course they could talk. They absolutely could talk. He came to his feet, pushing the chair out behind him.

"Deacon?" Aaron's voice penetrated.

Deacon looked up to three expressions of astonishment.

"I have to go," he said.

"What?" Beau demanded.

"I'm…" Deacon started for the door. "I'll…talk later. I have to go."

He all but sprinted down the hall. He didn't know what would happen in the boardroom behind him, but he didn't particularly care.

He texted while he walked: I'm on my way. Where are you?

He hopped into his car, tossing his phone on the passenger seat, watching it to see her answer. It was taking too long. It was taking way too long for her to respond.

He stopped at a light and picked up the phone, thinking something had gone wrong. He'd have to resend.

But then it pinged: At the bakery. But on my way home.

He glanced at the red light and typed in a message: Be there in an hour.

A horn honked behind him. He hit send and switched to hands free, contacting an air charter company.

They had a jet with immediate availability. He didn't ask the price, all but threw them his credit card in the boarding lounge and leapt on board.

He barely noticed the opulent white leather surroundings. He did say yes to a single malt, hoping it would calm his nerves. The pilot was able to radio ahead for a car, and Deacon came close to his time estimate.

One hour and twenty minutes later, he was at Callie's front door.

She opened it, and he had to fight an urge to wrap her immediately in his arms.

"Hi," he said, instead, feeling breathless.

"Hi," she returned.

He could hear the boys in the kitchen.

"Is everything okay?" he asked.

He searched her expression for a sign of her mood or her state of mind. At first, he'd taken her request as a good sign. But as the minutes dragged by in the jet, he was assailed with doubts. The truth was, he had no idea what she wanted.

"You came," she said.

"Of course I came." Nothing could have kept him away. "Is it the boys?"

"They're fine. We're all fine. Well, maybe not so fine."

Deacon was leaping from hopeful to worried to confused.

"Come in," she said, stepping out of the way.

He walked over the familiar threshold, feeling more at peace and at home than he had in weeks.

"I can't live in the castle," she said.

Hope flooded him. "I would never ask you to live in the castle."

The castle was a terrible place. He had no intention of living there either.

"I know it's a lot of money," she said.

"The money doesn't matter." The money couldn't matter less. "You matter. The boys matter."

"You said you loved me."

"I do."

"What do you love about me?"

"Everything." Without conscious thought, he moved closer to her.

"You haven't talked yourself into it, have you? You know, because of the potential perks of loving me."

He couldn't help but smile at that. "I haven't talked myself into a thing. After you left, if I could have talked myself out of loving you, I would have done it in a heartbeat to save my sanity."

She tilted her head to the side as if she were considering him. "I didn't exactly understand that, but I'm going to assume it was a good thing."

"It was a good thing. It is a good thing." He gave into his desire to reach for her, cradling her face with his palm and stepping closer still. "I love you, Callie, more than anything else in the world."

"You'll give up the money, hundreds of millions of dollars."

"See, the thing is—"

She put her fingertips across his lips. "There can be no equivocation. You have to make your choice."

"There is no equivocation. It's you, Callie, and James and Ethan, over and above anything else in the world."

"Good. Then we'll get by. We have the bakery. We'll work as hard as we have to."

He opened his mouth to explain again, but then thought better of it. "I know we will."

"Good," she repeated.

"So…" He searched her expression. "We're doing this? We're making it real? We're making it work?"

"I love you," she said.

His heart sang, and his grin broke free. "Thank goodness."

He swooped in for a heartfelt kiss.

"Daddy!" came Ethan's excited voice.

"Daddy!" James chimed in.

Ethan's compact body hit the side of Deacon's leg, his little arms going around it. James came up on the other side to give his hip a hug.

Deacon gave Callie another quick kiss. "Hold that thought." Then he crouched down to hug the boys.

"We *are* a package deal," she said with a thread of laughter.

"Best package in the world," Deacon said to the boys.

"Daddy, come and see the new castle," Ethan said, tugging on Deacon's hand.

"It has a moat," James added. "Mommy made us build it in the kitchen."

Deacon looked up at Callie. "Mommy's very smart."

Deacon followed the boys, his boys, to the kitchen, duly admiring their creation.

After a few minutes, he stood, leaning on the counter next to Callie. He took her hand. He touched her cheek. He gave her another kiss.

"There's something you need to know," he said.

She drew back to look at him. "Will I be unhappy?"

"I don't know. It's about the money and the Clarksons."

"That never makes me happy."

The boys squealed and zoomed rubber alligators through the makeshift moat.

"It's Aaron and Beau. They want us to be real brothers."

She searched his expression. "Is that what you want?"

"It is." It was what Deacon wanted. He was surprised by how much he wanted it.

Callie wrapped her arms around his waist. "Then that's wonderful."

Deacon didn't want to leave anything out. "That's not the crux of it. They want to join forces with me in running Hale Harbor Port. They blocked Tyrell's plan to write me out of the company."

She pulled back again. "The money?"

"It's still mine. It's ours. We own Frederick's share of Hale Harbor Port. And someday it will belong to James and Ethan." He held his breath, waiting to see if she'd be angry.

She didn't look thrilled, but she didn't look angry either.

"You don't mind?" he dared ask. "That we're rich and we're connected to the Clarksons? I promise you don't have to worry about Tyrell or Margo or anyone else. Any relationship with them will be on your terms."

"We were always going to be connected to the Clarksons," Callie said with resignation. "I just didn't know it for a while."

"Between me and my brothers—that's so odd to say. With the three of us together, Tyrell won't be able to bully anyone ever again."

James shouted out, "The alligator ate the princess!"

"Owie alligator," Ethan called.

"I'm not afraid of Tyrell," Callie said, molding against him. "I'm through being afraid of bullying men."

"Good."

She gave a little laugh. "I'll send them to you."

"Absolutely."

"You can bribe them."

"Ouch," he said.

"I'm teasing. I have complete faith in you to protect us."

"I always will," Deacon said, feeling a deep and enormous sense of satisfaction. He tightened his hold. "I have a family," he whispered in wonder. "A true and wonderful family. And I love you all so very much."

"We love you back, Deacon. All three of us love you right back."

* * * * *

AN HONOURABLE
SEDUCTION

BRENDA JACKSON

To the man who will forever be the love of my life,
Gerald Jackson, Sr.

To all of my readers who asked for Flipper's story.
This one is for you!

To the Brenda Jackson Book Club/Facebook fans.
Over 4,000 strong and after fourteen years,
you guys still rock!

Many waters cannot quench love;
rivers cannot sweep it away.
—Song of Solomon 8:7

Prologue

The Naval Amphibious Base
Coronado, San Diego, California

"What kind of trouble have you gotten into?"

David Holloway, known to his Navy SEAL teammates as Flipper, glanced at the four men surrounding him. They were like brothers to him. More than once they'd risked their lives for each other and they would continue to have each other's backs, on duty or off. That bond was what accounted for the concerned looks on their faces. He wondered how they'd known he'd been summoned to the admiral's office.

"Let's hope I'm not in any trouble, Mac," Flipper said, rubbing a hand down his face.

He had to admit he was wondering what was going on, just like they were. Usually, you were only summoned to a meeting with the admiral when you were getting reprimanded for some reason, and he never got

into trouble. At least he *rarely* did. As the son of a retired SEALs commanding officer and the youngest of
five brothers—all Navy SEALs—he knew better.

"Maybe there's an event on the base and he wants
you to escort his daughter now that you're the single
one among us," Coop said, grinning.

Flipper didn't grin back. They'd seen Georgianna
Martin, the admiral's twenty-three-year-old daughter.
She was beautiful, but they'd heard the horror stories
from other teammates who'd been ordered to take her
out on dates. According to them, those evenings had
been the dates from hell. The young woman was spoiled
rotten, selfish as sin and had an attitude that sucked.
That's why Flipper didn't find Coop's comment at all
amusing. He hoped that wasn't why the admiral wanted
to see him.

It didn't surprise Flipper that it was Mac who'd asked
if Flipper had gotten into trouble. Thurston McRoy—
code name Mac—was older than the other four men on
the team, who had all started their careers as SEALs
around the same time. Mac had been a SEAL five years
before the rest of them. Mac seemed to like to think
he was the big brother looking out for them, almost
like he figured they couldn't take care of themselves.
He was forever giving them advice—even when they
didn't ask for it.

In addition to Mac and Flipper, their SEAL team
included Brisbane Westmoreland, code name Bane;
Gavin Blake, whose code name was Viper; and Laramie Cooper, whose code name was Coop.

Flipper checked his watch. "Since I have a couple
of hours to spare before meeting with the admiral, let's
grab something to eat," he suggested.

"Sounds good to me," Bane said.

Less than an hour later, Flipper and his four team-mates shared burgers, fries and milkshakes at one of the most popular eating places on base. They decided to sit outside at one of the café tables in the front instead of inside where it was crowded since it was such a beautiful May day.

No one brought up his meeting with the admiral again or the notion of him taking the admiral's daughter on a date. He was glad. Instead, the guys had more important things to talk about, namely their families.

Bane's wife, Crystal, had given birth to triplets last year and he had new photos to share, so they passed Bane's cell phone around.

Viper's wife, Layla, was expecting with only a few months to go before Gavin Blake IV would be born. Viper was excited about becoming a father, of course.

Like Bane, Mac had plenty of photos to share; he was married and the father of four.

And Coop had a two-year-old son he hadn't known about until he'd run into his old girlfriend about six months ago. They'd reconnected, gotten married and were now a happy family.

Earlier in the week, the teammates had gotten word from their commanding officer that next week was the start of a four-month leave. For Flipper, that meant heading home to Dallas and he couldn't wait. His mother had a birthday coming up and he was glad he would be home to celebrate.

"I don't care what plans you all are making for your leave, just as long as you remember my mom's birthday celebration. I understand you not showing up, Viper, with a baby on the way. The rest of you guys, no excuses."

"We hear you," Bane said, grinning. "And we will be there."

When Viper ordered another hamburger, everyone teased him about being the one to eat for two instead of his wife. And then everyone talked about what they planned to do with their four months off.

It was two hours later when Flipper walked into the admiral's office. He was surprised to find Commanding Officer Shields there as well. Flipper saluted both men.

"At ease. Please have a seat, Lieutenant Holloway."

"Thank you, sir," he said, sitting down. He was used to being under his commanding officer's intense scrutiny, but there was something in the sharp green eyes of Admiral Norris Martin that was making him feel uncomfortable.

"You come highly recommended by your commanding officer here, Lieutenant Holloway. And the reason I asked to meet with you is that we need you. Your country needs you."

Flipper was happy to step up. He was a Navy SEAL, and the reason he'd enlisted, like his father and brothers, was to protect his country. "And what am I needed to do, sir?" he asked.

"Our investigators have provided intelligence and a preliminary report that says acts of espionage are happening in Key West. Someone is trading valuable government secrets to China."

Flipper didn't respond immediately.

The one thing he hated was a traitor, but he'd discovered that for the right price, a number of American citizens would perform acts of treason. He understood that. However, what he didn't understand was why he'd been singled out for this meeting. He was part of a SEAL team. He didn't work in naval intelligence.

Confusion must have shown on his face because Admiral Martin continued, "The report was given to me, but I don't believe it."

Flipper raised a brow. "You don't believe a report that classified documents are being traded in Key West, sir?"

"Oh, I believe all that, but what I refuse to believe is that this suspect is guilty of anything."

"Is there a reason why, sir?"

"Here is the information," said Commanding Officer Shields, speaking for the first time as he handed Flipper a folder.

Flipper opened it to find a picture of a very beautiful woman. She looked to be around twenty-four, with dark, sultry eyes and full, shapely lips. Then there was her mass of copper-brown spiral curls that flowed to her shoulders, crowning a cocoa-colored face. A pair of dangling gold earrings hung from her ears and a golden pendant necklace hung around her neck.

He knew he was spending too much time studying her features, but it couldn't be helped. The woman was strikingly beautiful.

Reluctantly he moved his gaze away from her face to check out the background of the photo. From the tropical vegetation captured by the photographer, she seemed to be on an island somewhere. She stood near a body of water that showed in the corner of the eight-by-ten photo. Scribbled across the bottom were the words:

Miss you, Godpop 1
Love, Swan

Swan? It was an unusual name, but it fit.

He moved to the next document in the file. Attached to it was a small family photo that showed a tall Caucasian man with sandy-brown hair and brown eyes standing beside a beautiful woman who closely resembled Swan. Her mother. In front of the couple was a beautiful little girl who looked to be around eight.

Flipper studied the child's face and knew that child had grown up to be the gorgeous woman in the first photo. The shape of her face was the same, as were her eyes. Even as a child, she'd had long curly hair.

The family photo was clipped to a profile of the young woman. As he'd guessed, she was twenty-four. Her name was Swan Jamison. She was an American, born in Key West. Presently, she owned a jewelry store on the island. That was all the information the document provided.

Flipper lifted his gaze to find his commanding officer and the admiral staring at him. "I assume this is the person naval intelligence believes is the traitor."

"Yes," Admiral Martin said. "She's my goddaughter. I am Godpop 1."

"She's my goddaughter as well," added Commanding Officer Shields. "I am Godpop 2."

Flipper's gaze moved from one man to the other. "I see, sirs."

Admiral Martin nodded. "Her father was part of our SEAL team and our best friend. His name was Andrew Jamison."

Flipper had heard that Commanding Officer Shields and Admiral Martin were part of the same SEAL team a number of years ago.

"Andrew was the best. He lost his life saving ours," said Commanding Officer Shields. "He didn't die immediately, and before he died, he made us promise to look after his wife, Leigh, and his daughter, Swan." The man paused and then said, "Over twenty-eight years ago, when we were taking some R & R in Jamaica, Andrew met Leigh, who was a Jamaican model. They married a year later, and he moved her to Key West, where our team was stationed. After Andrew was killed, Leigh returned to Jamaica. When Swan graduated from high school, she returned to the Keys and moved into her parents' home."

"How old was she when her father was killed?" Flipper asked.

"She was fifteen," Admiral Martin said. "Swan was close to her dad. Leigh was so broken up over Andrew's death that she didn't want to live in the States without him, which was why she returned to Jamaica. She passed away two years ago."

Flipper's commanding officer then took up the tale. "Leigh sent for us before she died of stomach cancer, asking us to look out for Swan after she was gone. We would have done that anyway, since we always kept in touch with both Leigh and Swan. In fact, Swan rotated summers with us and our families even after Leigh returned to Jamaica. We took our roles as godfathers seriously. We were even there when Swan graduated from high school and college."

"Did Swan have any American grandparents?" Flipper asked.

He saw both men's lips tighten into frowns. "Yes. However, her paternal grandparents didn't approve of their son's marriage to Leigh," said Commanding Officer Shields.

"So they never accepted their granddaughter." It was more of a statement than a question.

"No, they never did," Admiral Martin confirmed. As if it was a topic he'd rather change, the man added, "We've been given some time to find out the truth, but not much. Luckily, Swan's Godpop 3 has a high-level position at naval intelligence. Otherwise, we wouldn't know about the investigation. We have thirty days to prove Swan is not a traitor and identify the person who is. That's where we need your help. Instead of releasing you to go home as we're doing for the other members of your team, we are assigning you to a special mission, Lieutenant Holloway. You are being sent to Key West."

One

Key West, Florida

Swan Jamison was beside herself with excitement as she opened the huge box on her desk. Although it contained only her jewelry-making supplies, the package served as affirmation that while rebuilding was still taking place in certain areas, the majority of the island had recovered from the hurricane that had hit eight months ago.

"Anything for me?" Rafe asked, sticking his head through the office door.

Her shop was in a very trendy area so she could capitalize on the tourists visiting the island. To help with high operating costs, she leased out one of the large rooms in the back. Rafe was her tenant, who'd converted the back room into a tattoo shop. On some days, he got more customers than she did.

"Nothing for you, Rafe, just supplies for me." She

checked her watch. "You're early today." Usually he didn't open up until noon.

"I have a special appointment at ten thirty and I need to ready my ink." And then he was gone. Rafe didn't say a whole lot except to his customers.

The door chime alerted her that *she* had a customer. Jamila, who worked part-time and usually only in the mornings, had taken time off for a day of beauty—hair, nails, pedicure, bikini wax, the works. Her boyfriend worked on a cruise ship that was due in port tomorrow. Swan was happy for Jamila and happy for herself as well. The cruise ships always brought in tourists who wanted to purchase authentic handmade jewelry.

She walked out of her office as a man perused her jewelry display case near the door. That was good. While he checked out her jewelry, she would check him out.

He had a nice profile. Tall, broad shoulders that looked good in a T-shirt and a pair of muscular thighs that fit well in his jeans. He had diamond-blond hair that was neatly trimmed and his hands were the right size for his body.

There was something about the way he stood, straight and tall, that all but spelled out *military man*. And the way his legs were braced apart, as if he had to maintain his balance even on land, spelled out *navy*.

Too bad. She didn't do military men. In all honesty, lately she hadn't done men at all. Too busy.

And then there was the issue of Candy's divorce. Swan knew she shouldn't let what had happened to her best friend darken her own view, but Swan was known to claim whatever excuse suited her and that one did at the moment.

And speaking of the moment, she had looked her

fill. She needed to make her first sale of the day. "May I help you?"

He turned and looked at her, and every cell in her body jolted to attention.

Wow! She'd seen blue eyes before, but his were a shade she'd never seen. They were laser blue; the intense sharpness of the pupils captured her within their scope. And his features... Lordy! The man had such gorgeous bone structure! There was no way a woman had ever passed by him and not taken a second look. Even a third, while wiping away drool.

"Yes, you can help me."

And why did he have to sound so good, too? The sound of his voice—a deep, husky tone—made her throat go dry.

"All right," she said, walking over to him. She knew she had to get a grip. Her store had been closed for two months due to the hurricane, and now that the tourists were returning, she needed to catch up on sales.

"And how can I help you?" She didn't miss the way he was looking at her. She saw interest in his eyes. There was nothing wrong with that. She took pride in her appearance because she had been raised to do so. Leigh Rutledge Jamison, who'd been a Jamaican model, had taught her daughter that your appearance was everything.

Pain settled in Swan's heart. She missed her mom so much.

"I'm looking for a gift for someone."

Swan nodded as she came to stand beside him. Not only did he look good and sound good, but he smelled good as well. She glanced down at his hand and didn't see a wedding ring. He was probably buying a gift for his girlfriend or soon-to-be fiancée.

"What do you have in mind?"

"What do you suggest?" he asked her.

"Well, it depends," she said, looking into those gorgeous eyes.

"On what?"

"What the person likes. I make jewelry from stones, but as you can see, there are a number of them, in various shades, colors and styles."

He smiled and Swan felt a tingling in the pit of her stomach when a dimple appeared in one of his cheeks. "I honestly don't know what she likes. Her tastes change from year to year. It's hard to keep up."

Swan nodded. "Oh. Sounds like the two of you have known each other for a while."

His smile widened even more. "We have. I would have to say I've known Mom all my life."

"Your mom?"

"Yes. Her birthday is next month. I was passing by your shop and thought I would drop in to see what you had."

A racing heart for starters, Swan thought. So the woman he was thinking about buying jewelry for was his mother. "Well, I'm glad you came in. Let me show you what I have."

"All right. There looks to be a lot of nice pieces."

She appreciated the compliment. "Thanks. I made most of them myself."

"Really? Which ones?"

She led him to the area set aside for Swan Exclusives. "These. Most of the stones come from India, Argentina and Africa."

He leaned in to look. "You did an excellent job."

Whoever said flattery, especially coming from a

good-looking man, would get you anywhere knew just
what they were talking about. "Thank you."

"I'm David, by the way. David Holloway." He offered her his hand.

She took it and tried to ignore the sensations that
suddenly flowed through her from the contact. "Nice
to meet you, David." She quickly released his hand.
"And I'm Swan."

"The name of the shop."

"Yes."

"It's a unique name."

"Yes, my parents thought so. On their first date, my
father flew Mom from Jamaica to New York to see
Swan Lake."

"Some date."

"Yes, he was trying to impress her."

"I take it he did."

Swan chuckled. "Yes, because he actually flew them
there. He had his pilot's license."

"Now I'm impressed."

She didn't like bragging about her father but there
were times when she just couldn't help it. "He served
in the air force — that's where he learned to fly. And
then he went into the navy after deciding he wanted
to be a SEAL. That's when he met Mom, while he was
a SEAL. She hadn't known about his stint in the air
force until the night he rented a plane to fly them to
New York."

Why was she telling him all this? Usually she wasn't
chatty. "What about this one?" she asked as they moved
to another glass case. "I call this piece *Enchantment*."

"Why?"

"Look at it," she suggested, leaning closer to the
glass. He followed suit. "This is one of my favorite

pieces because the teardrop gemstone necklace is pretty similar to my very first piece." No need to tell him that she'd made that one for her own mother.

"It is beautiful."

Something in his tone made her glance over at him, and she found him staring at her and not at the jewelry in the case. His eyes held her captive and their gazes met for a minute too long before she broke eye contact with him.

She swallowed. "So are you interested...in this piece?" She wanted to ignore the way her stomach seemed to be filled with all kinds of sensations, but she could not.

"I'm interested in a lot of pieces, Swan, but I'll start with this one."

Swan Jamison was even more beautiful than the photograph he'd seen last week.

The photographer hadn't fully captured the rich creaminess of her skin. And the shade of red lipstick she wore today seemed to make her lips plumper, more well-defined. Luscious.

He had read the dossier on her. He knew his commanding officer and Admiral Martin were operating based on a personal connection with her. He was not. If Miss Jamison was guilty of any wrongdoing, he would find out. And if she wasn't the one handing out classified data to China, then he would discover who was.

"So you want to buy this particular piece?"

Her question brought his thoughts back to the present. "Yes."

"Wonderful. I think your mother will like it."

"I'm sure she will. What about earrings?"

She lifted a brow. "Earrings?"

"Yes. Do earrings come with the necklace?"

"No, but I can make you some."

He'd been hoping she'd say that. "When?"

"It will take me a couple of days. The cruise ship docks tomorrow, so the shop will be busy. Two days from now will work for me, unless you need them sooner."

"No, I can wait. My mother's birthday is next month."

He would have an excuse to return to her shop.

Flipper watched her open the case and pull out the necklace. He knew his mother was going to love it.

"If you don't mind, please complete this ticket," she said. "And I will need full payment for the earrings before I make them."

"That's no problem," he said, taking the document from her.

After he completed the form, he handed it back to her. She glanced at it. "So you're from Texas?"

"Yes. Dallas. Ever been there?"

"Yes, once. I thought it was a nice city."

"It is. I was born and raised there."

"And what brought you to Key West?" she asked him.

"Work, at least for the next thirty days." That wasn't a total lie.

"Hurricane relief?"

"Something like that."

"You're military?"

"At one point but not now." He would let her think he was no longer military.

"I knew immediately."

He lifted a brow. "How?"

She shrugged. "Military men are easily recognized, at least by me."

"Because your dad is military?"

"He *was* military. Dad died years ago in the line of duty."

"I'm sorry." Flipper was always sorry whenever a fellow soldier lost their life.

"Thank you. Your package will be ready in two days, David. Your mobile number is on the form you completed. If I get to it sooner, I will call you."

"Two days is fine. I'll be back."

"'Bye, David."

"'Bye, Swan." He then turned and walked out of the shop.

As much as he wanted to invite her out to lunch today, he knew he couldn't rush things. He needed to earn her trust, even though he had less than thirty days to prove her innocence and determine who had no qualms about making her look guilty.

Swan was cheerful that night as she let herself into her home. Sales today had been better than normal. A tour group from New York had converged on the island and they'd come to spend money. She'd been happy to oblige.

Opening a jewelry shop had been a risky business move, but one that had paid off. She'd earned a degree in business management from the University of Miami and returned to the island after college to work as a manager at one of the elite hotels on the island. She'd enjoyed her job but had felt something was missing in her life. She hadn't been using her jewelry-making talent.

She'd promised her mother on her deathbed that she would find a way to use that talent.

Even after taking care of all her mother's funeral expenses, there had been more than enough money left to buy a little storefront. It had been a good investment because of its location. Some days were busier than others. This had been one of those busy days.

Now she was ready to wind down for the evening. She pulled her hair back in a ponytail and eased her feet into her favorite flats before heading to the kitchen for a glass of wine. As she did so, she couldn't help but think about her first customer of the day.

David Holloway.

He was a cutie, she had to give him that. And the memory of those eyes had stayed with her most of the day.

David Holloway had come into her shop to buy a birthday gift for his mother. How sweet. His mother was lucky. A lot of men didn't even remember their mothers' birthdays. She'd dated quite a few of those men and never developed lasting relationships with any of them. She figured if a man didn't treat his mother right, then there was no hope for a girlfriend.

As she opened the French doors to step out on the patio, she again remembered those blue eyes and how she'd felt whenever she'd looked into them. No man's eyes had ever made her feel that way before.

The effect was unsettling.

Okay, so what was wrong with her? Cutie or no cutie, she normally didn't get caught up over a man. She dated when it suited her, but she would admit that no one had suited her lately. At least not since her best friend, Candy, had left Key West to go live in Boston. Candy had refused to live on the island with her ex and his new wife—the one he'd married before the ink had even dried on the divorce papers.

Refusing to dwell on how shabbily Donald Knoll had treated Candy, Swan looked out at the water. It was calm tonight. When she had evacuated due to the hurricane, she hadn't known what to expect when she returned. Between her home and her shop, there had been some damage, but not as much as she'd feared.

The thought of losing her home had been devastating. This was where her father had brought her mom after they'd married. This home held so many childhood memories—of her father leaving on his missions as a Navy SEAL, of how happy she and her mother would be whenever he returned.

But then he hadn't returned.

Swan felt a knot in her throat as she recalled that day. She'd never seen that sparkle in her mother's eyes again. Swan recalled her mother telling her once that when you met a man who could put that sparkle in your eyes, then you knew he was a keeper.

Swan often wondered if she would ever find her keeper.

She had plenty of time. Besides, she needed to re-think her opinion about men first. If what Don had done to Candy wasn't enough to keep her single, all Swan had to do was remember William Connors, the businessman she had met while working at the hotel.

At the time, he had convinced her he was a bachelor without a care in the world but claimed that he wanted to make her Mrs. William Connors one day.

For some reason, Candy hadn't trusted him. She had a friend who worked for a private investigator check him out. Swan had been devastated when the investigation revealed there was already a Mrs. William Connors, along with three Connors children.

William had been playing her. He had been a lesson well learned. Her only regret was that she'd shared her body with him. She'd been young, naive and impressionable. He had been her first and he should not have been.

She was not naive now and she went into relationships with caution and even a little mistrust. Her mother once told her that being mistrustful wasn't a good thing. Swan knew she would have to learn how to trust again.

She took another sip of wine. Unfortunately, she hadn't gotten there yet.

"So how did things go, Flipper?"

"Have you met her yet?"

"Does she have a traitorous face or just a pretty one?"

"Do you think you'll be able to prove she's innocent?"

Flipper heard the questions coming at him nearly all at once. While unpacking, he had placed his mobile call on speaker to engage in a five-way conversation with his SEAL teammates.

"I think things went rather well, Mac. And yes, I met Swan Jamison today, Viper. I went into her jewelry store to purchase Mom a birthday gift."

Flipper eased open the dresser drawers to place his T-shirts inside. "She doesn't have a traitorous face or just a pretty one, Coop. The woman is simply gorgeous. Beautiful beyond belief. And yes, I hope to prove she's innocent, Bane, because Commanding Officer Shields and Admiral Martin truly believe she is."

"What do you believe?" Viper asked.

Flipper leaned against the dresser for a minute and thought about Viper's question. "Too early to tell."

"Did you ask her out on a date?" Coop wanted to know. They could hear Coop's two-year-old son, Laramie, chattering in the background.

"No, not yet." Flipper's attraction to her had been instant. He'd felt it the moment he looked into her face. Discussing her now wasn't helping matters. All it did was force him to recall what a beautiful woman she was—a woman he would have to spend time with in order to discover the truth.

"Then how do you plan to see her again if you don't ask her out?" Mac wanted to know, interrupting Flipper's thoughts.

"I ordered a pair of earrings to go with the necklace I bought for Mom. She has to make the earrings and I'll make my move when I pick up my purchases in two days."

"And if she turns you down?" Viper asked.

"Not an option. I now have less than thirty days to get this all straightened out."

"We should be there with you, watching your back," Bane said.

"No, you guys are just where you need to be, which is home with your families. I've got this."

"Well, some of our families don't appreciate us being home," Mac grumbled.

Flipper rolled his eyes. They'd all heard the complaints from Mac before. After every extended mission, their teammate went home to an adjustment period, where he would have to get to know his wife all over again and reclaim his position as head of the house. Sometimes the adjustment didn't go over well. Mac had a strong personality and so did Mac's wife, Teri. "Do we have to send both you and Teri into the time-out corners?"

"Hell, I didn't do anything," Mac exclaimed.

Flipper chuckled. "Yeah, right. You better get your act together, Mac. No other woman is going to put up with your BS."

"Whatever. So what did you notice about the place today?"

Mac was changing the subject and Flipper decided to let him. "Everything matched the architectural report I was given. Even with the repairs due to the hurricane, there were no major changes. Front door. Back door. High windows. Glass storefront. No video cameras outside. There are several rooms in back. One is being used as a tattoo parlor. I didn't see the person who runs it. I think I'll go out tonight and do a little more investigating," he said, sliding into a black T-shirt.

"Be careful, Flipper," Viper said. "Although you might not have seen any video cameras, that doesn't mean there aren't any."

"I know. That's why I'm wearing my Pilf gear."

Everybody knew how much Flipper liked digital technology. In addition to all the futuristic developments the military used, Flipper had created a few of his own high-tech gadgets behind the scenes. Some had been so impressive the federal government had patented them as Pilf gear to be used by the military. Pilf was the name Flip spelled backward. On more than one occasion, Flipper had been offered a position with the Department of Defense's Research and Development Department and had turned down each offer, saying he loved being a Navy SEAL more.

"We don't give a damn if you plan to parade around naked tonight, Flipper. Be careful."

He knew Mac was in his big-brother mode. "Okay, Mac. I hear you and I will be careful."

"Call to check in when you get back to the hotel tonight," Bane said.

"It will be late and I wouldn't want to wake up any babies, kids or a pregnant woman. I'll text everyone."

A short while later, wearing undetectable military gear under his clothing, Flipper left his hotel using the stairs.

Two

Two days later, Swan didn't leave the shop for lunch. Instead she accepted Jamila's offer to bring her something back from the sandwich shop on the corner. Although she'd tried convincing herself her decision to hang around had nothing to do with the fact that David Holloway would be returning today to pick up his items, she knew it did.

And her anticipation was so bad that every time the door chimed, her heartbeat would kick up a notch, only to slow back down when someone other than him walked in. She checked her watch. The shop would be closing in an hour. What if he didn't make it before closing time? What if...?

The door chimed, and her heart nearly stopped when David Holloway walked in.

She'd told herself the man hadn't *really* looked as good as she remembered from that first day, but now she saw that he did. In fact, today he looked even better than she remembered. Maybe it had something to do with the unshaven look. Men with a day-old beard had sex appeal. But it could also be his tan, which indicated he'd probably spent the last couple of days lying in the sun.

If he'd been at the beach, there was a good chance he hadn't been there alone. But didn't he say he was in the Keys working?

Why did she care?

She quickly dismissed all those questions from her mind as she continued to watch him walk toward her in a strut that had blood rushing through her veins. His blond hair and blue eyes seemed brighter against his tanned skin. He was deliciousness with a capital *D*.

But then that capital *D* could also stand for *dangerous* if she wasn't careful. Or it could stand for *delusional* if she didn't get control of her senses. Right now, she would play it safe and claim the capital *D* stood for *David*. She couldn't allow herself to think any other way for now, no matter how tempting.

She smiled. "Hello, David."

"Hi, Swan."

"Your tan looks nice."

He chuckled. "So does yours."

She grinned. "Yes, but mine's permanent."

"I know and I like it."

She didn't say anything to that because she understood what he was implying. He was letting her know he had no problem with interracial dating. She didn't have a problem with it either. Neither had her father, although his family had had conniptions about his marriage to Swan's mother. She pushed that thought to the back of her mind, refusing to dwell on an extended family that had never accepted her or her mother.

She reached behind the counter and retrieved a box. "I hope you like the way the earrings came out." She opened it to show him the final earrings.

"Wow!" He ran his finger over the stone that came closest to matching the color of his eyes. "You're very gifted."

"Thank you, and I believe your mother will love them."

"I'm sure she will. I think I've outdone my brothers this time."

She closed the box and placed it, along with the one containing the necklace, into a shopping bag. "You have brothers?"

"Yes, four of them. I'm the youngest."

"My goodness. Any sisters?"

"Not a one. Three of my four brothers are married, so I have sisters-in-law. They are the best."

"And the fourth brother is still single?"

"He's divorced but has a beautiful little girl. And she's my parents' only granddaughter. They have six grandsons."

"Sounds like a nice family. Is your father still alive?"

"Yes, Dad is still alive. He and Mom own a medical supply store."

She nodded as she offered him the bag. "Here you are, David. Thanks again for your business."

He accepted the bag. "Thanks. Now that this is taken care of, there's something I want to ask you, Swan."

She lifted a brow. "What?"

"Would you go out to dinner with me tonight?"

Normally Flipper was good at reading people, but he was having a hard time reading Swan. He definitely needed to remedy that. Although both Commanding Officer Shields and Admiral Martin were convinced of her innocence, the jury was still out for him. He had to remain impartial and deal with the facts, not speculations.

For two nights, he'd searched the area around her shop. Getting inside without triggering her alarm hadn't been easy, but he'd done it. Once he'd picked up the location of the interior security cameras, it was a small matter to make sure he stayed out of their range and within a certain perimeter until he could deactivate them and do what he needed to.

"Go to dinner with you?"

"Yes."

She was apparently mulling over his invitation in her mind and he would give her time to do that. He had no problems studying her while he waited for her answer. Today she looked even prettier than the other day. He figured it had to be the lighting in this place.

"Yes, David. I'll go to dinner with you. You name the restaurant and I'll meet you there."

She wasn't going to give him her address and he had no problem with her being cautious. Little did she know he already knew where she lived and had visited yesterday while she'd been here at her shop. She had a beautiful home on the ocean. Inside it was as neat as a pin with no clutter. She'd even made up her bed before leaving.

"I noticed a restaurant off the pier. Summer Moon. I've heard only good things about it since I've been here." And he knew the place was within walking distance from her home.

"Everything you've heard is true. Summer Moon is fabulous and one of my favorite eating places. I'd love to join you there. What time?"

"What about seven? Will that be a good time for

you?" He figured since it didn't get dark until close to nine, he wouldn't have to worry about her walking to the restaurant in the dark. After dinner, he would walk her home or put her in a cab regardless of the fact that she lived only a few blocks away.

"Seven is perfect."

"Good. I'll see you then."

Swan watched him walk out of the shop.

David had the kind of tush that made a woman want to squeeze it...after doing all kinds of other things with it.

She jumped when fingers snapped in her face. Frowning, she looked at Jamila. "What did you do that for?"

"To keep you from having an orgasm in the middle of your shop."

Swan rolled her eyes. Jamila, the attractive twenty-two-year-old green-eyed blonde, evidently thought reaching a climactic state was that easy. "It would take more than ogling a man for that to happen, Jamila."

"I don't know. Your eyes were about to pop out of their sockets and your breathing sounded funny."

"You're imagining things."

"Denial can be good for the soul, I guess. So who is he?"

Swan and Jamila had more than an employer-and-employee relationship. Their friendship had started when Jamila first moved to the island a couple of years ago and patronized Swan's. It didn't take long to discover that Jamila liked nice things and decided Swan's was one of her favorite places to shop. Last year, Jamila had been looking for work after she lost her job as a day cruise ship captain.

As far as Swan was concerned, it hadn't been Jamila's fault when an intoxicated customer had tried coming on to her and she'd kicked him in the balls. Surgery had to be performed and the man had sued the ship company. They'd settled out of court but not before firing Jamila for all the trouble she'd caused.

Jamila had gotten an attorney herself so she could not only sue her former employer for an unfair firing but also sue the intoxicated customer. To avoid negative publicity, her former employer wanted to settle out of court with her as well. The intoxicated customer was also trying to settle since the woman he'd been with on the ship hadn't been his wife. If things worked out in Jamila's favor, she wouldn't need a job at Swan's much longer.

"He is a customer who came into the shop a couple of days ago to buy a gift for his mother."

"His mother and not his wife?"

"He says his mother."

Jamila snorted. "Men lie all the time."

How well she knew, Swan thought. Then she wondered why Jamila was men-bashing today. This wasn't the first comment of that type she'd made since arriving to work. Her boyfriend had come to town a couple of days ago with the cruise ship, right? So what was going on?

Swan decided not to ask. She didn't want to hear another sad story about a man that would ruin her date tonight with David. It was a date she was definitely looking forward to. She figured going out to dinner with him wouldn't be risky as long as she kept things in perspective.

She knew what could happen if she let her guard down when it came to a man.

* * *

Flipper deliberately arrived at Summer Moon early
so he could see when Swan arrived. His stomach felt
floaty the moment she turned the corner from the street
where she lived.

Be still, my...everything.

She was wearing a printed sundress and a pair of
high-heeled sandals, but what caught his attention—
and was still holding it tight—were her long shapely
legs that seemed to go on forever. He would love to see
where they stopped under that dress. He forced that
thought to the back of his mind.

But the closer she got, the more that thought wiggled
back to the forefront. He shouldn't let it. He was on assignment and she was the subject of an investigation.
He shouldn't see her as temptation. Letting his guard
down around her could be a dangerous and costly mistake. He had to keep his head screwed on straight, no
matter how innocent she seemed and how beautiful
she was, and she was definitely one gorgeous woman.

Men, even some with female companions, were giving Swan second looks, and Flipper tried to downplay
his anger. He had no right to be upset about other men
checking her out when he was checking her out himself.
The best thing to do to control his crazy reaction was to
stop looking at her, so he glanced down at his bottle of
beer and thought about the reports he'd finished reading a short while ago on her employee and her tenant.

Jamila Fairchild had worked for Swan for a year.
He knew all about her former job as a captain of a day
cruise ship, why she'd gotten fired and her litigation
against not only her former employer but also the man
who'd caused the ruckus in the first place. Naval intelligence hadn't left any stone unturned in Ms. Fair-

child's report and she'd come up clean. Flipper would verify that she was.

Then there was Rafe Duggers, the tattoo artist. Although his parlor was located inside Swan's shop, there was a back door for his customers to use without entering through the jewelry shop. Flipper hadn't gotten a chance to look around the tattoo parlor and he intended to do another visit in a few days. Rafe was too squeaky-clean to be true.

No wonder naval intelligence was trying to point the finger at Swan. After all, it was her shop and they had somehow traced activity as originating there. But how? When? He hadn't found anything.

He had searched Swan's office, the small kitchen in the back, the bathrooms and another room that she used as a workshop where she made her jewelry. He'd come up with nothing, even after checking out her computer. So what were the grounds for accusing her?

Flipper's mind flicked back to Swan and he stood when the waiter escorted her to his table. "Hello, Swan. You look nice."

"Thanks and so do you. I was trying to be early and you still beat me here," she said, sitting down across from him.

"I was thirsty," he said, sitting back down and indicating the beer. Now that she was here and sitting directly across from him, he was more than thirsty. If he wasn't careful, he could have a full-fledged attack of desire. She had a pair of beautiful shoulders and her skin appeared soft and smooth to the touch.

Then his mind drifted to wanting her and he quickly snatched it back. "You walked here. Does that mean you live close by?" he asked, deciding it was best to keep the conversation moving.

"Yes, not too far," she said. He knew she was deliberately being evasive.

The waiter handed him another beer and gave them both menus. "What would like to drink, miss?" the waiter asked her.

"A glass of Moscato please."

When the waiter left, she glanced over at Flipper before picking up her menu. "You're not working so hard that you're not enjoying the Keys, are you?"

"I'm doing a bit of both. I admit the ocean is beautiful tonight."

She smiled. "I think it's beautiful every night."

He nodded as he took another sip of his beer, straight from the bottle. "So are you a native or a transplant?"

"A native. I was born and raised right here on the island in the same house I live in now. My mother never made it to the hospital before I was born."

He raised a brow. "She didn't?"

"No. Mom came from a part of Jamaica where the belief was that when it comes to delivering a baby, a midwife is better than a medical doctor. My father promised to find her a midwife here. Otherwise she would have insisted that I be born in Jamaica and he didn't want that. He wanted me born in America."

"So he was able to find a midwife?"

"Yes, but I was born a few weeks early and the midwife wasn't here."

"So who delivered you?"

"My dad, with the help of three of his closest military friends. They were stationed at the base here and were visiting, watching a football game at the time. Needless to say, over the years I've gotten four different versions of what happened that night. My mother didn't remember a thing other than it took four men to deliver me. Although Godpop 1 claims my father passed out trying to cut the umbilical cord."

Flipper laughed. He then asked, "Godpop 1?"

"Yes, my father's three closest friends, the ones who assisted that night, became my godfathers. That's how I distinguish them. Godpop 1, Godpop 2 and Godpop 3."

Flipper nodded. No wonder the three men felt such strong ties to her. "You're lucky to have three godfathers. I don't have a one."

"Yes, I'm lucky," she said, after the waiter set the glass of wine in front of her. "They were my and Mom's rocks after we lost Dad, especially when my grandparents showed up at the funeral trying to cause problems."

Then, as if she realized she might have shared too much, she asked, "So what do you plan to order?"

Swan thought David had picked the right place for them to have dinner. When he asked for recommendations on what to order, she suggested Summer Moon's crab cakes and, as usual, they were delicious. The mango salad was superb, and after dinner they enjoyed listening to the live band.

When the band played their last song, she glanced over at David to discover him staring at her. The intensity in his gaze nearly scorched her and she took a sip of her wine. "Thanks for dinner, David."

"Thank you for accepting my invitation. The place is about to close. Are you ready to go?" he asked her.

"Yes." Because she knew he would suggest that he walk her home, she added, "If you still have a little bit of energy, I'd like to treat you to something."

He lifted a brow. "What?"

"A laser show that officially kicks off the summer season. It's a short walk from here." Since it was in the opposite direction from where she lived, she would have no problem catching a cab back later—alone.

He smiled as he beckoned for the waiter to bring their check. "Then by all means, let's go."

Once the show began, it didn't take Swan long to decide that David was wonderful company. She could tell he was enjoying the laser lights as much as she was.

She attended the event every year and it seemed the displays only got better and better. Each year, they honored a different state and tonight that state was New York. The New Yorkers in the crowd showed their happiness with whistles and shouting. And when a huge display of the Statue of Liberty flashed across the sky in a brilliant variety of colors, Swan caught her breath.

After that, the showrunners took the time to honor the servicemen in attendance with a flag salute. She couldn't hold back her tears as she remembered how much her father had loved his country and how, in the end, he'd given his life for it and for her.

David must have detected her weepy state. He pulled her closer to his side.

"Sorry," she said. "I get all emotional about our servicemen and servicewomen, especially those who sacrifice their lives."

"You sound very patriotic."

She pulled back and looked up at him. "Of course I'm patriotic. Aren't you? You did say you used to be in the military, right?"

"Yes, I'm very patriotic," he said, wrapping his arms around her. She wished she didn't think the arms around her felt so strong and powerful.

"I thought you would be, but you said I sounded patriotic as if you thought that perhaps I wasn't."

"I apologize. I didn't mean it that way. I'm glad you're so patriotic."

She nodded, accepting his apology. Scanning the area around them, she said, "They are serving complimentary wine coolers over there. Let's go grab a couple."

"Sure thing." He placed his hand on the small of her back.

The contact sent a rush of desire through her that was so strong she had to force herself to breathe. Swan quickly glanced up at him and noticed he'd been affected by the feeling as well. However, he hadn't removed his hand.

Instead, he pressed his hand more firmly into her back and she felt him urging her away from the crowd and toward a cluster of low-hanging palm trees. Once they stood in the shadows, he turned her in his arms, stared down at her for a long moment and then lowered his mouth to hers.

The moment their lips touched, he slid his tongue inside her mouth, and she recalled her thoughts from earlier that day. He was delicious—and dangerous—with a capital *D*. And it wasn't just because he tasted of the beer he'd consumed at Summer Moon, but because he tasted like a hot-blooded man. All the sexiness she'd seen in him was reflected in his kiss.

When she began kissing him back, he wrapped his arms around her and deepened the exchange by crushing his mouth to hers.

She didn't mind his eagerness. In fact, she welcomed the pleasure of his hunger, his taste, which was getting more provocative with every stroke of his tongue. It had been a while since she'd been kissed, and certain parts of her were reminding her of just how long it had been. Not only that, those certain parts were goading her to keep up with the forceful demands of his mouth. She hadn't been kissed so thoroughly or possessively before in her life. Or so passionately.

Swan wasn't sure how long they stood there kissing. It wasn't until they heard the sound of fireworks that they disengaged their mouths. She glanced up as more fireworks exploded in the sky. Instead of looking up, David trailed his tongue along her neck and collarbone with wet licks.

"Say you'll go out with me again, Swan."

There was no way she wouldn't say it. She looked at him and saw deep desire in the eyes looking back at her. "Yes, I'll go out with you again."

"Good."

And then he lowered his head and kissed her again.

Flipper had tried everything possible to get to sleep. He'd counted sheep, counted backward, rolled his eyes for a full thirty minutes and had even tried hypnotizing himself. None of those things helped.

He couldn't remember ever feeling this tight with need. So here he was, close to four in the morning, and still wide awake. Nothing he did could erase the taste of Swan from his mouth and the act of kissing her from his mind.

The kiss would complicate his mission, but it hadn't been an act. It had been the most real thing he'd done in a long time. He had wanted that kiss. Needed it. It had been inevitable.

Sitting across from her at dinner and watching the movement of her mouth had caused a throbbing need to erupt in his gut, making him rock hard. There had been no way to ignore the delicious heat of carnal attraction spiking between them.

And the patriotism he'd seen in her eyes when she'd gotten teary-eyed in support of servicemen, and then when she'd told him about her work with the city to find lodging for homeless vets, hadn't helped. Neither had the fact that she'd looked stunning and had smelled irresistibly hot tonight.

Kissing her had made his entire body feel alive. Had revved up his passion to a degree that his libido had him tied in knots and had his pulse tripping. He could feel himself riding the fine edge of intense desire heightened by more sexual energy than he'd felt in a long time.

While kissing her, he hadn't cared that they could have been seen in spite of the low-hanging trees. He'd been beyond the point of caring. He'd been tempted to drag her to the ground right there.

Damn. How was he going to clear her of anything when the only thing he'd wanted to clear her of was her clothes?

He had access to women whenever he needed them. There were always women who went bonkers for men in uniform and he had no problem engaging in one-night stands. Those types of relationships had always been the way to go for him. He liked being single, coming and going as he pleased, with no one to worry about but himself.

It had been a long time since any woman had kept him up at night and that wasn't cool.

Grabbing his phone he texted the message: If anyone is awake. Call me.

Within seconds, his phone rang. It was Bane. "What's going on, Flipper?"

"Why are you up?" Flipper asked his friend.

"Feeding time. Crystal and I rotate."

"Oh? You're breastfeeding now?"

"No, smart-ass. The trio are on bottles now. What are you doing up?"

Flipper stretched out across the bed. "I couldn't sleep. I tried everything. I even tried to hypnotize myself."

Bane chuckled. "I guess it didn't work."

"No, it didn't work."

"So why can't you sleep, Flip?"

He wasn't one to kiss and tell, no matter who the listener was, so he said, "I still haven't figured out anything about the situation down here and the CO and the admiral are depending on me."

"Maybe they're going to have to accept naval intelligence's report that she's guilty."

"I don't think so." Flipper paused. "She cried tonight."

"What do you mean, she cried?"

"Today was the first day of summer and there's an annual laser show to commemorate the change in season. One of the laser displays was a salute to New York, where they did an awesome light replica of the Statue of Liberty and American soldiers. She got emotional and cried. Dammit, Bane, a person who is betraying their country doesn't cry for those in the service. Call me a sucker for tears but I don't believe she has a traitorous bone in her body."

"Then it's up to you to prove it. What about those two people who hang around her shop?"

"The woman who works for her and the tattoo guy? Both seem clean. But I will dig further. I have to."

"Okay, but make sure while you're digging for answers that you're not burrowing yourself into something you can't handle."

"What do you mean?"

"I think you know what I mean, Flip. You were sent there to prove her innocence—not to prove she has a passionate side. Remember that. Good night."

Flipper clicked off the phone and rubbed a hand down his face. Little did Bane know that after the kiss with Swan tonight, Flipper was driven to do more than prove her innocence, or her passion.

He wanted to possess Swan completely.

And he had a feeling the desire wasn't one-sided. He'd seen the look in her eyes during dinner. He'd felt how her body had responded to his touch. He was certain the same sensations that rushed through him had affected her, too. Kissing her had been inevitable, something they both wanted and needed.

The genie called desire was out of the bottle and Flipper honestly didn't know how to get it back inside.

Three

Swan pushed away from her desk and took another huge gulp of ice-cold lemonade. It had been that way for her all day. Instead of concentrating on the online orders she needed to fill and ship out, her mind was wrapped around that kiss from last night.

All she had to do was close her eyes to remember every single detail, specifically every sensuous lick of his tongue inside her mouth. Even now, the memory sent multiple sensations coursing through her body, causing pleasure the likes of which she'd never encountered before.

She looked up at the sound of a knock on her door. "Yes?"

Jamila stuck her head in. "Mr. Make-you-have-an-instant-orgasm is back."

Swan didn't need to ask Jamila what she meant or who she was talking about. "Any reason you can't wait on him?"

Jamila smiled naughtily. "I could use the pleasure but he specifically asked for you."

Swan nodded. "I'll be out in a minute."

"Okay, I will let him know."

Swan reached over and took another gulp of her lemonade. She didn't want to admit it, but after that kiss last night, David could become an addiction. Besides putting down a gallon of lemonade, she'd been twitching in her seat most of the day, thinking that if his tongue could do that to her mouth, then Lordy…she could only imagine what else he would be able to do…

She quickly stood, refusing to go there even as a naughty part of her mind wished that he would. Leaving her office, she rounded the corner and stopped.

David stood in the middle of her shop wearing a pair of khaki shorts and a muscle shirt. The sight of his muscled abs and strong legs made Swan bite back a groan. Just when she thought he couldn't get any sexier, he'd proved her wrong.

He must have heard the sound of her footsteps because he turned and smiled.

As if on cue, she smiled back. "Hello, David, you came to make more purchases?" Hopefully he would take the hint that she didn't expect him to just drop by without a reason.

"Yes. I'm buying jewelry for my three sisters-in-law and would love for you to offer suggestions."

Swan couldn't help but smile since she liked making sales. What store owner wouldn't? "I'd love to help you pick out pieces of jewelry for them."

An hour later, Swan stood at the cash register to ring up all of David's purchases. With her assistance, he'd selected some really nice pieces, with a number of the stones chosen specifically because that's what he'd said

they would like. Then he wanted earrings to comple-
ment the necklaces, which he paid for in advance. They
decided to select stones for the earrings tomorrow since
they'd spent a lot of time on the necklaces today and her
shop would be closing in less than an hour.

From their conversation, she knew the Holloways
were a close-knit family. He'd even pulled out his phone
to show her pictures of his young niece and nephews.

"No pressure for you to marry?" she asked when
he tucked his phone back into the pocket of his shorts.

"None. My parents have been married for more than
forty years and are still very much in love. They make
sure their kids and grandkids know that. They believe
we will know when it's time for us to marry without
any pressure from them. We'll be the ones to have to
live with the people we choose. They just want all their
children to be happy."

She nodded. "I like the way your parents think. I
want to believe that, had my parents lived, they would
have a similar philosophy. Dad used to tell me all the
time that he wanted me to grow up and be whatever I
wanted to be and do whatever I wanted to do, and that
he and Mom would always have my back."

She suddenly felt a deep sense of loss. "Appreciate
your parents, David. You never know how truly great
they are until they're gone. But in all honesty, I think
I've always known I had great parents."

At that moment, he did something she wouldn't have
expected from him—he reached out and took her hand.
"They sound great and I know they're proud of your
accomplishments."

"Thanks." That was a nice thing for him to say. To
avoid thinking about just how nice he was, she slid the

bag with his purchases toward him and gave him the credit card slip. He signed it and gave it back to her.

"How would you like to go to happy hour at Danica's with me?"

After talking about her parents and missing them like crazy, she could use more than just an hour of happiness. She would love to be able to have a lifetime of that feeling.

It wasn't that she was *unhappy*, because she wasn't, but there were times when she wondered if maybe there was more out there for her than what was currently in her life. Perhaps she was shortchanging herself on some things. What those things were, she had no idea.

"I would love to go but good luck getting a table at Danica's. They have the best hot wings and are always crowded, *especially* for happy hour. I think the entire island heads over there at five."

"Since I know you don't close your shop until five, how about if we meet over there at five-thirty? I guarantee we'll have a place to sit."

"Um, sounds like you might have connections, David Holloway."

"We'll see." He took the bag and turned to leave, and just like before, she watched his movements until he was no longer in sight.

"Wow. You do have connections, don't you?" Swan said, sliding into a stool at the bar. "I've been here a number of times and the best seat I've ever gotten is at one of those tables outside."

Flipper smiled. Like at Summer Moon, he'd arrived early and was waiting for her. He liked seeing her stroll down the sidewalk looking as beautiful as ever.

Today she was wearing a pair of shorts and a pretty

top. Her legs were long and shapely and he could imagine them wrapped around him while...

Whoa, he didn't need to go there. Ever since that kiss, he'd been trying *not* to go there—no matter how tempted he was to do so. Quickly, he changed the direction of his thoughts.

"I know Danica personally," he said, trying hard to keep his naughty thoughts in check.

She lifted a brow. "Really? How?"

There was no way he would tell her the whole story. Danica was the godmother of former SEAL team member Nick Stover. Nick had given up being a SEAL a few years ago to take a job with Homeland Security after his wife had triplets. Instead of the whole history, Flipper gave her a modified version. "Her godson and I used to work together."

"Oh." The bartender chose that moment to take their drink order.

"I know you used to be in the military at one point but what do you do now?" she asked once the bartender had walked away.

Flipper had expected that question sooner or later and had a prepared answer. "I travel a lot and my job deals with ocean marine work. I guess you can say I'm a specialist in that area."

"Sounds interesting."

He chuckled. "Trust me, it is."

The bartender set their beers in front of them along with a huge plate of hot wings. They dug in.

"Your assistant at the store seems nice," Flipper commented. "I hope she didn't get offended when I asked specifically for you."

"No, very little offends Jamila, trust me."

"You've known her a long time?"

If his question seemed odd, she didn't mention it. "We met a couple of years ago when she moved to the island. The first time she came into my shop she nearly bought out the place. Like you, she has a huge family living up north and wanted to buy holiday gifts for everyone. Thanks to her, I made my month's quota in that one day. She earned a friend for life."

Flipper took a long swig of his beer. What Swan had just told him was interesting. Based on the naval intelligence report he'd read, Jamila didn't have any family. No parents, siblings, aunts, uncles or cousins. She'd been adopted and her adopted parents had been killed in a car accident in her last year of high school. And they hadn't lived in the north but out west in California.

Why had Jamila lied?

"So you hired her that day?" he asked, grinning, trying to make a joke of what she'd told him.

"No, she had a job as a ship captain at one of the day cruise companies in town. When things didn't work out for her there, I hired her on part-time."

He'd read the report and knew why Jamila had been let go and knew about her pending lawsuits. There was a big chance both cases would be settled out of court in her favor. "Is the reason she's part-time because she's a student?"

"Sort of. She saw how much money Rafe makes and—"

"Rafe?" He knew who Rafe was, but Swan didn't know that.

"Yes, Rafe. He rents space in my shop where he operates a tattoo parlor. He's good and always has a steady stream of customers. Some are so pleased with his work that they recommend him to others. I've known people to fly in just to use his services."

She took a sip of her beer, grinned and added, "Jamila decided to give him some real competition by becoming a tattoo artist as well. I have to admit she's pretty good. But Rafe doesn't seem worried. He even allows her to assist him sometimes. I guess you can say he's taken her under his wing. I think that's nice of him."

Flipper took another swig of his beer. "Yes, that is nice of him. Real nice."

Later that night, as they waited for a car at the taxi stand, Swan turned to face David. "I had a wonderful time this evening."

Once again, she had enjoyed his company and hated that their time together was about to end. It didn't come as a surprise to her that the sexual chemistry between them was more explosive than ever. The kiss they'd shared the night before had ignited something within her. From the way she'd noticed him looking at her, she believed something had ignited within him as well.

More than once, her smooth bare legs had brushed against his hairy ones. The sensual contact had sent a gush of desire through her.

The first few times it happened, she'd pulled away. But finally, she'd decided not to pull her legs back and he'd given her one of those *I know you did that on purpose* looks and she had smiled innocently and sipped her beer.

He had initiated the next physical contact and she could envision his mind at work trying to decide how to push her sensual buttons. She doubted he could push them more than he was already.

"I'm glad I got to meet Ms. Danica. After all the years I've been living here, this was my first time meeting her. She's nice."

"Yes, she is."

"And I definitely appreciate this," she said, holding up the bag of hot wings the older woman had given Swan to take home.

"I think she appreciated how much you enjoyed them."

She chuckled. "You're probably right."

"What do you have planned for later?" he asked in a deep, husky tone that seemed to have dropped a purposeful octave.

He had taken her hand when they left Danica's to walk to the taxi stand. The feel of his fingers entwined with hers had stirred something within her, something that grew with every step they took. She was aware of every detail about him as they walked together. Because of his long legs, more than once he had to slow his pace so she could keep up with him.

Swan could have walked home but figured he would suggest walking there with her. She was still cautious about letting him know where she lived. When she left Jamaica to begin living on her own, her mother had drilled into her the danger of letting a man know where you lived too soon. In her heart, Swan felt David was safe, but still...

"It's near the end of the month and I need to work on the books for my accountant." No need to mention she had tried doing that very thing today at work and hadn't been able to concentrate for remembering their kiss from last night.

"How about dinner tomorrow night?" he asked her.

She didn't answer right away. Instead, she broke eye contact with him and glanced down at the sidewalk. Hadn't they seen each other enough these last few days?

Where was this leading? Wasn't he leaving the Keys in less than a month?

She glanced back at him. "Why? We've gone out twice already. I wouldn't want to dominate your time."

"You're not. And the reason I want to take you out again is because I enjoy your company."

She certainly enjoyed his. "Can I ask you something, David?"

He nodded. "Yes?" Considering her history with William, it was something she probably should have asked David before going out on their first date. She'd discovered the hard way that a man not wearing a wedding ring didn't mean anything these days.

"What do you want to ask me, Swan?"

She met his gaze and hoped she would be able to see the truth in his eyes. "Do you have a wife or a significant other?"

Instead of guilt flashing in his eyes, she saw surprise. "No. I'm not married and I've never been married. I dated a woman for years but because of my frequent travels, she decided to end things. That was over six years ago." He then leaned against a light post and asked, "What about you, Swan? Have you ever been married or is there a significant other?"

"Of course not."

He nodded slowly. "Then I assume there is a reason you thought that maybe I was in a relationship?"

"I needed to be sure."

He didn't say anything. Instead, he looked at her as if tumbling her answer around in his head. "But like I said, I assume there is a reason you needed to know."

"Yes." However, she didn't intend to go into any details.

"Well, rest assured there is not a Mrs. David Hollo-

way out there anywhere. Nor is there any woman wearing my ring. Satisfied?"

"Yes."

At that moment, a taxi pulled up. "Thanks for dinner
again." She was about to move toward the taxi when
he reached out, took hold of her hand and tugged her
to him. He lowered his mouth to hers and kissed her
quickly but soundly on the lips.

"I'll see you tomorrow," he said, his words a soft
whisper against her wet lips.

"Tomorrow?" she asked in a daze from his kiss.

"Yes, we're supposed to go over designs for the earrings, remember?"

It was hard to remember anything after a kiss like
that. "Yes, I remember," she said.

"Then I'll see you tomorrow."

She nodded, and when he opened the door for her,
she quickly got into the taxi and headed home alone.

The moment Flipper entered his hotel room he went
to the small refrigerator beneath the wet bar and pulled
out a beer. Just then it didn't matter that he'd already
drank a couple at Danica's. He needed another. There
was just something about Swan that was getting to him,
touching him on a level he wasn't used to when it came
to women. He had truly enjoyed her company tonight.

He and his SEAL teammates had just returned from
a two-month mission in South Africa and more than
anything he had needed to unwind. He would be home
in Texas doing just that had he not been summoned to
the admiral's office.

So here he was, and although he was in Key West
on official military business and he was supposed to be
investigating Swan, he loved spending time with her.

Tonight, when she'd met Danica, it had been price-less. You would have thought Swan had met a Holly-wood celebrity. He had sat there while the two women conversed, immediately as comfortable as old friends.

The sound of Swan's voice had been maddeningly sexy with a tinge of sweetness that had stroked his senses. For the first time since returning to the States, he had allowed himself to uncoil, to loosen up and relax while appreciating the richness of her personality. Her persona was uniquely hers and the sensuality of her very being called to him in a primitive way.

And that wasn't good.

Taking a huge swig of his beer, he switched his thoughts to what he should be focused on—what she'd told him about Jamila and Rafe. Remembering what she'd said, he pulled his phone out of the pocket of his shorts and with one click he connected to his friend Nick Stover.

"This better be good, Flipper. Natalie is taking an art class at the university tonight and I have babysit-ting duties."

Flipper couldn't help but smile. Like Bane, Nick had triplets and from the sound of the noise in the back-ground, the triplets had him. "Stop whining. Taking care of a trio of three-year-olds can't be too bad."

"Then you come do it."

"Sorry, I'm on assignment."

"So I hear. In the Keys, right?"

He figured for Nick to know that much meant he'd either talked to Bane, Viper, Mac or Coop. "Yes, I'm in Key West."

"While you're there, be sure to stop by Danica's. Give her a hug for me."

"I did that already. Tonight, in fact."

"Good."

"I think she has more photos of the triplets than you do."

"I wouldn't doubt it. So if you can't be a backup babysitter, why are you calling?"

"When you arrive at your cushy job at Homeland Security tomorrow, there are two people I need you to check out for me. I've read naval intelligence reports on them, but something isn't adding up. Call me a suspicious bastard, but after that situation with Bane, when those traitors within the agencies were exposed, I'm not taking any chances."

He then told Nick about the discrepancies between what the reports said and what Swan had told him. "Somebody is lying. Either Jamila lied to Swan or someone falsified the report, and I want to know which it is."

Four

"He's *baaack*," Jamila said.

Swan pushed away from her desk. She didn't have to ask who Jamila was talking about. "I was expecting him," she said in what she hoped was a professional tone. "He needs to look at designs for earrings."

"If you say so. I'll send him in here."

Swan was about to tell Jamila they could use the computer out front, but Jamila was gone after closing the door behind her.

Standing, Swan inhaled deeply. How she had finished the books last night, she wasn't sure. Thoughts of David had been stronger than ever after their night out. When she'd gone to bed, she had dreamed about him. Okay, she'd dreamed about him before, but the dreams last night had been so hot it was a wonder they hadn't burned her sheets. She had been tempted to do something she hadn't done in a long time, reactivate her vibrator.

She drew in a deep breath when she heard the knock on her door. "Come in."

And in walked David, looking sexier than he had the other times she'd seen him. Last night, to stay focused, she had come up with every reason she could think of for why she shouldn't be attracted to him and why a relationship with him wouldn't work.

She'd even thrown in the race card. But of course that was thrown out when she remembered her parents and how happy they had been together. Yet she also couldn't forget how her father's family had ostracized him for his choice in love. Would David's family be the same way? There was no reason to think they wouldn't. And wasn't she getting ahead of herself for even throwing love in the mix?

"Hello, David."

"Swan." He glanced at her desk, taking in all the folders spread across it. "You're busy."

"That's fine. Besides, I need to get those earrings ready for you."

Now that he'd seen her desk, it would make perfect sense for her to suggest they use the computer out front to design the earrings. But now that she had him behind closed doors, she liked it.

Not that she planned on doing anything about having him here.

"Please have a seat while I clear off my desk." Today he was wearing jeans and she couldn't help but watch how fluidly his body eased into the chair. How the denim stretched across a pair of muscular thighs. She quickly switched her gaze before he caught her looking.

"Nice office."

"Thanks." She closed the folders and placed them in her inbox tray. She then glanced over at him and caught him looking at her. She followed his gaze and soon figured out why he was staring.

She was wearing a skirt with a V-neck blouse, and when she'd leaned over to place the folders in the tray, her shirt had shown a portion of her cleavage. Instead of calling him out for trying to cop a view of her breasts, the fact that he was interested sparked a distinct warmth between her legs.

She quickly sat down. "Now if you would roll that chair over here, I am ready." Too late, she realized how that sounded and quickly added, "To look at designs."

He smiled. "I know what you meant."

He rolled his chair behind her desk to place it right next to hers. When he sat down, their legs touched. Moving away would be pretty obvious so she let the denim of his jeans rub against her bare legs.

"Now, then," she said, trying not to notice how good he smelled. "What do you think of these?" she asked, bringing up a few designs on the computer screen.

When he didn't answer, she glanced over at him and found him staring at her. Sitting so close to him, she could look directly into his laser-blue eyes. It was as if his gaze was deliberately doing something to her, causing a surge in her breath and arousal to coil in her core. She saw the dark heat in his eyes and desire clawed at her even more.

"May I make a suggestion?" he asked in a voice that seemed to wobble in a sexual way.

"It depends on what that suggestion is," she heard herself say.

He leaned in a little closer and whispered, "I want to kiss you again. Only problem is that I don't want to stop until I get enough. And I'm not sure I would."

She had been staring at his lips, watching how they

moved while he talked. She slowly dragged her gaze back up to his eyes. She saw need flare in his gaze at the same time that anticipation for his kiss thickened the air flowing in and out of her lungs.

"I don't know what to say."

"Don't say anything, Swan. Just bring your mouth closer to mine."

She knew she shouldn't, but she found herself doing it anyway.

Flipper drew in a deep breath when Swan's lips were almost touching his. He flicked out his tongue and she gave a sharp intake of breath when he began licking her lips from corner to corner with the tip of his tongue.

"What are you doing?" she asked on a wobbly breath.

"Since you asked…" He captured her mouth and when she closed her eyes on a moan, he reached up and cradled her face in his hands while he kissed her with a greed he didn't know was in him.

What was there about her that made him accept the primitive part of himself that wouldn't be satisfied until he made love to her? Was it because she crept into his dreams at night and into his every waking thought? Or was it because an arrow of liquid heat shot straight to his groin whenever he saw her? Or could he blame it on the fact that whenever she touched him, he burned? She made him edgy and aroused him as no other woman could.

It was all of those things and more.

Right now, he didn't know how to back away. So he didn't. Instead he accepted the stream of heat in his gut and the crackle of energy passing between them.

Their lips were copulating in a way that sent blood coursing through his veins like a raging river. It was raw, hot and explosive, causing a hot ache to erupt in his gut. It wouldn't take much to lose control and take her here on her desk. At that moment, his entire body was tight with need, totally entranced by everything about her.

The phone rang and they quickly broke off the kiss, drawing in deep breaths of air. He watched as she reached across her desk to press the speaker button. "Thank you for calling Swan's."

At first, no one said anything and then a deep male voice said, "Swan? Are you okay? You sound out of breath."

He watched as she pulled in another deep breath before a smile touched her lips. "I'm fine, Godpop 1. How are you?"

Knowing who she was talking to on the phone was like a pail of cold water drenching Flipper. He was quickly reminded why he'd been sent to Key West. His admiral would have him court-martialed if he knew what Flipper had just done with his goddaughter. If the man had any idea how many times Flipper had kissed her already and how each time he'd wished they had gone even further...

She turned off the speaker so he heard only one side of the conversation, and from the sound of her voice, he knew she was happy about receiving the call.

Feeling a tightness in his crotch from his still-aroused body, he got up from the chair and walked to the window. If she could have this sort of effect on him just from a kiss, he didn't want to think about what would happen if he were to make love to her. Just the thought of easing his body into hers had his stomach churning and caused an ache low in his gut.

Knowing he needed to think of something else, he

glanced up into the sky. It was a beautiful day. Monday was Memorial Day and he wondered if Swan had made any plans to celebrate. He'd heard there would be a parade and unlike some places in the States, where stores remained open on Memorial Day, the laid-back businesses in the Keys closed up for one big party.

He liked the Keys. When he retired from being a SEAL, he could see himself moving here to live out the rest of his days. The island was surrounded by the ocean and they didn't call him Flipper for nothing. He loved water. Being in it and being a part of it. Living this close to the sea would certainly be a plus for him. But then there was the question of how he would deal with Swan if he chose to retire here. Even if he could prove she was not guilty of espionage, there was always that possibility she would hate his guts regardless of the outcome, because he had not been truthful with her.

"Sorry about that, David."

He turned, not caring that she could see his still-hard erection. It was something he couldn't hide even if he had tried. Was she sorry they'd been interrupted or was she regretting that they'd kissed in the first place? He hoped it was the former because he doubted he could ever regret kissing her. "I take it that was one of your godfathers?" he asked, knowing it had been.

She was staring at him below the waist, but after his question, her gaze slowly moved upward to his face. "Ah, yes, that was one of my godfathers. The other two will be calling sometime today as well. It always works out that they all call within twenty-four hours of each other."

He nodded and slowly walked back over to his chair to sit down. "I know you're busy so let's look at the designs."

Had he just seen a flash of disappointment in her eyes? Did she want them to continue what they'd been doing before she'd gotten that call? Didn't she know how close they'd both been to going off the edge and falling into waters too deep to swim out of? Even for him, a SEAL master swimmer.

Somehow they got through the next half hour looking at earring designs. Just as each one of the necklaces were different, he wanted the earrings to be different as well and reflect each one of his sisters-in-law's personalities.

When he was satisfied with his choices, he stood, convinced he needed to rush back to the hotel and take a cold shower. Sitting beside Swan and inhaling her scent without touching her was one of the most difficult things he'd had to do in a long time.

She was so female that the maleness in him couldn't help responding to everything about her. A part of him felt drugged by her scent and the intense physical awareness of her. Even now, desire was racing through his bloodstream.

"I owe you additional monies, right?" he asked. A couple of the designs he'd selected cost more than what she'd originally estimated.

"Yes. I'll let you know the difference after I finish designing them, when you pick up everything."

He hadn't missed the fact that when he stood her gaze had immediately latched on to his crotch once again. Was she still hoping to see him with a hard-on? If that was true, then she wasn't disappointed. He could get aroused just from looking at her.

And why did she choose that moment to lick her lips? She had no idea that seeing her do such a thing sent the pulse beating in his throat and desire hammering against his ribs.

On unstable legs and with an erection the size of which should be outlawed, he moved around her desk and looked at her. "Yesterday I asked you to go to dinner with me again, but you never gave me an answer."

He figured that seeing how aroused he was, she probably wouldn't give him an answer now either. She surprised him when she said, "Yes, we can dine together this evening."

He nodded. "Okay, you get to pick the place."

She took a slip of paper off her desk, wrote something on it and handed it to him. He looked at it and he must have stared at it too long, because she said, "It's my address, David. I'm inviting you to dine with me this evening at my home."

He broke eye contact with her to glance back down at the paper she'd given him. He looked back at her while trying to downplay the heat rumbling around in his gut.

"Do you need me to bring anything?" he asked her.

"No, just yourself."

Swan glanced around her home and felt the knots beginning to twist in her stomach. She hoped she hadn't made a mistake inviting David here.

Today marked a week since they'd met and if she was going to continue to see him while he was on the island, she couldn't take advantage of his thoughtfulness and expect him to invite her out without ever returning the kindness. However, more than anything else, she needed to keep things in perspective. She needed to remember he was someone she could have a good time with and that's it.

She didn't want anything more than that.

One day, she would be ready to explore her options and consider a future with a man, but that time wasn't now. She liked being single and responsible only for herself.

She knew from Candy that a serious relationship was hard work. And on top of all that hard work, you could assume you had the right person in your life only to discover you didn't. By then, you would have opened yourself up to hurt and pain in the worst possible way.

The thought that a man had caused her best friend that kind of agony bothered Swan whenever she thought about it. Candy loved Key West as much as Swan did, and for a man to be the reason she had moved away was disheartening.

Swan tried telling herself that not all men were like Candy's ex, Don, or like William. On days when Swan wanted to think all men were dogs, all she had to do was remember her dad.

Andrew Jamison was the yardstick she used to measure a good man. She'd watched how he had treated her mother, had seen the vibrant and sincere love between them. She had not only seen it, but she'd felt it as well. Both her parents had been demonstrative individuals and Swan had often interrupted them sharing a passionate kiss or embrace.

She still felt it here, within the walls of her house and in the very floor she walked on. All the love that had surrounded her while growing up was in this house she now called home.

She was glad her mother hadn't sold it after her father died, when Leigh had made the decision to move back home to Jamaica. Instead, she had kept the house, knowing one day Swan would want to return. It was almost too spacious for one person but Swan knew she would never sell it or move away. This house had everything she needed.

She could see the water from any room, and at night, whenever she slept with the window open, the scent of the ocean would calm her.

Her favorite room in the house was her parents' old bedroom, even though she had not moved into it. It had floor-to-ceiling windows and a balcony she liked sitting on while enjoying her coffee each morning. A couple of years ago, she'd had the balcony screened in to keep the birds from flying into her house, although she loved waking up to the sound of them chirping every morning.

Although neither one of her parents would tell her the full story, Swan knew her father had come from a wealthy family. And she knew he had been disowned by them when he had fallen in love with her mother and refused to give her up. Before dying, Leigh had given Swan a beautiful leather-bound diary to read after her death. That's what had helped keep Swan sane, reading the daily account of her mother's life and love for her father and believing they were now back together.

For weeks following her mother's death, Swan had wanted to be alone to wallow in her pity and read about what she thought was the most beautiful love story that could exist between two people. Her mother had always been expressive with the written word and Swan enjoyed reading what she'd written.

It had made Swan long for such a man, such a love. Maybe that's why she had been so quick to believe in William and why, once she'd found out about his duplicity, she'd been so reluctant to get serious with a man since.

From her mother's diary, Swan discovered her moth-

er's appreciation for her husband's agreement to make
Key West their home. The people on the island em-
braced diversity and tolerated different lifestyles.

Swan had read the account of when her father had
been stationed at a naval base in Virginia and had sent
for her mother to join him there. In the diary, her mother
had written about the hateful stares they would receive
whenever they went out together. The unaccepting and
disapproving looks. The cruel words some people had
wanted them to hear.

Her father hadn't tolerated any of it and hadn't
minded confronting anyone who didn't accept his wife.
But to avoid trouble, Leigh had preferred to live in Key
West, where people's issues with an interracial marriage
were practically nonexistent.

However, people's attitudes never kept Leigh from
leaving the island to join Andrew whenever he would
send for her. Oftentimes, Leigh would take Swan along
and they would both join Andrew in different places
for weeks at a time.

When she heard the sound of the doorbell, Swan
drew in a deep breath. The time for memories was over.
The only plans she had for *this* evening were for her and
David to enjoy the meal she'd prepared and later enjoy
each other's company.

She had no problem with them deciding what the
latter entailed when that time came.

"Hello, David. Welcome to my home."

Flipper pushed from his mind the thought of how
Swan would feel if she knew this wasn't his first time
here. How she would react if she knew he had invaded
her space without her knowledge. If she ever found out
the truth, would she understand it had been done with

the best of intentions? Namely, to keep her from wasting away in a federal prison after being falsely accused of a crime?

He forced those thoughts to the back of his mind as he smiled down at her. She looked absolutely stunning in a wraparound skirt and yellow blouse. "Hi. I know you said I didn't have to bring anything, but I wanted to give you these," he said, handing her both a bottle of wine and a bouquet of flowers.

He had decided on the wine early on, but the flowers had been a spur of the moment thing when he'd seen them at one of those sidewalk florist shops. Their beauty and freshness had immediately reminded him of Swan.

"Thank you. The flowers are beautiful and this is my favorite wine," she said, stepping aside to let him in.

He chuckled. "I know. I remember from the other night." There was no way he would also mention having seen several bottles of Moscato in the wine rack the time he had checked out her house.

He glanced around, pretending to see her home for the first time. "Nice place."

"Thanks. I thought we would enjoy a glass of wine and some of my mouthwatering crab balls out on the patio before dinner."

"Mouthwatering crab balls?"

"Yes, from my mom's secret recipe. You won't be disappointed," she said, leading him through a set of French doors. The first thought that came to his mind when he stepped out on her patio, which overlooked the Atlantic Ocean, was that it was a beautiful and breathtaking view. This had to be the best spot on the island to view the ocean in all its splendor.

He recalled how, as a boy, he would visit his cousins in California and dream of one day living near the beach. Over the years, being stationed in San Diego had been the next best thing. He owned an apartment close to base that was within walking distance of the beach.

However, his view was nothing like this. All she had to do was walk out her back door and step onto the sand. It was right there at her door. If he lived here, he would go swimming every day.

He glanced over at her. "The view from here is beautiful."

"I love this house and appreciate my mother for not selling it when she decided to move back to Jamaica after Dad died. She got a lot of offers for it, believe me. So have I. Mom said being here without Dad was too painful, but she knew I'd feel differently. For me, it was just the opposite. Being here and recalling all the memories of when the three of us shared this place makes me happy."

Hearing how the loss of her parents affected her made Flipper appreciate his own parents even more. Colin and Lenora Holloway had always been their sons' staunch supporters. Their close and loving relationships had been the reason none of their sons had had any qualms about settling down and marrying. All the marriages had worked out, seemingly made in heaven, except for his brother Liam's.

When Bonnie had gotten pregnant, Liam had done the honorable thing by marrying her. Bonnie had always been a party girl and didn't intend to let marriage or being a mommy slow her down. While Liam was somewhere protecting his country as a Navy SEAL, Bonnie was conveniently forgetting she had a husband.

No one, not even Liam, had been surprised when he returned from an assignment one year and she asked for a divorce. Liam had given it to her without blinking an eye. Since then, Bonnie had remarried, which had introduced another set of issues for Liam. He was constantly taking Bonnie to court to enforce visitation rights to see his daughter because the man Bonnie married didn't like Liam coming around.

Flipper had no qualms about marriage himself, but he had too much going on right now. Namely, resisting the temptation of Swan while he continued his investigation. That was his biggest challenge. The more he was around Swan the more he liked her and the more he wanted to prove her innocence. It was hard staying objective.

"Here you are," she said, handing him a cold bottle of beer. "I figured you would like this instead of the wine."

He smiled. Like he had picked up on her drinking preferences, she had done the same with him. "Thanks. I've never been a wine man."

She chuckled. "Neither was my dad. That's how I knew when it was time for him to come home because Mom would have his favorite beer in the fridge."

He opened the bottle, took a sip and noticed her watching him. He licked his lips, liking the taste of the beer, which was the brand he'd chosen the other night at Summer Moon. When he took another sip and she continued to watch him, he lifted a brow. "Is anything wrong?"

She smiled. "No, nothing is wrong. I just love to watch how you drink your beer."

He chuckled. That was a first. No woman had ever told him that before. "And how do I drink it?"

"First there's the way your mouth fits on the beer bottle. I find it very sensuous."

He tried ignoring the quiver that surged through his veins at the tone in her voice. "Do you?"

"Yes. And then there's the way you drink it like you're enjoying every drop."

"I am."

"I can tell." Then, as if she thought perhaps she'd said too much, she took a step back. "I'll go get those crab balls for you to try."

When she turned to leave, he reached out and touched her arm. He couldn't help it. The air all but crackled with the sexual energy between them. "Come here a minute before you go," he said, setting his beer bottle aside. "Although I do enjoy drinking beer, I've discovered I enjoy feasting on your mouth even more."

And then he lowered his mouth to hers.

Perfect timing, Swan thought, because she needed this. She'd wanted it the moment he tilted his beer bottle to his mouth and she'd watched him do so. And now he was doing her. Showing her that he was enjoying her mouth more than he'd enjoyed the beer. Just like he'd said.

There was a certain precision and meticulousness in how he mastered the art of kissing. First, as soon as his tongue would enter her mouth, he would unerringly find her tongue, capture it with his own and begin gently sucking in a way that made the muscles between her legs tighten. Then he would do other things she didn't have a name for. Things that made desire flow through her like sweet wine, kindling heated pleasure and burning passion within her.

He rocked his thighs against her and she felt him pressed against her. His arousal was massive. Instinctively, she moved her hips closer, wanting to feel him right there, at the juncture of her thighs.

When he finally pulled his mouth away, she released

a deep, satisfied breath. Her mouth was still throbbing and there was an intense ache in her limbs. Right now, their heavy breathing was the only sound audible, and the laser-blue eyes staring down at her sent a tremor to her core.

She licked her lips when she took a step back. "Ready for a few crab balls?"

"Yes," he said, after licking his own lips. "For now."

Five

He wanted her.

Flipper knew he shouldn't, but he did. All through the delicious dinner Swan had prepared and while engaging in great conversation with her, the thought of just how much he wanted her simmered to the back of his mind. Now with dinner coming to an end, desire was inching back to the forefront. Images of her naked tried to dominate his mind, the thoughts made him shift in his chair to relieve the ache at his crotch.

"Ready for dessert, David? I made key lime pie."

Right now, another kind of dessert was still teasing his taste buds. "Yes, I would love a slice, and dinner was amazing by the way. You're a good cook. My mother would absolutely love you."

Too late, he wondered why he'd said such a thing. From the look on her face, she was wondering the same thing. So he decided to clean up his mess by adding, "She admires other women who can cook."

Swan smiled. "You don't have to do that, David."

"Do what?"

"Try to retract the implications of what you said so I won't get any ideas."

He *had* done that, but not for the reason she thought. He'd done so because it wasn't right for either of them to think something was seriously developing between them. More than likely, she would hate his guts when she learned why he was really in Key West, when she discovered she was his assignment and nothing more. He couldn't tell her the truth, but he could certainly set her straight on what the future held for them.

"And what ideas do you think I wanted to retract?"

"The ones where I would think we were starting something here, the ones that meant I would be someone you'd take home to meet your mother."

He sat down his glass of ice tea, which she had served with dinner. "Any reason why I wouldn't want to take you home to meet my mother *if* we shared that kind of a relationship, Swan?" Although he didn't think he needed to let her know—again—that they didn't share that kind of relationship, he did so anyway.

"Honestly, David, do I really have to answer that?"

"Yes, I think you do."

She stared at him for a minute. "I'm well aware when it comes to interracial relationships that not all families are accepting."

He chuckled. "My family isn't one of them, trust me. Interracial or international, we couldn't care less. My brother Brad met his wife, Sela, while working in Seoul, South Korea, and my brother Michael met Gardenia in Spain. Like I told you, my parents would accept anyone who makes us happy, regardless of race, creed, religion, nationality or color."

She didn't say anything to that. Then she broke eye contact with him to glance down into her glass of tea. Moments later, she raised her gaze back to him.

"My father's parents didn't. They threatened him with what they would do if he married Mom and they kept their word. They disowned him. Still, my mother reached out to them when Dad died to let them know he'd passed. They came to his funeral but had no qualms about letting Mom know they still would not accept her. They would only tolerate me since I was biracial. They even tried forcing Mom to let me go back with them. That's when my godfathers stepped in."

Flipper shook his head, feeling the pain she refused to acknowledge, the pain she'd obviously felt because of her grandparents' actions. But he'd heard it in her voice nonetheless.

"It's sad that some people can be such bigots. At the risk of this sounding like a cliché, some of my closest friends are black," he added, immediately thinking of Bane, Viper and Coop. Like her, Mac was of mixed heritage and had a white mother and black father.

"I'm sure some of your closest friends are, David."

He wondered if she believed him. One day, she would see the truth in his words. Then it suddenly occurred to him—no, she would not. There would be no reason for her to ever meet the four guys who were just as close to him as his biological brothers.

"I'll be back in a minute with the pie," she said. Then she stood and left the room.

Flipper watched her leave, feeling that he hadn't fully eradicated her doubts the way he'd wanted to do. That bothered him. He didn't want her to think he was one of those prejudiced asses who believed one race of people was better than another. What her grandparents had done to her father and mother, as well as to her, was unforgivable. Regardless of how she'd tried to come across as if their actions hadn't hurt her, as if they still didn't hurt her, he knew better.

She needed a hug right now.

He pushed back his chair and left the dining room to enter her kitchen. Instead of getting the pie like she'd said she would do, she was standing with her back to him, looking out the kitchen window at the ocean. And he could tell from the movement of her shoulders that she was crying.

"Swan?"

She quickly turned, swiping at her tears. "I'm sorry to take so long, I just had one of those miss-my-daddy-and-mommy moments."

He crossed the room to her, knowing that her tears were about more than that. He knew it and he intended for her to know he knew it. "Not wanting to get to know you—that was your grandparents' loss, Swan."

She gazed into his eyes and nodded. "I know, David, but their actions hurt Dad, although he never said it did. I knew. Mom knew, too. I think that's one of the reasons she loved him so much, because of all the sacrifices he'd made for her. That's why she did anything she could to make him happy so he would never regret choosing her. But it wasn't fair. He was a good man. Mom was a good woman. They deserved each other and should have been allowed to love freely and without restrictions, reservations or censure. It just wasn't fair, David."

And then she buried her face in his chest and cried in earnest. Wrapping his arms around her, he held her, leaning down to whisper in her ear that things would be all right. That her parents had had a special love, one she should be proud of, one the naysayers had envied.

Emotions Flipper hadn't counted on flowed through him as he continued to stroke her hair and whisper soothing words next to her ear. Inwardly, he screamed at the injustice of trying to keep someone from loving the person they truly wanted to love. It was something he'd never understood and figured he never would. And never would he accept such a way of thinking from anyone.

Swan knew she should pull out of David's arms, but found she couldn't do it. Being held by him felt good. His fingers, the ones that were stroking through the strands of her hair, seemed to electrify her scalp. They sent comforting sensations all through her—and something else as well. A need that he was stroking to fruition. As a result, instead of pulling out of his arms, she closed her eyes and enjoyed being held by him while inhaling his masculine scent.

She wasn't sure how long they stood there, but it didn't take long for her to notice his breathing had changed. But then so had hers. His touch had shifted from comforting to passionate. He was using the same strokes, but now the feelings within her were beginning to build to an insurmountable degree of desire.

Opening her eyes, she lifted her head to stare up at him. The minute she did, she caught her breath at the intense yearning she saw in his gaze. That yearning reached out to her, jolted her with a level of throbbing need she hadn't known existed. She'd heard of raw, make-you-lose-your-senses passion, but she had never experienced it for herself.

Until now.

"David…" She said his name as something burst to life in the pit of her stomach. It made a quivering sensation rise at the back of her neck. He implored her with his eyes to follow this passion, as if letting her know he understood what she was experiencing even if she didn't.

"Tell me what you want, Swan," he said in a deep voice while gently caressing the side of her face. "Tell me."

The intensity in his eyes was burning her, scorching her with the sexual hunger that was coming to life inside her. She wanted more than his erection pressing hard against the apex of her thighs. She wanted him on top of her. She wanted him to slide into her body and begin thrusting in and out. She needed to lose herself in more than just his arms.

Suddenly, she felt emboldened to tell him just what she wanted. "I want you, David. In my bed."

Flipper wanted to be in her bed as well. Lord knows he shouldn't want it, but he did. He would have to deal with the consequences later. He felt too tight and hot to try to fight the demands his body was making. Sweeping her into his arms, he quickly walked out of the kitchen and headed toward her bedroom.

"You think you know where you're going, David?"

He slowed his pace, remembering that she had no idea that he knew the layout of her home. Not only did he know where her bedroom was located, he knew the blueprint of the plumbing underneath her floor. He looked down and met her gaze, grateful she wasn't suspicious. "I figured you would stop me if I went in the wrong direction."

"Yes, I would have stopped you, but you're going the right way."

"Good." When he resumed his swift pace, it didn't take him long to reach her bedroom.

Swan had gotten next to him in a way he hadn't counted on happening. Seducing her had not been part of the plan and he should not have allowed things to get this far. He didn't want to think of the major complications involved, and not just because she was the goddaughter of three top naval officers.

But something was happening that he hadn't counted on. His mind and body were in sync and a rare sexual aura was overtaking him. He could no more stop making love to her than he could stop being a SEAL. For him to even make such a comparison was pretty damn serious.

Instead of placing Swan on the bed, he eased her to her feet, loving the feel of her soft body sliding down his hard one. "If you're having second thoughts about this, Swan, now's the time to say so."

She shook her head and then in a wobbly voice, she said, "No second thoughts, David."

Hearing her affirmation spoken with such certainty, Flipper released a low, throaty groan as he lowered his mouth to kiss her again, needing the connection of her lips to his as much as he needed to breathe. Wrapping his arms around her waist, he pulled her body closer to him as he deepened the kiss, wanting her to feel his erection, the hard evidence of his need for her.

He had never wanted a woman with this much intensity in his life, and he had no idea why Swan was having this kind of an effect on him.

Why she, and no other woman before her, had tempted him to cross a line during a mission. His mind didn't function that way. He had yet to prove her innocence, so technically, she was still naval intelligence's prime suspect, but at the moment that didn't matter. For all he knew, he could be about to sleep with the enemy.

But right now, that didn't matter either because deep down, a part of him believed she was innocent.

What was happening between them was definitely out of the realm of normal for him. He'd known he would have to get close to her, but he hadn't counted on this—his intense desire to do inappropriate, erotic and mind-blowing things to Swan Jamison.

But he wanted her and there would be no regrets. At least not for him, and based on what she'd just said, there would be no regrets for her either.

The moment he ended the kiss, his hands were busy removing her skirt, followed by her blouse, and when she stood in front of him in her lacy panties and bra, he couldn't help but growl his satisfaction. She looked sexy as hell and the rose-colored ensemble against the darkness of her skin was stunningly beautiful. *She* was beautiful.

He reached up and traced a finger along the material of her boxer-cut panties. This style on a woman had never done anything for him. Until now.

"You should have been a model," he said in a deep, throaty voice, filled with profound need and deep appreciation. She had such a gorgeously shaped body.

"My mother used to be a model. I was satisfied with being a model's daughter."

"And a strikingly beautiful one at that," he said, lowering to his knees to rid her of her panties. He couldn't wait to touch her, taste her and do all those erotic things to her he had dreamed of doing over the past few nights.

He breathed in deeply, getting more aroused by the second while easing her panties down a pair of long, beautiful legs.

After tossing her panties aside, he leaned back on his haunches and gazed at her, seeing her naked from the waist down. Her small waist, her stomach, the shape of her thighs and longs legs were perfect. She was perfect.

After looking his fill, he leaned forward and rested his forehead against her stomach, inhaling her luscious scent. He loved the way it flowed through his nostrils, opening his pores and causing his body to become even more erect.

And then he did something he'd wanted to do since their first kiss. He used the tip of his tongue to kiss her stomach, loving the indention around her naval and tracing a path around the area. Then he shifted his mouth lower, licking his way down and enjoying the sound of her moans.

When he came to the very essence of her, he licked around her womanly folds before leaning in to plant a heated kiss right there. It was as if sampling her special taste was as essential to him as breathing. His hands held firm to her thighs when he slid his tongue inside of her, loving the sound of his name from her lips.

Then he went deeper, using his tongue to taste her, claim her and brand her. The latter gave him pause but not enough to stop what he was doing. He'd never claimed a woman as his own and had never thought about doing so. But with Swan, it seemed such a thing wasn't just desired but was required.

And he didn't want it any other way. She was the first woman he wanted to claim. Forcefully, he pushed to the back of his mind what it could mean to make any woman his and decided he would dwell on that aspect of things at a later time. For now, he wanted to focus on the delicious, succulent, enjoyable taste that was Swan.

He took his time, wanting her to know just how much he loved doing this to her. He wanted her to feel the connection his tongue was making with her flesh. However, he wanted her to do more than feel it, he wanted this connection absorbed into her senses, into her mind, into every part of her body.

Moments later, Flipper knew he'd achieved his goal when he felt her fingers dig into his shoulder blades, followed by the quivering of her thighs. Tightening his hold on her hips, he knew what would be next and he was ready.

She screamed his name when she was thrown into an orgasmic state. Her fingernails dug deeper into his skin, but he didn't feel the pain because knowing he was giving her pleasure made him immune to it. What he felt was a desire to take things to the next level, to slide into her body and go so deep it would be impossible to detect where his body ended and hers began.

He finally pulled his mouth away and looked up at her, saw the glazed look in her eyes. Without saying a word, he traced his fingers around the womanly mound he'd just kissed before inserting his finger inside of her. She was ultra-wet and mega-hot and he had every intention of capitalizing on both. The orgasm she'd just experienced would be small in comparison to the one he intended to give her.

Pulling his finger from her, he licked it clean, knowing she was watching his every move. "Sweet," he said softly, holding her gaze.

He slowly eased to his feet and reached behind her to

remove her bra. When she stood totally naked in front of him, he feasted his gaze on her. "And I'm about to show you just how sweet I think you are, Swan."

Six

Swan was having difficulty breathing and the blue eyes staring at her made getting air to flow through her lungs even more difficult. Never had she felt this energized from a sexual act. And when David got to his feet and leaned in to kiss her, letting her taste herself on his lips, she felt weak in the knees. But he held her around the waist, holding her up as he kissed her more deeply, making her wish the kiss could last forever.

She released a low disappointed groan in her throat when he pulled his mouth away.

"Don't worry, there's more coming."

He swept her off her feet and carried her over to the bed, placed her on it and joined her there.

"You still have clothes on," she said, reaching out to touch his shirt.

"I know and they will be coming off. Right now, I just want to lie here with you and hold you in my arms."

She smiled at him. "You're not going to fall asleep on me, are you?"

Chuckling, he said, "Asleep? With you lying beside me without a stitch of clothes on? Sleep is the last thing I'd be able to do, trust me."

He'd already pleasured her with his mouth, so she couldn't help wondering what was next. She soon discovered his intent when he reached over and cupped her breasts.

"You are perfect," he said in a deep husky voice.

The words triggered a memory of overhearing her father whisper the same compliment to her mother, after she surprised him with a special dinner after he returned home from one of his missions.

Swan knew she was far from perfect. Those were just words David was speaking. But still, hearing them filled her with joy. Maybe she shouldn't let them, but they did.

Then any further thoughts dissolved from her mind when David eased a nipple between his lips. She moaned at the pleasure she felt all the way to her toes. Just when she thought she couldn't stand anymore, he began torturing her other nipple.

When he finally eased away, she opened her eyes to watch him undress. When he removed his shirt, she saw the tattoos covering his tanned skin on both of his upper arms—huge dolphins emerging from beautiful blue ocean waters. Another tattoo of even more dolphins was painted across his back in beautiful vivid colors. She'd never been into tattoos but she thought his were stunning.

"I like your tattoos," she said.

He glanced over at her and smiled. "Thanks."

When he lowered his shorts, her gaze moved to the area between a pair of masculine thighs. His shaft was massive and marvelously formed. Just the thought of him easing that part of himself inside of her sent her pulse skyrocketing.

"You okay?"

She lifted her gaze to his. She wasn't sure if she was okay. A thickness had settled in her throat when she saw how he was looking at her. Not only did he intend to join his body with hers, she had a feeling he planned to keep them connected for a while.

"Yes, I'm okay."

Swan continued to check him out, thinking he had a mighty fine physique. His body was all muscle and it was obvious that he worked out regularly. A man didn't get those kinds of abs if he didn't.

She watched as he pulled a condom from his wallet and sheathed himself in a way that was so erotic, she felt herself getting wetter between the legs just watching him. Then he was strolling back toward the bed. To her.

"I'm about to make sure you feel more than okay," he said, reaching down and easing her up to rest her chest against his. Her breasts were still sensitive from his mouth and rubbing them against his chest caused a multitude of arousing sensations to swamp her.

"What are you doing to me?" she asked in a ragged breath, barely able to get the words out.

"Anything you can imagine," he whispered, lowering her back on the mattress and then straddling her. He stared down at her as he gently moved her legs apart. She felt him, that part of him, lightly touch her feminine folds and then he was rubbing back and forth across them, sending even more sensations racing through her bloodstream.

"Trying to torture me, David?"

"No, trying to pleasure you. Ready for me?"

The movement of his manhood against her was making it impossible for her to concentrate. "What do you think?"

"You're wet and hot, so I think you're ready." And then he entered her in one deep thrust.

She gasped at the fullness and was glad he'd gone still for a minute. This gave her the chance to feel him fully embedded deep within her. It had been a long time for her and her inner muscles were greedily clamping on to him, tightening their hold.

"You're big," she whispered.

"You're tight," was his response. "But we're making this work."

And he did. First he began moving again, gently sliding in and out of her. That only lasted a few seconds before he picked up the pace and began thrusting harder.

She responded by wrapping her legs around his waist. Then he lifted her hips to receive more of him. When he established a slow and deep rhythm, touching areas in her body that hadn't been touched in a long time, or ever, she fought back a scream. She grabbed hold of his hair and pulled it, but he didn't seem to mind.

"Rule number one, Swan. Don't hold back."

Was he kidding? It wasn't a matter of holding back. It was more like she was trying to keep her sanity. David was so powerfully male that he was pushing her over the edge with every deep stroke. Every cell within her vibrated in response to his precise thrusts.

"Hold on, baby. Things are about to get wild."

Flipper had given Swan fair warning. When he began pounding harder, making strokes he'd never attempted with another woman—going deep, pulling out and then going deep again—he felt a quivering sensation start at the base of his testicles and move toward her womb with each and every thrust. He had to hold on tight to her to keep them on the bed. He was determined to show her wild.

Simultaneously, he leaned down to have his way with her mouth, licking it corner to corner and then inserting his tongue inside with the same rhythm he was using below.

What he was feeling right now was more than off the charts, it was out of the atmosphere. When she finally let go and screamed his name, the sound vibrated in every part of his body, especially in her inner muscles. They clamped down on him, trying to pull everything out of him while her hands tightened even more in his hair.

"David!"

She screamed his name again. The sound drove him. He wanted more of her. Wanted to go deeper. Throwing his head back, he felt the veins in his neck strain. There was pain but not enough to dim the pleasure.

And he knew at that moment Swan had gotten under his skin in a way no other woman had.

He began rocking hard into her with an intensity that made him go deeper with every thrust. Then he was the one hollering out in pleasure, saying her name as an explosion ripped through him. Then like a crazed sexual maniac, he leaned in to feast on her mouth and breasts. It was like his desire for her could not end.

"David!"

He knew she was coming again and, dammit to hell, so was he. Marveling at such a thing, he tightened his hold on her. His control had not only gotten shot to hell and back but had died an explosive death as the result of the most powerful orgasms he'd ever endured.

This was what real lovemaking was about. No holds barred. No restrictions. Every part of him felt alive, drained, renewed. The room had the scent of sex and more sex. But that wasn't all. Emotions he'd never felt before touched him and swelled his heart.

He quickly forced those emotions back, refusing to go there. Knowing he couldn't go there.

The husky sound of deep, even breathing made Swan open her eyes. She was still in bed with David. Their limbs were entangled and his head was resting on her chest as he slept.

This man had been the most giving of lovers. He didn't come until he made sure she came first. He had kissed every part of her body, some parts more than others, and he had stoked passion within her in a way that had made her reach the boiling point. No man had ever made love to her with such intensity.

He had warned her about them getting wild. As far as she was concerned, they had gotten more than wild, they had gotten uninhibited, untamed. She hadn't known she had so much passion within her. He had brought it out and made her do more than own it. He had made her so aware of it that she doubted she could undo what he'd done.

David Holloway had done more than push a few of her buttons. He had turned on all the lights.

That thought made her smile and pull him closer. Feeling exhausted, she closed her eyes and drifted into sleep.

Flipper slowly opened his eyes, taking in the sight and scent of the woman lying beside him, snuggled close to his body. He was so sexually contented, he could groan out loud. He didn't. Instead he tightened his arms around her.

Things had gotten wild. They had finally fallen asleep after four rounds of the most satisfying love-making possible.

While making love with Swan, he had discovered there was a vast difference in making love to her versus making love to other women. He'd known it before but she had made that point crystal clear tonight.

With other women, he'd usually had one goal in mind—seeking sexual pleasure and making sure she got hers. With Swan it had been about that, too, but it had also been about finding closeness. No other woman had made him want to stay inside her. It had only been the need to replace condoms that had forced him from Swan's side. And then he had been back inside her in a flash...like that was where he belonged. Hell, he was still thinking that way and the twitch in his aroused manhood was letting him know just what he desired.

Flipper was known to have a robust sexual appetite. When you lived your life on the edge, engaging in covert operations as his team did, then you needed a way to release.

Usually, unerringly, he found his release in some woman's bed. He made sure she knew it was one and done. Due to the nature of his occupation, he didn't have time for attachments or anything long-term. Some SEALs did; he didn't. He'd tried it once and it hadn't worked out. Now he preferred being a loner. It didn't bother him that he was the lone single guy among his close friends. To each his own.

So how could one night in Swan Jamison's bed have him thinking things he shouldn't be thinking, especially considering why he was in Key West in the first place?

It had everything to do with the woman he'd had mind-blowing sex with for the past four hours or so. Now he saw her as more than an assignment. Now she was also a woman who had the ability to match his sexual needs one-on-one, something he found invigorating and energizing on all levels. He was a totally physical male and Swan Jamison was wholly, utterly female. Almost to the point that she'd blown his ever-loving mind.

Now she was sleeping peacefully while he was lying here thinking, knowing his honor was being tested. As a military man, he always did what was honorable. On top of that, his mother had drilled into all five of her sons that honor was not just for their country but extended to humans just as much, especially women. Why had that thought settled deep into his mind now?

One reason might be that he'd read the report on her. He knew about those elderly people residing at the senior living complex that she visited on her weekends off and how she'd championed so hard for the homeless. She was working with the mayor to help find funding to build a housing complex for them.

She was a caring person. He'd witnessed her love for her country, for her father, that night at the fireworks and the more he was around her, the more he believed in her innocence.

She made a sound now and he glanced down and met beautiful brown eyes staring at him. Immediately his senses connected with those eyes. She trusted him. He could see it in the gaze staring back at him. Otherwise he would not be here in her bed.

What would she think when she learned the truth? Would she still trust him? He pushed the thought to the back of his mind.

She gave him a beautiful, sleepy smile that melted

his insides. Made him wish he had come here to the Keys for a real vacation, a much-needed one. He wished he had entered her shop with no ulterior motive but to do as he claimed, which was to buy his mother a birthday gift. He would still have tried his hand at seducing her, but things would have been different. Specifically, he wouldn't feel as if his honor was being compromised.

"You didn't try my key lime pie," she whispered.

"We can get up and eat some now if you want," he said.

"No, I like being just where I am. We can always eat some later...or even for breakfast."

He leaned down and brushed a kiss across her lips. "Um, breakfast sounds nice. Is that an invitation to stay the night?"

"Only if you want to."

He wanted to. And when he brushed another kiss across her lips, he slid his tongue inside her mouth to kiss her deeply and let her know how much he wanted to stay.

He knew at that moment that his commanding officer and the admiral weren't the only ones with a personal interest in Swan Jamison. He now had a personal interest in her as well.

Seven

The next morning, Swan woke up to bright sunlight flowing in through her window and a powerfully male body sleeping beside her.

Last night was rated right up there with *Ripley's Believe It or Not*. It had been just that spectacular. They'd made love a couple more times before getting up after midnight to eat the pie she'd prepared for dessert. After clearing off the table and loading the dishes into the dishwasher, he'd suggested they walk on the beach.

So at one in the morning, they had strolled hand in hand along the water's edge. It had been a beautiful night with a full moon in the sky. The breeze off the ocean had provided the perfect reason for him to pull her close while walking barefoot in the sand. He told her more about his family; namely about his parents' medical supply company.

Then at some point, they began talking about her

company and she found herself telling him just about everything about jewelry making. He was curious about her stones and complimented how beautiful they were and inquired how she was able to create so many pieces.

No man had ever taken an interest in her work before and she was excited that he thought what she did for a living was important. She had found herself explaining the day-to-day operations of Swan's. He couldn't believe how she found the time to handcraft a number of the items sold in her shop.

David also thought it was great that Rafe, through his connections with a huge distributor in California, was able to get some of Swan's more expensive stones at a lower cost and had even helped her save on shipping by including them in the packaging with his ink.

She glanced over at him now as he shifted in bed. He kept his arms wrapped around her while he slept. She studied his features and saw how relaxed he looked.

She drew in a deep breath, still amazed at the depth of what they had shared last night. It had been the most profound thing she'd ever experienced with a man. Making love with David had touched her in ways she hadn't thought possible. He had made her feel things she hadn't ever felt before and those things weren't just sexual in nature. While in his arms, she had felt safe and secure. Protected.

As far as she was concerned, what they'd shared last night was more compelling and meaningful than any other time she'd shared with a man, even more meaningful than the time she'd spent with William. She'd never really allowed herself to fully let go with William. Now she could admit to herself that she'd known in the back of her mind that something didn't add up with him.

Yet she'd been so desperate for companionship after

losing her mother that she had wanted to believe William was honest, even though he'd seemed too good to be true. She was glad Candy had become suspicious when he'd never wanted them to be photographed together or when he'd insisted that they spend the night at Swan's place instead of the hotel.

At the time, his requests hadn't bothered her because she hadn't wanted her employer or her coworkers to get in her business. But Candy had seen through all that and knew something in the milk wasn't clean, as she would often say. It had been Candy who'd unveiled her own husband's secret affair with a flight attendant. And once confronted, Don hadn't denied a thing. He'd said he was glad she'd found out because he wanted a divorce.

Pushing thoughts of Don's and William's betrayals to the back of her mind, Swan continued to study David. She couldn't help but recall the number of times he'd made her climax. Now that was simply amazing all by itself.

She was enjoying her time with him, even knowing it wouldn't last. Later this month, he would leave the island and she would probably not hear from him again. She knew that, accepted it. She had long ago learned to live for the now and not sweat the small stuff. Especially those things she couldn't change.

"You're awake."

She couldn't help but smile at the slumberous blue eyes staring at her. The dark shadow on his chin made him look even sexier. "Yes, I'm awake. I guess I should be a good host and prepare breakfast before you leave."

"Um, I've overstayed my welcome?"

"No, but today is Sunday and I have a lot to do."

"Maybe I can help you."

"You don't know what I'll be doing."

He reached out and pushed her hair back off her shoulders so he could completely see her face. "Then tell me."

She gazed into his eyes. "The shop is closed on Sundays and I use my day off to visit Golden Manor Senior Place. My mom used to do volunteer work there when we lived on the island years ago. I would go with her on Sundays to visit everyone. I guess you could say it's become a family tradition that I decided to continue."

"I think that's a wonderful thing you're doing. I'm sure the residents there appreciate it."

"Yes, they do, although those who knew my mom are no longer there. They've passed on. I'm establishing new relationships and friendships."

"Good for you. I'd love to join you."

"You would?" she asked, surprised.

"Yes, and don't worry about preparing breakfast. I'll go home and refresh and be back here within an hour. We can grab breakfast somewhere before heading over. Afterward, we can spend more time on the beach. I enjoyed the walk last night with you."

And she had enjoyed it, too. The thought that he wanted to spend more time with her made her feel really good inside. "Okay, that sounds wonderful."

"I'm glad you think so, and before I leave…"

"Yes?"

He leaned over to kiss her and she knew where things would lead from there. She looked forward to getting wild again with him.

Flipper clicked on his phone the minute he walked into his hotel room. He noted several missed calls since he'd deliberately cut off his phone last night. One was from the admiral, who was probably calling for an update. But first Flipper would return the call to Nick.

"Flipper, should I ask why I couldn't reach you last night?"

"No, you shouldn't," Flipper said, flopping down in the nearest chair.

"You have heard the saying that you shouldn't mix business with pleasure, right?"

Too late for that, Flipper thought, running a hand down his face. Instead of responding to Nick's comment, he said, "I hope you have something for me. There's another angle I want you to check out."

"Okay, and yes, I have something for you. I found out the initial investigation was handed off to a group of civilian investigators, which means naval intelligence didn't rank it at the top at first."

Flipper was very much aware of the part government bureaucracy played in certain investigations. If someone thought a case should be under naval intelligence's radar, then they made sure it got there. "Why?"

"Not sure yet, but first, let's talk about Jamila Fairchild."

Flipper leaned forward in his chair. "Okay, let's talk about her. What do you have?"

"Not what you obviously think. What she told Swan was the truth. She does have a huge family who lives in the north."

Flipper raised a brow. "Then who made the error in the report from naval intelligence?"

"Don't know, but it's worth checking out, although I don't think it's anything suspicious on Ms. Fairchild's end. Especially when I tell you who her family is."

"And who is her family?"

"Her mother's brother is Swan's grandfather."

A frown covered Flipper's face. "The grandfather who disowned Swan's father?"

"Yes, from what I've gathered. But I can find no record of her grandfather ever reaching out to her."

"Interesting."

"Yes, it is. I take it Swan Jamison doesn't know about the family connection."

"No, she doesn't." Flipper decided not to try to wrap his head around this bit of news just yet. Instead he asked, "What about Rafe Duggers?"

"Personally, I think something is going on with him."

Flipper lifted a brow. "What?"

"First of all, certain aspects of his info are sealed."

"Sealed?"

"Yes. I would think if naval intelligence was checking into something related to Swan and her story, they would see that sealed record for her tenant as a red flag. For them not to have flagged it raises my own suspicions about a few things."

That raised Flipper's suspicions as well. Was Rafe a double agent? Someone working undercover? Was someone in naval intelligence deliberately setting Swan up as the traitor? If so, why?

"You weren't able to find out anything about him?"

There was a husky chuckle. "I didn't say that. There are ways to find out anything you want when you know how to do it."

And Nick knew how to do it. He'd been an amazing SEAL, but as far as Flipper was concerned, Nick's natural investigative talents were better served at Homeland Security. "When will you let me know something?"

"Give me a couple of days. In the meantime, don't say anything to anyone about my suspicions about Duggers."

"Not even the CO and admiral?"

"Not even them for now. You mentioned Swan had a third godfather who was someone high up at naval intelligence. Was his identity revealed to you?"

"No, it wasn't but then I didn't ask," Flipper said.

"It wasn't hard to find out," Nick replied. "All you have to do is find out who Andrew Jamison's SEAL teammates were at the time he died and do a little research to determine where they are now."

"I take it you've done that."

"Yes, and would you believe Swan Jamison's third godfather is Director of Naval Intelligence Samuel Levart?"

Flipper would not have considered Director Levart in a million years, but it all made sense now. In order for someone to have delayed making formal charges against Swan, that person would have to be someone in power. The admiral had alluded to as much. "Swan doesn't know how favored she is to have three powerful men in her corner."

"Yes, but we both know it wouldn't matter if one of her godfathers was the President. If naval intelligence believes they have enough evidence to prosecute her, they will," Nick said.

Flipper knew that to be true. Now more than ever he had to find the person intent on framing Swan. To him, it was beginning to look like an inside job.

"So what else do you have for me to check out?" Nick asked, reclaiming Flipper's attention.

"It's about something Swan told me." He then shared with Nick the information about Rafe Duggers's association with some huge distributor in California. "I need you to check that out."

"I will. I know time is of the essence so I'll get back to you soon, Flipper."

"Thanks, I appreciate it."

"If you're so concerned about me, then why not return to the Keys and keep an eye on me, Candy?" Swan asked. She moved around her bedroom getting dressed while talking to her friend on speakerphone.

"You know why I won't return, just yet. But I did hear something that's interesting."

"What?" Swan asked as she shimmied into her skirt.

"I talked to Francola the other day and she said Marshall mentioned to her that Don is thinking about moving away from the island."

Swan paused. Francola and her husband, Marshall, had been close friends of Don and Candy's while they were married. The two couples often did things together. Personally, Swan didn't care much for Francola because the woman had been aware Don was cheating on Candy but hadn't told her friend. "I would take anything Francola says with a grain of salt these days," Swan said as she continued dressing.

"I know you still fault her for not telling me about Don and I admit I was angry with her, too, but now I understand her not doing so."

"Do you?"

"Yes. Her relationship with me is not like our relationship, Swan. You and I have been best friends since grade school and we have no secrets. You would have told me about Don had you suspected anything."

"Darn right."

"Well, Francola and I didn't have that kind of relationship. We only met through our husbands, who worked together. Besides, I'm not sure I would have believed her even had she told me. I would have been in denial." Candy paused. "Now, enough about me. Tell me more about this David Holloway."

Swan smiled while putting hoop earrings into her ears. "He's a real nice guy. Thoughtful. Considerate. Handsome as sin." She glanced over at her made-up bed. Although there were no signs of anyone sleeping in it last night, it didn't take much for her to remember all the wild action she and David had shared under the sheets. "And he's great in bed. More than great. He's fantastic."

"Just be careful, Swan. Protect your heart."

Swan slipped her feet into her sandals. "My heart? It's not like I'm falling for the guy, Candy."

"Aren't you? I can hear it in your voice. You like him a lot."

Yes, she did like him a lot. "It won't go beyond me liking him," she said, trying to convince herself of that more so than Candy.

"Can you honestly say that?"

"Yes, because I can't let it. His work brought him to the island and he'll be leaving soon. In less than thirty days."

"Doesn't matter."

Swan knew for her it *did* matter. She only wanted short-term. The last thing she wanted was to do long-term with any man.

Eight

"I enjoyed my time with you today, Swan," Flipper said, looking down at her.

They'd had brunch at Summer Moon before heading to the senior living complex where they spent the next four hours. She assisted the staff by reading to groups of people and even taking a few of the seniors for walks around the complex. Some, she'd explained, had family who rarely visited so she had become like their surrogate granddaughter.

On the flip side, considering what she'd missed out having in her life, he couldn't help but wonder if they had become her surrogate grandparents.

From the moment she walked into the facility, everyone brightened up when they saw her. It was amazing to him. She knew just what to say to elicit a smile or to get them to engage in more conversation. The majority of the seniors knew her by name and he couldn't help noticing a number of the women wearing what looked like necklaces she'd made.

When he inquired about the necklaces Swan confirmed they were her designs but she had taught the women to make them from stones she'd given them. It had taken longer than normal since a lot of the older women's hands weren't as nimble as they used to be.

After leaving the nursing home, they'd grabbed lunch at a sidewalk café before returning to her house where they'd spent the rest of the day on the beach. Later, after ordering takeout for dinner from Arness, they were back at her place.

No matter how tempting Swan was making it for him to stay longer at her place, he would leave when it got dark. The information about Rafe Duggers's sealed records bothered him and he'd decided to poke around in the tattoo parlor later that night to see what he could find.

He glanced over at Swan as she sat across the table from him eating dinner. Earlier today, when he had returned to take her to breakfast, she had opened the door looking fresh and perky and dressed simply in a pair of shorts and a tank top. Seeing her dressed that way reminded him of just what a gorgeous pair of legs she had, as well as how those same legs had wrapped around him while they'd made love that morning and the night before.

When they had gone swimming, she'd worn one of the sexiest two-piece bathing suits he'd ever seen. He had totally and completely enjoyed his day with her. They would be attending the Memorial Day festivities together tomorrow in town, which included a parade.

Because he needed some investigative time, he'd

come up with an excuse for why he couldn't see her a couple of days this week. Time was moving quickly and he had yet to find anything to clear her of wrongdoing.

Because of Nick's warning, Flipper hadn't told Admiral Martin everything when he'd called him back yesterday. Namely, he'd left out the discrepancies between what Nick had found out and the actual reports from naval intelligence. Until Flipper discovered what was going on, he would follow Nick's advice and keep that information to himself for now.

"Although I won't be seeing you for a few days because of work, will you still be on the island?" Swan asked.

It was hard not to be totally truthful about why she wouldn't be seeing him. She was the last person he wanted to be dishonest with but he had no choice. His goal had always been to prove her innocence and now that was doubly true. He would check out the tattoo shop tonight and look around in both Rafe's and Jamila's homes this week while they were here at work. Although it had been established that Jamila was Swan's relative, as far as Flipper was concerned, she was still a suspect.

"Yes, I'll still be on the island but I have to concentrate on this project I was sent here to do." No need to tell her that the project involved her.

"I understand how things are when work calls."

He reached up and caressed the side of her face. "We still have a date for the parade tomorrow, right?"

"Yes."

"What about dinner on Friday evening?" he asked her.

Her smile touched something deep within him. "I'd love that, David."

"Good. I'll swing by your shop at closing time Friday and we can go to dinner directly from there. You pick the place."

"All right."

"What time do you want me to come get you for the parade tomorrow?"

"It starts at ten in the morning and we need to get there early to get a good spot. How about if I prepare pancakes for us in the morning around eight?"

"You sure? I wouldn't want you to go to any trouble."

She waved off his words. "No problem. I told you I enjoy cooking."

After they finished dinner, he told her he needed to leave to read some reports for work, which wasn't a lie. She walked him to the door. He leaned down to kiss her, intending for it to be a light touch of their lips.

But the moment his mouth touched hers and she released a breathless sigh, it seemed the most natural thing to slide his tongue inside her mouth and deepen the kiss. Wrapping his arms around her waist, he pulled her tight against him and knew the exact moment the kiss had changed to something more.

It was no longer a *goodbye and I'll see you later* kiss. Instead it was one of those *I need to have you before I go* kind. And Swan seemed to be reciprocating those feelings as she returned the kiss with equal fervor.

The next thing Flipper knew, he was sweeping her off her feet and moving quickly toward her bedroom. When he placed her on the bed, they began stripping off their clothes.

For him, she'd become an itch he couldn't scratch and a craving that wouldn't go away. There was something about making love to her that made every part of his body ache with need. She had imprinted herself on his soul and in every bone in his body and there was nothing he could do about it but savor what they had for as long as he could.

When she was completely naked, his pulse kicked up a notch and his breathing was forced from his lungs when he looked at her. She was beautiful and perfectly made.

He pulled a condom from his wallet in the shorts she'd helped him remove and toss aside. Knowing she was watching his every move, he rolled it over his aroused manhood.

"I want to do that for you the next time."

He looked at Swan. "All right." So she was letting him know she intended there to be a next time for them. He was glad because he wanted a next time, too.

There was a big chance when she found out the truth about why he was here on the island that she wouldn't want to have anything to do with him again. But he forced the thought from his mind.

"You don't have all evening, you know," she teased.

She was right, he didn't and it was a good thing she didn't know why. He moved toward her. "Impatient?"

She smiled up at him. "Yes, you could say that."

"In that case, I can help you with that problem." He leaned in. "I've got to taste you again," was all he said just seconds before his mouth came down on hers.

Swan automatically lifted her arms around his neck the moment his lips touched hers.

Capturing her tongue, David drew it into his mouth. Blood rushed fast and furious to Swan's head, making her feel both light-headed and dazed as his tongue began mating with hers. His technique was rousing her passion to a level that electrified every part of her. Insistent need rushed up her spine, spinning her senses and mesmerizing her with his delectable taste.

He suddenly broke off the kiss and they both panted furiously, drawing deep gulps of air into their lungs.

She rested her head against his chest and inhaled his scent as she continued to catch her breath. She knew she was losing herself to passion again when she felt the hardness of his erection brushing against her thigh, energizing the area between her legs.

Then she heard him whispering erotic details of what he wanted to do to her. His words spread fire through her body and when he gently cupped the area between her legs, she moaned.

"You're torturing me, David," she said, before twisting to push him down on his back so she could straddle him. Before he could react, she lowered her head between his masculine thighs and eased his erection into her mouth.

"Ah, Swan," he growled huskily, gripping her hair. She was fully aware of him expanding and felt a sense of triumph in her ability to get him even more aroused than he already was. The feel of his hands locked in her hair sparked even more passion within her and motivated her to use her mouth in ways she'd never done before.

"Swan!"

She felt his thighs flex beneath her hands before he bucked forward. She wasn't prepared when he quickly switched their positions so that she was the one on her back. The blue eyes staring down at her flared with a passion that sent tremors through her.

Before she could whisper his name, he slid inside

her. He kept going deeper and deeper, stretching her in ways she didn't know she could be spread, inch by inch.

"Wrap your legs around me, baby," he whispered in a throaty voice.

When she did as he asked, he began thrusting hard. It was as if his total concentration was on her, intent on giving her pleasure. She felt every inch of him as he rode her hard, not letting up.

"David!"

She screamed his name as he continued to make love to her, throwing her into a euphoric state that seemed endless. He was using her legs to keep their bodies locked while relentlessly pounding into her. Her world was spinning and she couldn't control the need to moan, moan and moan some more.

She was unable to hold anything back when her body erupted into an orgasm so powerful it propelled her toward utter completeness. She screamed his name once again as a deep feeling of ecstasy ripped through her entire body.

Flipper eased off Swan to lie beside her. Pulling her into his arms, his nostrils flared as he inhaled the scent of sex. The scent of woman, this woman. A woman he still desired even now.

He was not new to lust. Been there, done that and he figured he would be doing it some more. A lot more. With Swan lying in in his arms, snuggled close to him, close to his heart, he knew something had changed between them.

Bottom line, Swan Jamison was not only intoxicating, she was addictive.

"I don't think I'll be able to move again, David."

A smile touched the corners of his lips. He definitely

knew how she felt, but he knew he had to move. He had somewhere to be tonight and as sexually drained as he was, he intended to be there.

"Then don't move. Just lie there. I'll let myself out," he said, reluctant to go, although he knew he must.

"You sure?" she asked in a lethargic voice.

"Positive. I'll be back in the morning for the parade and then we have a date on Friday."

"Yes. I'm going to need it. I'll be working late Wednesday doing inventory. I probably won't leave work until around ten."

"With your worker's help?"

"No. The cruise ship comes in Wednesday."

He released her to ease out of bed and put on his clothes. "What does a cruise ship have to do with anything?" He could feel her gaze on his body. He couldn't disguise the impact of knowing she was watching him. He was getting aroused all over again.

"Jamila dates a guy who works on the cruise ship and they only see each other whenever the ship comes to port. She always requests the day off to spend with him. I guess they made up."

He had planned to check out Jamila's house when he'd assumed she would be at work. Good thing he now knew otherwise.

"Made up?" he asked, pulling his shirt over his head.

"Yes. I got the impression they weren't on good terms last week. Not sure what happened but it's all good now since they've apparently kissed and made up."

He nodded. "How long have they been together?"

"About six months now."

Flipper didn't say anything as he continued dressing. There hadn't been any mention of a boyfriend for

Jamila Fairchild in the report he'd read. Another discrepancy. There were too many inconsistencies for his liking and he was determined to find out why. One thing was certain, he didn't like the idea of Swan being at her shop alone late at night.

He moved back to the bed, leaned down and brushed a kiss across her lips. "I'll see you in the morning."

"Looking forward to it."

He smiled down at her and then turned and left.

Later that night, Flipper, dressed all in black, moved in the shadows, careful to avoid streetlights and security cameras. He had scoped out the area and was familiar with where the cameras were located. More than once, he'd had to dart behind a shrub when people were out for a late-night stroll.

He reached the area where Swan's shop was located and when he heard voices, he darted behind a building to hide in the shadows.

Two men stood not far away. One of them was Rafe. Neither of the men saw Flipper. The other guy was a little taller and appeared to be a foreigner. Their conversation sounded like an argument and was in a language Flipper wasn't familiar with and he spoke four. Most SEALs spoke at least that many, except for Coop, who had mastered seven.

When the men lapsed into English, they lowered their voices and could barely be heard. Flipper did make out the words *ink* and *roses*. Was someone getting a tattoo of roses painted on their body? If so, did it mean anything?

Flipper was glad when the men finally moved on. More than ever, he was determined to check out the tattoo parlor. He waited a half hour to make sure the men didn't return. When he was certain they had gone, he went to work bypassing the security alarms and cameras.

Using a sort of skeleton key, he opened the back door and walked inside the tattoo parlor. Using night goggles, he glanced around.

The place looked like a typical tattoo parlor. He should know since he and his brothers had frequented a number of them. He was proud of the images on his body. Luckily, Swan hadn't asked him about them. He was glad because the last thing he wanted to do was lie about why he was into dolphins.

Pulling off the camera attached to his utility belt, he replaced the night goggles with a high-tech camera, which was his own creation. This particular piece of equipment detected objects underground and under water. Looking through the lens, he scanned the room. It wasn't long before the camera light began blinking.

He moved toward the area and aimed the camera lower, toward the floor, and the blinking increased. Evidently something was buried beneath the wooden floor, a portion covered by a rug. The architectural report he'd been given of Swan's shop had not exposed any secret rooms or closets.

Putting the camera aside, he moved the rug and felt around to find a latch. He opened the trapdoor to find a small compartment beneath the floor. He saw more containers of ink. Why? There was a supply case full of ink on the opposite side of the room. Why was this ink hidden?

The first thing he noticed was the difference in the labeling. Was there something different about this particular ink? There was only one way to find out, he thought, taking one out of the cubby. He would overnight one of the containers to Nick instead of naval intelligence.

At this stage of the game, he wasn't taking any chances about who could be trusted.

Nine

Swan had just finished the last of her inventory when she heard the knock on her shop's door. Crossing the room, she peeped through the blinds to see who it was. A smile touched her lips as she unlocked the door. "David, I didn't think I'd see you until Friday."

He glanced around her empty shop before looking back at her. "I finished work early and remembered you saying you were working late tonight doing inventory. I wanted to make sure you got home okay."

That was really nice of him. "You didn't have to do that." But she was glad he had. They had spent Monday together celebrating Memorial Day. He had arrived at her place for breakfast and then they'd walked to where the start of the parade would take place.

After the parade, they'd gone to the island festival marketplace where various vendors had lined the streets with booths and a huge Ferris wheel. They had taken one of the boat rides around the islands and had ended up eating lunch on Key Largo.

She had thought about him a lot since Monday, remembering in explicit detail how he'd made love to her before leaving.

"I know you said Jamila would be off today," David said. "What about your tattoo guy? Is the parlor closed on Wednesdays as well?"

"Yes, but Rafe dropped by earlier. He was expecting a shipment of more ink to come in today but it didn't. He wasn't happy about that."

"He wasn't?"

"No. He said there was a particular shade of blue he was expecting."

Flipper nodded and checked his watch. "Ready to go?"

"Yes, I just need to grab my purse from my office." She was about to turn to get it when there was another knock at the door.

"Expecting anyone?" David asked her.

"No. I'll see who it is."

She walked to the door and David went with her. After glancing out of the blinds, she turned back to David and smiled. "It's Jamila and Horacio."

She unlocked the door. "Jamila, hi."

"Hey, Swan. Horacio and I were in the neighborhood and I remembered you would be here late. I thought we'd drop by to say hello."

Swan smiled at the man with Jamila. "Horacio, it's good seeing you again."

"Same here, Swan," he said in a heavy accent that Swan always loved hearing.

"And this is my friend David Holloway. David, you

already know Jamila. This is her friend Horacio Jacinto," Swan said, making introductions.

The two men shook hands. Swan wondered if she'd imagined it but she thought David had tensed up when he'd seen Jamila and Horacio. "Nice meeting you, Horacio," David said. "I can't place your accent. Where are you from?"

"Portugal."

"Nice country," David said.

"Thanks."

"I hope you'll leave before it gets too late, Swan," Jamila was saying.

"I will. David came to make sure I got home okay." Usually whenever she worked late, either doing inventory or making her jewelry, she would catch a cab home even though she lived only a few blocks away. But since David was here, she would suggest they walk. It was a nice night and she would love to spend more time with him.

"We'll see you guys later," Jamila said. "We had dinner at Marty's Diner and now we're going to Summer Moon for drinks and live music."

"Okay. Enjoy. And I hope to see you again the next time the ship ports, Horacio," Swan said.

Horacio smiled. "I hope to see you as well."

After they left, Swan went to her office to get her purse. She returned and noticed David was standing in the same spot where she'd left him, staring at the door. "Are you all right?"

He turned to her. "Yes, it's just that Horacio looks familiar and I was trying to remember when I might've seen him. Maybe I've run into him before, here on the island."

She nodded. "That's possible. He's a chef on the Century Cruise Line that docks here once a week. Whenever it does, he comes ashore and meets up with Jamila. I think I mentioned that to you."

"You did, but I could have sworn I saw him a few nights ago. Sunday. After leaving your place."

Swan shook her head. "It wasn't him. The ship didn't arrive in our port until today. But you know what they say about everybody having a twin."

He chuckled. "You're probably right, but I'm sure you don't have one. I'm convinced there's not another woman anywhere who is as beautiful as you."

Swan knew better than to let such compliments go to her head, but she couldn't help the smile that spread across her lips. "You, David Holloway, can make a girl's head swell if she's inclined to believe whatever you say."

"I hope you do believe it because I spoke the truth." He took her hand in his as they headed for the door.

Flipper pulled out his phone the minute he walked into his hotel room later that night. He'd felt it vibrate in his pocket when he was walking Swan home but figured it would be a call he needed to take in private.

Swan had invited him inside but he'd declined, telling her he had a ton of paperwork waiting on him back at his hotel. That wasn't a lie. He'd begun rereading all those naval intelligence reports to see if he could determine why those investigators had failed to do their job and instead intentionally went after Swan as a scapegoat.

He checked his phone and saw Nick had called and Flipper quickly returned the call. "What do you have for me?"

"More than you counted on. All I can say is whoever handled that investigation did a botched-up job."

Or they did the job they'd been expected to do, Flipper thought. "I guess there's a reason you feel that way."

"Yes. That ink you sent to be analyzed isn't what it's supposed to be."

"It's not ink?"

"Yes, it's ink, but coded ink. When applied to the skin as a tattoo, it can be decoded by a special light. It's my guess that's how the classified information is leaving Swan Jamison's shop—with people's tattoos and not with any of her jewelry. Guess where the ink is being shipped from."

"Swan mentioned from some place in California."

"Yes, that's right and the distribution company is a few miles from the naval base in San Diego. That means someone on the base must be passing classified information that's being shipped in the ink."

Flipper frowned. "And because Rafe Duggers is conveniently including Swan's stones with each shipment, it makes sense for her to be suspect."

"Right," Nick agreed. "Someone is setting her up real good, Flipper. They are definitely making her the fall guy."

Flipper wondered who in naval intelligence had targeted Swan and why. "I have another piece of the puzzle I need you to check out."

"What?"

"The guy who was with Rafe Duggers two nights ago. The one I told you he was arguing with. I saw him today."

"You did?"

"Yes. He came into the shop when Swan was closing up. His name is Horacio Jacinto and he's Jamila Fairchild's boyfriend."

"That's interesting. I'll find out what I can about

him," Nick said. "I wonder if Ms. Fairchild knows what's going on or if she's being used as a pawn."

"I don't know, but I'm going to make sure I keep an eye on all of them."

"Be careful, Flipper."

"I will."

A few hours later, after taking a shower, Flipper was sitting at the desk in his hotel room suite when his cell phone went off. Recognizing the ringtone, he clicked on and said, "What's going on, Coop?"

"You tell us."

Us meant Bane, Viper and Mac were also on the phone. "I guess Nick called you guys."

"Yes, he called us earlier today," Bane said. "What's going on with Swan Jamison sounds pretty damn serious. Don't you think it's time to call the CO?"

Flipper ran a hand down his face. He glanced at the clock on the wall. It was close to three in the morning. "If Nick told you everything, then you know it's an inside job at the base. There's a traitor somewhere and until I know who I can trust, then—"

"You know as well as we do that you can trust our CO, Flipper," Viper said. "Once you tell Shields what you've found out, if he suspects Martin or Levart of any wrongdoing, he will know what to do."

"Yes, however, the three of them share a close friendship. What if the CO is blinded due to loyalty?"

"We're talking about our commanding officer, Flipper. Shields would turn his own mother in if he thought she was betraying our country. You know that."

Yes, he knew it. But still… "I don't know if Martin or Levart is really involved. Like Shields, they are Swan's godfathers and I would hate to think they are shady. I just know it's an inside job and right now I'm suspicious of just about everybody."

"We figured you would be, so open the damn door," Mac said.

Flipper frowned. "What?"

"We said open the door," Coop said, knocking.

Flipper heard the knock, clicked off his phone, quickly went to the door and snatched it open. There stood his four best friends.

"What are you guys doing here?"

"What does it look like?" Mac asked as the four moved passed Flipper to enter the hotel room.

"We figured ten pairs of eyes were better than two," Bane said, glancing around. "Besides, we need to keep you objective."

"But what about your families? Viper, your wife is having a baby!"

Viper chuckled. "And I plan to be there when she does. According to Layla's doctor, we still have a couple of months, so I'm good."

"And our families are good, too," Coop said. "They know we look out for each other and they agreed we should be here for you."

"Teri is glad I'm gone," Mac said, grumbling. "Maybe when I go back, she'll have a new attitude."

"Or maybe you'll have one," Bane said, frowning at Mac.

"Whatever," Mac said, picking up the hotel's restaurant menu book. "Is it too late for room service?"

Flipper closed the door and drew in a deep breath as he watched the men gather around the table, already rolling up their sleeves, ready to help him figure things out. They worked together as a team and he would admit that whenever they did so, good things happened.

"There's something all of you should know," he said, getting their attention.

They glanced over at him. "What? No room service at this hour?" Mac asked in a serious tone.

"That, too."

"What's the other thing we should know, Flipper?" Viper asked, sitting back in the chair he'd claimed as soon as he came in.

Flipper leaned against the closed door. "Investigating Swan Jamison is no longer just an assignment for me. It's become personal."

The men nodded. "And you think we don't know that, Flipper?" Coop asked in a steely tone. "That's why we're here. Someone is trying to frame your woman and we're going to help you find out who and why. But first things first. You know what you have to do, right?"

Flipper stared at the four men. Yes, he knew. Instead of answering Coop, he picked up his cell phone from the table and placed a call to his CO.

Ten

As far as Swan was concerned, Friday hadn't arrived fast enough. With every passing hour, she would glance at her shop's door expecting to see David walk in. One would think his surprise visit Wednesday would have sufficed. Unfortunately, it hadn't.

She'd had two days to think about how irrational her thoughts about David were becoming. He didn't come across as a forever sort of guy and she wasn't looking for a forever kind of relationship, so what was up with this urgency to see him?

The only reason she could give herself was that she'd been alone and without a man's attention for so long that now that she had it, she was in greedy mode, lapping it up like a desperate woman. And she had never done the desperate thing before.

The door chimed and she looked up to see that it was Rafe who walked in. Lately she'd noticed him using the front door a lot more, instead of the back door to his parlor. They had decided at the beginning of his lease that the entrance to her shop was off-limits so his customers wouldn't trounce back and forth through her shop on the days Rafe worked late.

"Did your box of ink finally arrive?"

He stopped and looked over at her. "Why would you be asking about my ink?"

Now that, she thought, was a silly question. Did the man have a short memory? "Because you came by Wednesday looking for the shipment and left in a tiff when it hadn't arrived."

"I wasn't in a tiff and yes, I did get my box of ink."

Yes, he had been in a tiff, but if he wouldn't acknowledge it, then she would leave it alone. "Good. I'm glad you got it."

She watched him walk off toward his parlor. He hadn't been in a good mood lately. But then, maybe she'd been in such an extremely good mood that she had a distorted view. In fact, come to think of it, it was pretty normal for him to be moody.

Moments later, while she worked with a customer, Swan watched as Rafe walked back through her shop and toward the front door. She decided if he did that again she would remind him of their agreement about which door he should use whenever he went in or out of his tattoo parlor.

After her customer left, she glanced at her watch. Her shop would be closing in a couple of minutes. David usually arrived early. It would be understandable if he'd gotten detained, but she hoped he hadn't been. She was so anxious to see him.

The thought of how much she was looking forward to being with him should bother her, but for some reason it didn't. Like she'd told Candy, Swan wasn't expect-

ing anything from her relationship with David. There
had been no promises made, so none would be broken.
The only thing she was expecting was exactly what she
was getting—a good time. He was excellent company
and great in bed.

It had been almost three years since William, and
during that time, although she'd dated, she hadn't allowed herself to get serious over a man. Instead she
had concentrated on opening her shop and making it
a success.

She had put her mind, heart and soul into Swan's.
Especially her heart, deciding that if she put it into her
business, she wouldn't run the risk of placing it else-
where. Now it seemed there might be a risk after all and
that risk had a name. David Holloway.

A part of her wanted to protect herself from another
possible heartbreak by calling David and canceling any
plans for tonight and then to stop sharing any time with
him after that. He had given her his number so she could
reach him. She could certainly come up with a plausible
excuse. But did she really want to do that?

No, she didn't.

David would be her test. If she could handle a casual affair with him, then she would ace the test with
flying colors.

The door chimed and she glanced up and there
he was. She watched him lock her door and put the
Closed sign in place before pulling down the blinds.
Then he slowly sauntered toward her wearing a pair
of khaki pants and an open white shirt and holding
her within the scope of those laser-blue eyes. There
was his too-sexy walk and a smile that made her heart
beat rapidly.

Suddenly seeing him, when she'd been thinking of

him all day, took complete control of her senses. Without much effort, the man had turned the sensuality up more than a notch. He had his own barometer of hotness.

Finally moving her feet, she strolled across the floor to meet him halfway and walked straight into his arms. The moment he pressed his body to hers, she reached up and looped her arms around his neck. He responded by wrapping his arms around her waist, drawing her even closer so she fit against him.

"I missed you, Swan."

She shouldn't let his words affect her, but they did—to the point where she was having difficulty replying.

"I missed you, too."

And she had, although they'd seen each other Wednesday. Even when she'd tried to convince herself that missing him to such a degree meant nothing. Now, as she stood wrapped in his arms, with her body pressed tight against his, hip to hip and thigh to thigh, she knew it meant everything.

"That's good to know, sweetheart," he said in a throaty voice.

Sweetheart? The endearment left her defenseless. She was trying to summon all her senses to regroup. And it wasn't helping matters that his arousal was cradled in the apex of her thighs. Good Lord, he felt so good there.

"Ready?" she found the voice to ask him.

His gaze studied her face as if he was seeing her for the first time. As if he was trying to record her features to memory. And then a mischievous smile touched his lips. "I'm ready for whatever you have in mind, Swan."

Shivers of desire skittered down her spine and Swan

wished his words hadn't given her ideas, but they had. Ideas that were so bold, brazen and shameless she felt her cheeks staining just thinking about them. But at that moment, she didn't care. She could and would admit to wanting him.

She should wait until later to act on her desires. That would be the safe thing to do. But she knew she would be tortured during dinner whenever she looked at him. The way his mouth moved when he ate, or the way his hands—those hands that could turn her on just by looking at them—gripped his beer bottle. There were so many things about David Holloway that would do her in if she were to wait until later.

"You sure about that, David?"

"Positive. Do you want me to prove it?"

Did she? Yes, she did. "Where?"

"I will prove it anywhere you want. Right here in the middle of the floor if you like," he said. "But I suggest your office."

Flipper could tell by the way she was looking at him that she was giving his offer serious thought. He had no problems tilting the scale in his favor and he decided to do so. Lowering his head, he kissed her, trying to be gentle and finding gentleness hard to achieve. Especially when her taste made him greedy for more.

He knew she'd ceased thinking when she responded to his kiss by sinking her body farther into his embrace and tightening her arms around his neck.

Some things, he decided then and there, were just too mind-blowingly good, and kissing Swan was one of them. What they'd shared these last few days was a dimension of pleasure he hadn't felt in a long time—or maybe ever—while devouring a woman's mouth. And when his hands shifted from around her waist to cup her backside, he groaned at the feel of her body pressed tightly against his erection.

When he finally broke off the kiss, he buried his face in the curve of her neck and drew in a deep breath. This woman was almost too much. She looked good, tasted good and as he drew in another deep breath, he concluded that she smelled good, too.

"You want to come with me, Mr. Holloway?" she asked, stepping out of his arms.

"Yes." The answer was quick off his lips.

She took his hand. "Then follow me."

He had no problem following her and the minute he crossed the threshold into her office, he recalled the last time he'd been in here. Namely, when they'd shared a kiss that had nearly brought him to his knees.

"It appears dinner will have to wait."

He glanced over at her. She had stepped out of her sandals. After locking the office door, he leaned against it and watched her undress. She was wearing a burnt-orange sundress with spaghetti straps. It looked good on her and the color of the dress seemed to highlight her hair and skin tone.

He had gotten little sleep since his friends had arrived in the Keys. But then they hadn't come here to rest. They had left their families to come here and help him solve a sinister plan of espionage against the country they loved.

And to protect the woman *he* loved.

He suddenly swallowed deep when that last thought passed through his mind. As he watched Swan remove her panties, he knew without a doubt that he had fallen in love with her. He wouldn't try to figure out how it happened but just accept that it had. Now more than ever he was determined to make sure whoever was trying to screw her over didn't succeed.

"Are you going to just stand there?" she asked, standing before him completely naked.

"No, that's not my intention at all," he said, moving away from the door to stand a few feet from her in what he considered his safe zone. If he got any closer, he would be tempted to take her with his clothes on. He removed his shirt and eased both his khakis and briefs down his legs at the same time. Quick and easy.

"I love your dolphins," she said. "I meant to ask you about them a number of other times, but always got sidetracked. So I'm asking you now. Any reason you chose dolphins?"

He decided to be as truthful with her as he could. One day he would have to explain to her why he'd lied about so many things. "Like the dolphins, I love being in the water. But this isn't just any dolphin."

"It's not?"

"No. This dolphin's name is Flipper. Surely you've heard of him."

"Not as much as I know Willy from *Free Willy*."

He chuckled as he moved toward her. "Willy was a whale. Flipper was a dolphin. That's what my friends call me. Flipper."

"Flipper?"

"Yes. Like I said, I love being in the water."

"You don't look like a Flipper."

He came to a stop in front of her. "Don't tell that to my family and friends. They wouldn't agree with you."

She reached out and touched the tattoo of the dolphin on his arm. Her fingers felt like fire as she traced along the design with her fingertips. "Beautiful. Not just your tattoos but all of you, David."

"Thanks." And in one smooth sweep, he picked her up and sat her on the desk, spreading her legs in the process.

"Did I tell you how much I missed you?" he asked, running his hands over her arms.

"Yes. Just a few moments ago when you arrived here and I told you I missed you, too. You also told me that you missed me when you walked me home Wednesday night and I invited you to stay."

Flipper heard the disappointment in her voice. If only she knew how much he'd wanted to stay. But once he'd found out Jamila would be out for a while with Horacio, he needed that time to check out her place. "I couldn't, but I intend to make it up to you when we have more time."

He was letting her know this little quickie didn't count. He had something planned for her when all this was over and he could sit her down and tell her everything.

"Not here and not now? What do you call this?" she asked when he reached up and cupped her breasts in his hands, marveling at just how beautiful they were.

"This is an I-can't-wait-until-later quickie."

"Interesting."

Shifting his gaze from her breasts to her eyes, he said, "Let me show you, Swan Jamison, just how interesting it can be." He leaned forward and kissed her while placing the head of his erection against her wet opening. The contact sent heat spiraling through him.

While his tongue mated greedily with hers, he entered her in one hard stroke. Pulling his mouth from hers, he let out a guttural moan when her muscles clamped down on his throbbing erection. That made him push harder and sink deeper.

And when she moaned his name, he knew she could feel the fire of passion spreading between them as much as he could.

Swan wrapped her legs completely around Flipper, loving the feel of him moving inside her. He was giving her body one heck of a workout on her desk. She could feel the heat in his eyes as he stared at her.

He used his hands to lift her hips off the desk's surface for a deeper penetration. When his erection hit a certain part of her, she gasped and arched her back.

"David…"

She whispered his name when she felt him going deeper and deeper. The intensity of their joining sent emotions skyrocketing through her.

She needed this. She wanted this. Like him, she needed it now, not later. This was more than interesting. This was a hot, frenzied, torrid mating. More than a quickie. David was thorough, meticulously so, and not to be rushed. It was as if he intended to savor every stroke.

Suddenly, she felt herself falling. Not off the desk but out of reality when an orgasm rammed through her at the same time as he shuddered with the force of his own release.

They stared at each other, realizing something at the same time. Wanting to make sure he didn't stop, she whispered, "Pill."

It seemed that single word triggered another orgasm and she felt him flooding her insides again while his deep, guttural groan filled the room. His release sparked another within her. His name was torn from her lips when her body shattered in earth-shaking and mind-blowing ecstasy.

As the daze from Swan's orgasmic state receded, she felt David slowly withdraw from inside her. That's when she forced her eyes open to stare at him and accepted the hand he extended to help her off the desk. Once on her feet, she wrapped her arms around his waist, feeling weak in the knees.

"It's okay, baby, I got you. I won't let you fall," he whispered close to her ear as he leaned down.

Too late, she thought. She'd already fallen. Head over heels in love with him. The very thought suddenly sent her mind spinning.

Hadn't she just given herself a good talking to moments before he'd arrived? Told herself he was someone she could enjoy, both in and out of bed and nothing more? That he was someone she knew better than to give her heart to because she hadn't wanted to take the risk?

What on earth had happened?

She knew the answer as she moved closer into the comfort of his warm naked body. David Holloway had happened. As much as she hadn't meant to fall in love with him, she had.

It didn't matter that she had known him less than three weeks. Somehow he had come into her world and turned it upside down, whether that had been his intent or not. When his work on the island was finished, he would move on and not look back. But still, knowing that he would leave hadn't stopped him from winning her heart.

"Ready?"

She lifted her head and look up at him. "You know, David, that lone question will get us in trouble."

He held her gaze for a long moment and then caressed the side of her face. "Or take us to places we really want to go and inspire us to do things that we really want to do."

Then he lowered his mouth to hers and kissed her.

Eleven

"Great work finding out about that ink, Lieutenant Holloway. I knew there was no way Swan would have betrayed her country."

"Yes, sir. Those are my thoughts as well," Flipper said. He had placed his CO on speakerphone so his SEAL teammates could listen to the call. "There's no doubt in my mind the persons naval intelligence should be concentrating on are Rafe Duggers and Horacio Jacinto."

"I agree. I met with Admiral Martin and Director Levart this morning and they concur there's a mole within the organization."

"By meeting with them, sir, does that mean you feel certain they can be totally trusted as well?" Flipper felt he had to ask.

"Yes, Lieutenant Holloway. I do. I know that because of what you discovered and what went down with Lieutenant Westmoreland a few years ago involving those moles at Homeland Security, you're not sure who you can trust. I understand that. However, I assure you that you can trust the three of us to protect Swan with our lives if we have to. We knew she was innocent, which was why we sent you there to prove we were right. You have. Now it's up to us to find out who's behind this and bring them to justice."

"And in the meantime?"

"In the meantime, Lieutenant, you are free to consider this assignment completed. Go home to Texas and enjoy the remainder of your leave."

There was no way he could consider this assignment completed, although under normal circumstances it would be once the CO said so. "I think I'll hang around Key West for a while."

"Why?" Commanding Officer Shields asked. "Do you think Swan's life might be in immediate danger?"

"As long as Duggers and Jacinta don't know they're suspected of anything, then no. However…"

"However what, Lieutenant Holloway?"

Flipper had no problem being truthful to his CO. "However, Swan has come to mean a lot to me, sir."

"Oh, I see."

Flipper figured since his CO knew him so well, he did see. "In that case, Lieutenant Holloway, how you choose to spend the rest of your leave is your decision. But keep in mind, since this is an ongoing investigation, you cannot tell Swan anything, including your reason for being in the Keys in the first place. That in itself will place you in what might be perceived by her as a dishonorable situation."

"I'm aware of that, sir, but I refuse to leave her until I have to. How long do you think it will take to wrap up the investigation?"

"Not sure. We will not only be investigating the original investigators but we'll have to restart the entire
case, making Duggers and Jacinta the primary suspects.
If you remain in the Keys and notice anything I need to
know, don't hesitate to bring it to my attention."

In other words, Commanding Officer Shields was
pretty much giving Flipper the green light to do his own
thing, unofficially. "Yes, sir."

When Flipper clicked off the phone, he glanced up
at his friends. "So what do you guys think?"

"Personally, I think you're doing the right thing not
leaving here until you're certain Miss Jamison's life is
not in any danger," Bane said.

"And since we don't plan to leave until you do, it's
time we figure out just who is behind this," Coop added.

"I agree with all the above," Viper tacked on.

They all looked at Mac, who rubbed his chin as if
contemplating something. Then he said, "Someone
needs to play devil's advocate, so I guess it has to be
me."

"No surprise there," Bane said.

Mac shot Bane a glare and then glanced back at Flipper. "Think about what the CO said. You can't tell Miss
Jamison anything. Once she finds out the truth, that she
was nothing more than an assignment to you, she's not
going to like it, no matter how noble or honorable your
intentions might have been."

Flipper drew in a deep breath. He knew Mac's words
to be true. Although Swan had yet to tell him anything
about her affair with William Connors, it had been in
the report. The man had betrayed her and there was a
chance she would probably see Flipper as doing the
same. "So, Mr. Know-It-All, what do you suggest I do?"
he asked.

"Start drawing a line in your relationship and don't cross it. In other words, stop seducing her," Mac said.

Too late for that, Flipper thought. All he had to do was remember what they'd done yesterday in Swan's office and again when he'd taken her home after dinner. Especially when he'd sat in one of her kitchen chairs and she'd straddled his body. The memories of what had started out in that chair and ended up in her bedroom made him feel hot. He hadn't left her place until dawn this morning. There was no way he could put a freeze on his relationship with Swan like Mac was suggesting.

"That's not an option, Mac. I'm going to do what I have to do now and worry about the consequences later."

"What's this about you having a boyfriend? I can't leave you alone for one minute."

Swan smiled when she glanced up at Rosie McCall, one of her frequent customers. Rosie, an older woman in her midforties who'd been away for the past three months visiting her family in Nevada, had returned to the Keys just yesterday. "I see Jamila has been talking again."

"Doesn't matter. So tell me, who is he?"

Swan closed the jewelry case. "First of all, he's not my boyfriend. He's just someone I'm seeing while he's here on the island working, which won't be much longer."

"Um, short meaningless flings are the best kind. What's his name?"

"David. David Holloway."

"Where he is from?"

"Texas."

"You said he's here working. What does he do for a living?"

"Whoa, time-out," Swan said, using her hand for the signal. "You don't need to know all that. David's a nice guy and that's all you really need to know."

She knew how Rosie liked to play matchmaker. She'd been the one who'd introduced Jamila to Horacio. Rosie had met him at one of the nightclubs and thought he was cute, too young for her but just the right age for Swan or Jamila. Swan hadn't been interested in a blind date but Jamila had. Horacio and Jamila met, hit it off and had been an item ever since.

"You can't blame me for being curious, Swan. You seldom date."

"My choice, remember? Besides, you do it enough for the both of us." And that was the truth. After her second divorce, Rosie had made it known she would never marry again but intended to date any man who asked her out as long as they were the right age. Not too old and not too young.

Rosie smiled. "Yes, I do, don't I? But that doesn't mean you shouldn't go out and have fun every once in a while. There's more to life than this shop, Swan. I hope you're finally finding that out."

"Whatever." Swan had heard it before and all from Rosie. She liked the older woman and thought she was a fun person who had a zeal for life. There was never a dull moment around her.

At that moment, the shop's door chimed and Swan knew without looking in that direction that David had walked in. She also knew when he saw her with a customer that he would wait until she finished before approaching her.

Rosie leaned in. "Looks like you have a customer.

Let's hope he buys something since he came in a minute before closing."

Swan inwardly smiled. "We can only hope, right?"

"But then he's such a cutie. Look at him."

Swan didn't have to look at David to know what a cutie he was, but she did so anyway. He was browsing around the store wearing a pair of shorts and a sleeveless T-shirt with flip-flops on his feet. He looked laid-back and sexy as sin. "You're right, he is a cutie."

"I love those tattoos on his upper arms. Nice."

"Yes, they are." She knew Rosie was into tattoos and was one of Rafe's frequent customers. The woman had them everywhere, visible and non-visible.

"You need to go wait on him. See what he wants. If he's not sure, offer him a few things."

Swan smiled. Little did Rosie know, but she intended to offer David a lot. "I will. Come on, I'll walk you to the door. I'm officially closed now," Swan said, coming from around the counter.

"You honestly want me to leave you here with him?" Rosie whispered. "For all you know he's not safe."

Swan chuckled and decided it was time for her to come clean. "He's safe, Rosie. That's David and he's here to walk me home. I'll introduce you on your way out the door."

"You mean that gorgeous hunk is your guy?"

Swan glanced over at David again. He was definitely a gorgeous hunk but she couldn't claim him as her guy. "Yes, he's the guy I've been seeing a lot of lately."

"Smart girl."

David glanced up when they approached and gave her a huge smile. "Hi," he greeted.

"Hi, David. I'd like you to meet Rosie McCall. A friend who has been away for the past few months and just returned back to the island. Rosie, this is David Holloway."

David extended his hand. "Nice meeting you, Rosie."

"Same here, David. I like your tattoos."

"Thanks and I like yours," he responded.

"Thanks. Well, I'll be going. I hope you guys enjoy yourselves."

"We will," Swan said, smiling up at David. "I'll be back after seeing Rosie out," she told him.

He nodded. "Nice meeting you, Rosie."

"Same here."

Swan returned to David a few moments later, after putting up the Closed sign, locking the door and pulling down the shades. She turned and studied him as he stood across the room, looking so amazingly sexy. She felt a lump in her throat. She loved everything about him, especially the muscles beneath his shirt, the masculine thighs and his tanned skin.

"Got more sun today, I see."

"Yes, I had to go out on the boat today."

"One day you're going to have to explain to me in detail just what your ocean duties entail."

"I will. But for now, come here. I missed you today."

She crossed the room to walk into his arms. "I missed you, too."

"That's good to know. Rosie seems like a nice person."

"She is."

"She has a lot of tattoos."

Swan chuckled. "Yes, she does. She's one of Rafe's best customers."

"Is that right?" David asked, still smiling. "He did an awesome job."

She checked her watch. "We can leave as soon as I

grab my purse." They would be having dinner at Nathan Waterway and afterward would attend an art show. "I'll be back in a second."

Flipper watched Swan walk off toward her office while thinking of what she'd told him about Rosie McCall. He recalled what he'd overheard Rafe and Horacio arguing about that night behind this building. Ink and roses. Or had they said Rosie? Was she a part of the group? If she was, that meant she had an ulterior motive for befriending Swan.

Pulling his phone from his pocket he texted Nick. Check out Rosie McCall.

He received an immediate reply. Will do.

He then texted Bane. Excursion tonight.

The reply was quick. On it.

Most of today he and Viper had pretended to go fishing after Mac, who'd been tailing Rafe for the past two days, reported that Rafe had rented a boat and headed in the direction of another island close by. Today Flipper and Viper had also rented a boat, making sure they stayed a good distance behind Duggers.

The man had docked in Fleming Key. Bane and Cooper, who'd arrived ahead of them, picked up the tail on Rafe. It seemed the man had gone into a sports shop where he'd stayed for three hours.

Pretending to be two guys enjoying their time out on their boat, Flipper and Viper had waited at the pier and knew when Rafe had left the island to return to Key West. Mac had been there to pick up the tail and reported that the man had been carrying a package when he went inside his tattoo shop. A package Rafe had gotten from the sports shop, according to Bane and Coop.

"I'm ready."

He looked up and when Swan met his gaze, she quickly clarified, "I'm ready *for dinner*."

He placed his phone back into his pocket and smiled. "That's all?"

The smile she returned made his insides quiver in anticipation. "For now, Mr. Holloway."

Twelve

It was getting harder and harder to leave Swan's bed, Flipper thought as he and his teammates docked at Fleming Key close to two in the morning. But at least he'd left her sleeping with the most peaceful smile on her face.

Without waking her, he had brushed a kiss across her lips and whispered that he loved her, knowing she would remember neither. But he decided to tell her how he felt when he saw her later today. He couldn't hold it inside any longer. She deserved to know. He wanted her to know. And when all this was over and she knew the truth, he would do whatever he needed to do to win her forgiveness and her love.

He jumped when fingers snapped in his face. He glared at Mac, who glared back. "Stay focused. You can daydream later."

"I wasn't daydreaming," Flipper countered. He then

realized he was the only one still in the boat. The others had already gotten out.

"Then night-dreaming. Call it what you want" was Mac's reply. "Just get out of the damn boat."

Flipper didn't have to wonder why Mac was in a rotten mood. Teri had texted him earlier in the day to say the new washer and dryer had been delivered. They were new appliances Mac hadn't known they were buying.

Moments later, dressed in all black military combat gear, the five of them circled around to the back of the sports shop Rafe had frequented lately. Being ever ready and not taking any chances, Glocks were strapped to their hips and high powered tasers to their thighs. Due to Viper's hypersensitive ears—known to pick up sound over long distances away—he would stay outside as the lookout. Flipper, Bane, Cooper and Mac bypassed security cameras to enter the building.

Once inside, they used Flipper's cameras and it didn't take long to find a hidden room. Making swift use of their time, they took pictures of everything. It was obvious this was the group's operation headquarters. More tattoo ink was stored here along with several specific tattoo designs. One design Flipper quickly recalled seeing on the side of Rosie's neck.

Flipper scanned the room with his camera and then opened several drawers in the huge desk and took photos of the contents. When he came across a photo in one of the drawers, he suddenly froze. "Damn."

"What is it, Flipper?" Bane asked.

Instead of saying anything, he motioned his head to the photograph he'd found. Mac, Bane and Coop came around him to see it as well. They looked back at him and Mac said, "We've been royally screwed."

An uneasy feeling settled in the pit of Flipper's stomach. "I need to get back to Swan as soon as possible."

Swan was awakened by the knocking on her door. She glanced at the clock on her nightstand and wondered who on earth would be at her house at four in the morning. Was it David returning? She didn't recall when he'd left but knew it was the norm for him to leave her place around midnight to return to his hotel because of his work. Usually she would be awake when he left but tonight sexual exhaustion had gotten the best of her.

Pulling on her robe, she tied it around her waist as she headed for the door. Looking out the peephole, she saw it was Jamila and Horacio. What were they doing out so late and why were they at her place? She found it odd that Horacio was on the island when the cruise ship wasn't due back in port again until next week.

From the look on Jamila's face, it appeared she wasn't happy about something. In fact, from her reddened eyes, it appeared that she'd been crying. Swan wondered what on earth was wrong. Had something happened?

Suddenly filled with concern, she quickly opened the door. The minute she did so, Jamila was shoved inside, nearly knocking Swan down.

"Hey, wait a minute. What's going on?" Swan asked, fighting to regain her balance.

"Shut the hell up and don't ask questions," Horacio said, quickly coming inside and closing the door behind him.

Swan frowned. "Horacio? What do you mean, I can't ask any questions?"

"Just do what you're told," he barked.

Swan glanced over at Jamila and saw the bruise on

the side of her face. "Did he do this to you?" Swan demanded, getting enraged. At Jamila's nod, Swan then turned to Horacio. How could he have done this when he adored Jamila? "I want you to leave now."

"If I don't, what are you going to do? Call the police? Or call that SEAL you're sleeping with?"

Swan frown deepened. "I don't know what you're talking about. Now leave or I *will* call the police."

"You won't be doing anything other than what I tell you to do. When I get the word, the two of you will be coming with me."

Swan placed her hands on her hips. "We're not going anywhere with you."

A cynical smile touched Horacio's lips as he pulled out a gun from his back pocket. "This says you will."

Swan stared at the gun, not believing Horacio had it pointed at both her and Jamila. She was about to say something when Horacio added, "I'm giving you five minutes to go into your bedroom and put on clothes. Bring me your phone first. I don't want you to get any crazy ideas."

Swan had no idea what was going on, but from the pleading look in Jamila's eyes, she knew it was best to do as she was told. She went and got her cell phone and handed it to him, but not before she noticed several missed calls from David. Why had he been trying to call her? Her mind was filled with so many questions.

"You got five minutes to get dressed. If you're not back in five minutes or try some kind of funny business, your cousin here will pay for it."

Cousin? Why did he refer to Jamila as her cousin? At what was obviously a confused look on her face, he said, "That's right. Secrets. There are plenty more where those came from, Swan, and you'll be finding out about them later. Now go."

Swan got dressed in less than five minutes. If she hadn't thought Horacio was serious about hurting Jamila, she would have escaped through her bedroom window. That bruise along the side of her friend's face indicated the man was serious.

Swan was walking out of her bedroom fully dressed when Horacio's phone rang. Instead of answering it, he said, "That's my signal that things are ready. We'll go out your back door to the beach. The boat is waiting."

"What boat?"

"Please don't ask him anything, Swan," Jamila pleaded, reaching out and grabbing her arm. "All of them are crazy."

Swan wondered just who were *all of them*. But she decided not to ask.

"Move!"

Following Horacio's orders, she and Jamila walked toward Swan's kitchen to go out the back door.

As soon as their boat docked, Flipper raced through the streets of Key West toward Swan's home with his teammates fast on his heels. He had tried reaching her on the phone but didn't get an answer. He immediately knew something was wrong because she kept her phone on the nightstand next to her bed and the ringing would have woken her up. He had tried several more times with no luck, which was why his heart was beating out of control and fear was gripping his insides, especially now that he knew who was involved.

They had contacted their CO and told him what they'd discovered. He was as shocked as they'd been and they knew Shields would be taking the necessary actions on his end. Flipper hadn't had to tell the man there would be hell to pay if anyone hurt one single hair on Swan's head.

When they reached her house, they found the door unlocked. Her cell phone had been tossed on a living room table and a quick search of her bedroom indicated she'd change clothes.

"Take a look at this, Flipper," Mac called out.

When he reached them in the kitchen, Mac pointed out the window. Flipper saw lights from a boat that was sitting idle in the ocean as if waiting to rendezvous with another vessel.

"I traced footprints in the sand that led to the water. A small watercraft probably took them out to that boat," Viper was saying. "There were three sets of shoe prints belonging to two women and a man. And they left around thirty minutes ago."

Flipper raced out Swan's back door and after putting on his night-vision eyewear, he stared out at the ocean.

"Intercept with our boat," he shouted over his shoulder to the others. Quickly dropping to the sand, he began removing his shoes, T-shirt and pants, leaving his body clad in a pair of swimming trunks.

"Don't try it, Flipper. The boat's too far out," Mac said. "It's too dangerous for anyone, even you."

Flipper glanced up at them while putting the waterproof military belt that contained combat gear around his waist. He then put a pair of specially designed water goggles over his eyes. "The woman I love is on that boat and I have no idea what they plan to do, so I have to try. Even if I die trying."

Without saying anything else, he raced toward the water and dived in.

* * *

Horacio had tied their hands before forcing them into a small boat, which carried them out into the ocean to a much bigger boat. Now they were sitting idle in the waves.

Swan wondered why. She glanced around and noticed that, other than the lights on the boat, there was only darkness. They were so far from land she couldn't see the lights from the homes where she lived anymore.

As if Horacio realized she was trying to figure out what was happening, he said, "I'm waiting for the rest of the gang, then we'll decide what we will do with the two of you."

What he said didn't make much sense. "Will someone please tell me what's going on?" Swan asked, getting angrier by the minute. None of this made any sense.

"I'll let your cousin go first since Jamila has a lot of explaining to do," Horacio said, grinning.

Swan turned to Jamila, who was sitting on a bench beside her. "What is he talking about? Why does he keep referring to you as my cousin?"

At first Jamila didn't say anything. In fact, it seemed she was refusing to meet Swan's gaze, but then she finally met Swan's eyes and said, "Because we are cousins, Swan. My mother is your grandfather's youngest sister."

"My grandfather?"

Jamila nodded. "Yes, Lawrence Jamison is my uncle. I knew for years that Uncle Lawrence disowned your father but I didn't know why until I was much older. Then I thought the reason was downright stupid and told the family what I thought. Everyone else in the family thought the same thing but were too afraid to stand up to Uncle Lawrence."

Swan didn't say anything. She was still trying to dissect the fact that she and Jamila were related. She'd known from her father that Lawrence had a sister and another brother. That was all she'd known.

"When I turned twenty-one and finished college, I decided to come find you. Uncle Lawrence didn't like it but I told him I didn't care. I'm one of the few who stands up to him. He said the family would disown me if I came here."

"Yet you came anyway," Swan said.

"Yes, I came anyway."

Swan glanced over at Horacio. He wasn't saying anything and didn't appear to be listening to what they were saying. Instead he stood at the bow of the ship looking through binoculars as if he was searching for someone. He'd said they were waiting for another boat with the gang and Swan couldn't help but wonder who the gang was.

She wanted to ask Jamila how much she knew and why they were being held hostage but figured that although Horacio was pretending not to listen to their conversation, he probably was.

Swan glanced over at Jamila. "Why didn't you tell me who you were when you first came into my shop that day? Why did you keep it a secret all this time?"

"Because I knew how my family had treated you and your mother. I figured the last thing you'd want was to meet a relative from that side of the family. I decided to let you accept me as a friend and then later I would tell you the truth that we were cousins."

"Now isn't that a touching story?" Horacio said, strolling back over to where they sat.

"Yes, it is touching," Swan said, defiantly lifting her chin. "Why are we here?"

He smiled. "You'll find out soon enough. And I hope you're not holding out any hope that your SEAL boyfriend will be coming to rescue you because he won't."

"Why do you keep saying David is a SEAL when he's not? He was in the military once but he was never a SEAL."

"Sounds like you've been conned by him just like your cousin here was conned by me," he said as if it was something to brag about. "Your lover boy *is* a SEAL and he was sent here to get the goods on you. Whether you know it or not, you've been his assignment."

Swan shook her head. "No, that's not true. I don't believe you."

"I don't care if you believe me or not but it's true. I only found out today what he's been doing and why he was sent here by naval intelligence."

Naval intelligence? Swan glanced over at Jamila, who said, "I don't know whether what he's saying is true or not, Swan, but he told me the same thing tonight."

"Why would naval intelligence suspect me of anything? It doesn't make sense." And more than that, she refused to believe David wasn't who and what he said he was.

At that moment, they heard the sound of a boat approaching. Horacio drew his gun and pointed the flashlight toward the oncoming boat. He put his gun back in place. "Hold on to that question, sweetheart. The person who will explain everything just arrived."

Swan kept her gaze trained on the boat that pulled up beside theirs and saw two people onboard. Both of them she knew. What in the world…?

She watched in shock as Rafe and Rosie came aboard. She was so focused on staring at them that she almost missed the third person who also came on board.

She gasped in shock when the person said, "Swan, you look well."

Suddenly losing her voice, Swan couldn't do anything but sit there and stare. There had to be some mistake. A very big mistake. There was no way the person standing before her was a part of this craziness.

No way.

She finally found her voice. "Georgianna? What are you doing here? What is this about?"

Thirteen

Flipper reached the boat and attached himself to the ladder on the side. Lucky for him, no one had thought to pull it up. Taking slow, deep breaths, he pulled air into his lungs while ignoring the pain in his arms and legs. He didn't want to think about just how far he'd swum, but like he'd told his friends, he'd had to try.

He quickly eased back into the water when he heard the sound of an approaching boat and was grateful the vessel pulled up on the other side from where he was hiding. He glanced at his watch. It was synchronized with the ones worn by his teammates, and he knew they would do their best to get here soon. In the meantime, there was something he had to do.

Pulling a micro audio recorder off his belt, he moved back up the ladder to peek over the railing and into the boat.

Good. Everyone's attention was on the approaching

vessel and no one saw him when he attached the audio recorder that was no bigger than a dime to the interior wall of the boat. He saw Swan and Jamila seated on a bench with their hands tied behind their backs and Horacio was standing not far away. Other than a man in the cockpit, there was no one else onboard. Flipper knew that was about to change when he heard voices.

Satisfied that the conversations would be recorded, he eased back down the ladder. When his watch began vibrating, he glanced down at the text message from Bane. On our way. Had 2 take care of a little problem 1st.

Flipper wondered what kind of problem his friends had to take care of. No matter. They were on their way and that's what counted. He listened to the conversation going on in the boat as he began pulling items from his belt. He intended to be ready to crash this little party when the time came.

He shook his head, knowing Admiral Martin would be heartbroken to discover his own daughter had sold out their country.

"I hate you," Georgianna said, glaring at Swan.

Swan was taken aback by the woman's words. "Why? What have I ever done to you? To any of you?" she asked, glancing around at the people she'd assumed were friends—Rafe, Horacio and Rosie. She hurt more at seeing Rosie than the others because she'd believed the woman had been a good friend.

"They work for me and did what they were told," Georgianna said.

"Work for you?" Swan was even more confused.

"Yes. I'm in charge of the entire operation. But I'll tell you all about that later. First, let me tell you why

I despise you so much. I've waited a long time to get this out in the open. When your father died and your mother would send you to us for the summer, my parents thought you were golden. They put you on a pedestal, especially my father. Did you know he called you his little island princess?"

Yes, Swan knew but she also knew her godfather hadn't meant anything by it. It was just a nickname he'd given her when she was born. All three of her godfathers called her that sometimes. "It was just a nickname, Georgianna."

"For you, it might only have been a nickname, but for me, it was Dad shifting his attention from me to you."

"Godpop 1 loves you. He wasn't shifting his attention to me, he was just being nice."

"Too nice, and I despised you for it. He had a daughter, yet any time your mother would call, he and Mom would drop everything and take off. Just because your father saved Dad's life—that meant nothing. They were all SEALs and your dad was doing his job when he died. But it was as if Dad blamed himself and he needed to make it up by being nice to you, like you were somebody special. So, with the help of some friends, I decided to change everyone's opinion of you."

It was hard for Swan to believe what she was hearing. She'd never known that Georgianna harbored such feelings. Granted she hadn't always been overnice and had a tendency to be moody, but Swan hadn't detected animosity like this.

"What did you do?" Swan asked her.

Georgianna smiled like she was proud of what she was about to say. "I set up an espionage operation out of your shop with the help of Rafe and Horacio. Then, with Rosie's assistance, I made it appear that the secret information being sent to China was being done through your jewelry."

"What!" Swan couldn't believe it. Her head was spinning from all the shocks she'd received tonight.

"I have to admit I put together a perfect plan. This guy I was sleeping with at the time assisted me by tipping off naval intelligence with what you were supposedly doing. They did their own investigation and my team and I made sure everything pointed at you. It should have been an open and shut case and you were to be arrested and charged with espionage."

As if she was tired of standing, Georgianna moved to sit on one of the benches. She frowned over at Swan. "Everything was going according to plan until the final thread of the investigation reached Director Levart's desk."

"Godpop 3?"

"See what I mean? You have three godfathers and I don't have a one," Georgianna said in a loud voice, pointing a finger at her. "You don't deserve such love and loyalty, and I intended to tarnish their image of you."

Flipper's watch vibrated and he glanced down at the text message. Here. N place. Coop got layout of boat.

He texted them back. 1 N cockpit. 4 others. 2 hostages.

He quickly received a reply from Viper. Eliminating cockpit.

Got 4 in scope. That particular text came from Bane, a master sniper.

Flipper knew that although everyone was in place, timing was everything. Georgianna had no idea her words were being recorded so he wanted to let her talk before making his move. Then there would be no way she could deny anything.

From listening to what the woman was saying, it was obvious she had mental issues. That could be the only reason to have such a deep hatred of Swan that Georgianna would go to such extremes. Georgianna assumed she'd had the perfect plan for Swan's downfall and Flipper was glad things hadn't turned out the way Georgianna intended.

Before inching up the ladder to listen to what else she was confessing, he texted the message: Will give signal.

Swan shook her head. It was obvious Georgianna's jealousy had blinded her senses and fueled her hatred. Didn't the others see it? Why were they following her blindly? Swan glanced over at Jamila and could tell by the look in her cousin's eyes that she was wondering the same thing.

"When Director Levart saw the report, he refused to believe you could be guilty of anything, especially betraying your country."

Thank God for that, Swan thought.

"He requested a thirty-day delay before agreeing to take any actions against you. Even after we made sure the investigation clearly spelled out your role in everything. There was no reason for you not to be charged," Georgianna said.

She paused a moment before continuing. "Unknown to me and the others, Director Levart went to your other two godfathers and they put their heads together to see what they could do to prove your innocence. They decided to send one of their top SEALs to find out what he could and to prove your innocence."

Swan drew in a deep breath. *Oh no, please don't*

let what Horacio said tonight be true. Please don't let David turn out to be someone other than what he said he was.

Georgianna's next words ripped into Swan's heart.

"The SEAL they sent was Lieutenant David Holloway. I guess you didn't know that all the time he spent with you was nothing more than an assignment. You meant nothing to him, Swan." Georgianna laughed as if she found the entire thing amusing while Swan's heart broke.

"Imagine how amused I was to find out just how taken you were with him, while not knowing the true purpose as to why he showed up here on the island. You were played, Swan," Georgianna was saying in between laughter. "But don't worry. I sent some other members of my group to take care of him for you. I think he's dead by now."

Suddenly a deep voice at the back of the boat said, "As you can see, I'm very much alive."

Swan gasped just as the others did. Standing with legs braced apart and wearing only a pair of swim trunks with a utility combat belt around his waist, David looked like a mad badass. It was obvious everyone was shocked to see him, especially Georgianna, who had assumed he was dead.

"Drop your gun," he ordered Horacio, who was still holding his weapon on Swan and Jamila.

"How the hell did you get here?" Horacio asked, enraged.

"I swam from Swan's home."

"That's impossible!"

"Not if you're a SEAL master swimmer," David said. "Now, do like I said and put your gun down."

"And if I don't? It will be a shame if I kill Swan or Jamila before you can get to anything on that belt you're wearing," Horacio sneered.

"Don't try it, Horacio. One of my team members who's a master sniper has all four of you within his scope. Before you could get off the first shot, you'd be dead."

"I don't believe you. There's no one else out here," Horacio said. When he lifted his gun to take aim at Swan, a shot rang out, hitting the man in the chest. The impact toppled him to the floor.

Jamila screamed and Swan understood. Jamila had fallen in love with a man who'd betrayed her and then gotten shot right before her eyes.

Suddenly, Rafe dived for the gun that had dropped from Horacio's hand. Before he could reach it, another shot rang out that hit him in the side. He fell to the floor as well.

"Either of you ladies want to join them?" Flipper asked Georgianna and Rosie.

Rosie looked like she was in shock and ready to pass out.

However, Georgianna looked furious. "You won't get away with this. No matter what you tell my father, he will never believe you over me," she said with absolute certainty. "I'll tell him that you decided to team up with Swan and she turned you against your country."

"I figured you would lie. That's why I've recorded your little confession to Swan detailing everything. I can't wait for your father to listen to it."

Suddenly the boat was surrounded by several naval vessels and sharp beams of light shined on them. A voice through a foghorn said, "Lieutenant Holloway, we are coming aboard."

A dozen men wearing SEAL gear rushed on board with their guns drawn, immediately taking Georgianna and Rosie into custody. Bane, Viper, Coop and Mac boarded the boat as well. Mac rushed over to check Horacio and Rafe. There really was no need since they were both dead.

Flipper rushed over to Swan and Jamila to untie their hands. More than anything, he wanted to pull Swan into his arms and tell her he loved her. He wanted her to put out of her mind what Georgianna had said about him until she'd heard his side of things. However, he knew when she pulled away from him to give her cousin a hug that she didn't want to give him a chance to explain.

He didn't intend to let her walk away.

"We need to talk, Swan," he said, looking down at her.

She glared up at him. "We have nothing to say to each other. Your assignment is over, Lieutenant Holloway. Now leave me alone."

Fourteen

Two weeks later

"How long are you planning to be mad at the world, Swan?"

Swan glanced over at Candy. Her best friend had returned to the Keys after hearing about what happened and she'd decided to stay. Swan was glad Candy had returned home but she was saddened by what had brought her back.

"I am not mad at the world," Swan said, taking a sip of her orange juice.

"But you are still mad at one particular man," Candy said, coming to sit beside Swan on the sofa.

Swan couldn't deny that was true so she didn't. "And what if I am?"

"He had a job to do, Swan. He was given orders. Surely you understand that."

Swan glared at Candy. "I'm sure none of my godfathers' orders included sleeping with me."

"I'm sure they didn't but David didn't force himself on you."

"No, but he deceived me."

"So did the others."

Did Candy have to remind her? "And I'm not talking to them either."

That wasn't totally true since Swan had reached out to Georgianna where she was being held at a federal prison in Orlando. The woman had refused to see her. Swan knew Georgianna was undergoing psychiatric evaluations to see if she was fit to stand trial.

Swan's godparents were heartbroken and she understood how they felt. Like her, they'd had no idea Georgianna harbored such hatred toward Swan, enough to do what she'd done. With both Rafe and Horacio dead, it was Rosie who was singing like a bird, telling everything she knew for a lessened sentence.

According to Rosie, Georgianna had manipulated a number of the men at naval intelligence into doing whatever she wanted them to do. When you were the admiral's daughter, you could wield that kind of power. She had even threatened a few with blackmail. She'd deliberately recorded several of the men having sex with her and then threatened to give the tape to her father and accuse them of rape.

Some of the men were not only married but a number were high-ranking military officers. Fearful of court-martial, the men had done whatever Georgianna asked, including falsifying records. So far, more than twelve men had been named in the scandal.

"I take it David hasn't called."

Swan drew in a deep breath. She had seen him last

week when they'd had to show up at the naval station to give statements. "Yes, he's called. Several times. But I refuse to answer. Like I told him, we have nothing to say to each other. His assignment is over."

"And do you honestly think that's all you were to him, Swan?"

"Yes, but it doesn't matter."

"I think it does," Candy countered.

"And you think too much," Swan said, easing off the sofa.

The first week after the incident on the boat, she had closed her shop while naval investigators did a thorough search of Rafe's tattoo parlor. She had used that time to take care of Jamila, who was still broken up over Horacio. Jamila had loved him and in a single night had seen him become an abusive monster, a man she hadn't known. Then in the end, Jamila had watched him die before her eyes.

Swan knew Jamila was going through something that only time could heal. That's why when Swan had reopened the shop this week and Jamila had asked for extra work hours, Swan had given them to her.

"So what are you going to do?" Candy asked her.

Swan glanced over at her. "About life? Work?"

"No, about David."

Swan just couldn't understand why Candy couldn't accept that David was no longer in the equation. "I'm a survivor, Candy. Although it was hard, I made do after my parents' deaths and I will make do now." She glanced at her watch. "I'm getting dressed to go into the shop today. The cruise ship comes into port tomorrow, so business will pick up. I want to make sure most of my new pieces are on display."

Another thing they had found out was that Horacio

had been fired from the cruise ship months ago but hadn't told Jamila. He had moved into Rosie's place while the woman had been gone. The duplicity of the people she'd thought she knew simply amazed Swan.

"And I need to be on my way," Candy said. "I promised my folks we would go out to dinner tonight. You can join us if you like."

"Thanks for the invite, but I'll pass. I just want to have a relaxing evening here tonight. I might go swimming on the beach later."

Swan had called Jamila and told her she would bring lunch from their favorite sandwich café. However, there were no clients in her shop when Swan got there, so she decided to do something she usually didn't do, which was close for lunch.

Normally, the shop remained open and she and Jamila would alternate lunch duties. But today she wanted to check on Jamila, talk to her to see how she was faring. Although Swan had been there for Jamila last week, they hadn't had a real honest-to-goodness talk since Jamila had admitted to being her cousin.

"What are you doing?" Jamila asked when Swan put up the Closed sign and pulled down the blinds.

Swan smiled over at her. "New store policy. From here on out, we will close at noon for lunch."

"What about the sales you'll lose?"

Swan shrugged. "Sales aren't everything. Besides, it's just for an hour. Come join me in my office."

"All right, let me grab some sodas out of the refrigerator."

A few minutes later, she and Jamila were enjoying their lunch when Swan gave Jamila a long look. "How are you doing?"

Jamila shrugged. "Okay, I guess. Trying to move on.

I loved Horacio so much only to find out he wasn't the man I thought he was."

"I know the feeling."

"No, you don't."

Swan snatched her head up, frowning. "Excuse me?"

"I said you don't know the feeling, Swan. David Holloway was nothing like Horacio. David intended to save you and Horacio would have killed me if that woman had ordered him to do so. Big difference."

"But like you, I was betrayed."

"How?" Jamila countered. "Your godfathers sent David Holloway here to prove your innocence and he did."

Jamila put her soda can down and then added, "And another thing. What man takes a chance and swims across the ocean to save a woman? Do you know how far from land we were? Think about that."

Swan had news for her—she *had* thought about it. She could never forget how David had appeared seemingly out of nowhere on that boat, looking tough and ready to kick asses while wearing nothing more than an outlandishly tight pair of swim trunks with a military belt around his waist. Even when she'd been in what seemed like a dire situation, that hadn't stopped the woman in her from noticing how dangerously sexy he'd looked at that particular moment.

"When I mentioned what an astounding feat he'd accomplished to his friends," Jamila said, reclaiming Swan's attention, "they said that's why they call him Flipper. Did you know that's his code name as a SEAL?"

Swan wiped her mouth with a napkin. "Yes, I knew he was called Flipper. But no, I didn't know it had anything to do with him being a SEAL because I didn't know he was one. I assumed Flipper was his nickname."

Swan forced from her mind the day she'd asked him about those dolphin tattoos. He'd told her then they represented Flipper. That had been the day they'd made love in this office. Right here on this desk.

She wished she wasn't thinking so hard about that now.

She looked over at Jamila. "Why are we talking about me instead of you?"

"Because I think you should and because I think I should," Jamila continued. "Talking about your situation actually helps me believe that not all men are jerks and that there are some who still possess real honor, Swan. Whether you want to admit it or not, David Holloway is an honorable man. He couldn't help being attracted to you any more than you could help being attracted to him."

Swan stuffed the wrappings from her sandwich into the empty bag. "Now you sound like Candy."

"Maybe there's a reason why I do," Jamila said, stuffing her own wrappings into a bag. "It might be because Candy and I can see things that you refuse to see. I often think about what could have happened to us had David and his friends not shown up when they did. Do you ever think of that?"

Swan drew in a deep breath. "I try not to."

"I think you should," Jamila said, standing. "Thanks for bringing lunch. It will be my treat the next time." She then walked out of the office.

Swan stayed in her office after Jamila left, trying to put their conversation out of her mind. She was working on her computer, verifying inventory, when her office phone rang. "Thank you for calling Swan's. How may I help you?"

"Hello, island princess."

She smiled upon hearing her godfather's voice. "Godpop 2. How are you?"

"I'm fine. I just wanted to check on you. So much has happened and I wanted to make sure you're okay."

She had spoken to each of her godfathers and had thanked them for believing in her. They had taken a risk with their individual careers to do that. "I'm fine. How is Godpop 3?"

"He's fine but as the director of naval intelligence, he has his hands full with the investigation. It seems that more names are popping up in this scandal each day."

"And how are Godpop 1 and Barbara?"

"They are as well as can be expected under the circumstances. Learning about Georgianna was a shocker for all of us. We had no idea. When we decided to send Lt. Holloway to prove your innocence, the three of us weren't sure just what he would uncover. The only thing we knew for certain was that you weren't guilty of anything."

"Thanks for believing in me."

"You have Andrew's blood in your veins. You could no more be a traitor to your country than he could. Considering all that happened, I'm glad Holloway remained in Key West when he could have left."

Swan sat up straight. "Wasn't David on assignment?"

"Not the entire time. His assignment officially ended when he sent that ink in to be analyzed and we discovered it was tainted. I told him that he no longer had to stay in the Keys since by then we knew you weren't involved and we would take over the investigation from there."

"Then why did he stay?"

"To protect you."

"He told you that?" she asked.

"Yes. I remember the conversation like it was yesterday. I told him he could consider his job assignment complete and go home to Texas and enjoy the remainder of his leave. But he said he wanted to hang around Key West for a while."

Her godfather paused. "I asked him if the reason he wanted to stay was because he thought your life might be in danger. He said he felt that as long as Duggers and Jacinto didn't know they were suspects, then no, your life wasn't in any immediate danger. He informed me that the reason he wanted to stay was because you had come to mean a lot to him. I told him in that case how he spent the rest of his leave was his decision. And, Swan?"

She drew in a deep breath. "Yes?"

"As his commanding officer, I felt the need to remind him that although he was no longer on assignment, since the issue that had started with you was an ongoing investigation, he could not tell you anything."

When Swan didn't reply, her godfather asked, "You're still there, Swan?"

"Yes, Godpop 2, I'm still here."

"Did you not know how Holloway felt about you?"

"No. I thought I was just an assignment."

"You were at first and I'm glad you were. Otherwise you would be in jail wrongly accused of a crime you hadn't committed. But on the flip side, I'm also glad that when you stopped being an assignment, Holloway had the insight to stay and look out for you because he cared for you."

Long after her telephone conversation with her godfather ended, Swan remained seated at her desk, leaning back in her chair and sitting in silence while thinking about what Candy, Jamila and her godfather had said. Some people never got betrayed, but she had been, a lot. William, Rafe, Horacio, Rosie, Georgianna and even Jamila. No one had been who she'd thought.

She remembered David and replayed in her mind all the time she'd spent with him since that day he'd first walked into her shop.

Was anything he'd told her true? Did he really come from a huge family? Was his mother even celebrating a birthday? Did he honestly have three sisters-in-law?

One thing was for certain, both Candy and Jamila were right. David hadn't pushed her into sleeping with him. In fact, Swan was the one who'd invited him to dinner at her place with the full intent of having sex with him.

She got up from her desk and walked over to the window. She knew from Jamila that David had left the island with his friends after that first week, after he'd completed all the questioning by naval intelligence. Was he back home in Texas? Did his parents really own a medical supply company? What parts of what he'd told her were true and what parts were fabricated for his assignment?

And why did she still love him so much it hurt… even when she didn't want to love him? Even when she didn't know how he felt about her? He might have told her godfather he cared for her but David hadn't told her anything. Shouldn't he have? But then, had she given him a chance to do so?

The answer to that flashed in her mind quickly. No, she hadn't.

He had saved her life that night, swam across the ocean to do so, and then she'd told him she didn't want to talk to him. And he had honored her wishes…for that one night. Then he had called her almost every single day since, and yet she had refused to take his calls.

He hadn't called today.

Did that mean he'd given up and wouldn't try contacting her again? Was she ready to put her heart on the line and contact him?

She wasn't sure. But what she *was* certain of was that they needed to do what they hadn't done before. They needed to get to know each other. She needed to know which parts of what he'd told her about himself were true and which were false.

She wanted to get to know the real David Holloway. *Then what?*

Hadn't she convinced herself she wanted no part of a man in the military? And what about her decision to never to get seriously involved in an interracial relationship like her parents had? Why did all of that no longer matter to her when she thought about her and David deciding to have a future together?

Maybe that's how love worked. It made you see the possible instead of the impossible. It made you want things you told yourself were not good for you because you were afraid to reach beyond your comfort zone.

Taking a deep a cleansing breath, she decided to call David tonight before going to bed. She had no idea what she would say to him but the words would come.

She doubted he would want to come back to the Keys anytime soon, so she would let him know she would come to him if he still wanted to talk. She would see what he said before asking Jamila if she could take care of the shop while Swan was gone. David might very well tell her that it was too late, that they had nothing to talk about. But there was a chance he would embrace her words. Embrace her.

Her mood suddenly lightened, knowing that was a possibility.

* * *

Flipper entered the hotel room and tossed his luggage on the bed. Different hotel but same city. He had given Swan two weeks and now he was back. They needed to talk and clear up some things. She hadn't accepted his calls, but now he was here and he wouldn't be ignored.

He shook his head when his cell phone rang. "Yes, Coop?"

"Have you seen her yet?"

"No, I just got here. In fact, I walked into my hotel room less than five minutes ago."

"Okay. And there's another reason I called. Bristol is pregnant."

"Wow, man. Congratulations. I didn't know you guys were trying."

Coop laughed. "We're always trying. But seriously, we figured it was time Laramie had a playmate."

"Sounds good to me."

"I hope things work out with you and Swan, Flipper."

"I hope so, too."

"And do me a favor."

"What?"

"For once, open up. Tell her how you feel. Don't beat around the bush. You have a tendency to do that. Women love a man to get straight to the point and share their feelings. I hate to say it, bro, but you're not good at doing that."

Coop was right, he wasn't. "I never had to do that before. I've never truly loved a woman before Swan."

"I understand. But you do love her, so make sure she knows it. A woman has to believe she's loved."

Flipper chuckled.

"What's so funny?" Coop asked him.

"You're giving relationship advice. Do you know how much like Mac you sound?"

Coop chuckled as well. "You would have to point that out. I guess it comes with loving a woman."

"I guess so."

"No guess in it, remember it. Know it. Feel it. Take care and good luck."

After ending the call with Coop, it wasn't long before Flipper got calls from Bane, Viper and Mac as well, all letting him know they hoped things worked out for Flipper and Swan. All giving him advice. They were married men who had the women they loved and they wanted him to have the woman he loved as well.

He appreciated good friends who not only watched his back but who also cared about the condition of his heart. They knew about the pain he had lodged there and it got worse every day he and Swan were apart.

Flipper glanced at his watch. Swan's store would be closing in less than an hour. He would give her time to get home and relax before paying her a visit. He refused to let her put things off any longer. They needed to talk.

He loved her and it was damn time she knew it.

Fifteen

Swan had just poured a glass of wine to enjoy while sitting on the patio when she heard the knock at her door.

She knew Candy had gone out to dinner with her family and Jamila had mentioned she would just stay in tonight and chill. Swan had invited Jamila to join her so maybe her cousin had changed her mind.

Her cousin.

That was taking a lot of getting used to but Swan knew her parents would want a family connection for them. Jamila was the only family Swan had and she appreciated their friendship more than ever.

She reached the door and glanced through the peephole. Her heart nearly stopped.

Was it really David? She blinked and looked again and saw it was really him. Back in Key West. And he was standing in front of her door looking like he always did, sexy as hell.

Drawing in a deep breath, she removed the security lock and opened the door. "David? I thought you'd left the island."

"I had but I returned today. May I come in?"

She nodded and stepped aside. The moment he passed her, she caught a whiff of his masculine scent, the same one she was convinced still lingered in her bedroom.

Swan closed the door and stood to face him. He was standing in the middle of her living room wearing a pair of shorts and a sleeveless shirt with a huge picture of a dolphin. *Flipper*. Her gaze moved beyond the shirt to his face to find his laser-blue eyes staring at her.

She cleared her throat. "I was about to sit out back and drink a glass of wine while enjoying the view. Would you like to have a beer and join me?"

She could tell he was surprised by her invitation. She hadn't bothered to ask why he was there.

"Yes, I'd like that."

Moments later, they were sitting side by side on a bench that overlooked the beach. They had been sipping their drinks for a few moments when he said, "I told you that night two weeks ago that we needed to talk, Swan. I think we still do."

Yes, they did. She would let him go first. "Okay, I'm listening."

"I want you to do more than just listen, Swan. I want you to engage by asking questions, giving me feedback, and I would like to be able to do the same with you."

"Okay, that seems fair because I do have some questions for you."

"Ask away."

She took another sip of her drink. "You didn't tell me you were a SEAL and I'd—"

"I couldn't tell you I was a SEAL, Swan," he interrupted to say. "That's why I lied and said I was no longer in the military."

"Yes, I know that now. I want to tell you, because of what happened to my father, I had made up my mind never to get serious about a military man...especially not a SEAL."

"Oh, I see."

She wouldn't tell him yet that she'd changed her mind about that. "Is your mother's birthday really next month and do you have four brothers?"

"Yes. Everything I told you about my family is true. I never lied to you about anything pertaining to them. I just omitted some details and couldn't elaborate on certain things."

She then put her wineglass down and turned toward him. "Why did you sleep with me, David, when I was just an assignment to you?"

Flipper knew this was the time of reckoning and what he told her would have an impact on their relationship for the rest of their days. He needed her to understand.

"You were supposed to be an assignment, Swan. But honestly, I don't think you ever were. From the moment I walked into your shop and saw you, a part of me knew I had to fight hard to be objective and do the job I'd been sent here to do."

He paused. "I tried to keep my attraction to you out of the picture but found it harder and harder to do. Each time I saw you while getting to know you, I fell deeper under your spell. It was hard pretending with you."

He decided to be totally honest with her. "Just so you know, that day you invited me to your place for dinner wasn't my first time there. I'd been to your home without you knowing anything about it. But at the time, it was just a house I was checking out as part of an investigation. The day you invited me to dinner, I saw it through another pair of eyes. Yours. And for me, it then became your home."

She drew in a deep breath. "You invaded my privacy by letting yourself into my home, but that's not why I'm upset. I accept that you had a job to do and I was your assignment but…"

"But what?"

"You still haven't fully answered my question, David. Why did you make love to me?"

David frowned, realizing that he *hadn't* answered her question. His teammates often teased him about beating around the bush, sometimes providing too much context instead of just sticking with the facts.

"The reason I made love to you, Swan, was because I desired you. Everything about you turned me on. Your looks, your scent, your walk…and then after our first kiss, it was your taste. Fighting my desire for you was no longer an option, although I tried being honorable enough not to seduce you."

"But then I seduced you," she said quietly.

He smiled. "No, I think that night we seduced each other. Everything we did was mutual."

"Yes, it was." She took another sip of her wine. "I spoke with Godpop 2 today and he told me your assignment ended but you decided to stay. Why?"

Okay, no beating around the bush this time, Flipper decided. "The reason is that by then I had fallen in love with you. In all honesty, in my heart you stopped being an assignment the first time I made love to you. I crossed the line of what was honorable, and I knew why. Because I felt you here, Swan," he said, pointing to his heart. "I felt you here in a way I've never felt before. No woman has ever been here, Swan. But during the one time you shouldn't have, you got there anyway."

"And now? How do you feel now?"

He placed his beer bottle aside and turned toward her. "Now you are still in my heart. Even more so. I love you so much I ache on the inside when I'm not with you. I love you so much I think of you even at times I shouldn't."

He reached out and took her hand in his. "Now I need to know, Swan, just how you feel about me."

Swan felt the gentle tug on her hand and, surprising even herself, she moved to sit in his lap.

When he wrapped his arms around her, she felt comfort flow through her. She turned in his lap to look down at him. He'd given her answers to all her questions, now she intended to give him answers to his.

"I love you, David. I fought it at first. I didn't know about you being present-day military, but I also had a problem...not with interracial dating...but with allowing anything to come of it. I saw how others saw my parents at times. Not as a beautiful couple in love but as an interracial couple in love. There should not have been a difference. I never wanted to deal with what they had to deal with in the name of love."

She paused. "But then I moved beyond thinking that way after I fell in love with you. Then I realized how my parents must have felt, believing nothing mattered but their love. Even if the world was against them, as long as they had each other, that's what truly counted."

"So you do love me?" he asked her as if for clarity.

Swan didn't have a problem clarifying anything for

him or anyone else. "Yes, I love you, David Flipper Hol-loway." And then she lowered her mouth to his.

Shivers of profound pleasure shot through every part of Swan's body when David slid his tongue into her mouth. Sensations bombarded her as she concentrated on his taste, his scent and the way he pulled her tongue into his mouth to mate with his. And when she felt his hands inch upward and slide beneath her top, his touch made her purr.

Both his taste and his touch were awakening parts of her, making her feel alive in a way she hadn't felt since the last time they'd been together. Here at her house. In her bed.

When his fingers touched her bare breasts, using his fingertips to draw circles around her nipples, she oozed deeper into the kiss, almost feeling like melted butter in his arms.

He slowly pulled his mouth from hers and looked at her. His blue eyes were sharp and filled with the same desire she felt. "Any reason why we can't take this inside?"

She wrapped her arms around his waist. "No, there's no reason."

"Good."

And then standing with her in his arms, he carried her into the house.

"Just so you know, David, I didn't ask you all my questions," Swan said when he placed her on the bed.

David glanced down at her. "You didn't?"

"No, but I can wait. None are more earth-shattering than this is going to be. And I need this."

He caressed the side of her face with his finger. "I need this, too. I know why I need it, tell me why you do."

She met his gaze and held it while she said, "I love the feel of you inside of me. I've never felt anything so right before. So pleasurable." She smiled. "Do you know I retired my sex toy?"

He chuckled. "That's good to know."

"Um, not too much information?"

"No. Nice to know what used to be my competition," he said as he began removing her clothes. Lucky for him, she wasn't wearing much. Just a top, shorts and a thong. Flipper had discovered outside earlier that she wasn't wearing a bra. He'd noticed more than once that she liked her breasts being free and so did he.

She reached out and tugged at his T-shirt and he assisted by removing his own shorts. Then he rejoined her on the bed. Reaching out, he lifted her by the waist.

"Wrap your legs around me, Swan. I'm about to join our bodies, to make us one."

As soon as her legs were settled around his waist, his shaft touched her core. She was wet and ready. Tilting her hips, he whispered the words, "I love you," before thrusting hard into her.

"David!"

Arching her back off the bed, she provided the prefect position for his penetration to go deeper. They were a perfect fit. They always would be. Not just in lovemaking but in everything they did from here on out. They had become a team.

He began moving, slowly at first and then harder and deeper, over and over again. The only constant sounds in the room were their breathing and flesh slapping against flesh. The air surrounding them was filled with the aroma of sex.

He felt on fire, like his entire body was burning and the flames fueled his need, his desire and his love. She was looking up at him, holding his gaze, and he hoped Swan saw the depth of love in his eyes.

He clenched his jaw when he felt it, the stirring of pleasure in his groin. The feeling was slowly spreading through his body and when Swan gripped his shoulders and dug her fingers into his skin, he continued to thrust inside of her like his life depended on it.

And when she screamed out his name, he knew the same sensations that were taking him were taking her.

He drew in a sharp breath only moments before calling out her name. Multiple sensations tore into him, causing an explosion inside of him that had him bucking his body in an all-consuming orgasm. The sensations kept coming until he let go and his release shot deep inside of her.

He knew right then that he wanted her to have his baby. If not this time, another time. One day, he intended to make it happen.

Moments later, he slumped down beside her and wrapped his arms around her as he tried to get his breathing under control. After recovering from his explosive orgasm, when he was able to talk, he said, "I feel like I've been burned to a crisp."

"Hmm, speaking of burning, do you know what I thought was hot?" she asked, drawing in deep breaths of air into her lungs.

"No, what?"

"You on that boat wearing nothing but swim trunks and that military belt around your waist. Now, that was hot."

He grinned. "You liked that, huh?"

She smirked up at him when he straddled her body again. "I liked it." Then her features became serious. "I still can't believe you swam all that way to save me."

He leaned in and brushed a kiss across her lips. "Believe it."

He then pulled back and looked down at her. His expression was serious. "I'm a damn good swimmer. I'm known to be able to hold my breath underwater for long periods of time. Longer than what most would consider normal. But I wasn't sure I was going to make it to the boat, Swan. I told my friends I had to try even if I died trying because the woman I love was on that boat. That's what kept me going. That's what fueled every stroke I made into the ocean waters. And when my body felt tired, like I couldn't possibly swim another lap, I would think of a life without you and for me that was unacceptable."

He drew in a sharp breath. For a quick minute, he relived the feel of the cold water as he swam nonstop to the boat to save her, not knowing if he would make it in time. "I had to save you."

"And then I rebuffed you. I refused to have that talk you wanted."

"I understood. I had been listening to what Georgianna Martin was saying, the picture she painted. I told myself that once I talked to you and told you the truth that you would believe me. I was just giving you time to think about everything. I figured you would realize that I did care for you."

She reached up and caressed the side of his face. "You never told me you cared."

"I did. Our last night together, when you were asleep, I told you before I left that I loved you. I had planned to tell you the next day when we were together but that's when you were taken."

"And you came back," she said.

"That was always my plan, Swan. I never intended to

let you go. I love you that much. And just so you know, my entire family is rooting for me. I told them about you and they can't wait to meet you. My brothers and I are giving Mom a party for her birthday next week. Will you go to Texas with me?"

When she hesitated, he added, "What I told you about them is true. My parents accept people for who they are and not how they look. Will you trust me about that?"

She met his gaze and nodded. "Yes, I will trust you and yes, I will go."

A huge smile spread across his face. "I can't wait to introduce you to everyone. And I've got the perfect thing for you to wear." He quickly eased off the bed.

She pulled herself up. "What's going on? You plan on dressing me that night?"

He glanced over his shoulder, chuckling as he pulled a small white box out of his shorts. "Something like that."

He returned to the bed and pulled her up to stand her on her feet beside the bed. Then he got down on one knee and looked up at her. "I love you, Swan. I know we have a lot of things we still need to overcome. But I believe we will do so together. Forever. Will you marry me?"

He saw tears form in her eyes when she nodded. "Yes, I will marry you."

He slid the ring on her finger and at that moment Flipper knew he was halfway to having his world complete.

He would get the other half the day she became his wife.

Sixteen

Swan glanced down at the ring David had put on her finger last week. Seeing it gave her strength and she definitely needed strength now, she thought as she entered a huge ballroom on his arm. It was his mother's sixtieth birthday party.

They had flown into Dallas last night so this would be the first time she met his family. Nervous jitters had tried taking over her stomach but a smile from David was keeping most of them at bay. He was convinced his family would love her and he had told her over and over that she was worrying for nothing. She was the woman he wanted and his family would love his choice.

"There's Mom and Dad," he said, with his arms around her shoulders as she carried his mother's gift. The same gift he'd purchased that first day he'd come into her shop.

A man she knew had to be one of David's brothers whispered something to the older couple and they turned with huge smiles on their faces.

At that moment, Swan knew David had inherited his father's eyes and that the smiles on the couple's faces were genuine. She could actually feel their warmth. David's mom was beautiful and did not look like she was sixty or that she had five grown sons.

When they reached his parents, David made the introduction. "Mom. Dad. I want you to meet the woman who has agreed to be my wife, Swan Jamison."

"It's an honor to meet you," Swan said, extending her hand to his mother.

Instead of taking it, the older woman engulfed Swan in a huge hug. "It's wonderful meeting you as well, Swan, and welcome to the family."

"Thank you. Here's your gift. Happy birthday."

"Thank you."

She received a hug from David's father as well. Then suddenly she was surrounded and a laughing David made introductions. All his brothers had those same blue eyes and like David, they were very handsome men. She could see why when she looked at the older Holloways; they were a beautiful couple. And Swan could tell from the way Mr. Holloway looked at his wife and the way Mrs. Holloway would look back at him that the couple was still very much in love.

A few nights ago, David had shared the fact that because his mother had been married to a Navy SEAL for over forty years and had five sons who were SEALs, she counseled a number of SEAL wives who had difficulties with the frequency and longevity of their spouses' missions. Swan had been glad to hear that since she would become a SEAL's wife soon.

Because David would be leaving in less than four

months on anther mission, they hoped to marry within a year. Surprisingly, David wanted a big wedding. She agreed as long as the wedding took place in the Keys.

The logistics of having a big wedding were enormous, given he had four brothers who were SEALs on different teams. Not to mention his closest four friends were SEALs as well. That meant Swan and David had to make sure everyone would be on leave in the States at the same time.

David also introduced Swan to her future sisters-in-law and they loved her engagement ring. The three were friendly and she liked them immediately. She was also introduced to other members of David's family—his grandparents, his niece, nephews, cousins, aunts, uncles—it was obvious the Holloway family was a huge one.

"Now I want to reintroduce you to four guys who are just as close to me as brothers. As you know, they came to the Keys to assist me in proving your innocence. And even when my assignment with you ended, they didn't leave. They stayed."

She had met his four friends that night after the incident on the boat, when they'd had to give statements. She had thanked them for their help but they hadn't been officially introduced.

"Did I tell you how beautiful you look tonight, sweetheart?"

She smiled up at him as they walked across the ballroom floor to the four men and their wives. "Yes, you told me. Thank you." She, Candy and Jamila had gone shopping in Miami. She'd known this was the perfect dress when she'd seen it on a store mannequin.

Within a few minutes, she had been introduced to Brisbane "Bane" Westmoreland and his wife, Crystal; Gavin "Viper" Blake and his very pregnant wife,

Layla; Laramie "Coop" Cooper and his wife, Bristol; and Thurston "Mac" McRoy and his wife, Teri.

After spending time with the couples, Swan felt that just like her future sisters-in-law, the four women were genuinely friendly and Swan looked forward to getting to know them better. They loved her engagement ring as well and told David he'd done a great job in picking it out.

"So what do you think?" David leaned down to ask, taking her hand in his and leading her to where his parents, siblings and their spouses were getting ready to take a group picture.

She grinned up at him. "Um, for starters, I think I need to start calling you Flipper, since everyone else does. And then, *Flipper*, I think I am one of the luckiest women in the world right now. I love you."

He chuckled as he pulled her to the side of the room and wrapped his arms around her waist. "And I, Swan Jamison, think I'm the luckiest man in the world, and I love you."

"A very wise woman, my mother, once told me that when you meet a man who puts that sparkle in your eyes then you'd know he was a keeper. You, Flipper, are a keeper."

He smiled. "You, my beautiful Swan, are a keeper as well."

Flipper then lowered his mouth to hers.

Epilogue

A year later in June

Bane Westmoreland leaned close and whispered to Flipper, "Don't get nervous now. You wanted a big wedding and you got it."

Flipper couldn't say anything because Bane was right. He stood flanked by his father, who was his best man, and twelve groomsmen—namely his brothers, best friends and cousins.

Only his SEAL teammates knew Flipper had a tendency to tap his finger against his thigh when he was nervous. He stopped tapping but not because he noticed that Viper, Mac and Coop were grinning over at him. But then he figured both Viper and Coop had reasons to grin since they'd both become fathers this year. Viper was the proud father of a son, Gavin IV, and Coop had a beautiful daughter they'd named Paris, since that was where he'd first met his wife.

It was a beautiful day for a beach wedding and so
far everything was perfect and going according to plan.
Swan had hired one of the local wedding planners and
the woman had done an awesome job. She had thought
of everything, including the super yacht that could hold
their five hundred guests that they'd be using for the
wedding reception. It was anchored in the ocean near
Swan's beachfront home. A fleet of passenger boats
had been chartered to transport the wedding guests out
to the yacht.

A ten-piece orchestra sat beneath towering balus-
trades draped from top to bottom in thin white netting.
Chairs were set up on the beach, auditorium style, facing the decorative stage where Flipper and the men in
the wedding party stood waiting.

Suddenly, the music began and all the ladies strolled
down the beach and up the steps.

Swan had chosen her wedding colors of purple and
yellow and Flipper had to admit the combination was
striking. It took all twelve women long enough to do
their stroll. His niece was a flower girl and Coop's son
and one of Flipper's nephews were the ring bearers.

Flipper almost held his breath when what looked
like a huge forty-foot golden swan was rolled onto
the beach. When the orchestra changed their tune for
the "Wedding March," the swan opened and his Swan
appeared in a beautiful, dazzling white gown. She
looked beautiful, stunning and breathtaking all rolled
into one.

Flipper stared at the woman who would be his wife
and felt so much love in his heart. He hadn't known
until now just how much he could feel for one woman.
They had spent the past year deepening their friendship
and their love. He looked forward to returning from his

covert operations, knowing she would be there waiting on him.

He watched as she slowly strolled toward him. All three of her godfathers participated in walking her up the aisle, passing her off to the other so many feet along the way. Then all three of them gave her away. When Swan reached his side and extended her hand to him, he accepted it while thinking she was *his* Swan.

His beautiful Swan.

The wedding ceremony began. What Flipper would remember most when he looked back was when the minister announced them husband and wife and told him he could kiss his bride.

Flipper pulled Swan into his arms and lowered his mouth to hers. She was his and he intended to keep her happy for the rest of his days. They would be flying to Dubai for a two-week honeymoon and then return to the Keys where they planned to make their permanent home.

When David released Swan's mouth, the minister said, "I present to everyone David and Swan Holloway."

Flipper knew they were supposed to exit by walking down the golden steps that led to the boat that would transport them to the yacht. But at that moment, he couldn't deny himself another kiss and lowered his mouth to his wife's again.

* * * * *

LET'S TALK
Romance

For exclusive extracts, competitions
and special offers, find us online:

 facebook.com/millsandboon

@millsandboonuk

@millsandboon

Or get in touch on 0844 844 1351*

For all the latest titles coming soon, visit
millsandboon.co.uk/nextmonth